THE
NEW GUY

THE
NEW GUY

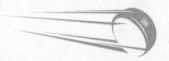

SARINA BOWEN

Tuxbury Publishing LLC

Author's Note:

If you watch a hockey game, you'll see the athletic trainer standing behind the bench. He (or she) is the one who runs out onto the ice if a player gets hurt.

Before writing this book, I didn't have a terrific grasp of what athletic trainers really do. They're not strength and conditioning coaches. They're certified healthcare professionals.

I owe a special shout out to reader and athletic trainer Corie H., who steered me toward appropriate resources and who assisted with Hudson's injury. Thank you! All mistakes are my own!

Cheers from New England,

—Sarina B.

ONE

Gavin

FEBRUARY

"GO OUT," my sister says. "Have fun." She literally pushes me toward the door to our new apartment. "What's the point of free babysitting if you don't take advantage?"

"Can I at least put on my coat first?"

"I suppose." She grabs it out of the narrow coat closet and thrusts it at me with one tattooed arm. "There. Now go. See a movie. Or find a bar. Meet a guy. Have some adult fun, before you forget how."

An argument forms on the tip of my tongue, but then my seven-year-old daughter, Jordyn, pipes up from the sofa. "Ooh! Aunt Reggie! 'Love is an Open Door!'"

"Awesome!" my sister agrees. "Let's hit it!"

The two of them are in the midst of a *Frozen* sing-along. I enjoy a good Disney movie as much as the next guy. But Frozen has been on heavy rotation in my home for a few years now. Adult fun is a barely recognizable concept at this point.

And half the reason I moved Jordyn to Brooklyn was so she could have more of a relationship with my punk rock sister.

So I do it. I put on my coat, give them a wave, and leave.

Outside, it's a crisp, February night, although Brooklyn is nowhere near as cold as New Hampshire, where Jordyn and I lived until a few days ago. Another perk of Brooklyn: I don't need a car here. My new neighborhood is within easy walking distance to everything we need.

At least that's what the real estate broker promised when she showed me the rental last month. I made the decision to move here in a single day, after accepting a new job working for the Brooklyn Bruisers hockey team.

In the past, I'd done many impulsive things. I used to be a fun, easy-going guy who lived for excitement. But that was the younger me. I used to have a lot less to lose, and fewer people depending on me.

Now, as I walk past the historic brownstones, I'm a little terrified at what I've done. New job. New neighborhood. New school for Jordyn.

It's a lot. And I think I'm already lost. Literally.

I don't want to look like a tourist, though, so I don't pull out my phone and check the map. I just keep going, turning corners and walking down every interesting block I encounter.

After a while, the quirky residential buildings give way to shops. I could do some grocery shopping, even though that isn't what Reggie meant by "adult fun."

When I turn onto Atlantic, the street becomes more lively. There are people out and about. It's 8:30 on a Tuesday night, and the restaurants are doing good business. Even if I've forgotten how to party, the rest of the people in my new neighborhood haven't.

Reggie says I'm the oldest twenty-five-year-old she knows. And maybe she's right. When my phone vibrates a moment later, I pull it out immediately, just in case my sister has an emergency at home.

Stop looking at your phone, Reggie has texted. *Go out and have at least half as much fun as we are right now.* There's a photo of her dressed up as Elsa, with my daughter Jordyn as Kristoff, because she is seven years old and determined not to do a single thing the same way that other seven-year-old girls do.

It's adorable. And the sight of Reggie and Jordyn together makes my heart happy.

We're going to be fine. Moving here wasn't a huge mistake, and we're going to love New York. I take another deep breath and then respond to the text. *Cute. But why are you texting me if you don't want me to look at my phone?*

I was just testing you, she says. *Now go find a hunky guy and don't come home until the wee hours of the morning.*

Right. Like that's going to happen. I shove the phone in my pocket and continue on my way.

There was a time in my life when I was exactly the kind of guy who looked at a night out as an adventure. But now I'm the kind of guy who is thrilled to simply wander alone for an hour while my sister babysits.

Atlantic Avenue has a bunch of restaurants, but I can't seem to make myself go in and ask for a table for one. I wander a little further and end up on Hicks, which is a quieter street. I stop in front of a sports bar that's not too busy. I could sit at the bar and order some wings.

As I open the door, I notice there's a hockey game playing on a TV over the bar. And it feels like a sign. In two days, I'm starting my new job with the Brooklyn NHL franchise. I've never worked with hockey players before, and I'm kind of nervous about it.

I'll take all the positive signs I can get.

There are plenty of empty seats at the bar, probably because it's only Tuesday. So I sit down and order a beer from a kind-looking older gentleman. "Should be a good game tonight," he says. "We're favored to beat Boston."

"Awesome," I say, as I wait for my beer.

I'm not a Brooklyn fan yet, though. I haven't started the job. Also, it feels disloyal to Eddie. My husband—he died two years ago —was a Boston fan. Big time.

Growing up, I watched a lot of sports, but hockey wasn't really on my radar. Then I met Eddie, and watching hockey together was part of our courting ritual. We had three great years together, and then he died in an accident at the age of thirty-two.

People always tell me, "You don't look old enough to have a seven-year-old daughter." And they're mostly right. Eddie was nine years older than I was, and he was already a dad when I met him. I never imagined dating a single father of a toddler. It wasn't on my bucket list.

But Eddie was special, and I fell hard. We watched a lot of TV together at home, because he had a kid to raise.

And then *we* had a kid to raise.

And now *I* have a kid to raise.

I miss him so much. It's one reason why I applied for a job with the hockey team. *Eddie would get a kick out of this*, I remember thinking. It was really just a whim.

When they offered me the job, I was floored. Now here I am, on a barstool, hoping I made the right call.

Meanwhile, my beer lands in front of me in a frosty pint glass, and I take a grateful sip. When I glance around the bar, I notice a *lot* of hockey paraphernalia. There's a signed Brooklyn Bruisers jersey framed at one end of the bar, and a signed Brooklyn Bombshells jersey at the other.

Eddie would get a kick out of that, too. But he'd still root for Boston.

On the screen, Brooklyn has the puck. But not a lot is happening. Nothing good, anyway. Boston is all over them. This is an away game, and the Boston fans are loud.

Not to contradict the bartender, but I'm not sure Brooklyn feels like winning tonight. I guess time will tell.

Just as I'm having this thought, a guy sits down on the stool beside me. Like, *right* beside me, even though there's a whole row of stools available.

It's been a million years since I was a single guy sitting alone in a bar. But somehow the old reflexes kick in, and I turn my head to check him out. And *hello*. He is a fine specimen. Broad shoulders. Sandy brown hair and deep brown eyes. And a handsome face with the kind of strong, scruffy jaw that might leave beard burns on my thighs.

Whoa. That fantasy escalated quickly. That's what happens when your dry spell is two years long.

Just as I remember to keep my tongue in my mouth, the hunk slowly cruises me, too. My pulse quickens, and our gazes lock.

"Hi," I say, because I'm brilliant like that.

He blinks. I swear his eyes dilate, too.

But that's when the bartender arrives in front of us, and the guy shuts it down so fast that I might already have whiplash.

"Hey, Pete," he says, his attention fully on the bartender.

"Evening," Pete returns with a chuckle. "Here to watch the game?"

"Of course. Can I have a lager and my usual?"

"Any time, kid." Then he turns to me. "Any interest in a menu?"

"Heck yes," I say. "Let's have it."

The older man slides it onto the bar, and I skim the offerings.

My new friend stays quiet until the bartender moves away. "Sorry to crowd you, but you have one of the best seats in the room."

I almost make a joke about how nice my *seat* is. Almost. But I rein it in. "You're not crowding me," I say instead, my voice carefully neutral. "Any advice on this menu? Looks pretty standard."

"Sorry, no." That perfect, scruffy face says. "I always order the same thing. But the guys tell me the burger and the nachos are about as adventurous as you're supposed to get."

"Good tip." I flag down the bartender again, and order the nachos.

Living large tonight. Chips for dinner!

It's a start.

TWO

Hudson

OKAY, yup. I probably made that awkward. A really cute guy checked me out, and I panicked.

Guys don't usually hit on me. Especially not in *this* bar. His smile, though? Caught me totally off guard. Made me forget for a minute all the reasons why I'm supposed to concentrate on hockey.

Only hockey.

Still, I sneak another look in his direction to try to figure out why he's so distracting. Dark blond hair. Tight T-shirt reading Hank's Gym, and muscular arms that have probably spent some serious hours in Hank's Gym, wherever that is. He's not bulky, though. Lean muscle, nicely defined chest. Blond hairs down his forearms.

He laughs suddenly, and I feel it in my groin. "Did you see that? Oof. So embarrassing."

My eyes flick back up to the TV in time for the replay. And, yeah, things are not going well. Castro got stripped of the puck by a Boston D-man, and Silas had to dive for the save.

It's chaos up there, but my eyes still turn back to their new favorite place. The world is full of attractive, toned men, and I usually don't bother staring at them. My neighbor is a total hottie, though. And just for a moment, I allow myself to imagine how it might play out: I buy him a drink. We watch the game. And then I invite him over for a little Tuesday night stress relief.

That's just a fantasy, though. I'm humoring myself, because it's been a bad day. Honestly, a bad year. And it's barely February.

The only reason I'm sitting here at all is because the Bruisers left me behind to go play Boston. The medical staff sent me to a specialist today to try to diagnose the pain and swelling I've had in my hip.

Luckily, the doctor said it's just bursitis. But it's sidelined me at an awkward time. Four weeks ago I was minding my own business in the weight room in Chicago. I'd had a recent string of bad games, and I'd been trying to stay positive and work hard.

But then? In my sweaty T-shirt, I'd been summoned to the GM's office. And I'd known exactly what was happening. *Here we go again,* I'd thought as the big boss quickly thanked me for my service and sent me off to pack for a flight to New York that very evening.

I'd been traded. For a third string goalie and a first round draft pick.

Trades happen. You're not supposed to take it personally. But I do. This was my fourth trade in five years. That's a very high number.

Getting traded is very disorienting, and super stressful. So it's no big surprise that I've been struggling on the ice in Brooklyn, too. I'm just not used to my teammates yet.

Tweaking my hip was just the latest indignity. So here I sit, watching my own damn team on TV, playing without me. So humiliating. And I can't even watch this at home, because someone is watching *Frozen* on the other side of my wall, and singing along at the top of their lungs. I couldn't even hear the damn game.

"Maybe this is the wrong bar to say so," says the hot guy beside me. "But Brooklyn looks a little shaky tonight."

My loyalty is a reflex. "Not *that* shaky." Except they do look skittish. "My name's Hudson, by the way," I add for no good reason.

"I'm Gavin," he says, offering his hand. "Nice to meet you."

And, shit. There's that smile again. Hot like a summer's day. His eyes are gray, and they crinkle in the corners when he smiles. His handshake is pleasantly firm.

Something crackles between us again. When he holds my gaze a little too long, I can't seem to make myself look away.

But then he lets go, just as Pete approaches with two plates. "Food, boys." He slides them onto the bar at the same time, as if we're dining together.

And I guess we are. After the game, though, I'll get out of here. I'll go straight home and watch some video for our upcoming game against Minnesota.

Eyes on the prize, Newgate. I remind myself. *Stay the course.*

I pick up my fork and cut into my burger patty, which is resting on a bed of salad greens. If my new friend Gavin thinks my no-carb dinner is weird, he doesn't say so. He just crunches into a cheesy chip with a sigh of happiness.

It's a nice sound, too. And my rebellious mind wonders what other sounds I could get him to make.

Yeah, like that's ever going to happen.

I tuck into my food, and the game picks up speed. Castro has possession of the puck, and my guys try to make some magic.

But the offense falls apart again a few minutes later, and I watch the puck get carried into our defensive zone.

My guys are struggling tonight. The schedule has been brutal. And I'm not there to help.

Then, just as the scoreless first period is winding down, a Boston player trips Castro, who goes down while trying to catch a pass. The puck goes right into the waiting stick of a competitor.

Even worse—the ref doesn't call the foul.

"Fuck that!" I shout. "Come on, Crikey. Time for payback. Can't let them get away with it."

Sure enough, the younger of our two enforcers looks for the first opportunity to pick a fight. The gloves are off before you can say *let's do this*.

The bar is quiet tonight. But every pair of eyes turns toward the TV screen.

Gavin shakes his head, though. "I just don't get the fighting."

"Yeah? It's an honor code thing," I explain. Although I realize this hottie has no idea who I am. "Not a fan of violence?"

"Well, no. But it's more than that. Here you've got twenty-three pampered thoroughbreds. They've got the best training money can buy, right?" He's gesturing at the TV screen, and his big eyes light up as he talks. "They get optimized fitness training. And specialists for every boo-boo. But then it's like, *go ahead and beat the crap out of each other. We'll just get out the gold-plated bandages and stitch you back together again.*"

I laugh so hard that I almost choke on my salad. He just called me a *pampered thoroughbred*, and he looked good doing it.

But I can't let him get away with it. "You think football is any better?"

"Hell no," he scoffs. "Football should be illegal. They're all going to have brain damage at fifty."

I give up watching the screen and just stare at him instead. "All right. So what sport makes more sense to you?"

"Oh, lots of them. I watch a lot of soccer—their fitness is amazing. Tennis is another favorite. I like endurance sports, too. And ski racing is fun to follow. I'm just a big fan of athletic bodies in motion." His eyes dip like he's a little unsure of himself all of a sudden. "Aren't you?"

"Definitely a fan of that," I agree. Holy crap, I'm flirting with him. I need to stop, but I don't really want to.

I glance up at the screen instead. And, fuck, I look right in time to see my guys fail to connect a pass. And then it just gets worse as I finish my dinner. We're down by two at the end of the second period.

Pete comes by to clear away my plate. "Are we having more than one beer tonight?"

"Absolutely," I surprise myself by saying. "Just a light beer, though. And one of whatever he's drinking." I gesture to my neighbor, who's polishing off his nachos.

"That's very kind," Gavin says in a low voice after Pete moves away.

"You've had to put up with my cursing. We're down two goals already."

"The way I see it, we're up by two goals."

I turn on my stool. "A Boston fan? Really? You know you're in Brooklyn, right?"

The guy shrugs his shoulders. "I'm from New England. And Boston is the better team this year. It's just the truth."

Lord. I bite back a laugh. I should probably let him know that he's spouting hockey wisdom to a professional hockey player. But I think I won't. It's more fun this way. And I'm not really in the mood to talk about myself.

Fuck it. Tonight I'm just a frustrated hockey fan. I really need Brooklyn to make it to the playoffs. I just need it a little more desperately than everyone else in this bar.

My guys make a beautiful attempt on goal, thwarted only by excellent goalkeeping from Boston. "Come on guys, let's do it again."

"They look tired," he says.

"They had back-to-back games earlier this week. No wonder they look tired."

I should be there with them, not sitting here like a loser.

"You know what?" Gavin says out of the blue. "I read that Castro used to play left wing."

"Yeah?" I say noncommittally. It's true, although I wasn't on the team then.

"They should switch him back," my new friend says decisively. "Or else make Drake play center. The first two lines are so lopsided."

"I like it," Pete says, passing by with clean glassware. "Good idea."

I let out a snort. "Maybe you should swing by and give your thoughts to management. The headquarters is right in the neighborhood."

Instead of getting offended, Gavin gives me a big, open smile that makes me feel like a jerk for taking a bitter tone with him. And he's so attractive that I feel that smile in my pampered groin.

"How do you feel about the defensive pairings?" I ask, because I can't help myself.

"I'm underwhelmed," he says, and I don't know whether to laugh or cry. So I take a gulp of beer instead.

Five minutes later, Boston commits another egregious foul, this time against Tank, my fellow defenseman. "Goddamn that cross-check!" I shout at the TV. "Ref! You're blind!"

And then it gets worse when those fuckers score on us thirty seconds later. Now it's three to zero. I groan.

"Ouch," Gavin says, draining his beer.

I set my beer down on the bar, half full. Watching my team lose is honestly excruciating, knowing I'm not there to help.

"Hey—feel like a game of pool?" Gavin asks suddenly. "I think I saw a table in that back room. And this game? It's all over but the crying."

"It isn't," I argue as a reflex. Because of *course* I'm going to watch the game all the way to the end. This is literally my job.

But then Boston scores again. And I'm in hell. It hurts to watch, and Coach Worthington is just going to make me watch it again during tomorrow's video session. "Is that pool game still on offer?" I hear myself ask. "Or even better—ping-pong?"

His gray eyes widen, and he pulls out some cash to settle his check. "I *love* ping-pong. Lead the way."

———

Confession: I am a stud at ping-pong. Most hockey players love it, and most teams have a table somewhere in the practice facility.

Except it turns out that Gavin is good too, so I don't have to take it too easy on him. He holds his gorgeous body in a loose, wide-legged stance. And he seems to find the ball no matter where I put it.

Watching him parry the ball back to me does nothing to dampen the attraction I feel for him, either. I'd like to take that shapely jaw in hand, testing its lines against my fingertips. And I'd like to run my hands through his wavy blond hair.

The game is fun. Really fun. I win the first game, but just barely.

"You're pretty good," he says. And there's that flirty smile again.

"I'm all right. My backhand is a little awkward tonight."

"No it isn't," he argues. "Your backhand is fine, but the way you unwind it slows you down."

I bark out a laugh. "Wait, really? What are you, a ping-pong guru?"

He shrugs. "I've taught tennis lessons. It's kind of the same principle. Watch."

Setting his paddle down, he moves around the table until he's standing behind me. Then he reaches around my body to grasp my wrist—the one that's holding the paddle. "So, the way you move your paddle is efficient." He guides my arm to move into the backhand position.

His grip on my wrist is firm. He doesn't do anything cheesy—like gratuitously stroking a thumb over my skin. But it doesn't matter. I *like* that firm grip. I want more of it on my body.

And suddenly I can picture it way too clearly. Those strong hands pulling my T-shirt over my head. And me, kissing that crooked smile off his face.

"...But you turn your body too much at the same time," he says, briefly tapping one finger against my back. "Square your body to the table the whole time, so that when you leave the backhand position, the angle is still good."

"Okay," I say uselessly as he moves my arm again. But I've lost my train of thought completely.

"See what I mean?" Gavin asks.

Instead of answering, I turn my head to look over my shoulder at him. His face is just inches away, and his eyes widen slightly. Like he can't believe I went there.

"You got any other tricks you want to show me?" I ask quietly.

The next few seconds seem to last forever. In the first place, I can't believe I'm doing this. And Gavin is a little off-kilter, too. He's clearly interested. But still, he hesitates.

I'm holding my breath now, afraid that he'll turn me down. And also afraid that he won't.

Slowly, he licks his lips, and drops my wrist. But he doesn't step back. If anything, he leans a fractional degree closer. "Yeah," he says under his breath. "I think I do."

Well *that* got heated fast. Go me.

And I don't *ever* do this. I must have lost my mind, picking up a guy in a bar where my team hangs out on the regular. So I need to downshift. "Let's finish the game," I whisper. "Want to put five bucks on it?"

"Sure," he says with a slow smile. "Only five?"

"Well, I've been holding back a little."

He laughs, and the sound of it is bright with promise. "Really? Why?" The question comes out sounding flirty. "Trying to flatter me?"

I shrug, suddenly embarrassed. But that's exactly what I've done. I'm in the mood to live a little. And by live a little, I mean take this guy home and strip his clothes off. It's been a long time since I had such a reckless urge.

It's been *years*.

But I'm pretty sure he wants me just as much as I want him. We're gazing at each other in a way that dudes in a bar just don't usually do.

Not *this* bar anyway.

Fuck. This is a bad idea. I drop my gaze, even though I don't want to.

Gavin moves back to his end of the table so we can finish the game. He taps his paddle on the table to let me know he's ready. "Bring it, man. Do your worst."

"All right. You asked for it." I take a breath that's meant to cool me down. And then I serve up a blazing fast ball, diagonally across the table.

Gavin returns it with a stroke so fast that it's almost invisible to the human eye.

I'd laugh, except I'm too busy yanking my paddle toward the ball. I get my shot off, but just barely. And he returns it again like gunfire.

"Jesus," I gasp as I dive for it. But this time he smokes me and takes the point.

I'm thinking I might be out five dollars. He hustled me. But I'm going to go down fighting.

THREE

Gavin

I HAVEN'T HAD this much fun in a *long* time. Hudson is a playful opponent with quick reflexes and a knowing smile which he deploys after every point.

Even though I'm winning. In fact, the match is evolving into a blowout. But something tells me this guy doesn't want me to take it easy on him.

Still, that doesn't mean it has to end too quickly. So I draw each volley out, testing his reflexes, upping the ante until we're both laughing and a little breathless. He ekes a point or two, but usually I ace him before he can find a way to get past me.

When I win the game, he laughs. "Holy shit. Didn't take you too long to finish me off."

I shrug, like it's no big thing. But my heart is thumping and my face is flushed. And I realize that I want this—I'd like to *finish him off* in a few other choice ways. It's the first time I've had that urge in a long time. A *really* long time.

I used to be fun, damn it. A party animal. But grief can change a guy. Tonight, though, I feel the old me bubbling to the surface. The handsome stranger at the other end of the table has helped me find him again.

"You're a shark. I owe you five bucks." He reaches for his wallet.

I hold up a hand. "Sorry, I don't take cash. You'll have to work it off in trade." Yup, that ridiculous line just came out of my mouth. And I don't regret it.

His hand stills on his back pocket. Then he braces his hands on the table and studies me. "Yeah?"

"Oh yeah." My words are full of bravado. But this is a big moment for me. I haven't been with a guy since Eddie died.

Across the table, Hudson might be having his own internal battles. His handsome face is thoughtful. Maybe even troubled. He sets down his paddle and actually glances over his shoulder to make sure there's nobody nearby. There isn't, though. We're the only ones in the ping-pong room. His gaze snaps back to mine. "I don't do this."

"Oh." That could mean so many things. "You mean pickups? Or guys?"

"Well, both."

Shit. "You're not married," I whisper. "Right?"

He actually laughs. "Nope. No way." He turns his chin toward the front of the bar, and I am suddenly worried that I've killed the mood. But instead of begging off, he says, "My place is only a couple blocks from here. But I have to settle up with Pete. You want to meet me outside?"

Ah. Now I get it. He doesn't want us to walk out together, and he doesn't know how to say so.

"Sure," I say with forced casualness. "I'll be outside. Don't take too long." I grab my jacket off the hook on the wall and stride past him, through the bar and out the door.

I don't glance at the bartender. They obviously know each other, and I am not going to think too hard about why Hudson doesn't want to be seen with a guy.

It's fine, I remind myself. Maybe he's experimenting. And we're not dating. This is just sex.

I feel a tremor in my chest, though. *Just sex.* Am I really going home with a stranger? After all this time?

The February air is bracing. I walk a few paces down the sidewalk, so that I'm not visible from the bar's front windows. And I hope Hudson doesn't spend too much time saying good night to the bartender. I might start thinking of all the reasons this is a dumb idea.

But I want this. I need to break the seal, even if it makes me feel a little trashy.

This is what moving on looks like, right?

Luckily, Hudson doesn't leave me alone too long with my thoughts. He emerges a minute later, his footsteps quick, a look of determination on his face. I love his sexy scowl—like he just can't wait to get at me.

The feeling is mutual, buddy.

"C'mon," he practically growls, and we walk side by side for a few paces. But as soon as we turn the corner, Hudson stops. He pushes me up against the side of the brick building. And then he kisses me hotly.

For a second, I'm too surprised to react. But his mouth is both firm and welcoming, and his hands grip my shoulders with a determination that totally works for me.

"Mmm," I say against his lips.

"Tell me about it," he murmurs. "Been wanting to do that all night."

Gripping his jacket, I dive in for another hot kiss. Our chests bump, and his tongue catches mine. He tastes of beer and hunger. Then he takes a half step closer and our hips meet. The hard column behind the fly of his jeans is unmistakable, and a zing of desire shoots like fire through my veins.

"Whoa," I say against his mouth. "Hi there."

His chest shakes with a chuckle as he pins me even more firmly to the wall with his cock.

He kisses me again, and it's a little desperate. He's physically aggressive in a way that's fun, not creepy.

But there's also something a little vulnerable about him that's hard to pin down. Like his aggression may be disguising a case of nerves. Maybe we're both a little outside our respective comfort zones.

And what's more fun than that?

"Goddamn," he pants, breaking our kiss. "You are just what I didn't know I needed."

This lights me up. Specifically my dick, which is fighting to get out of my boxers and into his. "I bet you say that to all the guys," I whisper. And then I nudge my hips against his.

He makes a sound that's half moan, half laugh. "It's been a long time for me. Now I'd better take you home and suck you off before I forget how that works."

Omifuckinggod. "Yes please."

He tugs me off the wall and steers me down a side street. It's not the same route I took to get here, but at least he's heading in roughly the same direction as my own Brooklyn street.

At least I think so. Hope I can find my way home after this little adventure is over.

Although it's hard to worry too much when there's a hot, horny man marching me down the sidewalk. When we reach the corner, the crosswalk light turns red, I almost let out an unmanly whimper of disappointment as the traffic begins flooding past us. I console myself, though, by placing a hand on Hudson's very firm ass.

And, wow, it's like a boulder. "You must spend a lot of time doing squats."

He whirls around, laughing. It transforms his face, honestly. He looks five years younger when he laughs. "Oh you have no idea." He looks over his shoulder again, and for a second I think he's checking for onlookers.

But nope. He was just searching out another surface against which to press my willing body. His firm hands land on my chest, and my ass lands against a sign kiosk. Then his tongue invades my mouth a second later.

Desire swamps me again. I fumble a hand between us and shamelessly cup his fly.

"Fuck yes," he grunts into my mouth. "Can't wait to get these clothes off you."

It's not Shakespeare, but it works on me nonetheless. I nip his lip and then use both hands to lift his jaw so I can lick a stripe up his neck. His stubble scrapes my tongue as he growls happily. The vibration goes straight to my balls.

And I realize with a start that I'd forgotten how this feels. Not just the promise of sex, but of adventure. My inner wild man is waking up after a *long* slumber. And he is ready to party.

"Let's go," he whispers hoarsely, probably because the light just turned green.

But then, changing his mind, he cups my face in one hand and gives me a steamy kiss. Our gazes lock, and I see my own joy reflected back at me in his brown eyes.

Tonight is turning into a fantastic, unexpected gift. And I don't intend to squander it. I push off the kiosk and grip his elbow. "We can make it," I insist, even as the walk sign is counting down its last few seconds.

Chuckling, he hurries across the street with me. "This way." We speed walk past some low slung buildings.

They're familiar, actually. I've been on this block before. "What street do you live on?" I ask.

"Henry," he says.

"So do I."

He glances toward me. "Really? What address?"

"Forty-one." I point up the block. I recognize the deli on the corner we're approaching, too. We're close.

He comes to a sudden stop. "You're shitting me."

Uh-oh. "No, I'm not. Just moved in yesterday. Three bedroom apartment. Second floor."

His mouth hinges open in an expression of pure horror. "Fuck no. There's a little kid next door. And a woman. I saw her. Lotsa tattoos. Are you *married?*"

"No!" I yelp. "That's my *sister.*"

He closes his eyes and then shakes his head. Like he hopes I'm not there when he opens them again.

I am, though. I'm just staring up at this attractive man and watching my night go up in flames. "So we're neighbors?"

"Across the hall," he barks. "Fuck."

"Is that so bad?" I have to ask. I'm still clinging to the possibility that my new neighbor doesn't care that much about our unlucky proximity. "I mean, think of the commute."

But it's no good. I can tell by the way his shoulders tense up. And by the way he looks up at the sky and yells "*FUCK*," and not in a fun way.

"No need to get ragey," I mumble. "I guess I'll just be going."

He lets out a sigh that carries the weight of total disappointment. I guess I should be flattered. "Look, I'm sorry. But I don't do pickups. Ever. For so many reasons. But we're gonna have to forget this happened."

"Yeah, I picked up on that," I grumble.

"Okay. Sorry." He grimaces and looks away. "Fuck," he says one more time.

And then he abruptly walks off, heading back the way we came. Away from his own home, and away from me.

Stunned at the turn of events, all I can do is watch his muscular ass power walk away from me, up the sidewalk.

"Okay," Reggie whispers. "Why do you look so flustered?"

We're seated side by side on my sofa, and Jordyn is finally in bed. She was almost too hyper to sleep. I guess moving to a new city can do that to a girl.

"Well..." I glance at her bedroom door. It's closed. "I almost did it. I met a guy in a bar. A *great* guy. And I was three quarters of the way to a hookup."

Her eyes light up. "Omigod, really? What do you mean almost?"

"He bailed," I whisper. "It turns out that he lives in this building. On this *floor*."

My sister's mouth flops open so far that I can see her tongue piercing. "Get out of here. Really? There's only one other apartment on this floor."

I nod violently. "When we both realized it, he freaked. I mean— hooking up with your neighbor is not super cool, right? Because you have to see each other every time you take out the recycling." I scrub my hands through my hair. "But his reaction was a little oversized."

"Oh shit," she whispers.

"Yeah," I breathe. "Maybe he's involved with someone. I really doubt it though. He must be, like, super deep in the closet?"

Reggie shakes her head. "I have another theory. That broker you rented from? She wrote something in her note with the keys. Hang on..." My sister pops off the couch and crosses to our messy dining table. We're at that ugly stage of unpacking where everything is chaos. "Oh, here." She plucks a sheet of paper out of the mess and returns it to me.

Gavin, welcome to the neighborhood. The Henry Street building houses several Brooklyn Hockey associates already. I'm sure you'll get a warm welcome!

"Oh yeah." When I'd been scouting apartments, the broker had told me that the power couple who owns the hockey teams also owns several neighborhood buildings. They only rent them out to people who work for one of their organizations. If you're on a budget, they're the best deal in town.

Since I'm most certainly on a budget, I'd asked to see anything in those buildings first. That's how we ended up here, in a three bedroom apartment that was priced the same as two bedrooms elsewhere.

"I guess it wasn't as warm a welcome as you'd been hoping for," Reggie says. And then she snort-laughs.

"Yeah, yeah. This could be bad." Really bad. I have a prickly feeling at the back of my neck. Are Hudson and I going to work together? Is that the reason he was so horrified to learn that we're neighbors?

Honestly, it would make me feel better. Hooking up with coworkers is a terrible idea. Maybe he'd figured this out before I did.

It's better than my other theories—that he's a cheater. Or that he's ashamed of his attraction to men.

But now I have to know. I get up and grab my laptop off my bed. Back on the sofa, I open a Google window and search "Hudson Brooklyn Hockey," since he never told me his last name.

The news article comes up immediately on a sports website, complete with a photo of the guy I was making out with an hour ago. *Chicago trades defenseman Hudson Newgate to Brooklyn.*

I make a strangled noise, and Reggie grabs the computer out of my hands. "Holy hell. *That* guy? That hottie right there?"

"Omigod," I whimper. "He's a *player*. That makes no sense. Why was he in the bar when his team was on the road?"

Unless...

I grab my computer back and google: "Hudson Newgate injury." Yup. Another news item pops up, from an injury roundup a few days ago. *Hudson Newgate out for three games for a lower body injury.*

"Oh shit. Oh shit oh shit oh shit..."

"Breathe," my sister says.

"Noooooo," I wail. "Not only do we work together, but I'll probably be massaging his *lower body* injury in thirty-six hours."

She cackles. "Perks of the job. And, wow little brother. I always knew you were cute, but look who can pull a professional athlete in a bar! Go Gavin!"

"Shhh." I snap the laptop shut, as if that could undo the damage. "You don't understand. I didn't know who he was, so I ran my mouth off about the team!"

"You did?" She's grinning ear to ear, like this is the most charming story she's ever heard.

"Stop smiling! He asked me what I thought of the defensive

pairings. And I said..." I want to die now. "I said I was *underwhelmed*."

She giggles.

I hate my sister.

"Oh Gavin! It must not have been that bad, if he still wanted to..." She drops her voice. "...Polish your piston."

My head drops into my hands, and I let out another moan. "Maybe he was just really horny."

"Who knew Brooklyn had a queer player? This is fascinating."

My stomach fizzes with anxiety. "Reggie? You can't mention this to anyone. He obviously isn't out."

"I am a vault," she says. "But maybe it's not a big deal. Maybe he's out to his teammates."

I shake my head. "I doubt it. When I had my interview, I made a point to tell the head trainer that I'm an out gay man. And then he made a point to tell me the team would never discriminate." I'd really liked Henry, and—up until a few minutes ago—I'd been excited to start this job.

"That's good, right?"

"Right. But then he said—'we have out players within the organization.' And I asked if any of them were men. Because hockey isn't historically welcoming to queer men. And he said 'So far the only out athletes are on the women's team.'"

"Ah." She bites her lip. "So your new friend has a secret."

"Sure sounds that way."

"Well, shit," she says. "He's not going to be very happy to see you again, is he?"

"Probably not."

She gives me a sad look. "I'm sorry, Gav. I hope that doesn't ruin your enthusiasm for meeting hot guys in bars. Eddie wouldn't want you to be lonely for the rest of your life, you know."

I know she's right. But that doesn't make this any less awkward.

Reggie retreats to her tiny bedroom after that.

My sister is living rent free with us for six months, until she goes off on tour as the bass player in a punk band. In exchange, she is going to pick Jordyn up from school most days and hang out with her until I get home.

It's a nice arrangement, even if the place will be a little crowded.

Alone with my thoughts, I lock the front door and tuck myself into bed. I stare at my unfamiliar ceiling and listen to the sounds of New York City beyond these walls.

It occurs to me, as I grow drowsy, that my bedroom shares a wall with Hudson Newgate's apartment.

I don't know the layout of his place, but it's conceivable that we are lying only a few feet away from each other right now.

Just not in the way I'd imagined.

FOUR

Hudson

AS I WIPE down the weight bench for my teammate, my phone starts singing "Under My Thumb."

Shit.

"Whose ringtone is that?" Drake asks with a snicker. "Your dad's?"

"Good guess. I'd better get it." My dad is also my agent. And he doesn't like to be ignored.

"Go ahead," says Drake. "You aren't supposed to spot me anyway."

This is also true, if overly cautious. Nobody wants my hip inflamed before I can skate again. As my phone continues to play The Rolling Stones, I walk into the corridor for a little privacy. "Hey, Dad," I say, answering when I'm out of earshot.

"Hudson, hey!" His voice is full of jocular enthusiasm that his other clients seem to love. Today, it just makes me tired. "How's the hip?"

"Better," I tell him. As if any other answer would be acceptable.

"You taking good care of yourself? Physical therapy? Good nutrition?"

"Yessir."

"Getting lots of sleep?"

"Yes," I lie. But it's not for lack of trying. I've spent the last two nights staring at the ceiling, wishing I could sleep on my side. And, fine, thinking about my neighbor. Wondering who he is, and what he thinks of me and my freak-out the other night.

I haven't run into him, though. Not on the sidewalk, or in the stairwell. And not here in the team headquarters.

But that's my fear. Our apartments are the only two on our floor. And billionaire couple Nate and Rebecca Kattenberger own the building—as well as the hockey team. So either Gavin or his sister must be a new hire.

Although the job could be anywhere in the Kattenberger empire. They own several companies as well as two hockey teams.

If there's a God in heaven, I'll never see him at work.

"You feel ready for tonight's game?" my father asks.

Here we go. "I'm not playing tonight, Dad."

"What? Why?" he barks. "They shouldn't overlook you like this! I'm going to put in a call to Karl..."

"Dad, *don't*. I mean—you don't have to." I close my eyes and regroup. It's rare for me to push back against the steamroller of Derek Newgate, and it has to be done delicately. "Coach spoke to both the specialist and the athletic trainer this morning. You don't need to worry. He's on top of this."

"Hmm." He mulls this over.

And I wait, like a good son.

My father is a two-time Stanley Cup winning veteran of hockey. And now a very in-demand agent. If he ranked the value of his clientele, I might not even make the top twenty. He knows everyone in hockey, including my coach. They were teammates at some point. He's well liked, and Coach would probably laugh off his invasive phone call.

But still. *Give it a rest, Dad.*

"All right. One more game," he says, as if it were up to him. "You're taking anti-inflammatories, and icing it?"

"Textbook, I promise. I practically live in that damn ice bath."

He chuckles. "All right. I know you're doing the work."

All I do is work.

"—It's just that four weeks in on a new team is a crappy time to be injured. They need to see you as their new powerhouse on the blue line."

I lean my head against the wall and let him talk. As if I don't have all these same thoughts every day.

Even before breakfast.

"—While you're waiting, don't slack off. Lots of upper body work. Get yourself to every video meeting."

Yeah, that's every day of my life.

"You're going to heal up and settle in. Pretty soon Brooklyn won't be able to remember how they lived without you."

"You know it," I say, because that's my line in this drama. Plus, I want to believe it.

"Chin up, Hudson. You can overcome this."

"Thanks, Dad." He's overbearing as fuck, but we both want the same things. And to his credit, he never expresses what we're both thinking—that five years bouncing around on different teams is not a good look.

I'm like the dog who's still looking for a forever home—but people keep returning him to the shelter after a few months. *He's great. Lots of enthusiasm, never pees on the rug, but he doesn't fit our family.*

My father and I sign off, and I wander back into the weight room. Someone else has taken my turn on the bench, and my hip has gotten stiff from standing still for ten minutes, so I head for the mats and stretch.

"Hey, New Guy?" Castro calls. "You got your phone on you? We need some tunes. Something retro? Maybe Santana."

"Sure," I say, reaching for my phone. A couple of taps later, and Santana is wailing away on his guitar.

"Thanks, New Guy."

I give him a friendly salute. But the truth is that I hate that nickname with the fire of a thousand suns. Not that Castro means anything by it—with a name like Newgate, "New Guy" is just low-hanging fruit.

But after four trades in five years, I'm damn sick of being the new guy—and trying to prove myself day in and day out for a new set of faces. It's exhausting as well as inconvenient. I've learned not to sign a long-term lease. I don't buy a lot of furniture, and I can never own a pet.

Those are just minor inconveniences, though. The grueling part is constantly adapting your style of play to fit in with the new team's needs. You have to be a sponge—learning your teammates names, nicknames and quirks. Listening to the coach like your job depends on absorbing every word.

Because it does.

I roll back and tuck one knee into my chest, and then massage the opposite hip. The athletic trainers usually help with this, but I haven't seen one today.

Just as that thought forms in my mind, I hear Henry's voice out in the corridor. "The men's weight room is usually about half capacity after morning skate. Some guys want to get in a quick workout, some go right home and take a pregame nap."

Henry's giving someone a tour of the facility. And suddenly I'm on high alert, like there's a noticeable change in the air pressure.

Two men walk through the door, and my heart practically explodes.

Oh no. Oh *shit*. It's *him*. Gavin from the bar. Gavin with the clear gray eyes, and the quick smile. In a Brooklyn polo, with an employee ID clipped to his khakis. That's the uniform for athletic trainers.

Holy hell. There's a clipboard hugged under one muscled arm, and I can see my own name on it. Fuck me. This is bad. He's going to work with the team?

It takes me about zero-point-five seconds to picture him kneeling down on this very mat and lifting my leg in his hands to pin it back against my chest, while I gaze up at his dark blond hair, and that rippling chest that I still want to explore with my tongue.

"Fellas, listen up!" Henry says, clapping his hands together. "I'd like to introduce you to Gavin Gillis. He joins the training staff today as my right-hand man."

The players all turn to listen, and O'Doul leans down and turns the Bluetooth speaker off.

The sudden silence is deep.

"Thanks, guys," Henry says. "Gavin joins us as senior training staff. He's never worked in hockey before, but that doesn't matter. His last full-time position was at the University of New Hampshire, where he worked with their D1 men's soccer team, as well as with the women's tennis team..."

I lose the thread of what Henry is saying, because I'm still staring at Gavin. He stands tall at Henry's side. He's wearing the half-smile of someone who's being forced to hear praise about himself and doesn't quite know what to do with it. As I watch, he makes eye contact with each player in the room, one at a time.

He gets to me last, though, because I'm on the floor, in the corner. When his eyes find me, he does a quick double take. His surprise is muted, though. On his second pass, he looks directly at me and does the world's quickest nod.

I forget to breathe, and my vision tunnels.

This can't be happening. He's a *trainer*? He'll be here every damn day. He knows things about me that nobody else knows.

And if he really wants to be a dick about it, my privacy could be shattered before the puck drops tonight.

Even if he's not a dick, it's still going to be awkward.

So fucking awkward.

I force some air into my lungs and try to stem my panic.

But this is bad.

So, so bad.

FIVE

Gavin

THIS IS the moment I've been dreading.

Sure enough, Hudson Newgate is scowling at me from the corner, as if I've done something wrong by showing up here.

Sorry, pal. It's not my fault.

Let the record show that he sat down beside me on that barstool.

Henry drones on, and I try to keep my cool. First days are always awkward. In this job you have to meet new faces all the time, though. You have to gain people's trust so they'll tell you their troubles, and also relax when you put your hands on their bodies.

I'm good at my job, damn it. I have every right to be here. Once I settle in, he'll get used to the idea.

When Henry is finished introducing me, we leave the weight room and settle into the training room. It's a big operation, and there's a lot to learn. Athletes wander in and out, and I watch Henry work on knees and ankles. I pull files for each athlete, and make notes, and make conversation.

My head is spinning, but that's just first day stuff.

Hudson Newgate does not turn up, though. And a trainer on the first day does not have a discreet way to pull an athlete aside for a private conversation. The main training room is a busy place, with multiple conversations in progress at any given moment, and athletes lurking nearby, waiting their turn.

Heck—that first day I can barely navigate the labyrinth of Brooklyn's deluxe practice facility. It's actually two facilities—the male and female athletes have separate floors of the building.

And I spend a solid hour signing personnel forms, and getting my new K-Tech phone. "Everyone who works for the organization has one," says Heidi Jo, the GM's assistant. "And there's an app for the medical system that Henry uses to track player injuries."

"Cool. Thanks."

It's a lot to learn. And when I get back down to the training room, I start skimming through case files, and memorizing every player's name.

As for Hudson Newgate, the files say that he's supposed to be seeing the training staff today for ongoing treatment of bursitis. But he's a no-show. A ghost.

The panic I saw on his face earlier was not my imagination. We need to talk. And soon.

When I arrive home that evening, laden with groceries, I eye his apartment door. I just stand there for a second, keys jingling in my hand, trying to talk myself into knocking. He's probably at the stadium, though. It wouldn't even work.

That's when my daughter throws open our apartment door. "Daddy! I thought you were never coming home."

I wince, even though she didn't mean it literally. Because that is something that already happened once in my daughter's life.

One day Eddie left for work and never came home.

"How's school?" I juggle one grocery bag so I can hug her.

"It stinks." She throws her arms around my waist. "I hate being the new girl. But guess what? There's a Scholastic Book Fair tomorrow. I need money."

"What else is new?" I tease, giving her ponytail a tug with my only free finger.

But she takes the question literally. "Well, did you know we live *right next door* to a hockey player?" She looks up at me, eyes like saucers. "I saw him! His jacket says NEWGATE on the back! Reggie and I googled him!"

Oh boy. I nudge Jordyn into the apartment, just in case he's home and listening.

"—He's a defenseman! Did you meet him? And the rest of the players yet?"

"Some of them," I say weakly. "I didn't memorize all their names yet."

Reggie smirks at me as I deposit the grocery bags on our kitchen table.

"We're going to watch the game on TV," Jordyn announces. "It starts at seven."

"Yeah, okay," is my automatic response, because that sounds like a good time. But then I remember it's a school night, and I'm supposed to be a responsible parent. "You can watch until your bedtime."

She wrinkles up her cute little nose. "Can we go to a game in the stadium? Do you get free tickets?"

"I'm not sure how that's going to work." Technically I could watch any game from the press box. But I don't think they allow children. "After I settle in, I'll ask around."

"Hockey players are cool," she says gleefully. "Do you think Hudson Newgate will give me his autograph?"

"Uh..." I honestly don't know how to get her off the topic of Hudson Newgate. It's bad enough that he's living rent free in my own head.

"Let your dad get to know the people first," Reggie says. "Before he starts asking for favors."

"Okay," she says. "Maybe he'll teach me how to play hockey! And Daddy can invite him over for dinner."

Reggie laughs. "Wouldn't that be fun?"

I hold back a groan and start unloading the groceries. This kitchen is decent for a New York apartment, but I'm not used to it yet. My mind is chaos, and so are my cabinets.

Uprooting your life is hard.

As if I weren't busy enough, my phone begins to trill from my pocket. "That must be Grandma," Jordyn says. "Everyone else texts."

Reggie and I laugh because it's true. And when I check my phone, I see that my daughter is right. So now I have a moral quandary. On the one hand, it's not good parenting if Jordyn sees me blowing off Eddie's mother.

But, Lord, I do not want to talk to that woman after a long day. She's never liked anything about me. Not my job, which she saw as inferior to her son's. Not my attitude, which she finds frivolous. She always saw me as Eddie's boy toy, and when he asked me to marry him, she was legit shocked.

The phone stops ringing, giving me an out. "I'll call her back after I get dinner going."

"Put me to work," Reggie says. "I'll help."

It's a nice offer, except that Reggie is useless in the kitchen. "Do you know how to prep potatoes for baking?"

She shakes her head. "Don't judge me. I can learn."

"Okay, start by running cold water over them and scrubbing them with the potato brush."

"The what?"

I love my sister, but how does she get through the day? When I travel for work—my contract specifies three road trips with the team, to give Henry a break—she and Jordyn are going to have to eat take-out food for lunch and dinner. Cold cereal is about as fancy as Reggie's cooking gets.

As I instruct her on the finer points of washing and scoring potatoes with a fork, my phone trills again, though.

"Might as well just deal with her," Reggie whispers. "She'll probably keep calling."

She's right, so I swipe to answer. "Hello Eustace. How are you this fine evening?" This is part of my strategy for dealing with her—always be pleasant, but then stick to my guns. In other words—smile while putting my foot down.

"I'm great! And how is the *best* little girl in the world?" Eddie's mother gushes.

I'm great too, thanks for asking. "Jordyn is doing well. Her bedroom is shaping up. Would you like to speak to her?"

"In a moment. First, I wanted to tell you something wonderful."

I brace myself, because Eustace has used this strategy against me before—she claims to have good news even as she arm-twists me into doing her bidding. "We're coming to New York for a visit at the end of the month!"

Already? I'd hoped for more of a reprieve. "That's lovely. I'm sure Jordyn will be excited to see you."

"Of course she will. And the best part is that we'll be apartment hunting in Manhattan."

My stomach drops suddenly, as if I'm on a roller coaster entering a sudden dive. "Is that so?" I manage to ask. But I really just want to throw my phone at the wall.

"We're looking at two-bedroom condos in new buildings. Jordyn can have her own room, for when she visits with us!"

I take a deep, calming breath. "That sounds like a very big expense for the occasional weekend visit," I say carefully.

"Well, you know Chad can work anywhere," she says. Her husband is the CEO of a medical equipment company. And a multi-millionaire. "Our plan would be to spend most of our weekends in the city with Jordyn."

Another deep breath. "I'm sure Jordyn would enjoy spending time with you in Manhattan. But it can't possibly be every weekend. She'll have her own friends and activities in Brooklyn." *And me!* I want to scream. *She'll have me.*

But that's not the way to win an argument with Eustace. There has never been a day when she accepted me as Jordyn's father. To her, it's just a legal accident that I became Jordyn's custodial parent after Eddie's death.

In fact, she didn't even wait for the funeral flowers to wilt before she asked me to relinquish custody. "Jordyn needs a stable home with two parents who love her. Chad and I are her best chance."

At that moment, standing in the kitchen of my dead husband's home, making a peanut butter sandwich for a five-year-old who'd spent the last seventy-two hours crying, I didn't even yell. I was too shell-shocked to yell. I just said "She's my child. End of story."

But Eustace is savvy. She never outright asked again about custody. Still, I know she thinks I'm not Jordyn's real dad, and everything she does feels like territorial warfare.

That first year after Eddie's death, I was in shock, and needed her help just to get through the day with a grieving kindergartner. After a few months, though, I pulled myself together and stopped leaning on her. I got grief therapy for both Jordyn and myself. I planned outings, even if I wasn't in the mood. I took pictures. I celebrated holidays with my child, like a normal person.

Since Jordyn is now in school for thirty-five hours a week, I realized I needed to get back into the workforce. I took on some private clients. But I didn't have the bandwidth to run my own business, so I started looking around for jobs.

That's when I saw the posting for the Brooklyn Bruisers. And when I showed it to my sister, she said: "Come to Brooklyn. Start a new chapter. I'll help."

On a whim, I applied to exactly one job, and landed it.

And then Eustace *freaked*. It's the only time I've ever seen her get red with anger. "Jordyn is my only link to Eddie! You can't tear her away from my bosom."

She actually used those words. I still cringe when I remember it.

But I'd rehearsed this. I calmly explained that Jordyn had an aunt who also loved her. And that I'd gotten a very good job with excellent health benefits and a retirement plan. I even said I couldn't "live off Eddie forever," which was exactly a thing she'd accused me of doing when Eddie was still alive.

So here we are, two hundred miles out of her clutches. And she wants to buy a condo across the river and put her nose in at every opportunity?

"We'll just see how the house hunting goes," she says calmly. "Jordyn loves her grandparents."

"Of course she does," I say without gritting my teeth. "And when you plan your visit, please email me the details so I can make sure she's free."

"Already have!" she says cheerily. "It's in your inbox. Now let me speak to that sweet girl."

Beaten, I carry the phone over to my child, who takes it eagerly.

And I resume making dinner.

The next few days are busy. I begin working full time with the players. I memorize injury reports. I sit down with Neil Drake to discuss his diabetes protocols, so I'll know how to intervene in a crisis.

I work with Ivo Halla on his ankle stiffness, and with Patrick O'Doul on his creaky shoulder. I do soft tissue work on everyone's aches and pains.

Except for Hudson Newgate's. He's still avoiding me.

The other guys are friendly and welcoming. That goes a long way toward easing my new-guy stress. But not Newgate. With a recent injury, he's near the top of the list of players with pressing physical issues. A close look at his chart reveals that he was sidelined from four games by a bursitis flare-up in his hip.

During which time I met him in a bar.

But can I find him to discuss the injury? Nope. Whenever I offer my services in the weight room, he's just leaving. When I walk into the players' lounge, he walks out.

It's nerve-wracking. He obviously doesn't want to talk to me. At all. And the longer it goes on, the more awkward it gets.

One morning I arrive just as the team is finishing a yoga session, and Newgate is there. From this distance, his hip movement looks smooth. So that's good news for him.

What's equally smooth, though, is the way he avoids me after the class. He strikes up a conversation with the team captain, which I am loathe to interrupt.

And then another player—Jason Castro—asks me if I have a minute. "My mid-back is cranky." He reaches awkwardly over his shoulder and frowns. "Like a rib is out of line."

"Can you feel it on a deep inhale?" I ask.

"Yup."

"Let's take a look." I point toward the treatment rooms, and we head in that direction.

"Hey baby," he says to a petite blonde woman in the corridor. "You look hot in that dress." Then he makes a *meow* sound. She rolls her eyes.

Well, okay, that's a little aggressive.

He follows me into the empty treatment room. "That's my wife, by the way. I'm not sexually harassing the staff."

"*Oh*." I let out an awkward laugh. "I *did* wonder."

Castro cracks a smile. "This is a very incestuous workplace. O'Doul is married to the yoga instructor. Trevi is married to the publicist."

"Ah. Which one?" I ask, quickly rubbing down the table with an antiseptic wipe. This place is *stocked*. I've never worked anywhere so clean and accommodating.

"Georgia. The, uh, female one." He sits down on the table.

"I was pretty sure that's who you meant. Just teasing, really."

"You married?" he asks.

"Actually, widowed." As I say it, I'm thinking *here we go*. It's important to me that I don't hide my sexuality. But I'm pretty sure I'm the only gay man on the staff, and you never know how that will be received. "My husband died two years ago in a car accident."

Castro's eyes widen sharply, and I brace myself for an awkward conversation. Or worse—maybe he won't want me to work on his cranky back.

"No shit?" he asks. But then he suddenly clasps my shoulder. "Man, I am really sorry to hear that."

I feel myself relax. "Thank you. Lie on your stomach?" He rolls, and I begin by placing my hands on his shoulders.

"You know," he says, his voice slightly muffled. "There's rules for when someone shares that, right? You're not supposed to say—oh, the same thing happened to me. Because they usually follow that shit up with—*my cat died last month*."

I let out a bark of surprised laughter. Because that *is* a thing people do. "Yeah, grief comparisons can be weird." And this conversation did not go in the direction I was expecting.

"Truth. But—just saying?" He raises himself on an elbow and looks over his shoulder at me. "When I was still in high school, my girlfriend died in a car crash. I know it's not the same thing, but it messed me up real good for a few years."

"Wow, I bet it did." I give him a nudge and he reclines again.

I work carefully on the muscles of his upper and mid-back, until I find a concentration of tightness. "This is the spot, right?"

"You know it." He's quiet a moment as I coax those muscles to loosen up. Then he sighs. "Humans aren't wired to look at their comfortable lives and understand that it can all be snatched away at a moment's notice. And when it happens, we can't even process it."

"The back pain is that bad?"

He snorts. "No, but your jokes are."

"Ooh, burn."

He shakes his head. "I used to do that, too. Always making a joke to get through it. Two years isn't very long, is it?"

"Nope," I admit. "Once a week I think of something and I'm like —oh, I should tell Eddie."

He nods. He gets it. Our club has a small membership, but we recognize our members.

"Welcome to Brooklyn," he says. "May your luck turn around. Mine did."

"Hey, you never know. I've always been an optimist."

But some days are easier than others.

"Hey, I'm heading over to set up at the stadium in a bit," Henry says on Monday. "But could you grab Newgate? He hasn't come into the training room."

Yikes. "I'm happy to try. He's been, uh, hard to track down." I'm about ready to put his picture on a WANTED sign in the weight room. *If you see this man, report him to the training office. May be armed and dangerous with a bad attitude...*

"Make sure you grab him before all the players head home to rest."

"Will do!" I say with more charm than actual confidence.

But, honestly, this avoidance has gone on long enough. I'm not about to let this arrogant man make me look bad to my new boss.

The minute Henry leaves, I march out of my treatment room and go looking for Newgate. I find him in the locker room, chest deep in the ice bath, a grimace on his face. *Finally.* A captive audience.

Also—why do irritating people have to be so hot? His chest is a work of art, even with goose bumps all over it.

"Excuse me, Mr. Newgate?" I ask politely, in a tone that suggests we have never had our tongues in each other's mouths. "I should see you before you go. Let's follow up on that hip."

He looks up at me like he's tasted something sour. "Sorry, can't. After this I've got a video session."

"Right." It comes out sounding bitter. "Another time then."

I want to scream into the void. But I leave the room instead.

SIX

Hudson

FUCK FUCK FUCKITY FUCK. I sit through the video meeting in a daze.

Gavin knows I'm blowing him off. It's obvious that we need to have a private talk. Emphasis on private. But here in this building? I feel claustrophobic just thinking about it.

It's not Gavin's fault that I'm a damned disaster. But every day I walk into this place and there he is. A hot, blond reminder of my own idiocy.

Even worse—I'm the only one who isn't Gavin's new BFF. My teammates love him. Castro sings his praises. And I overheard O'Doul thanking Henry for hiring "another true professional."

The problem is all mine, and I can't figure out how to solve it. We need to talk, but I don't even know how to do that. Keeping my trap shut has been my strategy for years.

God, I don't fuck up often. But when I do, I go big.

The meeting ends, and I have only a vague sense of what Coach has told us. I rise from the chair, and my hip complains immediately.

Okay, that's bad. I'm playing tonight—finally—and this much stiffness is a bummer. I head to the training room, and spot Gavin from the doorway. He's working on O'Doul's shoulder. Henry isn't there, but maybe I can find him.

Bingo. I find the head trainer putting on his jacket in the coatroom. "Hey, Henry? I know you're about to run over to the stadium, but I could use five minutes of your time." I sit down on one of the padded benches.

"*Here?*" He looks at me like I've lost my mind. But then he relents, removing his jacket and tossing it onto a hook. "Is Gavin not available?"

"Um..." I am such an asshole. "I'd just prefer your help, that's all."

"On your side, then," he says. "Let's make this quick. You're sore?"

"Yup."

Henry frowns. "Painkillers?"

"Not yet today." I lie down on my good side so he can manipulate the bad one.

"Then that's your next move. Don't panic, okay? You might have favored the joint in practice, and now the smaller muscles are complaining."

He digs in with his fingers and I exhale slowly, trying to relax. "Got any other tricks in your bag?" I ask. "I really need this to go away."

He shakes his head. "What did I say about not panicking? You're just going to get a lot of soft tissue treatment on the hip flexors, the IT bands—anything in the same zip code as the joint. And warm up like your life depends on it."

"Yeah, okay." I sigh.

"Can I ask you a question?"

"Sure."

"Is there some reason you won't see Gavin? He do anything wrong?"

"No," I say immediately. "Not at all."

Henry squints. "Is it that he's gay? Because in this organization we don't—"

"*No way.*" Horrified, I interrupt him. "It's *not* that. God no. It's…" I have to think fast. "A superstition thing. You stretched me before the Philly game, and I got my first goal for Brooklyn."

He hoots with laughter. "Athletes. You'd think I'd understand them by now." He stretches me with a firm grip. "Do yourself a favor and add the new trainer to your repertoire of good juju, okay? He was a good hire. Has a real way about him—people respond."

Oh I responded all right. "Yeah, okay. Sure."

"See you over there." Job finished, he stands up. "Find me again this afternoon, before warm-ups. You're going to have a great game tonight."

If only. "Thank you. See you over there."

Five hours later—after a lot of stretching and Advil—I take the ice for Brooklyn for the first time in ten days.

And it goes fine. Not amazing, but fine.

Then, while everyone else goes out to the Tavern to celebrate with beer and nachos, I go home and ice my hip and snack on carrot sticks, hummus and spring water.

My father calls, and I listen to him prattle on for a while about the angle of my shots from the top of the circle.

When I finally get away from him, I go to bed, wondering if Gavin watched the game tonight. Wondering if he's in bed on the other side of the wall.

And wondering why I care.

The next morning I go to the rink early. Morning skate doesn't start until ten, but I make sure to get there at eight thirty.

I park myself on the stretching mats. And ten minutes later, I hear Gavin's voice in the corridor, greeting the equipment manager, who's pulling a load of clean laundry down the hallway.

This is my chance to catch him alone, while the place is quiet.

I man up and head down to the training room. When I put my head inside the door, there's nobody else around. It's just Gavin, humming to himself while he wipes down a treatment table. He doesn't notice me at first, so I spend a second admiring his strong back muscles, flexing as he works.

Henry is right—there's something dynamic about his energy. He's the kind of guy who radiates competence and good intentions. No wonder everyone loves him.

But then he turns suddenly, catching me in the doorway like a creeper. He stops humming, and his expression shutters. "Morning," he says crisply. "Come on in."

I enter, and then close the door behind me. Nobody does that—the training room is always open. But we have things to discuss.

"Please have a seat," Gavin says in a crisp tone that suggests we've never met before. "Glad you're back on the ice. Let's see how that hip held up after last night's game." He's all business as he disinfects his hands.

I sit down on the edge of the table, but I don't lie back. "Hey. I'm sorry. We need to talk."

"About your hip," he says firmly. "I'm only here to do my job, Hudson. I'm not here to ruin your life. I know your time is valued at approximately a hundred times more than mine, but I have work to do. So if you're ready to stop treating me like a contagious disease, please lie back and bend your right knee."

"Can we just talk for a second? Please?" I beg.

He crosses his arms on his well-defined pecs and glares at me. "Fine. Talk. You have sixty seconds."

Yup, he's angry. This is why I was avoiding this conversation. "Look, I just wanted to say it's not you, it's me."

He actually rolls his eyes. "I know that, buddy. You didn't seem to have any issues with me when I was still an anonymous stranger. If that's your thing, great. We can pretend we never met. Just don't make me look like an asshole to my new boss."

Well damn. Fiery Gavin is just as hot and distracting as laid-back Gavin.

Not helpful.

"Look, I apologize, okay? I just don't know what to do with you."

"Oh please. Were you not listening? Lie down on the damn table. With my help, your only job here is to rehab that hip. So that is what we're going to do."

I hesitate for another second. Maybe it's questionable logic to put your body under the hands of a riled up, muscular man who's angry at you.

But he gives me another glare. So I do it. I roll onto my back and prop my right foot onto the table. Then I brace myself for the awkwardness of being close enough to Gavin that I can smell the clean scent of his deodorant.

When his hands land on my bare knee, they're warm and kind. "Please tell me if I hurt you."

"I'd probably deserve it, though."

He ignores that and begins palpating the muscles surrounding my hip. They include, of course, the muscles stretching around to my ass, and the ones in my groin area. But his touch is firm and businesslike. "Any tenderness here?"

"Some," I admit.

He wears a thinking man's frown. "Roll over for me. Let's work on that IT band."

In spite of the tension between us, his touch relaxes me almost immediately. I've been an athlete all my life, and we're used to a certain amount of handling. But I'm still human. The touch of another person on my sore spots feels like relief. I let out a little grunt of satisfaction as he begins to loosen me up with soothing fingers.

"When these muscles get tight, they can make the hip joint less fluid. That can make your bursae more susceptible to inflammation."

"Okay," I grunt as he moves his hands in a new spot.

"This hurt?" he asks.

"No," I lie. But then I reconsider. "Well, somewhat." It honestly feels great, and I wish he'd never stop touching me. He leans over me a few more degrees, and I get a whiff of piney cologne and peppermint.

When I steal a glance at his face, I see his brow furrowed in concentration. "No heat on this—only ice," he says. "You've probably been told that."

"Yeah." I try not to groan as he presses his strong hand against another stiff spot.

"Don't let up on your anti-inflammatories. You're not sensitive to them, right?"

I shake my head. "Advil is life."

"Agreed. See? We have one thing in common." He flashes me a quick smile that I certainly don't deserve.

I'm willing to bet there's a bunch of things we have in common. But I keep that idea to myself.

"Look," he says. "I reviewed the tape of this injury, and the hit didn't look that hard. But the hip is a vulnerable joint."

"Right," I say, trying not to gasp as his hand strokes my thigh muscle.

"And your chart doesn't mention any history with this hip. But you just got here a month ago so I gotta ask." He looks me right in the eye. "Hudson, is this a chronic injury?"

"Nah," I say immediately.

His hands pause right in the middle of this life-giving massage. "You sure about that?" he asks quietly.

Fuck. Fuckity fuck. "Well, it's happened before. Uh, twice. The first time was from a big hit last fall. I was out for three games."

The expression that flashes through his eyes is disappointment. And I hate it. I couldn't even tell you why, but I don't want Gavin Gillis to think badly of me.

"I'm sorry," I blurt out.

He sighs. "Why would you hide that from the people who are trying to heal you? It's only going to make our job harder."

"Because I can't afford to be seen as a liability."

He licks his lip, like he wants to say more. Then he resumes his excellent ministrations to my stiff muscles. "Do us all a favor and just tell the truth, Hudson."

My blood pressure spikes. "Are we still talking about bursitis? Or, like, my whole life?"

"Your *hip*," he says through clenched teeth. "You're the only one here who keeps bringing up that other thing."

He's right, but now that I've finally gathered myself to apologize, he's letting me twist over it. "I'm sorry I bailed on you, okay? I should never have left that bar with you in the first place. It's not something I usually do. But I was just so..." I don't know how to finish that sentence. *Attracted to you. Tempted by you.* "I'm just a hot mess."

His brow furrows. "But why? Is there more to the story?"

Oops. Having bursitis in *both* hips would be more fun than talking about my stupid life. "There isn't a story. I just don't usually pick up guys."

Finished with me, he releases my leg to the padded table. "Because...?"

This isn't a conversation I *ever* have, so I try out a few answers in my head.

Because of conversations like this.

Because it could cost me my career.

Because reminding myself what I'm missing just makes things worse.

"Because I can't," I say lamely. "Not at the moment." And when you're always the new guy, that moment never seems to arrive. "I'm bisexual, as I'm sure you, uh, noticed. But I don't date men. Or anybody, really."

His eyes widen. "And nobody knows?"

"Nobody but you. I'd prefer if you would keep it in confidence."

He makes a noise of surprise. "Of course I will. Jesus. But that sounds..." His voice softens, and his curious gray gaze pins me down. "Lonely."

Suddenly I feel vulnerable. I'm lying here like a beached whale, and I hate it. So I sit up and swing my legs off the opposite side of the table, turning my back to his prying eyes. I need to get out of here. "You probably think I'm a coward," I mumble. "But it's complicated."

"I bet," he says quietly. "Sounds like maybe you could use a friend, though."

My heart gives an ugly squeeze. Never mind that he's right, I don't like how pathetic it sounds. "Right, because the poor, confused hockey player doesn't have any of those?"

"*Hudson...*"

"No. You can fix my hip, okay? But you can't fix my life."

He makes another irritated noise. "Message *received*. I'll still keep your damn secrets, though. It's kind of insulting to ask. Maybe you could also refrain from mentioning that I shot my mouth off about Brooklyn's prospects that night in the bar. You're not the only new guy here."

I snort. "Hell, I'd forgotten that part. So disloyal. I guess we both have blackmail material. You were rooting for Boston, for fuck's sake. Why is that?"

"My husband was a big fan."

Husband. That startles me to such a degree that I turn and look him in the eye again. "Was?"

"Yeah." His eyes burn with sudden fury. "He passed away two years ago in a car accident."

"Oh *shit.*" Just more of my eloquence.

"...Your life is complicated, I get that," he says, grabbing a spray bottle and aggressively misting the table. "But maybe you're not the only one? Next time you're short with me, remember that my only sin was liking you. For a whole hour or two, you were the most exciting thing that happened to me in years. And the first person I kissed since the last one died. But hey—no big deal! You've got games to win. Go ice your hip and beat Philly."

He grabs a fresh towel and wipes the table down like it's on fire.

And it takes me an awkward minute to realize I've been dismissed.

SEVEN

Hudson

WE DO BEAT PHILLY.

Then I ice my hip.

My dad calls and tells me seventeen little things I could have done better.

They're all accurate.

"You okay, Son?" he asks when he's done with the litany. "Your hip solid?"

"Yup, fine." It's just my confidence that's battered.

When we hang up, I can't stop thinking about how neatly Gavin put me in my place. He didn't just bring me down a few steps on the ego ladder, he sent me sliding all the way to the basement.

I make another ice pack for my hip, and lie down in bed, wishing his capable hands were still stretching me. I strain my ears to hear sounds of life from his place next door.

But all I hear is silence.

The next morning we're off on a road trip—Minnesota and then Chicago. I'm just rolling my bag out into the hallway when I hear Gavin's door opening.

My first reaction is to wince, because I'm embarrassed by the way I've acted toward him. Twice.

Still, I man up, turn around and smile.

It's not Gavin at all, though. It's a girl—probably the same one who sings *Frozen* at the top of her lungs. She's not little, but not big, either. Sort of a medium-sized kid, wearing jeans, Chucks, and a black ski jacket.

"Hi?" I say, wondering if Gavin is about to reveal himself.

"Hi!" she squeaks. "I'm Jordyn. You're Hudson Newgate. Jersey number twenty-two. Defenseman."

"Uh, yup." Maybe she knows my face because Gavin—her... uncle? He's too young to be her dad—has already put my photo on the family dartboard.

"Could I..." She swallows. "Could I have your autograph?"

"You want..." *Really?* This is hilarious. "Okay. Sure. You got a pen?"

"Jordyn! Where are you?" Gavin's voice rings out. "Is your backpack ready?"

She glances over her shoulder. "Just a minute, Daddy!"

Daddy?

I'm sure there's shock on my face when Gavin appears behind her in the doorway. He frowns at me. "Problem?"

"No," I say after a beat of confusion. "She was just, um..."

"Asking for his autograph!" she says cheerfully.

Gavin's frown deepens. "I'm sorry," he says to me. "Jordyn, he's on his way to catch a plane. You can't badger him in his own hallway."

"But Daddy...!"

He pulls her back inside without a word to me, and closes the door. I can still hear them, though. "Is that why you've been hanging out in front of the door? This is his home. You can't pounce on a guy who's just trying to get through his day."

"He didn't mind!" she insists. "I almost had his autograph! I could show the kids in my class! I told them I live next door to

Hudson Newgate and Daddy, they didn't *believe* me. They said I'm a weirdo."

"Oh, baby," he says. "Is the new school that bad?"

"I don't have *any* friends."

Ouch. My phone buzzes in my pocket, though, reminding me that there's a car waiting outside. And I realize I'm just standing here eavesdropping like a creeper.

So I tiptoe toward the stairs and make my exit.

It's a long three days in Minnesota and Chicago. In the cab on the way home from LaGuardia, my hip stiffens into something resembling a rusty chunk of iron.

But I did it. I made it through, and I didn't let it affect my play. Coach is pleased with me. O'Doul complimented my game, and we picked up some league points on the road.

And I didn't spend the whole time thinking about Gavin.

Not often, anyway.

"You guys coming to the game tonight?" my teammate Anton asks as our cab approaches Brooklyn.

The Brooklyn Bombshells—the women's team—are playing a home game tonight against Albany. Anton is dating one of the goalies. And my teammate Drake is married to one of their star players.

"I'll go," I offer, in spite of my exhaustion. The truth is that I have made very little effort to socialize with the team. In January, I invited them all to a party that my father had heard about. And I was super relieved when they all turned me down.

Since then, I've ducked out of most everything. I don't hang out at the bar on the road, because I'm not really a drinker and I need my rest. I don't play cards on the jet.

But I know I should make an effort. And since the Bombshells game is played on the same ice where we practice, it's an easy jaunt in my own neighborhood.

After agreeing to meet my teammates at the rink, I get out of the taxi. When I reach my front door, and fumble for the key, I feel eyes on me. I look up, but I'm alone in the second floor hallway, except for the peephole in my neighbors' door.

I remember Jordyn hanging out there, trying to catch me. So I wave at the door, and I hear a sharp intake of breath.

Hilarious. "I can hear you breathing in there!" I call, and she giggles.

Smiling, I let myself into my stale apartment. Other players make arrangements for cleaning services and grocery delivery. But I haven't gotten around to it yet. So my fridge is empty, which is kind of depressing. But then I remember I'm going to the Bombshells game in a couple of hours, and I can eat stadium chow.

The life of a single guy, ladies and gentlemen. It has its moments.

A few hours later I'm standing in the lobby area of the team's headquarters with a dozen or so of my teammates, while Trevi's wife, Georgia, the publicist, is doling out signs for us to wave. *Go Bombshells*, and *Brooklyn Strong* are splashed across their shiny faces.

I didn't realize we were going to be part of a PR pony show, but I don't really mind. The new guy has to do his part. *Go Bombshells.*

Then Georgia comes down the line a second time with a lavender Bombshells jersey for each of us. I shed my jacket and pull the jersey over my head. Then I hear a little gasp.

When my head clears the neck of the jersey I spot Jordyn waving at me. She's standing beside Gavin, who's holding his phone to his ear.

"There he is!" the little girl says, shaking her father's free hand. "If I talk to him here, I'm not bugging him at home, right? Right." Without waiting for an answer, she leaves her father and gallops toward me. "Hi! Wow! Omigod. It's *all* of you!" She looks down the row of my teammates, wearing a starstruck expression.

Here's my chance to settle a score with a small hockey fan. "Hey, Georgia? You got an extra jersey? My friend here needs one."

Georgia looks from the little girl to me. Then she smiles. "Sure. Here." She tosses the jersey at me. And—even better—she tosses me a Sharpie, too.

"Here, buddy." I uncap the Sharpie and scribble my name on the arm of the jersey.

That's when Gavin ends his call and hurries over. "Jordyn, what are you—"

"Hey—don't drag her away just yet, okay? This is for her." I hand the jersey and the marker to Jordyn. "Quick, kid. Get the rest of these guys before we get herded to our seats."

Jordyn lets out a shriek as high-pitched as a dog whistle. "Thank you!" she and Gavin say at exactly the same moment.

With a reddening face, he watches her lunge at Leo Trevi for an autograph. "That was kind of you," he says.

"No problem." I clear my throat. "Everything all right? You look stressed."

He blows out a breath. "My job is only supposed to be daytime hours. That's my arrangement with management. But the Bomb-shells trainer is sick, and they called me. Didn't feel like I could say no. And now I can't reach my sister." He looks at his phone. "And I'm supposed to be in the locker room already."

Now I understand the problem. Jordyn can't stand behind the players' bench with him, no matter how much she'd like to.

"She can hang with us," I hear myself offer. Babysitting is like a foreign country I have never thought of visiting. But anyone can sit next to a kid at a game, right? "She'll be fine. Nice, wholesome entertainment. Except..." I glance down the row of players. "I predict some foul language."

Gavin actually laughs. "You think?" He looks at the time again. "Lord, I wouldn't even ask, but..."

52

"It's fine," I insist. "Have your sister text me if she shows up. Let me give you my number."

His sheepish eyes flip up to mine as he hands me his phone so I can text myself with it. "I'll owe you big after this."

"Nah," I say, waving that idea away with a flick of my hand. "I'd say we'd come out even."

Maybe I'll feel like less of an asshole if he lets me do this favor for him.

I doubt it, though.

It turns out that babysitting Jordyn is super easy—just as long as you're available to answer about four thousand questions.

Per minute.

"How did they hang that scoreboard from the ceiling? Why doesn't the ice melt? How do they get the lines painted *under* the ice?"

I know this last one. "It gets painted by hand on the floor at the beginning of the season. The ice is clear, so you can see through it."

She bounces in her seat. "Do you ever get to drive the Zamboni?"

"No ma'am. I don't have a Zamboni license."

She giggles. "Can we have cotton candy? Daddy would say yes."

Oh boy. "Let's put a pin in that until after we eat some real food. Are you a burger person or a hot dog person?"

"Oooh! Hot dogs. But no mustard because mustard is gross."

"Noted." I pull out my phone and text Gavin. *Any food restrictions? There has already been a request for cotton candy and hot dogs. Absolutely no mustard.*

He replies immediately. *God, anything goes tonight. Although cotton candy plus a soda will result in a level of hyperactivity you will probably not enjoy. I'll pay you back for whatever.*

I put in my food order with Leo, who's headed to the concession stand, just as the players take the ice for warm-ups.

"It's starting!" Jordyn shrieks. "Oh, a spotlight! That's fancy. The other team has white jerseys? That's boring. I hope they lose. Why does the goalie have a big fat stick? How come she's scratching up the ice with her skates? Are they gonna play music the whole time? OH LOOK! HI DADDY! HIIIIIII!" She jumps up and down and waves frantically as Gavin sets up behind the players' bench, with his first aid kit.

"He probably can't hear you because there are so many people here," I point out.

"It's okay," she says, flopping back down in her seat. "But will you take a picture of him? I can show the kids at school."

"You're the new kid in class, huh?" I pull out my phone.

"Yeah." She makes a face.

"Hard to make friends?" I use my camera to zoom in on Gavin's ridiculously attractive face. I take the photo for her, and then zoom out some and capture one of him with the players, too.

"All of them are already friends with each other. It's someone's birthday tomorrow, too. Some party they were all talking about, at the American Girl store..." She makes another grumpy face. "I've never been there."

"I bet you'll go there someday," I say quickly. Even if I don't have the first idea where or what that is. "I've been the new kid a lot. The trick is to smile a lot even when you don't want to. And don't try to figure out who's going to be nice, and who's mean. Just bring, like, a Hershey's Kiss for everyone in the class. Including the teacher. Everyone likes to feel included."

She frowns thoughtfully. "I dunno if you can just bring candy to school when it's not your birthday. My birthday was in the summer."

"Okay, okay." I think for a moment. "What about bringing it because they *missed* your birthday. Who doesn't like an extra birthday chocolate?"

Her eyes light up. "Ooh! That's *good*. Okay, now a selfie?" She leans against my shoulder. "Cheese!"

I raise the phone to frame us both and smile. Then I snap the picture.

"Awesome! Can I take some?" Jordyn reaches for my phone.

I hand it over. Saying yes is easier than saying no.

Sometimes there's hell to pay later. Ask me how I know.

EIGHT

Gavin

WORKING the women's game is a surprisingly fun time, so I'm too busy to worry about Jordyn. Mostly.

There are no further texts from Hudson, so I assume everything is fine. During the third period, I finally get a text from Reggie confirming that she got all my messages and that she's headed to the rink to collect my little girl.

I don't get home until ten o'clock, though, and Jordyn is already asleep. I hang up my coat beside the door and tiptoe to the sofa, where Reggie is waiting.

Her smile widens when I flop down. "Omigod," she whispers. "Our favorite neighbor is *super* hot in person! I practically passed out when I met him. You should go right over there and give him a thank-you gift."

"Yeah..." I consider the idea. "I owe him some cash for the concession stand stuff. But I guess it would be nice if I got him a good bottle of wine or something, too, right? I wonder if he drinks wine?"

"How about a blowjob? Every guy likes those."

"*Reggie.*"

She cackles. "But seriously, I don't think Jordyn ever had so much fun *in her life*. Look." She points at the table.

"What *is* all that?" The table is covered with lavender Bombshells swag. When I get up to inspect it, I find a set of pom-poms, and a Jordyn-sized T-shirt with Charli Higgins's number on the back. Plus a Bombshells program with the players' signatures, and the other jersey signed by the Bruisers.

And a hat. And a rain poncho.

"He got her one of everything at the gift shop." She shrugs. "He told me the new kid at school needs a leg up."

"Wow. That's...That's so nice I don't even know what to say."

"Sure you do. Go *thank* him. It isn't even late." She makes a shooing motion in the direction of the hallway.

I glance toward the door, wishing I didn't have to do it. When Hudson first blew me off at work, I was full of righteous anger. But that was before I went all emo on him in the treatment room.

I can't believe I word-vomited like that. *You were the most exciting thing to happen to me in two years.* It sounds so pathetic. Even if it's true.

Still, I gather up my courage and march myself out of my apartment to knock on his door.

For a lucky second I imagine he's not home. He might have gone out with his teammates after handing Jordyn over to Reggie.

But no such luck. I hear footsteps approaching, and then the door opens to reveal Hudson looking edible in a threadbare T-shirt and low-slung sweatpants.

Yowza.

"Hi," I say stupidly.

"Hi." His brown eyes give nothing away.

"Um..." It's really hard to think when his biceps bulge so perfectly in my line of sight. "I just wanted to say thanks. You didn't have to bail me out, and I really appreciate it. Jordyn is passed out already, but Reggie says you spoiled her rotten. So thanks for that."

"She's a cute kid." Mr. Serious flashes me a rare smile. "She got so excited seeing you on the bench, it was kind of hilarious. I don't know anything about kids, though. Hell, I didn't know you had a kid until the other morning. You don't look old enough."

"Yeah, I get that a lot. It's a long story."

He stares at me with that broody gaze for a beat. Then he opens the door wider, inviting me in. His expression is wary, though. Like he's not sure if this is a good idea. "Tell me. I have something for you, anyway."

Gulp. I follow him inside.

"Jordyn is, um, adopted," I say, following him inside. His door opens right into the living room, just like mine does. "My husband —Eddie—he was older than me by nine years. He and his long-time girlfriend were going to adopt, but she broke up with him before it went through."

"Whoa. And he adopted anyway?" He crosses to his sofa—it's charcoal gray. No throw pillows. It's also the only place to sit in this room, unless we're counting the stools at the kitchen counter across the room.

"Well, yeah. I didn't meet him until Jordyn was almost two. But she doesn't remember her life without me in it."

His broody eyes soften. "So you're her only family now."

"Well, almost. There's also my overbearing in-laws, and my sister. But, yeah. Eddie and I only got three years together before he died. After that I quit my job and stayed home to take care of her. She needed a lot of attention, and he had good life insurance." God, I'm rambling again. That's what Hudson does to me. "That's our story. It's a little unusual. But Jordyn is a great kid, and you made tonight special. So thank you for that."

"You're welcome." He grabs his phone off the coffee table. "There are, like, a hundred pictures of you on here. Maybe more. But I promise I'm not a creeper—Jordyn wanted pictures of 'Daddy at work.'"

"Oh!" I laugh awkwardly. "And I'm supposed to save them for her?"

He makes a gun shape with his hand and shoots me. "That's the idea. Do you have your phone?"

"Yeah, right here." I cross the room and sit on the other end of the sofa. I put my phone on the cushion between us, and he does the same, and then initiates the transfer.

"There's a lot," he says. "You've been warned."

My phone vibrates, and my inner teenager can't help but think that our phones are basically exchanging bodily fluids right now. My phone even makes a little grunt each time a photo lands.

This is what happens when you're widowed. Everything reminds you of the sex you're not having.

The photos transfer slowly. So I glance around at his apartment, which is almost completely bare. "I love what you've done with the place."

He waves a hand. "Yeah, yeah. The longest I've lived in any apartment was eleven months. I'm hoping to break that streak, although I don't want to jinx anything by furnishing it just yet."

"So you're basically a nomad?"

"Not by choice. You know how trades work in the NHL?"

I shake my head.

"Most players can be traded at any moment. One time I got traded on my birthday. My teammates were arguing about which restaurant to take me to, and the GM said *hey, I've got some news for New Guy.* Another time I found out I was traded while sitting on the john. Somebody leaked the trade before they could find me, and I read about it on Twitter."

Ouch. "Well that sounds awful. Does that happen all the time?"

"It does if you're me," he says, his cool eyes ducking mine. "I'm sort of special that way. But it's the reason I've never, uh, come out. I mean, I tried once."

My heart leaps with anxiety. "Really?"

"Oh yeah. Big mistake." He clears his throat. "I was twenty years old. First round draft pick. Big expectations—partly because my dad was a big name in hockey."

"*Oh.*" There's a lot I don't know about hockey.

"Yeah, so, I was playing for Colorado on my first national league team. It had also been my father's team before his retirement. Lots of Newgate history there. And during my first season I met this great guy. He was, um," Hudson looks suddenly embarrassed. "A trainer I met at the gym."

My laugh is sudden and a little loud. "You're *kidding* me."

He shakes his head. "He wasn't employed by the team, though. Just someone I met before training camp. Great guy. He made everything fun. Kind of like you. Hooking up with him answered a lot of questions I'd been having. I felt a lot of relief. Like, okay—I like girls *and* guys. I can stop wondering why I like to jerk off to Maroon 5 videos."

I clamp a hand over my mouth to try to stop my laughter. It doesn't quite work.

"Yeah, I know. It's funny." He flashes me a quick smile, but it's pained.

"So what happened with the guy?"

He rubs his forehead. "Well, life was great for a little while. I thought I'd made it, you know? Professional athlete. Hookups with a guy who likes to blow me. But eventually he says he can't be my dirty secret. And if I want to continue, I have to at least tell somebody."

"*Oh.*" I practically have PTSD from coming out to my own family, so there are lots of dark turns this story could take.

"So I man up and do it—I tell my dad. And he takes it surprisingly well. I'm kind of stunned. His only advice is *just don't tell the team.* He wants me to give it a whole season first." Hudson takes a deep breath. "Looking back, I think he was just hoping that I'd get sick of the guy, and maybe the problem would solve itself. But I didn't listen to him."

Uh-oh. I brace myself.

"...I mean, I really thought it would be okay. Coach was hard to read, but the assistant coach was a great guy, and I just had a good feeling—like the whole world should be just as happy as I am about this. You know what I mean?"

I nod, but I actually feel a little queasy.

"...So I pick a quiet day when management is around, and I ask for a quick meeting. Just fifteen minutes." He swallows. "They ask if it can wait, and I say no. So we tromp into Coach's office." He drops his eyes to his hands. "And I just go for it. The minute I sit down, I tell them I'm dating a guy, and I need my teammates to know. I want to be honest, because switching pronouns when I talk about my weekend makes me feel like a heel, you know?" His brown eyes flip up to mine, and they're pleading. "I didn't want to lie to my team about who I was."

"Oh I *know*." It's so hard to live that way. "But what did they *say*?"

"Nothing." He swallows hard. "Not one word. It was so quiet I could hear my own pulse. Lots of exchanged glances. Then the manager says—*thank you for telling us. Maybe just hold off a few days on telling the team. We'll call you in a day or so.*"

It's just as quiet right now as I wait for him to continue. He rubs his forehead again, like it pains him to think about this. But sometimes you just need to get it out.

"...So I figure they want to get the PR department on board. I'm waiting for a call. But when it comes, the GM calls me into his office alone. No PR person. He hands me a travel itinerary to Carolina. *Thank you for your service, but you've been traded.*"

I let out a gasp. "Really? Just like that? And you think it's because you came out?"

"I *know* it was." Those dark eyes flash with pain. "My father is my agent, and he's one of the most connected men in hockey. So he hears everything. And he was *pissed.*"

"At you?"

He winces. "A little. But mostly just pissed off. He gave a lot to that team, and when they traded me, he was ashamed. Like they were rejecting him. He sort of took it personally."

Ohhhhh shit. That is messy. "So, uh, I've heard a lot of coming out stories, and that's a prize winner."

He snorts. "Thanks, I think. But I wanted you to hear it. I've been waiting a long time to feel settled enough on a team somewhere to try again. But it hasn't happened for me yet. There's actually a Guinness Book entry for the most-traded hockey player. Nine times. I've got a few more to go."

Ouch. "So you basically live with an ax over your head? I'm sorry."

Those dark eyes lift to mine. "No, *I'm* sorry. Because you were pretty much the most exciting thing that happened to me, too."

"Oh."

Oh.

I'm suddenly aware of how close we are to each other. Again. He's right there, thinking all the same thoughts as me. Quiet apartment. Nobody else home. Late night. All I'd have to do is lean over and taste his mouth...

He rises abruptly and heads into the kitchen. "I'd offer you a beer but I have nothing more interesting than water."

"It's okay," I say, hiding my disappointment. I look down at my phone, where the photos have all loaded. This is probably my cue to leave.

I stall, though, opening up the photo gallery. The first thing I see is a pic of Jordyn on Hudson's shoulders. He's gripping her shins, and she's smiling like she just won the lottery.

Oh boy—a hot hockey player being nice to my kid. Is there anything more attractive than that?

Then there's a picture of her eating a hot dog with ketchup on her face. And a selfie of Castro and Jordyn and a bag of popcorn. And a photo of her wearing all her new Bombshells gear.

And—inexplicably—a picture of Jordyn signing Hudson's jersey with a Sharpie. The way he's smiling at my little girl makes my heart beat faster. "Hudson—these pictures are..." I gulp. "Perfect. Thank you. And let me pay you back for everything." I stand up and pull out my wallet to fish for some cash.

"No. You aren't going to pay me a dime," he says before taking a gulp of water. "I bought her that stuff because it's cool to support the women's team. And 'cause she said it's hard being the new kid. I, uh, kinda get that." He turns away and puts the glass on the counter, like it cost him something to admit that.

Now my heart is in danger of exploding. "Well, thank you. I'm sure it meant a lot to her. And I appreciate you stepping in to help me tonight when you had no need to."

He shrugs, and his face is a little red, as if hearing praise is hard for him. "No problem."

"I'd better go." I edge toward the door, wishing he'd stop me.

He doesn't, though. He thinks he can't.

At least now I know why.

"Good night," he says gently.

I show myself out.

NINE

Gavin

ON MONDAY MORNING, Jordyn puts on her new Bombshells shirt for school. And the baseball cap, too.

It's cold outside, and I'd prefer she wore a winter hat. But I let it go. It's already a quarter of eight. Her lunch is made and packed. Her hair is braided just the way she likes. "Okay, coat on! Let's do this! I have to get to work."

"Daddy?" She's just standing there with her coat. "I don't think I should go to school today."

Uh-oh. "Why?"

"I have a sore throat." She grabs her throat dramatically.

Ohhhhh shit. "That does sound bad," I agree. Except Friday, she had a tummy ache, and Thursday, a pain which magically jumped from one side to the other while we were discussing it.

And on the weekend? Nothing but smiles. Still, I am afraid to brush aside her concerns. What if today it's really strep? What kind of a parent would I be if I didn't listen?

"Open your mouth and let me take a look."

Her mouth opens like a little bird's.

I peer in. But all I see is a pink tongue and not much else. *A little help right now would be nice, Eddie. Can you send me a sign?*

He was a pediatrician. He always knew exactly what to do in

these situations. No, in *all* situations. He was the calm, solid one. A rock in the river. He'd quietly assess a situation, make a sound judgment and then patch you up, if necessary.

I had a different role. I was the party boy, the comic relief. The one who made balloon animals to distract you while Eddie stitched up your wound. To say that I'm out of my depth now is putting it mildly.

"Listen," I say as my daughter closes her mouth. "On a scale of one to ten, where one is an itchy mosquito bite, and ten is somebody trying to tell you the remake of *Miracle on 34th Street* is better than the original, how bad is your pain?"

She giggles.

"Well?"

"It's a two," she admits. "But it could get worse at any time."

"It could," I agree. "Your teacher should call me if that happens. If you don't go to school, you can't ask her for a specially timed birthday treat, can you?" This idea, apparently, came courtesy of Hudson. Jordyn woke up thinking about him.

I know the feeling.

"Okay," she says, zipping up her coat with careful fingers. "If it gets real bad, I'll ask her to call."

"Good deal," I say, relief coursing through me. My sister and I are both working today, and I don't want to be the new guy who calls in for childcare issues ten days after his hire date.

This single parenting thing is not for wimps.

Two hours later I'm at the practice facility. The players are coming off the ice from their morning skate, so I'm busy icing, taping and stretching various body parts.

"Thanks, man," O'Doul says after I apply the thumper to his sore muscles.

"No problem. Stay warm and limber!" I call as he slides off the table. "Real men wear a Snuggie until game time."

He laughs. "I'll bear that in mind."

"Next!" I call.

A sheepish looking Hudson Newgate enters the room. In a T-shirt and athletic shorts, he's just fresh from the shower. "Here I am. Not avoiding you."

"And I'm grateful. So are your hip flexors." I wipe down the table with forced nonchalance. It's important to me that we can work together. And not just because of my job.

I really like this hockey player. Grumpy, difficult Hudson Newgate is a gentler man than he lets on. And when I look at him, I see something familiar—a guy who's doing his best in a situation he can't control.

He kicks off his flip-flops and lies down on his back, and I get to work. "Bend this knee, please." I tuck his muscular knee into the crook of my arm, and rotate it across his body. Then I apply pressure with my fingertips up and down his quads. "You okay? You aren't breathing."

Hudson lets out a breath. "Fine," he mutters.

I massage his leg, waiting for him to relax into the stretch. Athletes are used to being handled like livestock. Still, everyone carries around unconscious associations with touch. Some people were taught at an early age not to trust it, but most of us learn to lean into it.

That's why I like my job so much. Training works at the intersection of mind and body. I never go home at the end of the day wondering if I've been useful. Because there's always someone who needs me.

I hear Hudson's breathing slow as he sinks into my practiced touch. I apply some easy pressure to his knee, asking the muscles for a little more stretch.

"You're making progress," I tell him. "This hip thing is going to be okay."

He narrows his eyes at me. "I've noticed you say that to everyone. Like it's your job to say that."

Busted. I chuckle. "Sure. But it's also *true.*"

"Not really. There's such a thing as a career-ending injury."

"And here I couldn't figure out why your nickname wasn't *Mr. Sunshine.*"

He snorts.

"The thing is? I see a lot of injuries. *All* the injuries. And most of them heal up just fine. Your perspective is different—you only see them from the terrifying point-blank range."

"I guess," he admits.

"It's not my job to blow smoke up your ass. My job is to help it *be* okay. And I'm good at my job." I press my fingers into the most stubborn muscles of his thigh, and his jaw flexes. "It's going to be okay. Okay?"

"Okay," he grunts.

"Good man." If I've read him right, this might be the only kind of touch Hudson ever gets—the careful, professional kind. So I do my best work. After I convince his IT band to release, I spend an extra moment on his calves, and then his ankle mobility. He makes a grimace, though, when I massage his foot with a firm grip.

"Hey, kids!" Henry, my boss, startles me from the open doorway. "Is New Guy having foot problems?"

"No," he says immediately. "Everything's fine here." He sits up suddenly.

"Say, Gavin?" Henry prompts. "Thanks again for bailing us out on Friday night."

"Oh, it was my pleasure."

"The Bombshells are big fans of yours now." He chuckles. "I'm a little worried they'll try to poach you. And if their trainer has any more issues on game night, I'm sure you'll be their first call."

I inwardly wince, because I don't need any more babysitting emergencies in my life. "Thanks, Henry."

"But you kind of put Gavin on the spot," Hudson says suddenly. "Maybe give him some more warning next time? He had to trust a bunch of hockey players to watch his kid. We did an excellent job, if I do say so myself. But Gavin was just lucky we were there. Fact is, as the new guy, he knows he has to say yes, even when it's inconvenient."

"Oh, shit." Henry's eyes jump to mine. "Didn't mean to put you on the spot. I know you're not supposed to work nights, but I kinda forgot why."

"It's all right," I tell him. "I won't always be able to say yes, but it isn't because I don't want to."

"Yeah, I get that." He rubs his chin. "I put a couple of road trips in your contract, though. Will that be a problem?"

I shake my head. "My sister can cover those road trips if we plan them in advance. It's cool. I know you need a chance to be home once in a while, too."

He grins. "My wife is pregnant, and there hasn't been anyone else that I trust for game night in a while. But when I interviewed you, I thought I might not miss the birth of my children after all. We've had trouble finding talent in the training room lately. Now the Bombshells are, like, *find us another Gavin*." He throws up his hands. "All suggestions welcome."

"I'll bear that in mind."

I'd been out of the workforce a couple years, so this kind of praise is very encouraging.

Meanwhile Hudson has slipped out of the treatment room while Henry and I were talking. So I don't get another chance to ask about that grimace.

Please be okay, I inwardly pray. Hudson needs a break.

Maybe it's selfish, but the dude has a really nice smile. I'd just like to see it again sometime.

TEN

Hudson

"INHALE TO PLANK POSITION. Full breath in plank," says Ari, the team's yoga teacher. "On your next exhale, lead with your hips into a downward dog."

Lead with your hips. My eyes slide sideways to find another pair of hips on a mat a few yards away from me. That same pair appeared in my dreams last night. And the night before that.

Gavin has invaded our yoga class.

I shouldn't say *invaded*. It's a perk of working with the team. But it isn't making my life any easier.

Before this year, I was damn good at focusing only on hockey. Now my focus has broadened to both hockey and lusty fantasies. I dream about him. And at night, when I'm lying in bed, I sometimes hear the muffled sound of his voice coming through the walls of our apartment building. I'm pretty sure his bedroom is on the opposite side of the wall from mine.

He's everywhere except—thank Christ—on the ice, or on the road. I still have my brain when I'm skating. And when we travel, I don't see him for days at a time. It's easier knowing I won't round a corner in our gym and find him laughing with Castro or Tank as he tapes up a knee or an ankle with strong, competent hands.

"Plant your left foot forward on the mat and rise to warrior two." Ari brings us through a series of lunging poses.

The class is crowded, and the room is pleasantly warm. That's kind of the point, I've learned. Yoga makes a guy extra limber.

I'd never done much yoga before coming to Brooklyn. But I actually like it. It's physical, but it's also a mental refuge. And a bonding moment with the team, and with yourself.

"There are no winners at yoga," Ari said during my first class. "And no losers. We aren't even competing against ourselves. I don't care how your last yoga class went. I don't care if you ever nail the half moon pose. The past and the future don't matter—on the mat, there is only the present moment. We are here to observe ourselves without judgment."

I kind of loved hearing this. There is no other moment in my week when winning doesn't matter. I'd honestly forgotten you could think that way.

But Gavin must like yoga, too. Lately he's always here, dressed in shorts and a fitness shirt that hugs his body in every twist and lunge. And sometimes rides up when he folds his body forward.

My mental database on Gavin now includes high definition imagery of his V-cut, and the way his thigh muscles flex when he bends. I know that his body hair is blond and soft-looking, and that his cheeks get red when he sweats.

It is slowly, privately killing me.

The class ends with some hip opening stretches and then a few minutes in Savasana, which I'm pretty sure means "corpse." You're supposed to use those final minutes to breathe deeply and appreciate that you're still alive. And to stay focused on the present.

I'm terrible at this. The moment we lie back my brain does a tour of my current anxieties. It knows that we're done with this relaxing bit, and it's time to go win more hockey games. We have practice right after this, in preparation for our road trip to Florida.

But before I put my skates on, Gavin will want to check the flexibility of my hip. Which means putting his hands on my body.

It's torture. And he has no idea.

I leave the yoga studio feeling warm and supple. I tape a new stick and pick up my skates from the equipment room, where the equipment manager has fitted me with a pair of new blades. Everything is going great until I arrive outside the treatment rooms.

There are two trainers working today, and Gavin is popular, so you'd think I'd have a shot at ending up on the other table.

But no. Gavin waves me toward his table as he finishes up a chat with O'Doul about his shoulder. "Ask Henry to tape that donut over it again before the game," he says.

"Will do!" O'Doul clasps Gavin's arm on his way out. "Thanks, man."

Everyone appreciates Gavin. Just not quite in the same way that I do.

"How'd that yoga class go?" he asks as he washes his hands. "Any tightness?"

Yeah, in my briefs. "Not really."

"Awesome! Feeling smooth in your downward dog?"

"Yup." *Dear Lord, I will do your bidding if I can get out of this room without picturing Gavin naked in downward dog.*

Or me *and* Gavin naked, in doggie style...

He palms my shin and prompts me to bend my knee. "Rotate for me. That's it. We're going to have to be vigilant with this IT band to keep your hip lubricated."

Ugh. I can't think about lubrication right now. His touch is firm and professional. But my body doesn't see it that way. I feel instantly warmer and wholly aware of how close he is to me. Then there's his touch, and the citrusy scent of his deodorant. It's overwhelming.

I'm *never* like this, either. I'm all business at the rink, and in the locker room. Just because I'm attracted to men doesn't mean I ever obsess about them. Keeping my head out of the gutter has never been difficult.

Until now. I close my eyes and think about a particularly

grueling bag skate my coach put us through in juniors. I vomited bright blue Gatorade afterward.

"Keep breathing," Gavin says. "Am I hurting you?"

Yes. "No." I inhale again, and get a whiff of his clean, masculine scent.

Fuck. I think about running a beep test at training camp. I think about that time I forgot to empty out my locker, and my jockstrap got moldy.

"It's going to be brutal, no?"

"Hmm?" I haven't been listening.

"Zoning out on me, Newgate? I said those back-to-back games in Florida sound brutal."

I clear my throat. "Yeah, it's a crappy schedule. That's the second and final time we have two games in two days, though."

"The schedule is the most shocking thing about hockey. I really had no idea."

"Yeah," I say lamely. He probably thinks I'm an imbecile. But that's better than him cluing in to my thoughts.

Anything is better than that.

"Well, I'll try to tape you all back together after the first game. Is there anything I should know about the Florida stadiums? Which one has the better setup?"

I replay that question in my mind, because it makes no sense. "You're coming to Florida?"

"That's what I just said. Henry put a couple of road trips into my contract so he could remind his pregnant wife what he looks like."

Well, fuck. I search my brain for something useful to say. But it's mostly just static in there now. I'll see Gavin on the jet. At the stadium.

In the *hotel.*

"Can I ask you a favor?" he says in a low voice.

"Anything." After I say it, I want to slap myself.

"If you see me messing up on game night, will you tell me? I'd rather be told than just keep screwing up."

"Sure," I say quickly. "You won't, though. It's just the usual stuff in another location. Except Henry brings snacks. He's always got a few boxes of protein bars in addition to all his medical crap and over the counter drugs."

"Right. Protein bars. That's on his packing list. Cool."

He runs skillful fingers down my calf, probing for tightness. "You still having charley horses at night?" he asks.

I should have never mentioned those, because now he's massaging my lower legs.

"They're better now," I lie.

"Awesome. Want to share a car to the airport tomorrow?" he asks. "We're leaving from the same place."

He digs his thumb into the arch of my foot and I fight the urge to moan. "Sure," I gasp. "Great idea."

No, it's a terrible idea. I'm in a dark mood as I pack the following afternoon. Just what I need—more alone time with Gavin. It's hard to look a guy in the eye after you've had dirty dreams about him.

When I walk out onto the sidewalk, though, I'm surprised to find Jordyn standing beside him.

"Hey, Hudson!" she calls happily. "Are you going to win in Florida?"

"I'm going to try. Are you coming, too?"

She shakes her head. "No. I want to, but it's a work trip. And Daddy promised he isn't going to Disney World."

I meet Gavin's eyes, and it's hard not to smile. "He's right—there's no Disney on this trip at all. Just the rink and the hotel."

She looks up at me with a disbelieving squint. "Does the hotel have a pool, though?"

"Um, probably not," I lie. "We'd be too busy to go to a pool anyway."

"Bummer."

"You know it."

Just then, a shiny SUV pulls up and a driver gets out. I think it's our car, so I lift my bag.

But nope. The back door opens to reveal a silver-haired woman in pearls and a dress. "Jordyn! There's my girl."

"Hi, Grandma!" she rushes over for a hug.

"Careful," the woman says, stepping back. "This coat is camel."

"*Camel?*" Jordyn asks, her eyes wide. "I didn't know you can make a coat out of that."

The woman smiles, but I'm not a fan. Who wears a fancy coat to hang out with a little kid? "Darling, where is your overnight bag?"

"It's here," Gavin says. "Hello Eustace. Good trip down from Boston?"

"It was perfect," she says. "No trouble at all." She stops and gives Gavin an appraising look. Then her eyes move to me. "Who is this? A boyfriend?"

My blood stops circulating.

"No!" Gavin sputters. "He's..."

"Our neighbor!" Jordyn says. "He's a hockey player! He signed my jersey!"

"Oh. I see." Her eyes slide away from me dismissively. "Does Jordyn have another pair of shoes? We're going to the ballet."

Gavin frowns. "She wears those with everything. You didn't mention the ballet."

"It's no matter." She waves a hand. "Get in the car, darling."

"Wait wait *wait*." Gavin holds his hands out. "Where is my goodbye?"

The little girl skips back over to her father and they say their goodbyes, and I look away.

Another car slides to a halt in the street, my name showing on a placard in the window. I hurry over and put my bag into the trunk. Then I slide onto the back seat.

"LaGuardia?" the driver asks.

"In a second," I say tightly. "We're waiting for him."

It only takes another minute until Gavin joins me. His daughter's car pulls away first. He tosses his bag into the trunk and climbs in.

The car glides down Henry Street and turns toward the airport before Gavin says, "I'm sorry about that," he says in a low voice. "Her assumption..."

"It was nothing," I whisper.

"Yeah, but..." He clears his throat. "It didn't have a thing to do with you. She is always just waiting for me to fuck up somehow. Lose my job. Date a loser. Something she can use as leverage."

"I think you just called me a loser."

"No! It was just an example! I..." He glances sideways at me. "Oh, you're joking."

I smile. "Yes, I'm joking." Although my heart has begun to race nonetheless. In another life, I'd be thrilled to be mistaken for Gavin's boyfriend.

But in this life, I can't have anyone guess that about me. Ever. So my greatest fantasy is also my greatest fear.

The car accelerates onto the highway, in the direction of the airport. And the start of a two game road trip, where Gavin will be with us constantly for a few days.

I cannot let it affect me.

I already chose my path. I just have to stick to it.

ELEVEN

Gavin

WHEN IT'S time to board the jet, I hang back and wait for the players to go first. They probably have favorite seats, and a pecking order. I don't want to step on any toes.

I notice that Jimbo, the equipment manager, does the same thing. He's a friendly kid a couple of years younger than I am. After the last player boards, he nods toward the jetway. "Shall we?"

The plane is luxurious—with the generous seats you'd find in business class, and upholstery in the team colors. I sit next to Jimbo, and after the plane takes off, I enjoy an Indian style chicken curry that's better than anything I've ever eaten on a flight before.

As night falls, the lights dim. Some of the players sleep or watch movies on their tablets. And there's a loud poker game at a table in the back.

I spend the flight wondering what Jordyn is doing with her grandparents in Manhattan, and worrying. There's no reason for me to think that she isn't being well cared for. But I have not spent a night away from Jordyn in over two years, and I feel unsettled.

I took this trip for a reason, though. When Henry offered it to me, I saw the date and realized that it was good timing on a number of levels. Eddie's parents would have Jordyn's company, which they crave.

And I'd be too busy—taping up ankles and knees—to remember that four years ago tomorrow was my wedding day.

When we deplane, there's a bus ready to take us to the hotel. I take a seat next to Heidi Jo, the manager's assistant.

"Do you mind if I make a quick phone call?" I ask her. "It's my daughter's bedtime."

"Go for it," she says. "I don't mind."

When I call Eustace's phone, Jordyn picks up. "Daddy! Are you in Florida? Is it pretty?"

"It's dark," I tell her. "And I'm on a bus. How is the hotel?"

"Pretty," she says. "Fancy. The juice was in a wineglass, and the carpet is swirly."

"Five stars! Are you going to the ballet tomorrow?"

"Yes! But..." She drops her voice to a whisper. "Grandma wants us to go to a salon first."

Uh-oh. "Maybe I should talk to her. There's nothing wrong with your hair." She hates having it cut, and I hate arguing about it. So what if it's a little shaggy?

"She says it's too long, and I would look so cute with layers. What are layers?"

"Baby, I have no idea. Hold on." I turn to Heidi Jo. "Any idea what layers are in hair? My daughter needs to know."

Heidi Jo beams. "Layers are just a fancy way of cutting the ends of your hair to give it more shape. It's not a big deal."

"Thanks." I return the phone to my ear. "Did you hear that?"

"Yeah." My daughter sighs. "That doesn't sound so bad."

"Agreed. But you do *not* have to get your hair cut if you don't want to. Let me talk to Grandma and I'll tell her."

Jordyn thinks this over. "No, it's okay. I like going places with Grandma."

"Are you *sure*?" My chest feels suddenly, horribly tight. She shouldn't have to navigate this alone. I just want to get back on the plane and go right home again.

"I'm cool," she says, a phrase she's picked up from my sister. "I get to see a ballet."

"Okay." I swallow hard. "I love you. So much."

"Love you, Daddy!"

After we hang up, I close my eyes and pinch the bridge of my nose. "I should have stayed in Brooklyn. My mother-in-law is a steamroller."

"That does sound awkward. I've been lucky—my in-laws are more laid-back than my actual family."

"Winning." I give her a fist bump.

The hotel, when we arrive, is sleek and luxurious. My room has a giant king-sized bed, and a balcony with a view of the darkened everglades.

So that's where I go, leaning on the railing, checking out the wide, flat horizon against the nighttime sky. Standing there in the warm breeze, I try very hard not to think about Eddie, and the joy on his face when he slipped a gold band onto my finger.

After our wedding, I used to stare at that ring sometimes, even though it made me feel vain. Jewelry had never been my thing, but I treasured that ring, and everything that it represented. *With all my love for Gavin* was inscribed on the inside of the band.

I'd never expected to get married. Eddie had shocked me by getting down on one knee by the fire pit in his backyard one night after Jordyn was asleep in her toddler bed. Even when he asked "will you marry me?" I almost demanded that he repeat the question.

Nobody—except maybe my sister—had ever loved me the way Eddie did, warts and all. My parents spent my entire childhood trying to mold me into someone like my father—a driven man without a sense of humor. They told me I lacked focus. That I lacked ambition. That I was too easily distracted. And when I came out to them at eighteen, it only got worse. It was like a confirmation of their worst fears.

Like I was some kind of alien they'd been sent by mistake.

But Eddie chose me. He looked at this messy, distracted, fun-loving guy I'd become and said—*that's the one for me*. He called me "wild-hearted" instead of distracted. He called me "energetic" instead of unfocused. "I love your creativity. You are never boring," he'd said.

Eddie, on the other hand, was all the things my parents wanted in a son. He was focused and quiet and rational. He was a doctor, for fuck's sake. But he was also the kindest man I'd ever met. He was spontaneous, too, once he trusted you.

He was basically a perfect human, although my parents never met him. They didn't approve of me, my sexuality or my marriage. They didn't attend our small wedding at a ski resort in the White Mountains.

Eddie's parents did, though, even if they didn't approve of me. Eustace never accused me to my face of being a gold-digger. But she *did* tell me that I was too young for Eddie. And that my post-grad program in athletic training was frivolous.

Nothing could take away my happiness, though. We had a fun wedding weekend, with everyone skiing—including Jordyn. She was our ring bearer at our ski-lodge ceremony. At three years old, she made it down the aisle without losing our rings, and then spent the rest of the ceremony perched on Eddie's hip.

When the officiant had said, "you may kiss your husband," Eddie had kissed me, and then Jordyn had cried out "me too!" to a round of laughter. In our wedding album, there's a photo of Eddie and me kissing either side of her round face.

After Eddie's death, I still wore my ring. I took it off only to do dishes, or to shower. There were exactly two places I was willing to put it down—the kitchen windowsill, and the medicine cabinet.

But then, during the difficult winter after Eddie's death, I took Jordyn skiing at the same resort where we were married. I guess my hands got cold, and the ring slipped off one of the dozens of times that I took off my gloves to help five-year-old Jordyn with her gear.

When I got home that night, it was just gone. I called the resort, frantic, and gave them a complete description, down to the inscription inside the band. They didn't find it. I went back myself the following week and looked around, by the lifts, but no such luck.

It was just gone. Like my husband.

New Hampshire gave me Eddie, and then it took him away again. He chose me, and then he left me, and that's just the way it is.

Life isn't fair. The best you can do is enjoy it while it lasts.

I take a deep breath of the salty Florida air. And I try to do just that.

CARRIE ROWAN

TWELVE

Gavin

"ICE TIME!" Jimbo says as he refills the last of a dozen water bottles and sets it into the caddy. "You need anything last minute?"

"Don't think so. But thanks." The day has been a ten-hour blur, and we're just getting started.

Jimbo and I arrived at the arena in the morning to set up. Then the players arrived for their morning skate, which meant that I taped elbows, knees, shoulders and ankles. I massaged stiff muscles and handed out ice packs.

Then, after lunch, Jimbo and I headed back to the arena to set up for the second wave. Before gearing up, players do a lot of stretching out and body-activating exercises. So I ran laps between the trainer's table and the stretching mats. I re-taped every single elbow, knee, shoulder and ankle that I'd seen earlier in the day.

Then, when the athletes moved into the dressing room to put on their skates, I checked and rechecked all my gear for the game. I've prepped several different kinds of ice packs. I've got pain relievers and glucose tabs and various antibiotic creams and sprays. I've got multiple kinds of tape, bandages, gauze and gloves.

I've given out protein bars in four different flavors, energy drinks and gallons of water. My table is ready for intermission adjustments. My on-bench bag is packed.

"Let's go!" Jimbo says, shouldering a dozen hockey sticks. "Best seats in the house, man. Metaphorically speaking. We can't actually sit down."

I'm probably too nervous to sit down anyway. I grab my emergency kit and follow him through the dressing room, where the last of the players are filing out into the tunnel beyond.

That's when the roar of the crowd hits us. Man, that is *loud*. And when we reach the end of the tunnel, I look up at the rows of seats. And up, and up. I've been to rock concerts with smaller crowds.

So this is what they mean by the big leagues.

"This way," Jimbo says as he steps onto the freshly resurfaced ice.

I follow him. And even though I'm wearing special grips on my shoes, I still say a little prayer. *Please, Lord, let me not fall down in front of fifteen thousand people.*

Meanwhile, forty-six warriors wearing pads and blades on their feet fly by at high speed. Yeah, this isn't intimidating at all.

But there's no time for nerves. Before I'm ready, the audience rises for the national anthem. Soon, it's game time. The ref drops the puck, Trevi snaps it to Drake, and off they go.

Watching from the bench is nothing like watching on TV—everything is louder and faster. I can hear every grunt, every chirp and every swish of steel against ice.

When people say that hockey is a physically brutal game, they're not kidding. No wonder I'm so busy in the treatment room. The stress on players' bodies is intense. Hockey requires rapid-fire lateral muscle movement, explosive acceleration and herculean core strength.

Our boys keep the battle mostly in our offensive zone for the first several shifts. As the minutes rack up, Brooklyn makes several attempts on goal. But Florida's keeper is having a good night, and we can't seem to put anything in the basket.

My job is to watch the hits closely. If anyone gets injured, it will help me to see the play unfold. Like when Trevi gets smushed against the boards by a monster of a defenseman, and gives his shoulders a couple of awkward shrugs after the hit.

Hell.

As he returns to the bench, I sidle up behind him. "Bad hit? Any damage?"

After a squirt of water from one of the bottles, he retracts his shoulder blades, as if testing them out. "No real damage. Just feels like my spine is a little out of whack."

"Lift your elbows a couple inches." When he does, I bend over and grasp him under the arms in an awkward hug from behind. "Deep breath in. Then out." When he exhales, I lift him up off the bench. His spine makes a series of pops as it releases in several places.

"Whoa. Cool. Thanks."

"Dude," says Hudson, who's sitting beside him. "Trevi's an inch taller after that." Then he rises suddenly and vaults over the boards for his shift.

I watch him go, and it's an awesome sight. Powerful muscles send him flying forward, like a Porsche accelerating on the autobahn. Then he spins effortlessly around to skate backward at high speed in his opponent's face.

Watching the spectacle from point-blank range, I feel like I'm seeing him for the first time. He's a fierce mix of raw power and beauty. As if I'm watching him do what he was put on this earth to do.

I'm so impressed.

All our boys skate hard, but the first period ends scoreless. We troop back to the locker room, where I spend a sweaty fifteen minutes stretching muscles and re-taping wrists. I check the app on my phone for a look at Drake's blood sugar, which looks good.

Then it's back out there for another bruising period. At the six-minute mark, Castro gets a goal, and we all celebrate. On the next play, though, a Florida player catches Newgate in the chin with the blade of his stick.

"Foul! High sticking!" I yell, as if the ref were looking for my opinion.

Luckily, I'm not the only one who saw it. The whistle blows. I see Newgate raise a hand to his face, and come away with blood.

Something twists inside me at the sight of it. I'm not squeamish, but I don't like to see someone I admire bleeding.

The whole bench cheers, though. And I remember that the penalty for drawing blood is a four minute bench minor, instead of two.

Newgate is smiling when he skates back to the bench for the power play. But I pull an antiseptic wipe out of my bag and lean over him to blot away the blood.

He grabs the wipe out of my hands and presses it to his skin himself. "I got it," he snaps.

I take a quick step back.

Henry warned me about this, actually. Some players don't want you to touch them during a game unless it's absolutely necessary, while others don't mind. He'd said, "It comes down to preference, and how they manage their focus during games."

So I'm not offended, although I would have liked to get a better look at the cut. I guess it can wait until the next intermission.

Florida scores, unfortunately. Then each team scores again, giving us a tie game as the second buzzer sounds.

I'm running on fumes during the second intermission, taping limbs and dabbing at cuts and stretching out O'Doul's shoulder.

When the third period begins, I'm rolling my own neck, trying to release the tension from my shoulders. The speed of the game picks up, and I barely breathe for twenty straight minutes. As the clock is ticking down, my eyes lock on Newgate. He's skating with fire and aggression, while sweat pours down his face.

Success in sports is often more about desire than talent. And Hudson wants this win badly. Even seated on the bench between shifts, his focus is locked onto the contest.

With only three minutes on the clock, he vaults over the wall again. Our forwards have the puck in play, and Newgate covers their winger like a wad of gum on a pair of new shoes. He's everywhere the opponent doesn't want him.

Drake sends Hudson a pass, and before I can even blink, he's flipped it to Trevi.

Who scores!

Suddenly the score is three to two, with thirty-seven seconds on the clock. And less than a minute later, we've won it.

"YEAH!" the whole bench shouts.

"We're going to party like rock stars tonight!" Castro yells. "Food and games in our suite later!"

"You got a suite?" Jimbo asks as he gathers up the extra sticks. "Big spender."

"Didn't want to go clubbing because I hate Miami traffic." The forward shrugs. "Let's eat a lot of room service and play poker. You guys are invited." He points at me and Jimbo. "Especially if you're bad at poker and flush with cash." Then he vaults over the wall one more time for the handshake.

———————

So that's how I find myself at eleven-thirty p.m., on a sofa in the Castros' suite, twenty dollars poorer than when I arrived.

Who knew Heidi Jo was a poker shark? She won everybody's cash, including her husband's.

I'm full of food, too. A surprisingly large mountain of nachos and chicken wings have been consumed. Plus a salad with a piece of salmon on it for Newgate. He eats healthy even on the road.

Not like I notice every single detail about him, all the time.

Okay, I do. It doesn't help that I'm a little bit drunk for the first time in ages. Partying with hockey players is fun. I'm living my best life right now, watching Trevi and Jimbo battle it out on a video game console that Jimbo brought.

"Does it frighten anyone that Jimbo is beating a bunch of hockey stars at a hockey game?" I ask. And then I belch. "Oops. Sorry."

Jimbo snickers. "At least I win at something."

"Huh," Newgate says, coming over to stand behind the sofa and watch. "O'Doul looks angry in this year's game. And Trevi's head is a funny shape."

"It does *not* look funny," Trevi complains as his on-screen player falls down again. "But they got Drake's tattoos wrong."

"That's because of copyright infringement," Drake says from the other sofa. "They don't want to pay licensing fees to my tattoo artist."

"But they gave you a *dragon* tattoo," Jimbo says. "You should sue them for making you into a cliché."

Everyone laughs.

"The dragon is dumb," Drake admits. "But they gave me a bitchin V-cut. The wife says it's hot."

"A dragon?" someone else hoots. "Injure Drake in the game, Jimbo. I gotta see this."

"Wait—" I sit up, tipsy. "Is there an athletic trainer in the game?" I ask. "Is he hot, too?"

Everyone howls.

And sure enough, when they injure a player to show me, a trainer runs out onto the ice with a medical kit bearing a red cross on it. He kneels down beside the injured player and whips out a bandage.

"That is not hygienic," I grumble. "Where are his gloves?"

I get another laugh.

Then Drake shows me how to play the game, and then I lose spectacularly, possibly because Leo Trevi pours me two shots of tequila in the middle of it.

I down them both, like I'm a college kid.

It's awesome. And everything is blurry.

Suddenly I hear a chime sounding from all corners of the room. "What the hell is that?" I slur.

"The bedtime chime," Drake says, pulling out his phone. "You have the team phone, right?"

"Right," I slur.

"When you're on the road with the team, you get a gold star when we win a game…"

"*Love* the gold star," I agree. It had appeared on the phone just as soon as we got onto the bus.

"It also prompts us for curfew," he explains. "If you're out at a club somewhere, it knows. And it nags you. If you're at the hotel, it only chimes once, to remind you to go to your own room."

"So bossy." I pull the phone out of my pocket. It shows the time —twelve midnight—and the date. I heave a big, drunken sigh. "I did it. I survived my wedding anniversary."

"Your anniversary?" Drake says. "Sorry you're here with us tonight."

"No, it's good," I slur. "Because he couldn't be."

Several more faces turn in my direction, while some of the alcohol in my system finds its way to the corners of my eyes.

"Uh-oh," Heidi Jo whispers. "Are you okay?"

"Yup." Hockey players don't cry. So I'm not going to, either.

I stand up instead. It doesn't go all that well, though. The rug seems to shift beneath my feet, and I tilt to the side.

I'm saved, though, by the firm grasp of a hockey player. "Easy," Hudson says in a husky voice. "Let's get you back to your room."

"Yes, let's," I agree. I've reached that state of drunkenness where I really need to go home.

Several people call out their good nights as we head for the hallway. Then Hudson steers me into the elevator, where I lean against the paneled wall in a way that looks more suave than wasted.

Hopefully.

"What floor?" he asks, his finger hovering over the button panel.

"Three." I'm pretty sure.

"Oh, we're neighbors. What a surprise," he deadpans.

I laugh, but that makes me wobbly, so I stop. "God, I'm a train wreck. Thanks for dealing with me."

His serious brown eyes look back at me. "It's nothing. In the first place, you are very entertaining. But didn't you just spend sixteen hours taking care of all of us?"

"Well, sure." I belch. "But they pay me for that. And I wanted to come on this trip because it's distracting. I just had to survive this day." I close my eyes as the elevator descends. "It was a really long twenty-four hours."

"Yeah," Hudson says softly. "Wedding anniversary, huh?"

"Yup. Some things in life you just have to get through."

"Right. Just power through. Like dental work."

"And colonoscopies," I add. "And phone calls from the in-laws."

"At least an anniversary happens only once a year," he says, trying to be helpful.

"Right. There's also birthdays, and Christmas. That one is a killer."

His expression drops, and now I've made another person sad. Oops.

The elevator door opens, and I slide my foot carefully forward. If only the wall could accompany me, that would be cool.

Hudson clamps a strong hand under my elbow. "You got this, come on. Do you have your key handy?"

"Sure." I pull it out of my pocket and walk toward my room's door. But I stumble. Twice. Hudson prevents me from falling, though. "This rug is awful," I complain. "Who chose this carpeting?"

Hudson laughs and I'm not sure why.

"Wait, all these doors look the same."

"That tends to happen in a hotel," he says gravely. "Do you have that handy sleeve the hotel gave you? With the room number on it?"

"No. But I'm sure it's this one." I wave the key card past the scanner, but it gives me a red light. "Wait, no. It's this one." I try the next door.

Rejected.

"This could go on all night. Do you have your ID? In case we need to ask the hotel which room you're in?"

"No, it's fine!" I lurch out of his grasp toward the door in the corner. "This is it. Trust me."

"No, I don't think..."

I swipe. Red light. "Damn it."

"Okay, let's cut this game short." Hudson nudges my hand, and finally! Green light.

"See? I found it." The door swings open. "Oh yay. A bed. I need that." I stumble forward, lifting my T-shirt over my head. It's surprisingly hard work. "Wow, I'm so drunk. I've completely lost my tolerance. My college buddies would be appalled." Parking my ass on the bed, I slither out of my jeans. And then, fuck it, my boxers too.

"Whoa there." Hudson covers his eyes. "Won't you be cold?"

"Nah. Kid-free trip, baby! I get to sleep naked."

He sighs.

I yank the covers up and slip between the sheets. "Oh, heavenly. I love hotels. I'm going to sleep so many hours."

"Are you now?" Hudson is fussing with something on the other side of the room. I don't care what. It was nice of him to put me to bed. "You want some Advil so you don't wake up at three with a pounding headache?"

"Good idea," I mutter. "It's in the travel kit, in the bathroom."

He returns a minute later and sits on the side of the bed. "Okay, sit up for me."

"Kay." I do that, but I keep my eyes shut.

He puts the pills in my hand, and after I toss them in my mouth, he puts a water glass in it next.

I take a gulp and hand it back.

"Good boy," he says softly, and goose bumps rise up on my shoulders.

"God, can you *not*?" I complain. "Don't use your sex voice. It's hard enough being near you all the time." I open my eyes to make my point, but that means I'm suddenly blinded by a lamp that Hudson must have turned on. I clamp my eyes shut again, but not before swaying precariously.

"Whoa!" He catches me with one iron-like arm, his palm on my bare shoulder. "Easy."

The warmth of him is irresistible. I lean in. My chin finds his shoulder, and my bare skin meets the warmth of his chest. I'm basically hugging him, so I slide my arm around his torso to make it official. He stiffens, but I don't know why. "This is nice. Nobody ever hugs me."

He stiffens even more. "Nobody?"

"Well, nobody older than seven. You smell nice. Like body wash and sex."

He makes a choking sound. But his arms close around me and he pats my back.

I sort of melt against him. "Hugs are nice. I almost forgot."

"Mm-hmm," he says gruffly.

My eyes are leaking for some reason. I push my face a little more tightly against the collar of his T-shirt, as if I could just retreat into his solid body until sleep takes me.

"Shh," he says. "You're going to be okay."

"That's...my line," I sniffle. "You think it's a lie."

"Nah. It's the truth this time," he says. "It's going to be fine."

I squeeze my eyes shut and just breathe.

And somehow it is.

THIRTEEN

Hudson

I WAKE up at four in the morning when Gavin gets out of bed.

He's on the side near the bathroom, which was by design. I maneuvered him over there after he passed out on me.

Literally.

I also left the ice bucket on the rug beside the bed, just in case he had to puke. But—luckily for both of us—he hasn't needed it. The bathroom door is still open, and I hear the sound of peeing. Flushing. And then teeth-brushing.

Huh. Okay.

He must have sobered up enough to maneuver in the dark, too, because it's pitch black in that bathroom and he hasn't turned on the bathroom light.

I hold very still, hoping he'll assume I'm asleep. As I should be.

A few moments later I feel the bed shift as Gavin rolls back into it. The covers jostle. "What's with..." he says as he wrestles with one of the extra pillows that I slotted between us.

And then? He grabs my arm, and suddenly shouts "AAAAGH! Jesus fucking Christ!"

I roll over. "Problem?"

He switches on a bedside lamp and then just kneels there, buck naked, a hand pressed to his heart. "You're still here? You scared the crap out of me."

"Of course I'm still here. Where else would I be?"

"Well…" He sits back on his haunches, obviously confused. "I remember you walking me back to the room. I do appreciate it. I never drink, and it hit me hard. But you can go, I swear. I'm not gonna choke on my own vomit and die or anything. And I'm done crying."

"Good to know." I tuck my hands behind my head and blatantly check out his bare body. I mean—it's *right there*. "But I'm still not leaving this room."

He frowns, crossing his arms in front of a nicely sculpted chest. "Too busy admiring the view?"

"You *are* naked."

"I caught that. But I have a habit of stripping when I'm drunk. My college nickname was *Buck*." He grins. "Besides, people take off their clothes in their own hotel rooms."

Lord, it's hard work keeping eye contact. *Do not look at his dick*, I beg myself. "Huh. Except this isn't your hotel room."

"What do you mean?" he blinks. "Of course it is. My key opened the door."

My ironclad self-control wavers, and I take one little peek. Just a glance, really. And, fuck, he's perfect *everywhere*. I feel my own body tighten in response.

Gavin clears his throat, and I realize we were right in the middle of an important conversation. I drag my eyes up off his cock, past the blond hair cradling his pubes, past his rippled abs, climbing by his shapely arms and finally up into his narrowed eyes. "Your key *didn't* open the door. Mine did. This is *my* hotel room. And that's why I'm still here."

He blinks. "What are you talking about?" But as I watch him, the idea sinks in. His eyes flit to the door, and then around the room. Even in the shadows, you can just make out my jacket on the back of the desk chair where I left it, and my suitcase on the floor. "Oh my God."

I start to smile.

"Fucking hell!" He glances toward the bathroom, and then back at me. "I just used your toothbrush. I *thought* that toothpaste tasted funny. I can buy you a new one."

"We swapped spit once before, right? I'll live."

Gavin blinks again, like he's still processing this confusing turn of events. Then he throws his hands down on the bed, and I wait for him to fold in on himself in embarrassment.

But that's not what happens. Instead, he howls with laughter. "Holy shit! *Buck* rides again! My college friends are going to be so impressed." His beautiful body shakes with laughter.

And it's contagious. I'm already grinning. "You know I'm never letting you live this down, right?"

His clear eyes lift to mine, his grin wide. "I deserve it. Fair's fair."

I feel a pang inside my chest when I look at his smile. Gavin is a special kind of guy—the kind with the nickname from all the drunk antics he pulled in college—the kind who laughs at himself instead of getting embarrassed. His personality moves the needle on his attractiveness from red-hot to blistering.

And suddenly I just don't want to fight it anymore. I pop up on an elbow and lean in, toward his smiling mouth. I cup his scruffy face in one hand.

He stops smiling. For a second I think I've wrecked it. But then he leans into my touch, pressing his face into my palm like a needy cat.

We get stuck there, gazes locked, hearts thumping. At least mine is. I'm so good at denying myself that I just watch him, while my cock grows heavy between my legs.

"What are you waiting for?" he asks in a voice that's textured with longing. "Last time you just pounced, and I fucking loved it."

Unnngh. He's right—that's exactly what I'd done. I pushed him up against a wall and ravished his mouth.

Then I ran away like a nervous freak ten minutes later.

Not much has changed. I'm still stupid. Still conflicted. But second chances don't come around very often. I'd better make the most of this one. So I rub the pad of my thumb across his top lip, and watch as his eyes go half mast with lust.

"Fuck," he groans. "You tease."

"Maybe that was *my* nickname in college."

"Accurate." He inches closer on the bed. "Are you going to make me beg?"

"That does sound kind of fun." But I don't want to be a tease anymore. I want to be the guy who just takes what he wants. So I roll closer and capture his mouth in a kiss.

It's not a pounce, either. It's not frantic. It's aching, sensual bliss. I anchor my hand in his soft hair and deepen the press of my mouth against his hungry one.

He opens for me, and somehow I manage not to rush. I slide my tongue between his lips with deliberate slowness.

When I finally taste him, we both moan. My body crackles like a wildfire—one deep kiss burns into another. And another. Teeth click. Tongues tangle. My hand finds its way down his flank, testing the smoothness of his skin, and the firmness of his chiseled abs.

But I still need more. I wrap an arm around his waist, roll onto my back and haul him on top of me.

He comes willingly, splaying his legs out on the tangled covers, his hands in my hair, his tongue in my mouth. His cock is trapped against my body, the covers doing nothing to disguise how hard he is for me.

I want to shout with excitement, but I devour his mouth instead.

Gavin doesn't hold back, either. He dives into the kiss, grinding his tongue against mine. This isn't even a kiss anymore—it's something dirtier. Weeks of corked up frustration, suddenly given its freedom.

His mouth wanders to my ear, my neck. He tries to taste me everywhere at once. But I miss his kiss, so I clamp one hand onto his bare ass and the other to the back of his neck, and I bring him back where I want him.

He allows it, and we spend some quality time trying to fuse our tongues together, until I'm grinding up against him, desperate for more.

"Fuck, you need it so bad, don't you?" he pants against my mouth. "You're gagging for it."

"Yeah. Since the night we met."

He groans. "Every time you give me that broody stare I just want to strip you down and suck you off."

My body screams for a demonstration. "I'm available for that."

"*Finally.*" With a horny chuckle, he rolls off me and yanks the covers down. His own dick bobs against his abs as he moves, and my mouth waters. He tugs on my T-shirt, and I have to stop staring to help him lift it over my head.

"Unngh," he sighs, reaching out to run his fingertips through the happy trail that snakes down the center of my belly into my boxers. "Who knew I had a thing for bruised up hockey players with chest hair?"

It's true that my torso is often smudged with purple and yellow bruises. That's life for a defenseman. And I don't wax, because nobody ever gets close enough to appreciate it.

But Gavin is loving it. He's exploring my lightly fuzzed abs and sucking on my nipple, like a kid with a new toy. I dig my heels into the bed and push up off the mattress, hooking my thumbs in the waistband of my boxers.

"Hold up," he murmurs. "That's mine to unwrap."

My body tightens with expectation as he takes over, tugging my underwear off my hips and flinging it over the side of the bed. Then he kneels between my legs and groans. "Fuck. Me. You are hot *everywhere.*" He dips his head and kisses my leaking tip. Then he runs his lips lightly down my cock.

Now I've lost my ability to speak. All I can do is grunt. And pray that he does that again.

"Hudson," he whispers, and now I have goose bumps, too. He looks up at me from between my legs, and the gleam in his heavy-lidded eyes makes me hazy with desire. Without dropping my gaze, he takes me into his hot mouth.

The slick heat makes me shudder and gasp. I drop a hand to his hair and tighten my fingers in it. "If you keep that up, I won't last long," I pant. "I dream about this. And when I'm on your table, I have to think about ugly thoughts just to keep myself in check."

He hums around my shaft, and my goose bumps double. Then he sucks me reverently, like he wants to draw it out. With a slow tongue and long glances and his thumb lightly stroking my sac, like a tease.

It's so hot. But I still want more. I want to make him feel as wild as he's making me feel. "Come here," I rasp. "Need to touch you."

He doesn't wait for a second invitation. He scales me like a tree, kissing me hotly, his hand still wrapped around my shaft, pumping slowly.

Although I'm proud of my top-notch self-control, it's a miracle I haven't come already. I knock his hand off my cock and take hold of his. He's satin over steel, and when I close my hand around him, he moans and shudders.

And I love it. My stroke is fast, and overeager.

"Yes," he pants against my mouth. "I like it rough."

Goddamn. The words make me want to come all over him. But I clench my thighs and concentrate on stroking him mercilessly. "Fuck my hand," I order. And when he thrusts his hips, I plunge my tongue into his mouth.

He moans, his body moving against me in a pulsing rhythm. He leans back just far enough that I can see the splash of color on his face, and the slick of his swollen lips from my bruising kisses.

Then he comes on a shudder, holding my gaze—red-faced and starry-eyed. Like he wants me to see how badly I'm wrecking him. The heat of his seed dripping through my fingers is the thing that pushes me past the point of no return. I take myself in hand and stroke. It only takes a second.

Lord knows what noises I'm making as I shoot, *finally*, coating us both and shuddering with relief.

Then silence, except for gasping breaths. He sags onto my body, his sweaty face nuzzled into my neck.

Wrapping my arms around him, I hold on tightly. My heart gallops happily inside my chest.

My imagination hadn't done him justice, either. Gavin is the hottest man to ever walk into my life. And I can't believe I resisted him as long as I did.

FOURTEEN

Gavin

MY CRAZY WEEKEND ends very suddenly at six-thirty on Monday morning, when Jordyn jumps onto my bed.

"Daddy! You're home!"

"Hi, angel," I say without opening my eyes. Unfortunately I've gotten less than five hours of sleep. We flew back after the Tampa game, landing in the wee hours.

"Wake up!" she says. "I missed you."

I pry my sleep-pasted eyes open. "Wow, nice haircut." It's shorter, barely to her shoulder. And cut in a skillful, flattering way.

She lifts a quick hand to her hair, as if I've reminded her it exists. "It's okay," she says gravely.

"Just okay? It will dry faster. You hate drying your hair."

"Daddy, it's too short to braid!" she says with great anguish. "All the girls at school wear braids."

"Turn around. Let me see." She rotates to face the bedroom door. "Huh. Let me get up and do a little research, pumpkin. I bet I can still braid it."

"Really?" She whirls around again. "I told the girl at the salon that I like braids, but the girl didn't listen."

"It's going to be all right," I say. "Let me get up and put on the coffee. I do hair better with coffee."

98

She gallops out. Fifteen minutes later, I'm working on something called a Dutch milkmaid braid, thanks to a YouTube tutorial that popped up when I searched *how to braid short hair*.

"This is going to work," I tell her. "Just don't wiggle around so much? So how was the ballet?"

"Long." She hunches her shoulders. "I didn't understand the story. It was supposed to be about swans. Mostly they just danced a lot. The hockey game was more exciting."

"You are definitely Daddy's girl! How are your grandparents doing?"

"Good. But Reggie got mad at something Grandma said about her tattoos."

Jesus.

"I don't know what it was. And Grandma wants me to go to a summer camp in New Hampshire. She said I would like it. They have horses there."

My fingers go still. "A sleep away camp?" She's *seven*.

Jordyn shrugs. "You can ask her."

"Do you *want* to go to horsey camp?"

"I'm not sure. Horses are very big and a little scary."

"You are a very sensible person. I like that."

She giggles, but I'm not joking.

Now that I'm awake, I dad so hard. That means homemade pancakes for breakfast on a school day, plus a banana smoothie and several knock-knock jokes I'd been saving up. Then I walk her to school, hand in hand.

My smile doesn't drop until she's safely inside the building.

After getting home at two a.m., I'm still exhausted. And I'm feeling a little hollow.

Fooling around with Hudson was kind of like indulging in a big cupcake with buttercream frosting. It is delicious, and you can try to savor it. But pretty soon it's gone, and you already regret devouring it.

A sugar high is always followed by a crash. Every time. Last night we shared a taxi home in the wee hours, sitting a respectful distance apart in the back seat, both of us groggy from sleeping on the jet. With the driver right there, we weren't about to discuss what happened.

Upon arrival, we'd carried our luggage upstairs in companionable silence. When we reached the second floor, he'd said, "I had fun." And it had sounded so final. Like his own sugar crash had already set in.

"Yeah, same," I'd whispered.

He'd cleared his throat. "I shouldn't, uh, go there again, though. I can't make a habit of it."

"I know," I'd said quickly. "I get it. My life is complicated, too." My job security is more perilous than his. If someone in the organization didn't like the idea of the trainer banging their athlete? I'd be jobless before I could even blink.

So that was it. One really awesome night, followed by this hungover feeling.

It's not guilt, exactly. I'm certain that Eddie—if heaven is real—had been cheering me on the other night.

Though I still feel hollow. I finally did the scary work of making an effort to connect with someone. But I chose a guy who can never love me back.

Plus, there's the sinking realization that the world is full of guys who can never love me back. Because they're not interested or straight or closeted or emotionally unavailable or kid-haters or commitment-phobes. I could go on and on. So many reasons.

Even when I was a young punk at twenty, I knew that Eddie's love was a miracle. When any two people find each other like that, it's not merely special—it's magic.

In my gut, I believe that I used up my lifetime allotment of magic. Nobody will ever make me feel that special again. I just hope

I did the same for him. God knows I tried, and not a day went by when I didn't remind him how I felt.

Whatever was going through his mind that day when he was T-boned at a stop sign, he must have known I loved him.

On that sad thought, I head to work.

FIFTEEN

Hudson

MARCH

IT'S NOT easy to steal the puck from Neil Drake during a scrimmage. But no player is infallible. At just the right moment, I use my stick to lift his, spoiling the pass he's trying to catch, and flicking the puck away to Trevi.

Trevi shoots, and it goes into the net.

I laugh. Drake curses, and then high-fives me anyway.

Coach blows the whistle. "All right. Good work. See you in the tape room in forty-five minutes."

We all skate for the exits. It's only ten-thirty in the morning, and we're on a game day schedule—a morning skate at the practice facility, followed by a strategy meeting. Then a nap at home, a late lunch or an early dinner, whatever you want to call it. Then it's off to the stadium for a home game against Colorado tonight.

This will be my third game since our Florida trip eight days ago. My hip is holding up. And so are my spirits.

It's weird, but I feel like a different man after my night with Gavin. Maybe that sounds dramatic, but it's true.

My life hasn't changed at all. I'm still a second line athlete battling every day for success and recognition. I still get up early and work hard and avoid carbs. I still go to bed alone every night.

But I feel different. As if I went on vacation for the first time in years, and suddenly remembered that life isn't always a grind. And maybe this part sounds corny, but I feel *seen*. Like there's one person in this building who really knows me.

That's one more than there used to be. It helps, and I couldn't even say why.

Whistling, I shower quickly. And while my body is still warm and limber, I head into the training room. Both Henry and Gavin are on duty, but Henry waves me over first.

And I'm actually disappointed. Gavin is my go-to these days. He always puts a little extra effort into keeping me supple. These days he has to treat my *other* hip, because I've tended to overcompensate with it by favoring my right one.

"Hey, Newgate," he says cheerfully. He gives me a smile and then goes back to cautiously trimming tape away from Trevi's ankle. "I heard you and Castro had a high-stakes ping-pong battle last night."

"That's right." I'd gone out to the bar for once with my teammates. "Turns out my backhand has really improved this year, and Castro couldn't keep up."

Trevi snickers. "You should have seen Castro's face when New Guy aced him. *Hilarious.*"

Henry moves around the table and repositions my knee, blocking my view of Gavin. "It was a good time," I say. "You should have been there."

I relax onto the table and think of ping-pong, and the quality of Gavin's smile. I'd like to play him at ping-pong again.

I'd like a lot of things.

"Hi, guys." We all turn to see Dustin Hart in the doorway. He's a player I don't know very well. But his arm is in a sling. Poor fucker.

"Hey!" Henry says. "Have a seat. What's the news?"

"Broken," the guy says with a grimace. "Hairline fracture. I brought the films." He's clutching a folder in his good hand.

"Let's see," Gavin says, taking it from him. He holds it up to the light. "That is a bummer—but I've seen much worse. You're going to be okay. You'll come back from this stronger than ever."

"I hope so," Hart mumbles.

"I *know* so," Gavin says. "We'll give you a regimen that keeps the rest of your body strong while that bone heals. Just think of all the extra time you're going to spend with Henry and me! You lucky man."

The guy grins probably for the first time all day.

"Hudson!" Jordyn yells my name as I lock my apartment door. "We're going to watch your game tonight! And we're having pizza."

I turn around, and the first thing I see is Gavin's easy-going smile. I feel it like a warm hand on my chest. "Hey, guys." I drop my gaze to the little girl. Aww. She's wearing the Bombshells hat that I bought her. "Pizza, huh? I sort of remember pizza. It's square, right?"

"No!" she shrieks. "Round! You could have pizza with us."

"Sorry, girly. I have to go to the stadium already."

"Is Colorado good?" she asks. "You can win it, right?"

I clear my throat, trying to decide what to say about my least favorite team in the league. "They're coming off a really good season. But we're having a good season, too. I think I can take 'em." *Or at least not embarrass myself.*

And it must be written all over my face. "Is it weird?" Gavin asks. "Playing them?"

"It's all right. I don't know that many players on the team anymore." Except for my old roommate. And Kapski, the star forward, who I used to idolize. And their new head coach, who I used to trust.

The truth is that I dread this game. But a hockey player never admits that.

And Jordyn doesn't notice. "Will you score a goal on them?"

"Well I'll *try*. Jeez, kid. Way to set the bar high."

"Do it! And then you can come over for dinner tomorrow. Daddy is making ramen! It's like soup with noodles and chicken. Not as good as pizza, because vegetables. But still good."

Gavin chuckles. "That's a nice offer, baby, but Hudson doesn't eat noodles."

"I eat noodles sometimes," I hear myself say.

"YAY!" Jordyn shouts. "You can come for dinner and show me hockey tricks. I have a stick and everything."

"You do? Cool." I think I just took advantage of a starstruck seven-year-old in order to see Gavin outside of work.

But it's worth it. He's leaning against the wall with an amused smile on his handsome face. "I'll set out an extra bowl, then. Text me if you want to come."

"Oh, I'm coming," I say, but then I want to kick myself, because he raises his eyebrows suggestively.

"Go win your game," he says with a smirk. "The kid and I will be watching."

"Will do. Later, guys." I give them both a wave and move my ass toward the stairs.

I'd better make it a good game, too. Wouldn't want to disappoint a little girl before our dinner date.

The energy in the dressing room tonight is in the red zone. Colorado is coming off a great season, and my teammates are fired up to beat them. "Who's warming up with some elimination soccer?" Castro asks, the ball tucked under his arm. "Trevi? Bayer? How 'bout you, New Guy? You never play."

"Fine," I say, rising from the bench, even though I'm not in the mood to knock the ball around. I like to keep to myself before a game.

But I don't want my teammates to think I'm aloof. So I follow them toward the loading dock, where there's enough space. Castro chucks the ball to Trevi, who kicks it to me. I use my knee to knock it at Bayer.

"I've been thinking about something," Bayer says. "I think Colorado's advantage is training at altitude. Aren't their lungs, like, stronger than ours because the air is thinner there?"

"I dunno," someone else argues as the ball continues its journey around the circle. "If that were true then Calgary would be a powerhouse."

The team is quiet for a moment, mulling over this paradox. I tap the ball back to Bayer.

"We should do a training camp in Switzerland next year," Bayer says, heading the ball at Castro. "It could be our secret weapon."

"Last year you said açai berries should be our secret weapon," Castro grunts. "I had the shits for a week."

Several people make gagging noises, and Bayer laughs so hard he gets eliminated for letting the ball hit the ground.

I'm the next to go out, missing a fiery punt from Trevi.

Okay then. Mission accomplished—I played the game and still have plenty of time to build my focus.

I'm in the corridor, using the wall for support and stretching my quads, when I hear footsteps.

"Hudson Newgate!" booms a familiar voice. It's Clay Powers, the coach for Colorado.

Fuck.

"How are you doing, kid? Nice assist against Florida last week."

"Thanks." I grudgingly turn to acknowledge him. "I'm having a good season."

That's only recently true. But I don't owe this guy anything. He was an assistant coach back when I played for his team, and now he has the top job.

And I used to trust him. He was right there in the room on the day I tried to come out. But those men had looked at me like I'd grown an extra head.

Then I'd left the room. And they must have unanimously

decided that having a queer player on the team would be a fatal distraction. Or maybe they were just plain repulsed.

Looking back on that day, I want to smack myself for being so naïve. I'll never make that mistake again. *Message received.* You don't get to be a special, distracting snowflake until you're the most valuable player on the team. The guy they can't live without.

So that's what I've got to become. It's just taking a lot longer than I thought it would.

"Yeah, this could be a big season for you," Powers says.

"Thanks."

I wait for him to move along, but he pauses there in the hallway and considers me. "Saw you missed a few games last month. I got worried."

Sure you did, pal. And now I understand why we're having this chat—he's fishing for information. There's a reason why teams report player injuries in the vaguest of terms. We say *a lower body injury.*

We are never specific, because if you tell the whole world your right hip is inflamed, the team goon can just target that spot and take you out for good.

"It turned out to be nothing," I say, forcing a grin.

"Glad to hear it," he says with a polite tone. "Have a good game."

"You too," I say stupidly.

He leaves, and I stretch my hamstrings. But I'm grumpy now. No —it's worse than that. I'm furious. *This could be a big season for you.* That's a backhanded compliment if I ever heard one.

This was just a drive-by mind fuck, right? I came out to that guy at twenty, back when the earth was green and I thought I had a great life in Colorado.

And he shipped my ass across the country for it.

Anger fizzes inside me as I finish stretching. But that's actually a good thing. Now I'm feeling the need to smash Colorado. And their star forward—Kapski—is someone I used to train with, so at least I know some of his tricks.

When game time comes, I stare Kapski down before the puck

drops. And once we're in motion, I stake him out, doing my best to block his sight-lines before he's even got the puck.

There's lots of ways to be a defender. There are defensive defenders—the classic shot-blockers. O'Doul is that kind of player—always near the blue line, preventing the opponent from getting its way. Then there are offensive-defenders. Our man Tankiewicz fits that bill—he's a flashy player who breaks formation to set up scoring chances wherever he can.

In the middle you've got what we call a two-way defender. That's me—I play wherever I'm needed.

But not tonight. I'm kicking it old school. Colorado is a good team, but they're awfully reliant on Kapski. Most of their goals go through him.

So I set myself up like a cork in that bottle—a stopper. The human incarnation of *no*. It's not flashy, and it's probably not fun to watch. I'm just a dude getting in another dude's way every time we're both on the ice.

Which is a lot of the time. Coach seems to like my strategy, and he keeps sending me on shifts with Kapski. I skate hard, and with the kind of tunnel vision that makes the first period fly by.

Pretty soon the buzzer sounds and we're clomping back toward the dressing room.

"Newgate! Over here," Henry says, waving me toward the table.

"The hip's okay," I insist. But I'm hella winded.

"Dude, I know. But drink this." He thrusts a bottle of energy drink at me. "We'll have to change your nickname. To, like, Iron Man. Those are some of your longest shifts this season."

I didn't even notice that, but I guzzle some of Henry's magic juice anyway. He makes his own blend for us.

"Good work, son," Coach Worthington says as I mop sweat out of my eyes. "If you keep it up for another period, guy's gonna snap. Just make sure you fall on your left side when it happens."

I snort. "Will do."

Coach was joking, but he's basically right. I go after Kapski in the same hellacious way during the second period, and eventually

Colorado's game breaks down. One of them trips me, and the ref calls it, giving us a power play. And the second it's over, another one of them slashes Castro with his stick.

Another power play, and Brooklyn scores.

As Trevi celebrates his goal, I skate by to check out Coach Powers' face on the visitors' bench. He looks like he wants to shake his own players.

I give him a big smile, which he probably doesn't even notice. But I'm having fun.

The third period unrolls like a dream. Colorado continues to spiral, their play riddled with errors. And I manage a beautiful stick-lift on Kapski while he's trying to receive a pass. It's exactly the same move I did on Drake this morning.

And it works the same way. I nab the puck and execute a fast turn. Everyone in the stadium expects me to pass, because I've spent the whole game playing a sturdy but dull defensive game.

But rules are made to be broken. I zip around Kapski, elude a startled defender and fire the puck toward the net. It sails in between the goalie's legs.

I've five-holed him. The lamp lights, and it feels a little surreal.

It also feels fucking great.

For the first time in forever, I'm the guy the journalists want to talk to. That's fun.

And when I'm done smiling for the cameras, my dad is already blowing up my phone with voice messages of congratulations.

Also rare. Go me.

But none of it is quite as fun as the text I get from Gavin. It's a photo of Jordyn jumping up and down in front of the TV screen. *I let her stay up late for this. And now you pretty much have to come for dinner tomorrow.*

Guess I can afford a few carbs, I reply. As if I'm not desperate to go sit in Gavin's kitchen while he serves me homemade soup. *I'll bring the drinks.*

After I send that, I wonder if it sounds flirty. But it's too late. I can't take it back.

It's just a harmless dinner, right? No reason I shouldn't go. Just a low-stakes night of breaking my diet, and salivating like a hungry wolf at Gavin.

No problem. I got this.

SIXTEEN

Hudson

THE NEXT EVENING, though, I hesitate in the wine shop. Is sauvignon blanc too much like a date?

Yes, probably.

Hell.

I turn around and go to the corner store instead. Because this is Brooklyn, there are a million beers to choose from. I grab a four-pack of Japanese beer, and then a bottle of fancy soda for Jordyn. It's a low-key, friendly offering.

That's fine, right? I wonder as I tap my credit card.

This kind of overthinking is new to me. I've kept my life simple for the last five years. No entanglements. Just hockey. But now Gavin has me all twisted up inside, which is weird because he and I are not a thing.

We can't be a thing.

My subconscious feels otherwise, though. Whenever I hear his voice, I gravitate toward it. And when he smiles at me, a nameless energy bounces off the walls of my empty heart.

I need to shut it down. Instead, I'm going to dinner at his place.

When I tap on their door, Jordyn comes running. I hear her pounding feet, and then the door is flung open. "Hudson Newgate! You came!"

My smile is automatic. Nobody has ever been that happy to see me. "Hi, kiddo. Thank you for inviting me."

"I'll get my hockey stick," she says, bolting away from the door again.

I let myself in. These apartments have open living spaces, so Gavin is just around the corner at the far side of the room, stirring something on the stove. "I brought beer," I announce.

"Awesome." He turns around and hits me with a smile. And, yup, I feel it like a throb in my chest. "Come on in."

I navigate around a sofa—gray, with blue and orange pillows, one of which is shaped like a cat. There are side tables and lamps in several shapes and colors. There are framed photos on the wall, and a rug underfoot. A coffee table is covered with math homework, a handful of pencils, and an eraser in the shape of a unicorn.

"Wow, your apartment looks so much more lived-in than mine."

Gavin laughs. "Is that code for 'messy?' We're kind of crammed in here. It was hard moving out of a three bedroom house."

"That's not what I meant."

"I know that." He's dropping spinach leaves from a salad spinner into the pot. "This will be ready in, like, ten minutes."

"Can I do anything? Not that I cook. But I can set a table as well as the next guy."

He shakes his head. "Like that's even an option for you."

I see what he means when Jordyn comes tearing back out of a bedroom carrying a toy hockey stick and a puck made out of foam. "Let's play!" she announces, dropping the puck on the floor. "Teach me tricks."

"Cool. See if you can shoot the puck between the legs of that dining chair."

She shoots and misses by a mile. "Almost!" she says happily.

I bury a smile. "Let's improve your grip on the stick..."

The next ten minutes are spent with me coaching her a little. But mostly we're just goofing around.

I've always been a little intimidated by younger kids. They cry a lot, and I don't really know how to talk to them. But Jordyn isn't a baby, and she's got a sunny energy that I admire. She's here for the experience, and she's not too hung up on details.

There's something bouncy about her that reminds me of Gavin.

"Dinner," he says, interrupting a game whereby I try to catch the flying foam puck in a butterfly net that Jordyn had in her room. "Honey, let Hudson drink his beer, and please set the table?"

Jordyn drops the game without too much of a fuss, and goes to the silverware drawer. "Spoons and forks?"

"Chopsticks, too, Ducky," Gavin says. He grabs a glass out of a cabinet and fills it with milk from the fridge.

I help Gavin carry wide, steaming bowls of soup from the kitchen to the family's dining table. "It's just the three of us tonight," he says. "Reggie is out at a rehearsal."

"What does she do?" I ask, easing myself into my chair.

"She plays the bass in a band." Gavin frowns. "Why are you moving like that? Like your hip is stiff?"

"I got a little banged up in last night's game, but it's not a big deal. Just a little tenderness." I probe the muscle just inside my hip, and it's sore, but not in a dangerous way.

"Hmm," he says as he takes his seat. "I could work on it later."

Yes, please.

No, wait. That's a terrible idea. I'm very good at maintaining a professional distance when we're both at work. But I shouldn't let this man put his hands on me in private. I don't have that kind of willpower.

So I gaze into my bowl instead of his eyes. "This smells amazing." My soup has shreds of chicken, carrots, fresh mushrooms, spinach and green onions in addition to the curly noodles. Oh, and a fried egg floating on the top. "The way you serve this, it's not very far off my diet."

"Daddy made it *fancy* this time," Jordyn says, poking the chicken in her bowl.

I swear Gavin blushes. "Ramen is one of those meals that I can dress up or down. Sometimes I throw it together in a hurry, and sometimes I go all out. And, uh, I know Hudson likes his veggies."

"Daddy put an egg in yours," Jordyn says, wrinkling up her nose. "It's weird, but he likes it."

"I like it, too," I admit. And Gavin ducks his head, like he's a little embarrassed.

He and I tuck into the food with chopsticks, although Jordyn uses a fork. God, the soup is so good. "Where do you get the broth?" I wonder. Because I could almost put this together myself.

"It's homemade in my instant pot," he says, slurping a noodle. "I make a big batch of stock and freeze it."

"You *are* fancy," I say with a flirty smile that he returns.

I ought to cut that out. But I don't want to. Nobody ever feeds me home-cooked meals. I'm just a guest, but I feel cared for—the same way I feel when he works on my sore muscles.

Although that's his *job*, for fuck's sake.

Shake it off, Newgate, I remind myself. "How's school going, Jordyn? Any better?"

"A little?" she slurps her soup. "I got invited to a birthday party at a skating rink."

"Sweet. You can skate, huh?"

"'Course." She shrugs. "Everybody can skate."

"Well, every kid who grows up in New Hampshire," Gavin says with a fond look at his daughter.

"Even you?" I put down my chopsticks. It hadn't occurred to me that Gavin could skate. "Did you grow up in New Hampshire?"

"Rural Pennsylvania." He shrugs. "But we had pond hockey in the winter. I played as long as the soccer fields had snow on them."

"A man of many talents." Shit, that came out flirty, too.

I take a big bite of chicken and mushrooms just to shut myself up.

"Hey, Hudson!" Jordyn says as we finish eating. "My birthday treat for school is next week. It's a lollipop, plus a Bruisers sticker that Daddy got at work."

"Cool. A hockey theme. I like it."

"We put a picture on the goody bag. It's from the Bombshells game—you and me and Neil Drake? The one we took after Neil stopped saying swear words."

I laugh so suddenly that I almost choke on my beer. Drake had done a lot of cursing during that game, and I'd hoped that she didn't notice.

Oops.

"You know, you could sign them," she says, with a serious expression. "Then they'd be *autographed* treats."

I'm not sure many second graders care about my autograph. But this one seems to. "Sure, kid. Whatever you want."

Jordyn slides off her chair and runs for her bedroom.

Gavin regards me with soft eyes as he drains his beer. "You don't have to spoil her," he whispers. "A kid can hear 'no' once in a while."

"I don't mind," I whisper back.

He stands up and leans in to take my empty bowl. But at the last second, he places a soft kiss on my neck.

And—whoa—every nerve ending in my body is suddenly standing at attention. But Gavin is across the room already, loading bowls into his dishwasher. And Jordyn is running back with a shoebox full of little paper goody bags and a purple marker. "You can sign in the team color!"

So I do that. Meanwhile, Gavin opens another beer and watches me with a private smile on his handsome face.

I'm in so much trouble right now. I'd told him we couldn't hook up anymore. I was very clear on that point for both our sakes.

But now I can't remember why. Suddenly, none of my objections seem all that important.

After a while, Gavin tells Jordyn that she has to take a bath. So I rise from the sofa and carry my beer bottle into the kitchen. "I'll leave you two to your evening. Thank you for dinner."

"Wait for me a few minutes?" Gavin says. "I'll be right back."

He disappears to get Jordyn into the bath, and I take the opportunity to wash out his soup pot, and the other dishes in the sink. I'm drying everything when he returns.

"Oh, hell. You shouldn't tease me like that," he says, a serious look on his face.

"Wait, what?" I go still in surprise. "I've been trying all night not to flirt with you."

His eyes twinkle. "Real talk—a guy who does all the dishes is honestly sexier than a naked stud with a giant woody."

I laugh so hard I almost drop the pot on my foot.

"Easy." He takes it out of my hands and sets it onto the stove. "How's your hip?"

"I don't know how to answer that," I admit. "It's too tempting to invite you over to work on it."

Gavin works his jaw while he hangs up the dish towel. "Can't help you with that decision."

"Is your sister home later?" I ask.

"Any minute now," he says.

I lift a hand and put it on his shoulder. With any other man, it would be a meaningless gesture. But between the two of us, it's practically foreplay. Gavin's body seems to flush, and his bright eyes lock on mine.

The sexual tension between us is palpable. So I make it worse by sliding my palm up his shoulder to his neck, and then rubbing my thumb across his top lip. "Come over later," I whisper. "I don't think ignoring you is working."

"You said we weren't doing that," he says with heated eyes.

"Maybe I lied."

He leans into my caress. "I'll knock at eight-thirty. If you answer, I'll assume you didn't change your mind. Think about it."

I drop my hand and take a step back, before I do something impulsive—like push him against the fridge and kiss him stupid. "I'll be thinking about it, all right. But not the way you mean."

Then I leave, but I'm already counting down the minutes until eight-thirty.

SEVENTEEN

Gavin

"I WON'T WAIT UP," Reggie whispers from the sofa as I head for the door. Then she giggles.

I leave without answering, because I feel sheepish.

When I'd offered to work on Hudson's hip, I'd meant it genuinely. But then he escalated things, so there's no point in pretending that this is a business visit.

Which makes me a fool. He doesn't want to date me. And I shouldn't fuck around with a guy I work with. I don't want to confuse Jordyn, either, so this is a stealth mission.

There are so many reasons why this is a terrible idea. And yet, I'm freshly showered, and there's a bottle of massage oil in my pocket. The edible kind.

I knock.

His footsteps approach a moment later, and it occurs to me that after an hour or so to think it over, he's probably changed his mind.

The door opens, and there he is, filling my vision with his big body and thoughtful expression. He's also freshly showered, in sweats and a soft-looking Henley. And I just want to scale him like a tree. "Hey," he says.

"Hey. You okay? Maybe this isn't a great idea."

"Oh, it's definitely not." He takes my arm and steers me into the apartment. He closes the door behind me. And then sets me back against the door.

But he doesn't kiss me. He tips his forehead against mine, and just looks at me. "I can't stop thinking about you. It's a problem. And I am never indecisive."

"I'm sorry," I say, even though it's not really my fault. "I'm sorry you can't decide whether or not to have some meaningless sex."

His chuckle is dry. "That's the problem. I don't think it would be meaningless enough."

"Oh."

Oh. I meet his brown eyes and see trouble in them. And I wonder how much it cost him to say that. "You really are a bit of a mess, Hudson Newgate," I whisper.

"Yeah," he agrees. Then I get a flicker of a smile before he finally leans in for the kiss. It's sweet, and a little sad. For a second, anyway. Until I kiss him back, and then his tongue brushes my top lip, and I shiver against his chest.

Hudson groans and dives into the next kiss, and I welcome him with a hungry mouth and eager hands.

He tastes me deeply, and my head swims.

Here we are again—making out in a fog of sexual desperation. But he's right—meaningless sex doesn't go like this. It doesn't start with soul-deep kisses after dinner. And it doesn't sound like that hitch in his breath when I pull him in closer.

I have a lot of affection for the lonely hockey player in 2A. I want to feed him soup and see the gratitude in his eyes when he tastes it. And I want a whole night together.

But that's not in the cards.

I break our kiss and ease him back. "Let's take a pause, Hudson. This is still a bad idea."

"Yeah." He blows out a frustrated breath. "But I was hoping to pretend for a little while that it wasn't."

His honesty makes this even worse. Couldn't he just go back to being a jerk?

"If you need to go, I'd understand." He takes another step back.

So this has to be *my* decision? I'm truly conflicted. "Give me a second to think. Maybe I could take a moment alone with your contusions from last night?"

His laugh is startled. "Sure. Fine. Where do you want me?"

I hesitate. "On the bed."

His eyes flare, but he doesn't say anything. He just turns around and marches toward his bedroom.

I follow him, and notice that the bedroom is more nicely furnished than the rest of the apartment. The big bed is made up with a flannel duvet in gray, with blue plaid flannel sheets. A bedside lamp casts a friendly glow on the wall. There's a plush blue rug on the floor, with a foam roller nearby. "Do you stretch here on the rug?"

"All the time," he says. "That rug is my best friend. It's followed me through four cities."

"Lie down there, then. If you don't mind."

"Oh I don't mind." He kneels down on the rug, peels off his shirt, and stretches out on his side. "I got hit hard last night, but luckily he didn't jam my hip bone. So I'm sore, but I don't think it's going to flare up my bursitis."

"Let's see." There's a nasty bruise, but it's higher than his hip bone, and more on his back than his side. I probe the joint gently with my fingers, and he doesn't flinch. "This okay?"

"Yeah. There's, like, a deep muscle soreness. But nothing sharp at the joint. Henry took a look at it this morning."

"I'm sure he did. But I will be personally offended if some asshole reinjured you already, so I need my own assessment."

He shakes his head with a grin. "Have at it."

I get to work probing him for tight spots and strains. He groans the way we all do when someone puts skilled hands on an ache. And after a moment I feel him relax under my touch.

"You were right, by the way," he slurs after a time.

"About what?" I work my way down his thigh.

"When you said I was lonely. It made me so mad, because it's true. I wanted you to shut up and vanish, and now I'm glad you didn't. I'm so tired of being caged up inside my head."

"But I'm still a problem for you," I point out.

"Oh, I know it. Just because I can admit how much I like you doesn't make the situation any easier."

"True." I massage his thigh with slow precision. "But you have to give me some guidance, here. I have massage oil in my pocket and I don't know if I'm supposed to strip you down and use it or go home instead."

He closes his eyes and lets out a groan of a completely different kind. "I think you'd better do that first thing. Not the second one."

I snort. And then I pat his very firm ass. "Let's put down a towel so I don't get massage oil all over your best friend."

He rolls over and gets up. He heads to the closet and returns with two giant bath sheets, which he spreads out on the rug.

Then he grabs his phone to turn on some music, and low-key house music begins playing from a speaker on the nightstand. *He prepped for this*, I realize. The nicely made bed, and the soft lighting. The music.

I don't have to feel guilty about it, I guess. I didn't talk him into anything.

Then? He shucks off his sweats and his underwear in one go, leaving nothing but a semi-hard cock pointing straight at me.

I lick my lips.

He groans.

"Lie down," I command. "On your stomach." I'm willing to have this massage get as dirty as a low-budget porn flick, but I plan to draw it out a little, first.

He doesn't waste any time settling down on the towels, his forehead propped onto his folded hands.

I leave him there a minute and prepare myself—unzipping my jeans and kicking them off. I remove my shirt and socks, too, for practical purposes. Massage oil is messy. Then I kneel down in my briefs.

Step one is opening the massage oil and rubbing some between my hands. Step two is starting in on his broad shoulders.

"Fuuuuck yes," he murmurs. "That feels so good."

"I *am* a professional, you lucky man." I can feel his smile even if I can't see it. We both know there's nothing professional going on right here at the moment.

I waste a couple minutes wondering if that Brooklyn Hockey employee's manual I barely skimmed says anything about fraternization between employees. But I guess I'll worry about it later, because my slicked-up hands are already doing a full tour of Hudson's upper body.

And he's loving it. He groans every time I find a new muscle to rub. "Your neck is tight," I complain, digging my thumb into the base of his skull. "Can you remember something for me?"

"What's that?" He turns his cheek on the towel, so he can see me.

"There's nowhere else you need to be right now," I whisper.

"Yeah, so?"

"That's it. That's the whole message," I repeat. "There's nowhere else you need to be right now. Just here with me."

"Oh," he says softly. "Okay."

"Now relax." He sinks a little further onto the towel. And I take my time moving down his body. I spend a few minutes on his lats, and then his waist—careful not to give him any pain in the bruised spots. By habit, I wrap my hands underneath his body to work his hip flexors. Still some tightness there. But he moans happily.

I apply more oil to my hands and let myself work his glutes. And it's true what they say about hockey butts—all that muscle is pretty spectacular. I'm a terrible tease. I run a thumb lightly down his crack, watching while he breaks out in goose bumps.

"Can I turn over?" he begs.

"Not yet. But spread your legs a little."

"Fuck yes." He separates his legs, and I slowly work his inner thigh muscles, but never quite touching his sac.

"You're killing me. Practically humping the floor here."

"Patience. Roll over so I can do your...feet."

With a snort, he rolls, and I move down to sit at his feet. Maybe he thinks it's a de-escalation—but that only means that he's never had a truly great foot rub. There are nerves in the soles of the feet that can take a turned-on guy straight to super horny.

I set both his feet in my lap and take a moment with his ankles. Hockey players put too much stress on these joints. After each one gets a little love, I grasp a foot and dig into the arch with my thumbs.

Before too long, he's moaning and cursing. And I have a perfect view of his godlike body, while his cock bobs and drips against his ripped abdomen.

"You are the hottest thing," I whisper, as the music throbs softly in the background. "But I'm about done torturing you, because it's torturing me, too."

He smiles suddenly, and then does a super human ab curl and sits up. "So can I get those briefs off you now?"

"Sure. Why not," I say casually. As if I'm not already throbbing for him. "But if you intend to take this to the bed, you might want to wash off that oil first."

"Yeah, I thought of that. But I have a question. Who treats you?"

"Me?" I don't understand the question. "I'm not injured."

"So? Doesn't mean you don't get stiff."

"Oh, I'm plenty stiff." I point at my cock, which is trying to escape these boxer briefs.

He doesn't even smile. "I'm not joking. You're always there, making sure I get patched up. And I appreciate the way you touch me—in every possible way. So why don't you lie down and let me be in charge for a few minutes?"

In charge? *Unngh.* I love it when he takes control. "If you insist."

EIGHTEEN

Gavin

I GET up and wash my hands, which are coated in massage oil. When I return, Hudson is waiting. He's chosen an acoustic guitar song, and he's dimmed the lights even further.

It shouldn't feel awkward switching places with him, but it does. I lie down on the towels, my cheek on my folded hands, feeling self-conscious.

"Sir, I'm going to need to remove these," Hudson says, his fingertips at the waistband of my underwear. "Do you mind?"

"No." And now I'm smiling. "I wouldn't want to make your job more difficult."

"Appreciate it." He gives a tug, I lift my hips, and the fabric slides off my body. "That's better. Now tell me—where do you usually carry tension?"

My poor ignored dick gives a throb. "Usually? My shoulders. But right this moment..."

"Shoulders it is, then," he says briskly. "Stay there."

I hear the click of the oil bottle. And then Hudson positions himself with one muscular knee on either side of my hips. Broad hands land on my shoulders, and he begins to stroke my traps with his thumbs.

123

"Unnngh," I say immediately. "Wow. You have nice, strong hands."

"Thank you, sir," he whispers. "Now just relax and let me work here."

And work he does. Those broad hands move up to my neck, his thumbs rubbing firmly at the base of my skull. It feels incredible. Then he works his way back down to my shoulders and picks up the rhythm.

I feel my neck relax. And my limbs grow heavy. I can't even remember the last time I had a massage. It's been two years at least. Hudson isn't phoning it in, either. He works tirelessly down my back. Then he spends some time on my hips, and then my glutes.

The massage oil is reapplied, and he moves onto my thighs. "Roll over, sir."

Oh, yes please. In a state of bliss, I sort of ooze my way onto my back. My dick is the only part of me that's still stiff.

But the massage continues. He spends some time on my feet, and then works his way back up my legs.

"Sir, our time here is almost up. But I specialize in happy endings. It's included in the price."

My stomach shakes with laughter. "As long as it's *included.*"

I hear the sound of the oil bottle once more. And I brace myself for the firm hand that lands on my...

...Thighs. He rubs my inner thighs, and I groan with disappointment.

"It's a special technique," he says quietly. "If sir would just be patient."

"Sir has some tightness in his balls," I complain.

"Mmm. I see." One slicked up hand moves to my sac and strokes lightly.

"Ohhhh fuck." I widen my legs to give him better access. And it feels dirty—like I'm offering myself to him.

"*Very* nice, sir," he says in a low voice. And before I can say a word, he leans over and slides my cock onto his tongue.

I'm so surprised that I practically arch off the floor. I let out a monster groan as he begins to lick me from base to tip.

My surprise doubles as I realize how good Hudson is at this. I wasn't even sure this was a thing he'd enjoy. But he obviously does. He slips the head into his mouth and sucks me just as attentively as he massaged my neck.

And his hands are everywhere—cupping my balls and naughtily stroking my taint.

"That is...wow," I stammer. "You're...unngh."

His chuckle is muffled.

My toes are already curling. "M-maybe take that down a notch. Sir is going to blow like a geyser."

He hums. But he also squeezes the base of my cock, and slows down his ministrations from wildly enthusiastic to merely amazing.

I lay there panting, trying not to come, and wondering how I got so lucky. Maybe I should make him soup for dinner again tomorrow...

Hudson hums again, and I push myself up on an elbow so I can watch the show.

He lifts his brown eyes and smiles at me around my dick. Then he reaches down and starts pumping his own cock in his fist.

A flare of heat sparks throughout my body. "Hey, give me that," I rasp. "I want a turn."

His answer to this request is even better than I'd hoped. Without releasing me, he maneuvers his body around until he's lying beside me on the towels, sixty-nine style, his thick cock right there where I can reach it.

All I have to do is roll toward him and latch on. He's heavy against my tongue, and leaking. And as I take him deeper, he groans, and I get tingles.

Adrenaline is coursing through me. I'm buck naked on the floor, sweaty, covered in massage oil and tangled up with a sexy professional athlete. My latent party boy has finally awoken, and he's loving his life.

Hudson's mouth is heaven. But I'm no slouch, either. I stroke his sac until he moans. We're basically a human pretzel of desire, two competitors in a heated contest to out-please the other.

We're both winning. But then Hudson presses his thumb against my ass and rubs my hole. And it gives me such dirty visions that I moan around his cock.

Suddenly, neither one of us is in the mood to hold back any longer. I suck him harder as he thrusts hotly into my mouth. And he deep-throats me like this is the final round of the All-Star tournament of sex.

And maybe it is, because my balls tighten wickedly. "*Look out*," I gasp, as pleasure drowns me.

But he doesn't back off. He lets me erupt against his tongue. Waves of joy pulse through me, and I pop off with a gasp.

His cock pulses suddenly in my hand, and then he shoots his load all over my chest, while I clumsily stroke him through it.

When he's done, we just lie there a minute, panting. I'm too sexually satisfied to move.

But Hudson props himself up on an elbow and surveys me. "Hope you don't mind that I made a mess of you. Because that was the hottest sex of my life." Then he gives me that scruffy, boyish smile. "Shower?"

My head slumps onto the towel. I still can't quite believe my good fortune. "Sure. Just a second, while I remember how to stand up."

NINETEEN

Hudson

UNDER THE WARM spray of my shower, Gavin looks blissed out.

While I'm over here trying to play it cool. Like this isn't a big deal—showering with the cute single dad with magic hands and a smile that breaks me in half.

I'm not trying to hide how much I like him. And I already admitted that I can't stop thinking about him. And that sex with him isn't meaningless.

But it would be nice if I didn't come off like a complete dork, even if I'm jumping up and down inside.

I pump some body wash into my hand and rub it gratuitously all over his chest.

He reaches for the bottle and helps himself to a squirt, which he reaches around to rub on my back.

I make an unbidden happy noise. The intimacy is so rare for me. I've never showered with a lover before. Not once. Since Colorado, my sex life has been an infrequent series of unsatisfying one-night stands.

Gavin steps closer, soaping the back of my neck, and I use that as a flimsy excuse to lean in and kiss him on the jaw. I just want to spend the rest of the night like this—his hands on my body, the taste of his skin on my tongue.

He doesn't seem to mind, either. He runs those slick palms down my back until he has two handfuls of my ass. Then he aligns our bodies so he can kiss me for real.

Now we're lazily making out. Well, Gavin's kisses are patient and slow. But mine are increasingly needy. I press him up against the tiles, and when his cock begins to harden against my belly, I reach for the body wash and slick my palm with it.

He groans when I begin to stroke him. "You are a good time, Hudson Newgate."

"Not a compliment that I usually hear."

He leans his forehead on my shoulder and thrusts into my hand. "They're wrong," he mutters. "Dead wrong."

It's a lucky thing that he can't even see how big I'm smiling.

―――――――――――

We don't leave the shower until we're both waterlogged and spent.

I grab a big towel and wrap it around his trim hips. "Want a soda?"

He lifts tired eyes to mine. "Wait—Mr. Low Carb drinks *soda?*"

"Not commercial soda," I scoff. "I'm not a degenerate. I make my own plain soda, with a splash of fruit juice."

"Oh. Well, yeah. I'd better sample that. For quality control."

"Hop in the bed. I'll bring it to you."

Clearly I'm a genius, because five minutes later I've got Gavin in my bed, reclining naked against the headboard. And I'm next to him, my hand on his knee, drinking pineapple-ginger soda.

Except he's a little quiet. "Are you okay?" I have to ask.

"Yeah," he says. "I really am. I just didn't expect to end up here tonight."

I clear my throat. "You don't feel guilty, do you? You told me once before that you hadn't, um, moved on."

"You're right—I hadn't." He rests his head back against the headboard. "But I don't feel guilty about what we did. He wouldn't want me to."

"Glad to hear that." It would crush me if he regretted this. And I'd feel like a heel for enjoying it so much.

"He'd hate me being alone. We even had this conversation once. It sounds morbid, but Eddie was a doctor, and he was a really practical person. He had a will, and life insurance, and he talked about this stuff more easily than most people." He turns those gray eyes to me, but they're a little sad. "So I know exactly how he'd feel about me spending the rest of my life alone out of some kind of misplaced duty to him. He'd kick my ass."

"Maybe, but it's still gotta be hard to process."

"Sometimes." He sets his glass on the nightstand, then puts his hand on top of mine, where it rests on his thigh. "But not so much tonight."

I feel a flush of happiness. "I won't lie—I really hope we get a chance to do this again. But I feel bad even asking for it. I don't have a lot to give."

"To be honest, I don't either." He rubs his thumb along mine. "Even if you were in a position to openly date me, I still don't know how I'd handle a boyfriend around Jordyn. I have to be cautious with her. She can't afford to lose any more people in her life, you know? And she's nuts about you already."

Well, yikes. "That does make it complicated."

"She's my number one priority," he says, giving me a sideways glance. "But she does have an early bedtime."

Thank you, Jesus. "Kids do need their rest."

"Kinda glad she invited you over for dinner tonight, though. I should have thought of it first."

"I bet."

He laughs. "I should probably go. It's getting late."

"Oh, is it?" I ask as my heart plummets. Then I set my drink down, too. "I guess we should both get some sleep."

We glance at each other. And neither one of us gets up.

"Tomorrow is game night, huh?" He puts a hand on my chest and rubs my sternum. "Are you going to morning skate?"

"Probably." I turn a few degrees and run a hand down his arm.

I'm not sure who moves first. But somehow we're kissing again. He nips my bottom lip as he rolls onto my chest. I wrap my arms around him.

Goodnight kisses are a thing, right? Any second now I'll break this off and go home.

But not just yet. My lips are already stubble-burned from earlier, but I just can't stop. His body feels so right against mine. We slide down the headboard bit by bit, until we're full-on making out on the comforter.

He groans, and then I groan, and we're probably just going to spend the rest of our lives here in this room, because neither of us can find the willpower to leave.

And I'm one hundred percent okay with that.

TWENTY

Gavin

APRIL

"BYE, DADDY!" Jordyn waves at me from the steps of the elementary school.

"See you at three!" I call, waving goodbye.

When she goes in, I turn around and hoof it up the block toward work. I'm running a little late, so I don't even stop for a cup of coffee.

Last night I got a good night's sleep. But lately that's not a given, because Hudson and I have made quite a habit of our late-night hookups. Once or twice a week, when he's in town, I get a text. *You around?*

And unless Reggie is out at a late rehearsal or performance, I always make myself available. Each and every time.

Our ground rules are unspoken, but very clear to both of us. Nobody at work can know, and Jordyn can't know.

And it's just a hookup. There's no future for us. Obviously. But that doesn't stop us from making a habit of it.

"This block of Brooklyn is very, very horny," my sister had said the other night as I grabbed my keys and headed for the door in my socks.

"You shut your gob," had been my reply. But I couldn't hide my smile.

"Be careful out there," she'd said in a low voice.

And I'd paused with my hand on the doorknob. "Careful? I'm right next door."

She'd shaken her head. "With your heart, dummy. You aren't really cut out for hookups."

"Sure I am." In college I'd been the king of hookups.

She'd given me a pointed look that saw right through me. "Okay. If you say so. See you in the morning."

And that had been the end of the conversation. But we both know I'm lying to myself about my little arrangement with Hudson. I can play it off as a casual, convenient fling. It's only three paces from my door to his.

But once I'm inside his apartment, we don't act like college boys who just need to get off. Usually, if we haven't seen each other for a few days, we sit down together for a soda and some conversation before the clothes start flying.

Although sometimes our needs are decidedly less verbal—unless you're counting *oh my Gods* and groans. I've gotten used to setting an alarm on my phone for 2 a.m., just in case I fall asleep on Hudson's bed. The man tires me out, he's got the stamina of a pro athlete—obviously.

It's not all just sex, though. When he's not around, we do a lot of texting. My phone lights up most evenings with sports memes and team humor. *Tankiewicz fell asleep on the bus, and Castro drew a dick on his hand in Sharpie.*

Then, of course, I'll ask for pics. And he'll ask me how my day was. Then two hours will have suddenly gone by without me looking up from my phone.

In spite of the fact that we're conducting a secretive, doomed relationship, things are really good between us.

The rest of my life is still tricky, though. Jordyn has a couple of friends now, but she's still not a hundred percent comfortable in her new class. The teacher makes everyone read aloud in class, and it's making her anxious.

Plus, there's a girl who gives her a hard time whenever she

messes up. "*Dahlia*," Jordyn says with an exaggerated grimace. "She says I have a boy's name. She's mean to *everybody*."

I try to say the right things, but what do I know about mean girls? It's hard to tell if this is a true bullying situation, or what. I should email the teacher and ask, I guess. Or maybe that will just make me sound like an overbearing jackass parent?

It's another *What Would Eddie Do* moment. So far I am not sure.

Then there's my job. I love it—but it's exhausting. And I can tell that Henry wishes I could give him more hours. His wife is pregnant with twins, so he's juggling her high-risk pregnancy as we head into the playoffs season.

But I'm doing the best I can.

I've made it almost all the way to work when my phone rings. The ringtone is the theme from *Jaws*. That's my new ringtone for my monster-in-law. She loves to call in the morning. I've told Eustace several times that I prefer to speak in the evenings, but she doesn't care.

My needs aren't important to her at all, and never have been. The phone is still trilling as I enter the lobby of the Brooklyn Hockey HQ, which is in a hundred-year-old renovated warehouse.

Cursing quietly, I take the call anyway. Maybe I can get rid of her quickly. "Good morning, Eustace. I'm just on my way into work. Was there something you needed?"

"Good morning, Gavin," she says crisply. "I won't take up much of your time. I just wanted to tell you that our offer on the condo was not accepted."

"Oh, I'm sorry to hear that," I lie. My in-laws have tried to buy three different New York condos so far, with no such luck. Their tastes are so fancy that nothing measures up to Eustace's standards.

"So we're going to change strategies. Instead of buying a place in Manhattan, we're going to purchase an exquisite property in New Hampshire instead. It just came on the market."

"Ah," I say, trying not to sound too excited. "That will be lovely for you." *And it's two hundred miles away.*

"Yes it will. There is a swimming pool. I'd like to host Jordyn this summer."

Oh shit. I lean against one of the lobby's brick walls, and close my eyes. "I'm sure we can visit. I get some time off in the summer."

"Gavin, I'd like to have her *all* summer. She would live here for ten weeks. And part of that time she'd attend the day camp I was telling her about."

A tension headache settles into my temples. "We can visit," I say slowly. "But summer is my big chance to spend time with her. It's one of the reasons I took this job." Hockey season is long, but it dovetails nicely with my daughter's summer vacation.

"But what child wants to spend summer in *Brooklyn* when she could spend it in the hills of New Hampshire?" Eustace says. "What would she do all day?"

Now I want to hurl my phone at the floor. Instead, I take a slow breath. "I haven't sorted out our summer plans yet. But I'm not willing to send her away from me. That's not going to happen."

She's silent for a moment, and I brace myself.

"Eddie wouldn't like this," she says in a low voice. "He wouldn't like us fighting about what's right for his daughter."

His daughter. As if I don't factor at all. I want to howl. "Nobody's fighting," I say through a clenched jaw. "You asked me to send her away for ten weeks, and I said no."

She sniffs. "I'll ask you to reconsider. I want what's best for Jordyn. You should want the same. Think about what I've proposed, please. Now I'll leave you to work."

"Yeah, I'll think about it." *At four in the morning for the next several nights.* "Goodbye, Eustace."

"Take care, Gavin." She hangs up.

My day is ruined, and it's only eight-thirty. I shove my phone in my pocket and leave the lobby for the glass-walled tunnel connecting the offices to the practice facility. I'm jogging now because I might be a couple minutes late. At the bottom I have to pass the rink entrance and swipe my ID for entry into the practice facility.

There are players milling around already, which means it's later than I thought. I skate down the corridor and hurry into the training room.

Hell. There are two athletes waiting, and another on a table with Henry. "Sorry, guys," I say tensely. "Got a phone call on my way into the building."

"Everything okay?" Henry asks, a roll of stretch tape in his hands.

"Mm-hmm," I mutter. "Thanks." I jam my coat onto the hook in the corner, and roll my supply cabinet toward the empty trainer's chair. But I'm in such a hurry that I roll it—corner first—right into my knee. "God...*darn* it. Sorry."

"Easy," says Henry. "Take a minute if you need it."

"I'm fine," I argue, furiously rubbing my sore kneecap. And when I look up, I finally register that Hudson is one of the athletes standing quietly against the wall, waiting his turn. We haven't seen each other in a few days, either. The guys were away on a two-game road trip in the Midwest. But now his brown eyes look worried. Like he wants to ask me what's the matter, but he's censoring himself around the team.

I take a deep breath and beckon to the guys on the wall. It's Crikey who comes over to my table in need of ankle taping. He must have been the first in line.

"Let's see what we've got here," I say to him as I furiously wash my hands.

"Just the usual," he says. And I get to work.

It's like rush hour at the deli, though. No breaks in between athletes. I work on Trevi next, and Castro after him. By the time they're all on the ice for morning skate, it's time to restock the shelves, then Henry's travel kit. And then players start trickling back in from the rink again. I can hear their voices echoing off the shower walls.

Having busy hands is good, though. It makes me less likely to put my fist through a wall. I'm not known for my temper, but I just can't shake off my anger today.

A whole summer without Jordyn? I can't do that. It's a *horrible* idea. Every time I think of it, I want to scream.

"Hey. You okay?"

I whirl around and find Hudson standing in the room with me, his hair wet from the shower. I didn't even hear him come in. "Yeah. Mostly. You need something? Your hip okay?"

"It's fine." He frowns. "But you're not."

I sit down on my empty trainer's table. "Just a rough call from my monster-in-law. She wants to have Jordyn stay with them all summer."

"Wait, what?" He folds his arms and squints at me. "Without you?"

I nod, miserable. "She dangled some day camp in front of Jordyn, too, without asking me first. I'm so pissed off I could spit."

Hudson crosses the room to me. Then he does something very unexpected—he grasps the back of my neck and gives me a gentle squeeze. And I actually get goose bumps because he never touches me at work.

Like *never* never. And when his hand falls back to his side, I miss it.

"What's her endgame?" he asks. "What's their deal?"

I rub my forehead. "I think they see Jordyn as their last tie to Eddie. And they have a lot of money, so they think she'd be better off with them. They've said this to my face before."

He hisses through his teeth. "That's cold."

"They're cold. But when it comes to them, I can't think rationally. On the face of it, it's a great offer—Jordyn has a summer in the countryside and learns to ride ponies. But I don't trust them."

"You think they'd actually try to take her?"

"I don't *think* so." But the idea makes me ill. "Probably not. So if I just say no out of misplaced paranoia, does that make me an asshole? I don't have a plan for August yet, either. I'll be working here for training camp and my sister will be on tour. What if this thing in New Hampshire is heaven on Earth? I could be depriving her of something amazing. I can't even get her into the good camp in Brooklyn. Her new friends go to this Academy of Arts thing, but it fills up fast with Academy members." I realize I'm babbling, so I clamp my jaw shut.

"Hey." He puts his hand on my shoulder and gives it a squeeze. "You got, like, four months to figure stuff out, though."

When Hudson is really sweet to me, I don't know how to handle it.

"Everything okay?" Henry asks, striding into the room. "Is the trainer hurt this time?" He laughs at his own joke.

Hudson drops his hand, but not in a startled way. "Nah, Gavin was just having a stressful day. Family shit. We've all been there. Hang in there, man." He walks out of the room, leaving me more emotionally unstable than when he entered it.

"Anything I can help with?" Henry asks. "Nice job on the restock, by the way."

"Thanks. I just wish I knew what my husband would have wanted me to do about his overbearing parents."

Henry wipes down his table. "That bad, huh? You guys never got along?"

"Eddie's parents are overbearing. My husband did most of the things that his father wanted him to do. Except one—I was the thing his father didn't want him to do."

Henry laughs. "He wasn't okay with the whole gay thing?"

"Actually, Eddie was bi. And his parents assumed he'd marry his medical school girlfriend and have kids in a nice suburban house somewhere. But she left him. He adopted Jordyn the following year. And then we met at the park—he was running with Jordyn in a jogging stroller, and I was working out with some college athletes near the playground. He stopped to let Jordyn play in the sandbox just so he could watch me work out."

"Good play, dude." Henry laughs. "Let me guess—he came back to the park again every day for the next week?"

"He only had to come back once." The memory makes me smile. "He asked me out, and that was that. We only dated for six months before he proposed to me."

"Wow."

"Yeah. He was nine years older, and ready to make all these big decisions. I was only twenty-one when he proposed to me, but I was all in. Kid and all."

Henry's face falls. "And then you lost him. What a lonely way to become a dad."

Hudson flickers through my mind, because lately I haven't been lonely at all. But then I push that thought aside. "I'm glad we had the time we had. He was a really good husband, and a great dad. Much better than me, honestly."

"Hey," Henry argues. "Don't scare the clueless guy who's about to become a dad. You look pretty competent to me. Some of us don't even know how to change a diaper yet."

I laugh. "That's the easy part, trust me. It's answering their questions that will really mess with your mind. *How big is the world? Who made God?*"

He shakes his head and grins. "Good talk, Gavin. I'm already terrified of this fatherhood thing. I guess we just muddle through? Maybe that's what everybody does."

"Guess so."

TWENTY-ONE

Hudson

HUDSON: *Hey.*

    Gavin: *Yo. You home safe?*

    Hudson: *Yeah. Come over?*

    Gavin: *I would but Reggie's not here.*

    Hudson: *Doh! Shot down.*

    Gavin: *Hey, I'd rather see you than sit here and flip channels alone. Watching anything good?*

    Hudson: *No, I just got in, hung up my jacket and texted you. Be flattered.*

    Gavin: *Oh I am. But I'm in a shitty mood. TBH I'm probably bad company tonight.*

    Hudson: *I might not notice tho because your dick would be in my mouth.*

    Gavin: *Grrr. Now I'm picturing that.*

    Hudson: *You're welcome. So am I.*

    Gavin: *Grrr.*

    Hudson: *Will Reggie be back soon?*

    Gavin: *Negative. She's playing a gig in the Catskills. IDK where, but she made it sound far. Might not come home tonight.*

    Hudson: ***loud sigh***

    Gavin: *Right back atcha.*

. . .

I toss my phone down on the sofa with a grunt of disappointment. All the way home from LaGuardia I'd been looking forward to seeing Gavin. Only stubbornness prevented me from texting him from the taxi.

And now here we sit, maybe twenty feet apart. For no reason.

On that thought, I grab up my phone again and locate my keys. Then—in my bare feet—I leave my apartment and cross the hall, knocking softly on Gavin's door.

When he opens it a moment later, he's wearing a soft-looking flannel shirt and sweatpants. "Hi, sexy," he whispers. "Something wrong?"

"Yeah," I whisper back. "Can't I just come over? Wouldn't that solve all our problems?"

He glances down at the floor, and I realize I could have chosen my words more carefully. Our problems are not so easily solved as changing the location of our secret hookups from my place to his place. "I'm not sure it's a good idea," he says eventually. "If Jordyn woke up and heard your voice, she'd be out of her bed in a flash."

"Oh." I let that sink in for a second and I realize it's not about Jordyn losing a few minutes of sleep. It's the hazard of his daughter catching us in compromising positions on the sofa.

There's a good reason why we hang out at my place. "Look, can't I just come hang out for an hour anyway? Kinda miss you, here."

He looks conflicted. "It won't be that much fun."

"Sure it will. You're the funnest guy I know."

"That's just the horny talking," he says, but he smiles anyway. "Come in, I guess. But prepare to be good."

"Uh-huh. One second, though. There's something I gotta do first."

He raises his eyebrows, waiting to see what I mean.

So I lean in and kiss him softly. "Okay, there. Now lead the way."

He blinks. And then he yanks me by the sweatshirt into another kiss—a much more forceful one than mine. His firm, generous mouth is everything I've been dreaming about for the last couple days.

It's over way too soon, though.

He sighs, and opens his apartment door. "Right this way. Don't mind the usual mess."

I wouldn't, though. I like his place, with the fuzzy blanket on the couch, and the Perplexus puzzle on the coffee table. I sit down and pick it up, locating the little metal ball inside. "Is this a hard one?"

"Medium. Jordyn got it once already. You want anything to drink?" When I shake my head, he sits down beside me and picks up the clicker. "What do you want to watch on Netflix?"

I glance up at the menu on the screen. "Have you watched this season of the British baking show?"

The clicker falls to his lap as he stares at me. "Seriously?"

"What? You don't like it? Can't handle the tension?"

He laughs. "I like it fine. But—and I'm surprised you didn't notice this—it's a show about carbs. Not really your thing."

"I like carbs. I just don't *eat* carbs. Besides—it's not about the sugar and flour. It's the thrill of sportsmanship. Risk and reward."

"Okay, dude." He laughs. "Let's watch some Brits bake."

The show comes on, and I set the puzzle down and kick my feet up onto the coffee table like Gavin's. The theme of this first episode is fresh fruit. We watch as all ten of the new contestants decide what to make.

"Okay, the chunky guy is already my favorite," I declare. "He sounds rough, but I think he's a ringer."

"Interesting," Gavin says. "Who do you think goes home first?"

"The fussy one with the curly hair. She talks a big game, but there's a lack of mental toughness. I bet she cracks under pressure."

Gavin snorts with laughter. "You are hilarious."

"I'm just observant. And this show is a lot like my life, you know? One fuck-up and it's all over. Bye bye."

He settles in to see if I'm right—but I will be. Someone makes a cherry clafoutis. Someone else bakes a complicated lemon tart.

And the curly-haired fussbudget? She panics when her strawberry torte starts browning too quickly around the edges. She pulls it out of the oven and tries using foil to deflect some of the heat. But then the edges of the foil catch the strawberry goo in the middle, so she has trouble removing it afterward.

I sling my arm over the back of the sofa and palm the back of Gavin's neck. If I can't make out with him, at least I can touch him a little.

"Wow," Gavin says, leaning into my touch. "You called it. I don't think she'll make the cut."

"Even if she survives this one, it won't last," I say with the confidence of an armchair quarterback. "She doesn't have what it takes. But hey," I say, changing the subject. "You didn't tell me why you were in a bad mood tonight. What's up with that?"

His smile is a gift that I don't deserve. The weird thing about Gavin is that he seems to enjoy my grumpy, overly analytical personality. "Honestly I don't even remember."

That's probably not true. But I don't get a chance to prod him because my phone starts ringing loudly with "Under My Thumb." And even though I don't want to speak to my dad right now, I answer it by accident because I'm in a mad rush to make the ringing stop. "Hello, Dad?" I turn to Gavin and mouth *Sorry*.

He pauses the show.

"Hey, you made it home? Good work today. I wanted to talk to you about skating coaches for this summer. I got three or four ideas."

I make what is probably an audible, rude noise. "I'm sorry, we can't have this conversation right now. I need some downtime."

"But schedules fill up, Hudson. If you want the best of the best —if you want to *be* the best of the best—"

"Tomorrow," I insist, cutting him off. "Or the next day. Promise."

"I've booked you a spot with that conditioning coach in L.A. He's really doing some interesting stuff with isotonic—"

"*Dad.*" I cut him off. "I'm spending some time with a friend right now, so I can't talk."

"What kind of friend?" he asks pointedly.

Fuck. I glance at Gavin, and his eyes are wide. He can hear this conversation, through no fault of his own.

It would be easy enough to lie, I guess. *Just a teammate. Hanging out. He's going through a hard time.* But I can't do that to Gavin. It's bad enough that I pretend at the practice facility that we're just buds.

"I'm seeing someone," I say to my father. "It's casual, but I can't talk right now."

"What kind of *someone*?"

"That's private," I say quietly.

He actually groans. "Hudson, don't *do* this." And by *do this*, we both know that he means with a man. "You're so close to what you want! You're skating so well. By July I could have you locked into a new contract with Brooklyn. We might even get that no-trade clause. All you have to do is keep your head down. Be smart for once in your life."

"For once in my life?" I hiss. "That is *so* unfair. This conversation is over now. Good night."

I hang up on him for the first time in years.

Gavin whistles softly. "What just happened?"

I blow out a frustrated breath. "Usually I don't push back if it's about my career, but he's trying to have a say in my personal life. So I just bought myself another awkward conversation."

Gavin gets up off the couch and goes into the kitchen. He puts a tray on the counter and begins adding things to it—a small dish of nuts, a couple of clementines. Two glasses. Then he pulls a bottle off the highest shelf of a kitchen cabinet. It's a single malt scotch. "Have a wee dram with me?"

I nod, and watch as he pours an ounce or so into each glass. Then he puts a few ice cubes into another dish and carries everything over to the sofa, placing the tray between us.

He sits down and hands me a glass, then he puts an ice cube into his and raises it for a toast. "To overbearing families, and the strength to push back at them."

I clink my glass against his, and take a sip. "Thank you."

He shrugs. "Is your dad going to make your life difficult?"

"Like that would be new?" I take another sip. "The man has no boundaries. Usually it doesn't bother me so much, though, because I don't have much of a personal life for him to invade."

Gavin looks thoughtful. He tosses an almond into his mouth, and studies me. "Do you think he just can't stand the idea of his son's attraction to men?"

"No," I say quickly. "It's not quite that bad. He can't stand the idea of my career being tanked by it, though. Things haven't gone the way they were supposed to. He's frustrated with me."

"Would he be just as irritated if you had said *I have a girlfriend*?"

Slowly, I shake my head. "He wouldn't love it. He'd say it's a distraction. But he wouldn't care so much, because nobody would write rude social media comments about me and my team just because I had a girlfriend."

"So..." He clears his throat. "I've been meaning to ask you something, and I know you don't owe me anything. But do you hook up with women on the road?" His face actually looks a little red now.

"I have, in the past. Like, a couple of times a year, maybe."

His eyes widen. "That's it? Why? Don't the women swarm the players after games?"

"They swarm," I say with a shrug. It's just a fact since I'm a single, attractive, professional athlete. Finding willing sexual partners is never a challenge.

"But you're not interested? I'm just trying to understand."

"I'm, uh, sexually interested, if that's what you mean. I'm attracted to women. But..." I rub my neck. "It's a little hard to explain."

"Try me," he insists.

I pick up a clementine and peel it, just to have something to do with my hands. "Picking up women is easy. And nobody blinks, right? I'm passing for a straight man. But sex is supposed to make you feel, um, connected to people, right?"

His eyes flash with amusement. "Unless you're terrible at it, yes."

"Yeah, well I am. Because afterwards I just feel stupid—like those women see me as the super straight dude they assume I am. As if I got away with something. It just leaves me feeling lonelier than I was before. Like I'm playing a role."

"*Oh.*" He sips his scotch. "One time Eddie told me about a medical study he'd read in a journal. This one stuck with me. He said that bisexuals have higher rates of depression than people who identify as straight or gay."

A section of clementine pauses halfway to my mouth. "Really?"

"Yeah. Maybe because they don't feel like they belong to either the straight community or the queer community."

I put the fruit in my mouth and chew, so that I don't have to speak. But something in my heart clicks into place. Because that sounds really familiar to me. I've always felt like I didn't belong with the straight bros but didn't really see myself as a gay bro, either.

It just never occurred to me that anyone else might feel that way, too. Or that I would ever meet anyone who understood that about me.

"You still want to watch this show?" Gavin asks. "We don't have to."

"Oh, I want to." I offer him a section of my clementine. "You're probably going to have to throw me out."

He nudges the snack tray closer to me on the sofa. "Have some more low carb, high fiber snacks. This show makes me hungry."

"Thanks. Didn't I say you were fun?" I take a handful of nuts and toss them into my mouth.

But all I really want to snack on is him.

TWENTY-TWO

Hudson

TWO MORNINGS later I'm sitting in the training room while Gavin applies kinesiology tape to my left wrist, which is giving me some pain.

"Does this happen a lot?" There's an edge of concern in his voice.

"Nah. It's an old repetitive stress injury. It doesn't act up very often."

"Okay. Let us know if it gets worse."

"Hudson! There you are!"

When I look up at the man in the doorway, my stomach lurches. "Dad? What are you doing here?"

He's standing there in a suit jacket and crisp white shirt, his usual jocular grin in place. That smile wins over athletes and managers the whole world over. But it works less well on me. He and I haven't even spoken since the other night when I hung up on him.

Gavin removes himself to the far end of the room, as if to give us privacy.

"What kind of greeting is that?" My father crosses the room and sits on Henry's empty treatment table. "I'm headed to Boston tomorrow so I thought I'd swing through New York and see how you're doing. Besides, I owe you an apology."

Well *that's* unexpected. I swing my feet off the table and face him squarely. "Okay, let's have it then."

His expression cools a little. "I'm sorry that I implied that you haven't been smart and dedicated. Nobody is more dedicated than you."

"Thanks," I say gruffly. Honestly, I needed to hear that.

"But there are still things we need to discuss." He glances toward Gavin, who's tidying up his assortment of athletic tapes. "Can we have the room? Just five or ten minutes."

"Nope," Gavin says crisply. "I can't do my job if I'm loitering in the hallway. But Henry's office is unoccupied at the moment. Try there."

My father makes an unhappy face. He's not used to hearing no from support staff. Or anyone, really. But he stands up and heads for the door without another word.

I follow him and point toward Henry's small, messy office, and my father closes the door on us. Then he gets right to the point. "So it's him, huh? The trainer?"

"It's none of your business," I say calmly.

"Does anyone else know?"

"What did I just *say*? Are you kidding me? I haven't seen your face in three months, and *this* is the big emergency that has you flying into LaGuardia? To snoop into the details of my sex life?"

"You're spoiling for a fight then?" He crosses his arms and stares me down. "I only came to make sure you're all right. And to let you know how hard I'm working to make sure you live your dream. This isn't the right time to take your eye off the goal."

"I haven't."

He nods. "Okay, good. Nobody works harder than you do. I know that. We're going to get you there. You've just been unlucky."

I lean back against the wall—my ass parked against Henry's anatomy posters. But this is a very small room, and I feel hemmed in by this man who controls so many aspects of my life. "If Brooklyn doesn't renew me early with a no-trade clause...then what?"

"Then you keep playing and let the clock run down on your contract. This team is very shrewd. I'll let them know that you want stability more than you want to auction yourself off to the highest bidder next summer. They'll make you a reasonable offer. I'll make sure of it. You can buy a condo. Get a dog. Put down some roots. All those things you've been missing."

God, I want that so badly. I'm so tired of anticipating that tap on the shoulder—another trade. Another city. "So what do I have to do?"

He opens the leather folio that's permanently affixed to his hands. "Let's plan your summer training and nutrition regimen. You'll come to L.A. immediately after your season ends. You'll see my new favorite conditioning coach for a few weeks."

"All right."

He scribbles on his pad. "If Brooklyn goes deep into the playoffs —and there's no reason to think they won't—any vacation longer than a few days is really off the table."

"Yeah. Okay." I'm tired just thinking about it. But this is nothing new.

"Good man," my father says. "Now let's talk about nutritionists. A few guys are doing some interesting work on building up the gut flora."

"Sounds cool," I say. "Love talking about my gut flora."

He doesn't even crack a smile. "Excellent. I have two different guys in mind..."

Of course he does. This is my life. I chose this. And I'd be a fool to give up now.

I'm sitting at my own kitchen counter, drinking a protein shake before I head to the stadium. And texting with Gavin.

Gavin: *You okay?*

Hudson: *You mean my wrist? Or my dad.*

Gavin: *I mean both.*

Hudson: *Fine and fine.*

Gavin: *Nobody asked me, but I thought his apology was a little flat.*

Hudson: *Agreed. But apologies from him are thin on the ground. So I grade on a curve.*

Gavin: *I'll shut up now. My parents have never apologized to me and never will.*

Hudson: *You never mention them.*

Gavin: *I'm dead to them. There isn't much to say.*

Hudson: *God, I'm sorry.*

Gavin: *I'm over it. But there's a reason I didn't come out until I left for college. It wasn't safe for me to do so. And that's why I don't judge you for making the decisions you make. I'm frustrated for you. But I don't judge you.*

I look up from my phone, thinking the same thoughts about him that I always have. I don't deserve him. And I like him way too much.

Instead of replying to his text, I hit his avatar and call him. "Is this a bad time?" I ask when he answers.

"I'm making dinner, but talk to me."

"I appreciate what you said. That you don't judge me."

"Because I really don't."

I fiddle with my straw. "I wouldn't blame you if you did, though. It's easier to listen to my father than to do the hard work of trying to come out again."

"True."

"But what if he's wrong? What if Brooklyn isn't like my old team?" For some reason, I'm full of word vomit tonight. "Maybe five years is enough time to change the world a little. Maybe nobody would give a fuck? There must be *some* part of you that thinks I'm just a fucking coward."

"You are *not* a bleeping coward," he says in a low voice.

I snort. "Let me ask you this—has anyone in our locker room ever given you a hard time for being queer?"

"You know they haven't." He says quietly. "But you've been burned before. And even if the world has changed, there would still be a big, splashy story about you. And after *that*, you're still not done. You'd have to navigate this with everyone you know in hockey. I don't like your dad, and you should do whatever the fuck you want. But when he says it would be a distraction, he isn't wrong."

"Yeah." *And it gives me the cold sweats.* "My father says I need to wait until we get the contract we'd want. Then it would matter less."

"And when is that?"

"This summer, if I'm lucky. Next summer if I'm not. And—just saying—lucky isn't very on brand for me."

He laughs. "Are you sure? Because Henry just asked me to go on the next road trip, and Reggie is cool with babysitting."

It takes me a second to process that. "Whoa. You're coming to Montreal and Ottawa?"

"That's right."

"Huh. You know, I do feel luckier all of a sudden." That's a comfortable road trip, too. Not the most grueling schedule. "Am I getting a whole night in a bed with you?"

"If you're up for it."

"Oh, I'll be *up* for it."

He snickers. "Glad to hear it. I'd better go—these onions won't chop themselves."

"Go. But you've done wonders for my mood. As usual."

"Later, sexy."

"Later."

TWENTY-THREE

Gavin

I'M in an underground bar in Montreal, with twenty-three hockey players and six ping-pong tables. After we flew in on the jet, I expected the first stop would be the hotel.

But no—we came directly to this place. Apparently it's a tradition. So I'm drinking a light beer and watching the end of a game between Jason Castro and Jimbo—the equipment guy.

"Aw, you fucker," Jimbo says as Castro aces him again. "Your game has really improved this year. I want some of whatever you're drinking."

"Gavin fixed my backhand," Castro says, nodding at me. "You can ask him for lessons, but I'm his manager now, and the price just went up. A thousand dollars an hour."

Jimbo rolls his eyes. "What were you charging before, Gavin?"

"Just a beer," I say with a shrug. "I'll coach you when he's not looking."

"Let's see you play," Jimbo says to me, offering me his racket. "I'm tired of getting destroyed."

"All right." I set down my beer and step up to the table. "Need a breather, Castro? Water? Electrolytes? I don't want to be accused of wearing you down before the game tomorrow."

"No, I'm good." He jumps up and down a few times, like a tennis player at Wimbledon. "Let's do this. Coin toss, Jimbo."

"Yessir."

I win the coin toss, so I serve. And I don't take it easy on Castro, because where's the fun in that? It's a fast game, the ball flying between us at a blur.

After the first five points, we've drawn a crowd. "Come on, Castro!" his teammates call. "Fight for it, man!"

The next serve puts us into a long rally. I lose count of how many times we send the ball back and forth across the net, but it's a big number. Then he hits one a little long, and I'm able to chop it.

The underspin does him in, and the ball drops short of where he expects it.

Everyone hoots.

We battle onward, but Castro loses the next point, too. "Oh God, I've miscalculated," the hockey player says from the other end of the table. "The young padawan cannot defeat his master."

I win the next point with a smile, and a little bit of luck. I'm playing great tonight, and he's probably just a little drunk and a little tired. It isn't even a fair fight.

But it's still fun. I win the game without too much bother.

"So who's willing to play Gavin next?" the team captain asks. "Let's put some money on it—with a cut to charity, of course. Jimbo —you're the bookie. I've got a hundred bucks on whichever one of you is brave enough to play him. Who's it gonna be?"

"Me!" Hudson steps up to the table. "I got this."

"You *don't* got this," I say automatically, because smack talk is my second language.

"Ooooh," says the crowd.

"Burn," says Castro with a snicker. "I'll put a hundred on you, New Guy. Don't let hockey down, bro."

"I've got a hundred on Newgate!" someone else calls.

Then I hear the head coach's voice. "Two hundred on the trainer."

The players roar.

"Aw, man," Hudson says, shaking his head. "Where is the love? Coin toss, Jimbo."

He wins the toss, and I brace myself for Hudson's serve. And it's fiery. My guy comes out swinging. I bear down and drive it back to him.

Neither of us is fooling around, here. I win the first point, but he takes the next. And that's how it works for the next fifteen minutes —a tight, sweaty game. But then I ace him on a serve, and he curses.

Someone runs off to retrieve the ball, and we both grab our drinks for a swig.

Then his eyes flip up to mine, and he smiles at me.

I put my cold beer bottle to my forehead and smile back. And I realize I went a couple of years without having this kind of fun in my life. Uprooting my little family to take the job in Brooklyn was a big gamble. But it's done a lot for me. It kick-started my career. It gave me a new set of interesting friends.

And it brought me face-to-face with the man across the ping-pong table—the one who's gotten under my skin every day since I met him across a different ping-pong table.

Suddenly, the most outrageous thought pops into my brain. *Everyone can play ping-pong at our wedding.*

Okay, what? *No.* I smack that thought aside, the way you smack a mosquito. I'm being ridiculous. The novelty of the road trip is obviously messing with my brain.

It's Hudson's serve, and I get back into my groove. This is probably the longest ping-pong game of my life. Neither one of us is willing to turn down the pressure. We've drawn a crowd, with players upping their bets on every point. It's loud and rowdy and I'm sweating like a marathoner.

And I wouldn't change a thing. Even as my hand slips a little on the paddle, making my return a little clumsy, I'm still having the time of my life.

Hudson capitalizes, though. He wins the point, and the score is eleven all.

"You got this, Gavin!"

"Smash 'im, New Guy!"

We lock eyes, and his serve is lightning fast. I return it in a flash. The rally is furious, but then he kills me with a backhand shot—and does it beautifully.

"Just like I taught you," I grumble, and the crowd laughs.

He only needs one more point.

It's my turn to serve. But as I get set up, my phone vibrates in my pocket. I hesitate for a second. But there are a lot of eyes on me right now, so it will have to wait a moment. The buzzing stops.

I serve, trying to ace him with a zinger to the far left. But he returns it. And off we go, our rally lengthening into four and then six returns. I send the ball back and forth across the table, making him work for it.

He's more unpredictable, which keeps me guessing.

My phone starts vibrating again, damn it. And the idea that there might be some kind of emergency at home is just distracting enough that I send him the ball right in the center of the table.

He returns it with a lob that shouldn't work at all. It's too slow. But it's also shallow, and very far to my left. I try to get there, but I only get the edge of my racket on it.

It yeets itself off the table, useless.

Everyone roars.

"Pay up, gents!" Jimbo calls, waving an envelope around.

"Oh Jedi master, you'll get 'im next time," Castro says. And I accept a bunch of high fives, but I'm working my way toward the edge of the room so I can check my phone.

The calls were from Eustace.

I lost that game to Hudson because of my mother-in-law?

Fuck.

The phone rings again in my hand. And even though I know better than to answer a call from her when I'm agitated, I do it anyway. Because I'm not home at the moment and what if there was some kind of emergency?

"Hello Gavin," she says primly. "We need to talk about summer camp before it's too late to enroll Jordyn."

"We *did* talk about it," I growl. "She's not spending a whole summer away from me."

"August, then," she says. "Four weeks."

Fuck. I walked right into that. "Absolutely not. She's too young, and..." The truth is that I will have trouble articulating all my objections in a way that doesn't sound like a declaration of war. "I'm not willing to send her away for more than a couple of nights."

She gasps. "That is not fair to Jordyn. You have to work in August! She could be riding horses and enjoying the fresh air!"

I lean against a paneled wall and close my eyes. Misery sets in, because I don't know if I'm doing the right thing. "I'll bring her for a visit in July," I say weakly. "That's all I can promise you right now."

"That's not good enough," she says in a voice that's still calm, but ice cold. "I've retained a lawyer, Gavin. He thinks I have a chance at getting visitation. Or maybe even custody."

My eyes fly open. "*What? A lawyer?*"

"She could have a stable home with two adults who love her. She could go to a better school, and see her old friends."

"That's...You're..." My head spins. "You'll never get custody. I'm her only legal parent."

"If the judge sides with us, it won't matter," she says. "You sold the house that Eddie bought for her, with the backyard and the swing. You took her out of the school that Eddie chose for her. You're too young, and you lead a single man's lifestyle."

"What does *that* mean?" I demand. And then I realize I'm just letting her lead me down the garden path. "Never mind. You're behaving like a troll. And you'll never win custody."

"I might lose, but I might win. But if you don't give us the summer, you'll be hearing from our lawyer."

She hangs up before I can even process the threat. But when I do, I gasp for air, and feel an angry pain behind my breastbone. I'm so upset I might detonate into fiery pieces right here in the bar.

My phone lights up with a text, and I almost can't bear to look.

But the message is not from Eustace. It's from Hudson. *Baby, what's wrong? Is there an emergency?*

I look up suddenly and spot him on the other side of the giant room. He's leaning against the bar and watching me with worried eyes.

Then he breaks eye contact to tap something new into his phone, and my screen lights up again. *Meet me out front. You can tell me in the cab.*

TWENTY-FOUR

Gavin

THE HOTEL ISN'T EVEN ten minutes away by cab. So my rant isn't over when we get out on the sidewalk.

"Hold that thought," Hudson says as he taps his credit card to pay the driver. "I need you to check in. Then swing by your room to get your bag."

"Why?" I look up at the brightly lit hotel tower. I'd been so excited to come here. But now I have only anger in my veins.

"Because you're coming up to my room. Trust me. Now come on."

We go inside, and I stop fuming long enough to get my room key and glower up the elevator to the fourth floor.

Hudson was correct to assume that my suitcase would be waiting. I grab it and follow him back into the elevator, where he presses the button for the top floor.

"They're threatening me," I growl as the elevator climbs. "They know cash is tight. They're counting on the fact that I can't afford to hire a lawyer. But if I give in and do what they want, this will just happen again next year."

"Yeah, I hear you. I really hate this for you. But it's going to be okay."

The doors part, and he beckons me out into a quiet hallway, where he unlocks a door with his key card.

"Is it? Because I honestly don't know how we come back from this. They're..." My rant ends midstream as I take in the room. It's a suite—a big one. There's a giant, sleekly modern four-poster bed visible in the adjacent bedroom. In front of me there's a sunken living space with low couches surrounding a candle-lit square table.

There's a meal for two laid out on that table. I see salads, plus other dishes on a warmer in the center. The table shimmers with candlelight, which makes the bottle of wine glisten in its ice bucket.

"Wow," I say stupidly. "All that's for us?"

Hudson lets out an awkward laugh, and then he tosses his suit jacket onto a coatrack. "I don't ever take you out to dinner. And you've cooked for me. So I was trying to treat you right, here."

"Oh." I watch the candles flicker for a moment, and my heart rate drops a few crucial beats per second. "You're...Thank you."

His smile is wry. "I know my timing sucks. As usual. But is there anything I can do for you? You probably need to do a little custody law research, if it would make you feel calmer. Or google some lawyers to call in the morning. I could help you. Or at least feed you." He unbuttons his cuffs and rolls his shirt sleeves up, revealing strong forearms.

And all I want is for him to wrap them around me for a minute. So I cross the room and lean into his chest. I press my face into the starchy collar of his dress shirt and breathe in.

"Hey," he says quietly. Those arms wrap around me firmly. "It really will be okay."

"I know," I mumble. "Probably."

"No, really." He runs a firm hand up my back, and it feels so good.

"I was having so much fun tonight. I thought—look at me, living a little. And now this. It's like I can't ever take my eye off the ball. I'm sorry."

He gives me a squeeze. "Don't apologize, unless you're only sorry for using a baseball reference on a hockey trip. Now come on.

Let's eat a little something, and then we'll come up with a game plan."

"Okay, whatever you say."

"Good boy. Now open that wine while I take off this suit. And figure out what's in those covered dishes."

When he releases me, I step down into the seating area and plop down on one of the sofas. I smell garlic, and my stomach rumbles on cue. I lift the lid of one of the dishes, and see two pieces of seared salmon in butter sauce, with green beans. The other dish contains some kind of whipped potato with paprika on top.

My mouth waters aggressively.

"Does it look good?" Hudson asks, emerging from the bedroom in a pair of flannel pants, and no shirt.

"Almost as good as you do," I say, and it comes out sounding flirty, in spite of my anxious mood. I'd have to be dead not to find a shirtless Hudson diverting.

He takes a seat beside me. "All right. Let's eat. That fish looks good."

"Good? It looks amazing." I grab a plate and capture a filet for him. "This can't have been sitting here very long, or it wouldn't look so fresh."

He gives me a sideways glance. "I texted the concierge the minute our ping-pong game ended. Don't skip me with those potatoes. It's cheat day."

I add vegetables and a big scoop of potatoes to his plate, and then douse everything with some of the butter sauce. I make myself a plate, too, and pour two glasses of wine.

He groans when he takes the first bite. "I'm sorry your evening turned ugly, but I'm not sorry I ordered this dinner."

"I'm not sorry, either." Although it kills me that Hudson had all of this planned. It's romantic—like the date we can never take.

There's a gulf between the things he wants, and the things he allows himself. Sometimes when we spend time together, I feel like I'm helping him close the distance.

Tonight, though, I feel melancholy. Like the river is just too wide to cross. For both of us.

Food helps, though. I polish off the hot food on my plate, and then mow down my salad. When we're done, I top up our wineglasses while Hudson removes all the dirty dishes to a cart, and parks it in the hallway.

"Okay, I feel better," I admit. "Still anxious, but not quite so hopeless."

Hudson brings his laptop over to the sofa and sits down beside me. "First things first. What do you need to be ready to go up against her? Do you need to find a lawyer?"

I take a sip of my wine and lean back against the sofa. "I have one. We needed someone in family law to complete my adoption. But the lawyer's in New Hampshire, and I don't know if I need one in New York."

Hudson opens the computer and googles "custody jurisdiction." He scrolls through the results and then reads aloud. "Jurisdiction in a custody suit follows the 'home state' of the child. The 'home state' is the state where the child has lived for the last six months.'"

"Oh." I do the math. "So I should call the New Hampshire lawyer."

"Yeah. But..." He does some more googling. "She doesn't have a case, Gavin. Not even for visitation. Grandparent visitation rights are not a thing."

This perks me up. "Are you sure?"

"Google is sure." He looks up. "But also, my aunt is a social worker. So I grew up hearing all these stories from her job. And it's *really* hard to take custody of someone else's kid. They'd have to accuse you of all kinds of horrible things. I'm not kidding. They'd interview her school teachers, and they'd need proof of neglect or abuse."

"*Oh*. God that's dark."

"I know. Fortunately, the law is set up to keep children with their parents. And that's you." He puts a hand in the center of my chest, and I like the weight of it.

So I put a hand over his. "Thank you for listening to me rant tonight. I'm sorry I killed the mood."

"What mood?" He leans over and slowly kisses my neck. "I'm not always Mr. Sunshine, you realize."

"Is that so?"

"Mm-hmm." He kisses my neck again. "Do you want to keep working on this? Or is it time for me to distract you?" He noses his way to my jaw, where he kisses me again. And now his tongue comes out to play, and I shiver.

"Distraction is good," I murmur as I slide a little more deeply into the sofa. "Besides, we have this amazing room all night. So we'd better make the most of it—like get naked in it."

He pushes me down on the sofa and then studies me from above. I like the view—he's all warm skin and scruff and serious brown eyes. "If you're not feeling it tonight, I'd understand."

"Oh please." I run a hand down his six-pack. "I'll be feeling it all right if you take off more of your clothes. Besides—there's nothing more for me to do tonight, other than worry. Go ahead and make me forget my bad day. You're doing God's work, here."

He laughs. And then he does a sexy reverse-push-up and lowers his hard body onto mine. His eyes grow serious again.

I expect his kiss. I want it. I'm made of expectation. But he studies me a little longer, his thumb tracing my eyebrow. His eyes heavy-lidded.

Then he leans in and traces my bottom lip with his tongue.

The gasp I make is like steam from a pressure valve. I need this release tonight. My life is a damn mess, and tomorrow I'll have to face all that.

But right this second it's okay for me to weave my fingers into his hair and tug his head down for more.

"Gavin," he whispers against my lips, and the hair stands up on my arms. Then he plunges us into a kiss, and I'm finally, blissfully, swamped with the taste of him. My eyes fall closed with happiness, but then I force them open again.

There won't be many nights like this. I'd better enjoy it while I can.

TWENTY-FIVE

Hudson

BEFORE I MET GAVIN, I never knew my neck was an erogenous zone. But the way he strokes my skin makes me crazy. And I'm not very subtle about it. When I groan into his mouth, he roughens his grip, running his fingernails down my back, and it almost destroys me.

This is exactly what I'd been craving. Some men spill their hearts with romantic words. I'm too big a coward for that, so I show my cards with a candlelit meal and a plush hotel room. Right after he told me he was coming on this trip, I practically sprained something in my haste to upgrade my hotel room and set up our dinner.

As if he wouldn't take one look at this setup and see right through me.

I'm so gone for him—all of him. From his patient gaze, to his quick smile, and the easy sound of his laughter. And, fine, it doesn't hurt that he has a tight body and muscular ass, too.

I swear to God that if Gavin had been too upset to fool around tonight, I would have been a gentleman about it. Lucky for me, he wants this as much as I do. I don't have to hold back. So I grind against him with deep kisses and questing hands. I'm like a summer heat wave—intense and unrelenting.

He groans beneath me. Then he pushes at the waistband of my pants.

"Oh no you don't." I sit up and begin to unbutton the soft flannel shirt he's wearing. "I've been thinking about unbuttoning this all day."

"Hurry up, then."

As soon as I get it off him, he tosses the shirt aside. But I'm not done. I go for his khakis next. Those come off right along with his boxers. My mouth goes dry at the sight of his hard cock standing tall, engorged just for me. "What do you want tonight?" I'm already licking my lips, and ducking down to swipe my tongue across his rosy cock head.

"Mmm," he bucks against my tongue. "I just want you."

"You can have me—all of me," I taunt. His eyes flare, so I up the ante. "Any way you want."

And, yup, I just threw down the gauntlet, there. We haven't had penetrative sex yet. But I think about it all the time. And I've got lube and condoms hidden in my suitcase.

I haven't asked for it, though, because that's awkward. I don't know his preferences, and I don't want to assume. Plus—my greatest obstacle—I haven't wanted to own up to my own inexperience.

Honesty is so tricky. It's easier to just lower my head to Gavin's dick, and take him into my mouth. So that's what I do. His cock is heavy on my tongue. I give a suck, and the result is a moan, plus the briny heat of his precum on my tastebuds.

I love this. I love making him wild with the tight grip of my mouth. When Gavin is really turned on, his cheeks redden, and there's a flush on his chest. The evidence of his desire makes me so fucking horny. My cock is screaming for attention, but I'm having too much fun to stop.

So I double down. While I suck him, I cup his heavy balls in one hand, and stroke them with my thumb.

"Listen, hunk," Gavin pants as he writhes on the sofa. "If you want this to be over really soon, keep doing that."

I pop off of him. But then I spread his ass cheeks, lick my finger and slide it across his hole.

He lets out another moan as I take him into my mouth again. "Seriously. Dying, here."

He isn't the only one. As I release him, the supplies I brought with me on this trip are practically shouting at me from the other room. "I really want to fuck you."

"You do?" He props himself up on one elbow. "Never asked for it before."

"I didn't know what you liked."

"Right—because you didn't *ask*." His eyes flare. "I'm pretty versatile. But you never brought it up. I thought you might be squeamish—like maybe anal was too gay for you."

My face heats with embarrassment. "That's not it at all. I'm just real bad at asking. Besides, I might be, uh, not so great at it."

He rises to a seated position. "Why the fuck would you think that?"

Here we go. "Because I've never done it before."

"Oh." The shock is evident on his face. "*Oh.*"

"Yeah." *Gulp.* "This is really killing my cred, huh?"

He laughs suddenly. "You're usually so bossy that sometimes I forget how sheltered you are."

"*Sheltered?*" I sputter.

"Totally," he insists. "If you had more queer friends you'd probably be more comfortable discussing all of this. Joking about it. Queer people are better at discussing sex than straight people. They have to be."

"I guess that makes sense," I admit.

"So I guess I'll need to take a survey," Gavin says with a shrug.

"What?"

"I need to ask you a bunch of questions, so I can suss out your interests. Get up."

Confused, I do what he asks and rise from the sofa.

He nudges me toward the bedroom. "I'm going to take a fast shower, and while you wait, you can pull down the covers."

My mind floods with images of Gavin in the shower. "I need one, too."

"Go on then. You first." He nudges me again toward the bedroom. "But don't take too long."

When it's his turn, Gavin actually whistles in the shower, while my heart practically explodes with anticipation.

Meanwhile, I peel the comforter off the stylish four-poster bed and set the supplies I brought on the bedside table. That seems really forward, though, so I open the drawer and drop them in, right on top of the ubiquitous hotel bible.

Huh.

Closing the drawer, I retrieve one of the candles from the table in the living room and set it by the bed, where it gives the room a sexy, golden glow. But then I wonder if that's just too much, so I carry it back out and leave it in the living room.

God, I hate situations where I don't know what I'm doing.

Gavin emerges from the shower, still whistling, a minute later, a towel tied around his trim waist, and a few drops of water still clinging to his sculpted shoulders. He gives me a glance where I'm perched awkwardly on the end of the bed. "You know what would be perfect? Hang on."

He trots out into the living room, grabs two of the candles and brings them into the room, where I'm still sitting there, dumbstruck as he sets one on each side of the bed. Then he makes another trip into the living room, retrieving something from his suitcase.

When he returns to the bedroom, he's carrying a bottle of lube, a pack of condoms, and a pack of those sterile wipes that fitness trainers always carry around. He sets them down on the bedside table in exactly the same spot where I almost left mine.

"All right. Where were we?" He grabs the knot in his towel, flicks it open and flings the towel onto a chair.

The candlelight catches the contours of his abs, and the sheen of his straining cock. I've never seen anything so appealing in my life. Like a zombie under a spell, I finally stand up and shed my own towel.

"Hot damn," he says. "Now, before we jump each other, we're going to have a chat. A naked chat. On the bed."

Yessir. I sit in the center of the bed, leaning against the headboard, my arms clasped behind my head. Talking isn't what I'm after in this scenario, but I'll try to follow instructions.

It must show on my face, because Gavin chuckles. "You're so impatient. Maybe that's why we've never had this discussion."

"Why would you want to *talk* when we could be sucking each other's dicks?"

"We're already good at that." He straddles my thighs instead, and then kisses me. "But there are other things about you that I need to know."

"Okay? Like what?"

He drops his mouth to my neck and runs his teeth lightly over my throat. "You like this, yes?"

I growl instead of answering. Whenever he kisses my neck I just want to push him down and have my way with him.

"Okay, thought so. Now how about this?" He licks his way down my chest. Then he lightly bites my nipple and I gasp in surprise.

Then, my dick leaks against my stomach.

"Mmm, yeah," he says, licking my nipple while I grip his hair in my hands and pin his tongue in place. "So you're not so toppy that you can't appreciate me playing with you."

"Nnnghhh," is all I have to say about that.

He lifts his head suddenly. "Would you ever let me blindfold you? Or is that a bridge too far?"

In response, I let out an achy gasp, then grab my cock and squeeze the base of it.

There's humor in his voice when he asks, "So that's a yes?"

"Maybe," I grunt. "Some other night, when I'm not about to push you down and hold you there until we both explode."

His eyes darken at the idea. "Fair enough. So you definitely want to fuck me."

"Definitely," I echo. "No confusion there."

He reaches for his own dick and strokes it. "There's an idea I could get behind. Or under." He licks his lips.

"But I don't know what I'm doing," I warn. "And I don't want to hurt you."

"You won't," he says confidently. And he reaches for the lube. "Might take some prep, though. It's been years for me."

"Hell," I whisper. "Since he..." *died*? Maybe I'm asking too much.

"No, longer," he says, opening the bottle. "I was the top in my marriage."

"*Oh.*" Suddenly my head is full of Gavin fucking another man. Forcefully. And I like that image a hell of a lot more than I ever imagined I would.

Huh.

"Have you ever prepped your own ass?" he asks, leaning over to kiss my neck again. "Or anyone else's?"

"N-no," I admit as his stubble gives me goose bumps.

"Hmm," he says, kissing my jaw. "Can I demonstrate—on you?"

"Okay, sure," I say immediately. I already trust Gavin's confident hands on every other part of my body. This is really no different.

He sits up, his eyes flashing in the candlelight. "Just tell me if I do anything you don't like, okay?"

"Yeah, no problem." I recline, hitching my hips down the bed, resting my head on the pillow. One at a time he bends my knees, placing the sole of each foot onto the mattress. And I purposefully spread my legs, making room for him to kneel between them.

For a split second, I'm wildly uncomfortable. It's not easy for me to do this—to offer myself to anyone. To be as *seen* as this.

But Gavin gathers my left knee in one strong arm and kisses it. He makes a sound of happiness from deep inside his chest. Then he drags his lips up my thigh, and I melt back onto the mattress as his hot mouth makes me crazy.

He licks the base of my long-ignored cock, and I shiver with anticipation.

He chuckles quietly and then continues to tease me with his tongue. I reach down and thread my fingers through his hair, urging him on.

If you do the math, I haven't known Gavin more than a couple of months. But I suddenly realize how thoroughly I trust him. He takes my balls in one hand—literally the most delicate part of my body—and I lean into his touch completely.

It's so easy. Because it's him.

I'm drifting happily on this thought as he finally takes my cock into his mouth. *Fuuuuuck* yes. Heat flashes across my pecs, and I roll my hips with enthusiasm.

After the click of the lube bottle, a slicked-up hand strokes my taint, and my sac. I huff out a surprised breath, because that feels exceptionally good.

Gavin pauses, massaging my taint. "All good?"

"Oh *yeah*," I say on a gasp. It's just that I didn't know how sensitive my body was there, or how wicked that could feel. "Don't stop."

And he doesn't. A blunt, slicked-up finger traces into my crack, teasing my hole, and I quiver with anticipation.

He's barely touched me yet, and I'm breaking out in a sweat.

Gavin's hot, eager mouth envelops my dick unexpectedly, and I give a horny shout. He gives me a good, hard suck. And just as my eyes roll back in my head, one naughty finger penetrates me.

It burns a little, but I don't hate it. Not at all. The burn and the stretch blur together with the pleasure of his tongue against my cock.

"Fuck," I gasp. Then I bear down on his finger, trying to get accustomed to the sensation. It's strange. Definitely foreign. But also thrilling.

"Breathe," he demands.

Oh yeah. I take in some oxygen. *Good plan.*

His finger retreats. I hear the sound of the lube bottle again. But before I can catch my breath, his mouth is back to its wildly distracting ministrations to my cock. And when his finger slides back inside me, it's easier this time. So much easier. I flex my hips, riding it. And Gavin moans around my dick.

Maybe it's the hum of his lips on my cock, but something clicks inside me. Something good. And when Gavin makes a beckoning motion with his finger, I feel it everywhere. Across my pecs. My aching cock. In my fingers and toes.

My groan is loud, and I clench my ass to try to hold onto that feeling.

Gavin releases my cock. "Yeah yeah," he encourages. "That's it."

It occurs to me that I'm supposed to be learning something here —studying up on how to make this good for Gavin. But who could think right now? "More," I demand. "Show me."

"Yes*sir*," he says, and my dick gives a throb.

Another click of the lube bottle. And now I'm lifting my hips for what feels like two of Gavin's fingers.

Once again there's a burn. But this time I'm ready for it. Gavin is talking to me. Something about a ring of muscle. Muscles relaxing. *Blah blah blah*. "Breathe," he says.

At least I process that last word. I take a deep breath and feel my body letting him in again.

"Good boy," he says, and the words slide like butter along my overheated skin. He licks the underside of my dick, and then begins to slowly scissor his fingers.

So many sensations. So overwhelming. The burn dissipates, and a new kind of heat begins to build inside me. A deep, needy pressure. Then Gavin somehow slides a little deeper, his fingertips colliding with the neediest, achiest point of my being. My breath stutters and my limbs tingle and I let out a moan.

"And *that* is why it's fun to get fucked," Gavin blabbers. "That right there."

I get it. God, do I get it. But I can't say it. Or anything, really. All I can do is ride those fingers and lean a little closer to the promised land. But it's just out of reach.

I gaze down at Gavin's muscular shoulders, as he leans in to pleasure me, and suddenly I can picture it so clearly—his body pumping into mine. More of that blunt fullness.

It's such a powerful image that I let out another achy groan.

"Are you ready to switch?" he asks.

"Fuck no," I snarl. "You have to finish what you started. Fuck me already."

He lifts his head quickly, his hand retreating, and I growl at the loss. "Wait, what?"

"You heard me."

Confusion flashes through those sexy eyes. "That wasn't the plan," he says slowly. "This was supposed to be a demonstration."

"Yeah, a real good one. And plans change. Unless you hate the idea," I add, trying to sound like less of a dick.

But I really want *his* dick.

He blinks. Then he reaches for one of those wipes on the bedside table and cleans his hands, a thoughtful expression on his face. "You're *sure*."

"Do I look unsure?" I growl, my hand stroking my engorged cock. My balls are hard as boulders.

"Not really." He smiles. "But you are a study in contrasts."

"Whatever," I growl. "Fuck now, study later." Then I sit up and grab the package of condoms off the bedside table and rip it in two. I grab one off the strip and pop the packet open.

Gavin takes it from me, and I watch as he slips it over the head of his dick, and then rolls it down. The muscles in his arm flex in the candlelight, and I just want to devour him. "How do you want it?" he asks. "I bet you have big opinions on that, too."

He's not wrong. My mind is like the menu page on a porn site. "Sure, I want very specific things from you. Like, a hundred of them. Where do I even start?"

Gavin tosses the pillows off the bed, except for one, which he props against the metal headboard. Then he leans back against it. "Come here. Straddle me."

I like it. Two seconds later I'm kneeling over him, while he squirts the lube all over himself and then lines his cock up at my entrance. This is it. No hesitation. I grab the headboard with two hands and bear down on him.

"Easy," he whispers. "Breathe."

But I don't care about easy. I feel raw and reckless. For once in my life, I just want to act without thinking about the consequences. And in this moment, that means sliding the blunt, oversized head of his cock into my ass, and enjoying the burn.

"Slow," he orders.

Yeah, no. My body suddenly gives up the fight and welcomes him inside. And I slide all the way down his cock and bottom out.

Now it's Gavin who's suddenly cursing and gripping my thighs with white-knuckled hands. "Fuck yes. Fuck," he babbles.

His cheeks are stained red as he lifts his chin and gapes up at me in wonder, and we both pant through the most intimate moment of my entire life.

"Go slow," he whispers.

"Why?" I demand. Then I dip my chin and give him the dirtiest, wettest kiss I can manage from this angle. "I'm fine."

He groans, and then leans back against the pillow, his face red, his pupils blown. "Go *slow*, or I'm going to blow before you're ready. There's only so much of this bossy hot bottom act a guy can take without shooting."

"Oh." I let go of the headboard and run my hands all over his fevered chest. "I thought you were a pro at this." I tweak his nipple and he moans. I lean in and put my tongue in his ear, and he gasps.

Screw the consequences. I can't stop. This is the most alive I've ever felt. I grab his chin in one hand and kiss the living hell out of him, plundering his mouth with my tongue.

He retaliates, though. He sucks on my tongue, and then fits a hand over my cock. Just one stroke, and I feel it everywhere. My nipples tighten and my back breaks out in a sweat.

I pull away from our kiss and grasp the headboard again, rocking cautiously onto my knees, experimenting with a slow thrust up and down his cock.

"Yeah," he hisses. "Find it. Hit your spot."

I'm so full of him, and it's so odd. But when I flex my hips a few degrees, I find a zing of that deep, otherworldly pleasure he'd shown me before. So I chase it, picking up the pace. The burn recedes. There's only fullness and slickness and drugging pleasure.

"Fuuuuck." He throws his head back. "You are...the...hottest..." He actually clenches his jaw as I ride him a little faster. His hands find my chest, and he groans deeply.

And I'm electric. Every thrust brings me a little closer to the bright, sparkly high that I'm chasing.

But then Gavin starts stroking my cock in earnest. My rhythm stutters as my synapses try to fire, my brain incapable of processing additional pleasure. I'm like an overloaded system, verging on glitching out.

"Gavin," I gasp. It's both a prayer and a warning.

"Go," he says. "Take it. Fly."

I let go of the bed frame and grasp his shoulders instead. I'm sweating as I pump my tension-primed body onto his. Everything is heat and crackling sensation. As I strain for the finish line, I stare into Gavin's heavy-lidded eyes.

He stares right back at me, his lips parted, breath sawing in and out of his sculpted chest. Then he raises his hand, and holding my gaze, he licks the palm and returns it to the engorged head of my dick.

I guess I shouldn't be surprised anymore when Gavin plays my body like his own personal fiddle. But somehow that's the tipping point—the match tossed onto the flames. With a twist of his hand, I'm spiraling. The pressure deep inside me erupts into fireworks. I give a shout, and I'm emptying myself into his hand.

Then Gavin shudders beneath me. His thighs lock up like iron, and his head tips back and the most beautiful groan emits from his kiss-swollen lips.

I ride him slowly, like I can't remember how to stop, until he relaxes against the pillow.

Breathing hard, I rest my hands against the mattress. I curl forward and kiss his sweaty face. And then I coax my body to unclench and separate from his.

"Holy..." That's as far as he gets with that sentence.

"Yeah," is my equally sharp reply.

He wraps his arms around me and pulls me down onto his body. "You are full of surprises," he slurs.

I even surprise myself. Smiling into the stubble on his neck, I return his embrace—holding him tightly—never wanting to let him go.

TWENTY-SIX

Gavin

WE TAKE ANOTHER SHOWER. This one together. But we're both too spent to do anything more than soap each other up, and make out sloppily against the tiles.

I feel drunk on him—truly inebriated by his kisses and the memory of watching him ride me like a rodeo champion.

So I follow him back to bed like a well-trained puppy. We curl up together under the comforter, our skin still damp and scented of expensive body wash. I use one of his meaty pecs as my pillow, and I trail my fingers through the damp hairs of his happy trail.

Reality is still out there somewhere, waiting to pounce in the morning. But we're in our own little world, and it can't touch us yet.

Hudson shifts in the bed, and I realize I'm probably lying on his sore hip. My hand fumbles down to squeeze his hip flexor. "You okay?" I ask. "How's the joint?"

"Don't worry." He chuckles. "My hip won't be the sore spot tomorrow."

I push up onto an elbow and look him in the eye. It's dark in here now, since one of the votive candles has already flickered out. "Are you all right? Was this, like, bad timing?"

He takes one broad hand and presses my head back onto his chest. "Stop it. I'm good. I'm *perfect*."

But my mind has come back online, so it wanders to the bigger crises in my life other than Hudson's potentially sore bottom. Like Eustace. And Jordyn. And a summer camp with ponies.

"Gavin?" he whispers.

"Yeah?"

"There's nowhere else you need to be right now, yeah?"

I take a breath. "No. There isn't."

"Good," he says, stroking the back of my neck. "Because I thought I lost you for a second there."

"How could you tell?"

He shrugs those big shoulders. "I'm pretty clued into you. I'm always paying attention to you, even if I don't let it show."

"Oh." I swallow hard. "Sorry. I got a little distracted thinking about the dickish people in my life."

He puts a firm hand on my back. "Okay, serious question. How can we use *dick* to describe somebody who's terrible? Aren't we doing a disservice to dicks?"

I snort. "I like dicks as much as the next guy. But a dick can't think on its own. This is a proven fact—if you let dicks make decisions, bad stuff happens."

"Fair point." His voice is laced with humor. "I can see you've given this some thought."

"I have. Because a dick is only great if it's attached to the right guy. I'm a fan of yours, for example. Ten out of ten. And I appreciate its skills of distraction."

His thumb strokes my back, and his voice turns serious. "I'm glad. But tonight was a lot more than just some fun for me. I care about you, and I hate seeing you stressed."

I run my fingers through his chest hair with a sweet touch, but I don't really know what to say to that. If I'm honest, it scares me a little. "You can probably tell that I like you a whole lot, too." After all, I'm curled up on his chest like he's my favorite teddy bear. "It's just that I don't know what to do about it."

"Hey, relax," he says, smoothing a hand across my hair. "I'm not asking you for anything. I just want you to know that meeting you has made a real impact on me. It's making me question all my choices, and that's a *good* thing."

"Because you weren't happy?" I whisper.

"Not happy enough," he says slowly. "I'm so tired of sacrificing my whole life for hockey, when hockey can never love me back. Not really. Even if I get a big contract—even if I get exactly what I want —it's only temporary. Hockey is like a grinder—it eats up everything you've got and eventually spits what's left of you out on the other side."

That does sound frighteningly accurate. Every professional sport works like that, too. And we don't talk about it enough.

"See...I know that maybe you can't love me back, either. And I'll just have to accept it. But it's still nice to care about something beyond the next game or the next contract. I don't think I can go on like that anymore."

"Wow." I kiss his impressive stomach. "That's some big thinking you're doing."

"Yeah, I know. It's not easy to admit that my life is essentially selfish. Everything for hockey. No time for anyone else. Christ— your husband was a freaking doctor, right? I could never compete with that even if I tried."

"He was a pediatrician who loved hockey," I point out. "But I understand your struggle. I love athletes. I love how crazy they are, and how committed. How they put everything else on hold for this one thing. I get it, but I also think it takes a strong man to admit that it isn't enough. Show me *one* athlete who didn't have trouble with the transition to the end of his career. It's a thing we don't discuss often enough in professional sports."

"*Right*. Retirement is like a monster under the bed. You can't even whisper its name or it'll come over you."

We both laugh.

"Now I kind of want to check under this bed," I tease.

"But I booked a suite," he says. "They don't allow monsters here."

"Of course."

We lapse into silence again, but then he sighs. "When I'm in a room with you, everything seems so clear. I want a life. I want to be myself, and stop hiding. But the minute I put on my jersey, everything gets more complicated. I'm part of a team. I'm paid a lot to do a job, but not paid enough to tell management to fuck itself."

"I know," I say soothingly. "Your job is not easy."

"Yeah, I used to think I would look up one day and say—okay, I made it. I'm successful. I don't care anymore what people think. Now I realize how dumb that sounds. I might play hockey another five to seven years, but every one of them could be exactly this hard."

I lift my chin off his chest, and look right into those brown eyes. And, yeah, this isn't just about sex anymore. I don't know if it ever really was. I like this difficult, tortured man. I like him a lot. "I really appreciate hearing the things in your head."

"Do you?" He lays his head back against the pillow. "Well I'm trapped in here a lot, and it gets old. Thank you for listening to me ramble."

"Anytime."

"I know I'm a wreck, and I've basically promised my father I won't come out until I get a new contract. What are you even doing here with me?"

"There are a few fun perks." I run two fingers down his abs, until his tummy flexes under my hand. "The view is really great." I run a hand up his thigh, grazing his sac with my thumb. "And you're decent at ping-pong. You show a lot of promise."

"Oh, bite me. I won!"

I bite him lightly on the pec. "Be careful what you wish for."

"Come here," he says suddenly.

"Why?"

"Just do it."

I hitch myself a little higher until my head is on the pillow beside his, and he rolls to study me in the darkness, just as the other candle gutters out.

"We should sleep," he says quietly.

"Probably."

"I don't want to, though."

I smile.

Then he leans in and kisses me with a soft press of his mouth against mine.

I wrap my arm around him and kiss him back.

Not a minute later he's rolled that exquisite body on top of mine, and we're making out in earnest again. I lift my knees and hold his hips in their grasp, and he lets out a low sound of longing.

Sleep is overrated anyway.

I'm sure of it.

At eight the next morning, though, I'm a little less sure. Grogginess sets in as I sit up in bed and force open my bleary eyes.

We didn't get to sleep before two.

"Morning," Hudson says, emerging from his bathroom.

"Hey," I say, and my voice is rough with disuse.

He flashes me an uncertain smile, and then leans over his open suitcase on the floor. "I've got a strategy breakfast before morning skate. I'm sorry, I wish I could stay."

"No—you need to go," I say, blinking myself awake. "I do, too." I slide off the side of the bed and look around for my clothes.

His room is a mess—with throw pillows and a condom wrapper on the floor. I stumble around the suite until I find my underwear and my clothes. My whole suitcase is here, because I never went back to my own room.

So I zip up my bag and frantically finger-comb my hair, until I'm tidy enough not to look like I just rolled out of bed.

"I guess, uh, I'll see you at the stadium?" Hudson's hands are jammed awkwardly in his pockets. Like he's not sure what to do with them.

"Yeah you will," I say lightly. I'm not sure how to play it, either.

I'm not accustomed to being anyone's secret lover. "Have a great game, okay? Maybe you should have slept more."

He shrugs. "We get a rest before the game tonight. I'll use it wisely."

"Good. Do that." We stare at each other for a long beat. And then—*fuck it*—I close the distance and wrap my arms around his barrel chest.

He hugs me to him, and just for a second everything is fine again. *When I'm in a room with you, everything seems so clear.*

But the trouble comes after, right? I step out of his embrace, and give him a stoic nod. "See you over there." Where I'll have to pretend indifference.

He chews his lip, and then crosses to the door. "Mind if I, uh, take a peek into the hallway?"

"Yeah, go ahead."

I wait as he sticks his head out into the corridor and looks both ways. Then he opens the door for me.

And it feels terrible. Like I'm doing a perp walk. Still, I place a palm on his chest just before I walk out the door, pulling my suitcase behind me.

The door closes with a firm click, and I hate the sound of it.

An hour later I'm setting up my station in the underbelly of an unfamiliar stadium while game-day chaos swirls around me.

The visiting team never gets the glamorous digs. I'm essentially in a basement alcove, stacking bandages and supplies on a cracked countertop, while the equipment crew hauls bags of gear to and fro.

Hockey players are beginning to assemble in the adjacent dressing room. I hear their teasing voices, and catch a glimpse or two of their purple jackets as they arrive for their morning skate.

My phone rings, and the number is my sister's. There's no athlete in my chair yet, so I answer. "Hey Reg, is everything okay?"

"Of course," she says cheerily. "I just called to tell you that our child is amazing."

"Our child?"

"I get to claim her when you're out of town," she says, as if this makes perfect sense. "She's just so smart. I tried to stump her on Disney lyrics on the walk to school, and it totally backfired. She has all the lyrics to every song in Moana down cold."

"She must get that from me," I tease, and she laughs. "Thank you for being there for her this week."

"I love it! Are you okay? You sound down."

"I'm fine. Just tired." Although that's not really true. There's the bullshit with Eustace, but I don't need to ruin my sister's day.

Plus, sneaking out of Hudson's room made me feel melancholy. It's not the same as being a high school kid again, and living in fear of my father's wrath. But I still feel like maybe I'm kidding myself.

In the harsh light of morning, it's hard to hang on to the fact that Hudson cares about me, and that our night together was magical. If you can't get coffee together in the hotel lobby, did it really even happen?

"Gavin?" my sister prompts. "Did you hear me?"

"No, sorry," I mutter. "Tired, here."

She chuckles. "Must have been some night."

"Oh it was. But I'm paying for it now." In so many ways.

"Wake up, little brother. I was trying to tell you that my summer tour got some added dates, and I'm not coming back to the city until August twenty-second."

Shit. That means I need to find a summer program for Jordyn. Stat. "Okay," I say evenly. "Thank you for telling me."

"Sorry," she says softly. "I know you're worried about childcare."

"Only because I haven't dealt with it yet." But it's possible that taking this job was a huge mistake.

"Jordyn told me about a day camp at the arts center. Her friends like it."

"Yeah, I'm trying. But they give preference to their Gold Circle members. That's, like, a two thousand dollar donation. And that's before the cost of the camp."

"Jesus," Reggie sputters. "They'd better be little Rembrandts for that money. I'll see you soon?"

We hang up just as Jason Castro sits down on my table. "Everything okay?"

"Yeah. Just a little under-caffeinated. Are you ready for tonight?"

"You bet. If we win this one, we clinch our spot in the playoffs. Nobody else can catch up to us in points."

"You'd better win, then." I reach for the tape and get to work. Two more players are waiting for me now. It's going to be a busy day. "Is there any coffee down here somewhere?"

"Oh totally." He puts two fingers in his mouth and whistles. Then he hollers toward the hallway. "Yo! Hot Pepper!"

Heidi Jo appears a moment later, her hands on her hips. "Did you really just whistle for me *like a dog?*"

A low murmur goes through the players. "Oooh, Castro is in trouble."

"Baby, Gavin needs to know if there's coffee available. He's got twenty-three players to look after so we can win this thing. And the man is under-caffeinated."

"Oh, heck!" she says, straightening up. "I got this. How do you like your coffee? I was heading that way anyway."

"Don't put yourself out," I say, my neck heating at the attention. "I'll drink anything, but a splash of milk is my go-to."

"No problem. Five minutes. And, guys?" She raises her voice, and the conversations around us cease. "Announcements from the coach in thirty minutes. And then PR needs a moment before you skate."

"Yes ma'am," Castro says as she departs.

"I'm getting the feeling that Heidi Jo practically runs this place," I say as I cut the tape, finishing his wrist.

"You wouldn't be wrong." He rises from the table. "I married up, obviously. Just don't tell her."

"She knows, man. She knows," his teammates tease.

I laugh and get to work on the next guy.

———

Game day is a scramble, so I'm still taping joints when it's time for the coach to address his players. I solve this problem by carrying my supplies into the dressing room, where players sit in front of their gear stalls.

Although I wouldn't want to work this way all the time, it's really no problem to kneel down on the rubberized floor and tape up Bayer's ankle while the coach delivers his game day speech.

"Tonight's your night. Keep your focus, and we can finish the regular season with the highest points in our division…"

When Bayer's ankle is squared away, I take a quiet seat beside Halla and quickly check the bandage on his arm, where somebody slashed him in the last game.

After Coach speaks, it's Georgia's turn. "One more second, boys. Let's do a publicity rundown. If we clinch our playoffs spot tonight, I'll want O'Doul and the high scorer to give quotes afterwards. You're *so excited* to have another shot at the cup! You're so *grateful* for this opportunity, etc. Got it?"

"Yes, Killer!" they answer in unison.

This must be a running joke, because she grins. "Good boys. And one more thing—our annual Hockey is For Everyone night is next week—last home game of the season. You'll be suiting up in rainbow practice jerseys for a photo op, and you'll have rainbow tape for warm-ups. We'll be auctioning off the jerseys and the sticks after the game. Plus I need six players to take turns doing pregame photos with fans."

"*Pre*-game?" O'Doul asks. "Seriously?"

"Yeah, the timing is unusual, but these fans are mostly children. If six of you volunteer, I'll only need each player for ten minutes, one at a time, in front of the banner. We can make a lot of memories in sixty minutes, guys. Who's in?"

Nobody speaks up, and I look pointedly down at a scuff mark

on the floor. Athletes have very intense, personal pregame rituals. It *is* weird to ask them to step outside before a game. That's kind of a big ask.

And to stand in front of a rainbow banner celebrating LGBTQ inclusivity?

The silence thickens. But then O'Doul and Castro raise their hands at the same time. "I'll do it," O'Doul says.

"Me too. But I was actually first," Castro says, lifting his chin defiantly. "Dude copied me."

Georgia rolls her eyes skyward. "Okay, thank you both. I'll need four more. The sign-up sheet will be on the portal, but does anyone else want to sign on right now?"

Another hand goes up. But it doesn't belong to Hudson. He's sitting a few seats away. And I risk a glance in his direction.

He must feel my gaze, too, because his eyes cut to mine. And then his expression does something complicated. I see pain, and irritation.

And also guilt.

Then he drops his chin and stares at his skates on the floor.

I don't know if it's fair of me or not. But I'm disappointed. How hard could it be to take some photos for ten minutes with a bunch of kids in LGBTQ families?

Too hard, somehow. I guess.

Annoyed with both of us, I heft my trainer's bag and cross to leave the room. And I wonder what's going on inside his head right now.

Nothing good, I'd bet.

TWENTY-SEVEN

Hudson

MONTREAL ISN'T HAVING a great year, but they're having a great night, apparently. So the game is a shit show. And not just for me.

Everything is just off. Our passes don't connect. Our shift changes are messy. Our shots on goal keep hitting the post, and Ian Crikey got bloodied in a fight, and Gavin spent the second intermission patching him up.

Gavin had kept up a quiet conversation with Crikey, while bracing the player's chin in one strong hand. He'd somehow speedily disinfected and bandaged his cuts one-handed. While Crikey had looked him trustingly in the eyes and tried not to flinch.

Competence is sexy.

And guess what's *not* sexy? Cowardice. I'm still anguished over Georgia's sign-up for the LGBTQ event. If I do that event, my father will blow up my phone with warnings and reminders. *You need that contract. Don't draw attention to yourself.*

It's only a few photos, though. Not a big pronouncement. But I can still hear my dad's voice in my ear. *Just be patient. Keep your head in the damn game.*

Right now my head is not in the game. And the scoreboard proves it. We're down by one as the third period opens. Luckily,

Montreal has only done a middling job of creating opportunities in front of the net, or the score would be even worse.

"Come on *let's go!*" Coach bellows from behind the bench. "You're better than this. You're the better team. But I'm gonna need receipts."

We need to clinch, and I want to be the guy who makes it happen. I want it so bad. It would make all the difference.

So when Coach finally taps me on the back, I vault over the boards with the energy of fresh legs and a burning desire to make a damn difference.

My speed doesn't go unnoticed, either. Montreal sends out someone faster against me. And I manage to be a real pain in their *derrière* for several shifts in a row.

Coach grunts his appreciation between my shifts. "Good hustle. Now just find yourself a shot on goal."

If only. I guzzle some Gatorade, and Coach taps me again. Over I go, skating hard for the puck. I try every trick in the book—lifting the winger's stick, blocking his shots, and generally making a nuisance of myself. The player I'm guarding has an unkempt mountain-man beard, and curses me out in a language I don't speak. The dude is getting frustrated with me.

Good. That's how I like it. This game isn't over, either. We've come back from worse.

The cursing winger has the puck now, though. It's up to me to get it back. And today I choose violence. We're both big guys, but sometimes you have to sacrifice your body to make your point.

So maybe my backcheck is rougher than it needs to be. Colliding with him, I destabilize us both as I poke that puck through his tree trunk legs. I get the pass off, but the world is tilting fast.

As the stadium's roof wheels into view, I hear the crowd start to make some noise. But then there's a loud crash as I hit the ice. Hard.

And the noise cuts out abruptly.

The world does a strange, slow blink. After a moment of quiet darkness, it flickers back into view. Like a glitch in the matrix. The first thing I see is O'Doul's worried face above mine. "Hey, you with us?"

"Yeah." The crowd is screaming. "What happened?"

"Trevi scored off the pass you fed him." He puts out a hand, and I take it so he can haul me to my feet.

The stadium sways for a second, but then rights itself. I turn to look at the scoreboard, but before I can, Gavin arrives on the ice, his medical bag in tow. "Did you just black out?"

"Yeah," O'Doul says, just as I say "No."

"Which is it?" he demands.

"He was out for maybe a few seconds," O'Doul says.

"What? I'm fine," I insist, glancing toward the ref, who's also watching me. "I didn't get a penalty, did I?"

O'Doul laughs, but Gavin's face turns stormy. He leans over and grabs something off the ice—my helmet—and brandishes it in front of me. I'm surprised to see that there's a crack in it. "Your head hit the ice and you *blacked out*. On the bench, please." He puts a hand on my arm.

I shake it off immediately. Like anybody would.

He gives me an angry glare and then jogs back to the bench, my helmet in his hands.

Coach is beckoning, too, so I quickly catch up. And I'm skating fine.

"Is he out?" Coach asks as we approach.

He means out of the *game*, so I say no, at the same time that Gavin says yes.

"He blacked out for a few seconds," Gavin says icily. "And the concussion protocol is very clear."

Coach nods and then turns away from us, assembling his next shift of players as the whistle blows for a face-off.

I sit down heavily on the bench, and Gavin kneels in front of me, a pen light in his hands. "Look at me."

With a sigh, I turn my tired eyes to his worried ones. He shines the light in a particular way—from the outside of my visual field inward—that's supposed to make my pupils constrict. "Ow," I grumble.

He doesn't bother responding. Instead, he pulls out a card and a stopwatch. "You know the drill," he says. "And *go*."

There are numbers arranged in small print on the card. They track across several lines, and I read them off as quickly as I can.

Every athlete does baseline tests periodically. After a possible concussive fall, you repeat the test and they compare it to your baseline. If you're within five seconds, a concussion is not indicated.

"How'd I do?" I demand, as Gavin looks up my baseline on his phone.

"Eh," he says. "Four seconds."

"Then put me back in. Jimbo!" I call over my shoulder to the equipment manager. "I need a helmet."

"No you don't," Gavin hisses. "You need another test in a few minutes."

"Come on, I'm fine. Ask me anything. I know we're in Montreal. I know who's president. Singing the Star Spangled Banner would be a challenge, but that's my baseline. I could still beat you at ping-pong," I add, because he needs to lighten up.

But it doesn't work. His scowl could set things on fire. If I weren't itching to get back into the game, I'd probably find it hot.

"I need to check your head for contusions," he says stiffly. "Bend over."

That's what he said. I lean forward on the bench, but I'm gritting my teeth. Precious seconds are passing in the game, and I need to get back out there.

A skillful hand palpates the back of my head, and I try not to flinch when he finds the goose egg that's forming.

The crowd makes a loud noise, and I yank my head back up so I can see what's going on. Montreal has the puck and they're making trouble for my teammates. "This is stupid. Send me back out."

"Now way," Gavin grunts, and my heart sags.

"Why?" I growl. "You can see I'm fine. This is bullshit. Henry would put me back in."

"That's low," Gavin growls. There's fury in his eyes. "Read the numbers on the next card, please. I'm not abandoning the concussion protocol just because you've got something to prove."

"Well fuck you very much," I insist, moving the card out of my field of vision.

"*Jesus.*" Trevi says from beside me. "Stop being an asshole and let the man do his job."

But Gavin has already shoved the card back inside his pack. And he's hustling around the end of the bench.

For one ugly second I think he's going to haul Coach over here to yell at me. But no—Crikey's bleeding again and Gavin is pulling on his gloves so he can tend to the cut.

The clock is winding down toward full time, and I can't believe I'm going to have to sit on this bench and watch my teammates go into overtime without me.

And I've never seen Gavin so angry. That's my fault, too.

I could burn the whole world down right now. Just hand me a match.

Just as I'm taking another mental tour through all of my flaws, Castro gets a breakaway, flies past the unlucky defenders and flips the puck into the upper right-hand corner of the net.

We won. We clinched it. We're going to the playoffs.

And still I feel an ugly darkness inside me that just won't fade.

TWENTY-EIGHT

Gavin

SOMEHOW THE GAME ends with Brooklyn up one point. But I couldn't tell you how we got there. I do my job on autopilot. In the dressing room I cut tape off limbs and massage muscles. I make notes on charts, and I dab antiseptic ointment onto Crikey's face.

Then I stand over a sheepish Hudson while he reads off another concussion card.

The whole time, I'm burning up with fury. It's the kind of anger that feels like fuel. All I have to do is picture his unconscious body on the ice, and I want to burn the whole building down.

And there he sits, reading numbers off a card like everything is fine. At least his score improves, even in a loud, crowded dressing room, while a reporter interviews O'Doul about two feet away.

"Did I do okay?" he asks, looking up, his eyes full of questions.

"Only three seconds off your baseline," I say through clenched teeth. "But you're still getting a full workup tomorrow in Brooklyn."

"Yeah, okay?" he says, searching my face.

I turn away from him and march back over to my station.

Hudson *probably* does not have a concussion. These field tests can correctly predict concussion in ninety-two percent of cases.

Knowing that doesn't really help, though. I pack up my stuff with jerky, angry movements. I can't wait to leave this place behind.

Tonight was the perfect storm—with me on duty, and Hudson injured. I'd never pulled a player out of a game before, and it had to be him?

Fuck my life. This is why I should never have gotten involved with him. If management knew...

I shudder.

An hour later we reach the airport by bus. Once in the terminal, I find a quiet corner and call Henry. He answers right away. "Hey! How's Crikey's face?"

"He'll have to see the doctor tomorrow, probably needs a couple of stitches. That's all. Bled a lot."

"Yeah, face wounds usually do," he says with a sigh. "And Newgate? Any sign of concussion?"

My stomach clenches. "He passed the tests, but you should see his helmet. And there's a bump on the back of his head."

"I replayed that fall a few times. He hit once with the helmet on, and then kind of bounced after it popped off."

"He blacked out," I say as a wave of nausea rolls through me. "Just for a couple seconds." My voice is casual, but there had been a moment when he didn't move. You never want to see that kind of awful, absolute stillness.

He *didn't* see it, either. Rationally, I know that's why he was so adamant that he was fine. To him, it was nothing.

To me, it was a horror movie made real.

"Ah," Henry says. "You made the right call, pulling him from the game."

"No question," I say. "The protocol is very clear."

"It still sucks, though, right?" Henry prompts. "The athlete is usually an ass about it. They feel like they have to be."

"Oh, is that why?"

Henry laughs. But he has no idea how upset I am about the whole experience.

In a normal workweek, there's no conflict of interest between me and Hudson. Henry is the head trainer, and it's his job to help the team doctor and the coach determine player fitness.

These rare road trips are an exception, though. And I'd been kidding myself when I thought I could have my fun and do my job, too.

"What were his scores?" Henry asks. And after I give him all the information, he says, "Come see me tomorrow. There's something I have to run by you."

"Of course." We hang up, and it's time to board the jet.

The flight home is quiet, the players sleeping or watching movies at their seats. But I can't relax. All I can do is replay the night's horrors. Hudson's brief incapacitation will probably haunt my dreams. But the part afterward was worse—with me trying to do my job with shaky hands and a janky heart, while he argued with me.

Now I have a splitting headache, and deep, deep regrets.

When we arrive, I sprint for the taxi line alone, and grab a cab by myself.

Hudson is texting me, though. *You left without me? I thought we could ride home together. Don't I get to say I'm sorry?*

I leave him on *read*, and try to figure out what to say.

Look, I know I fucked up, he continues. *In that situation I'm not supposed to argue with you. I know you were just doing your job. I'm sorry, okay? It won't happen again.*

I get it, I finally reply. *You were just doing your job, too. But this is why we're problematic. I'm the one who's really at fault here. I know better. And I really need this job.*

Those bubbles appear—the indication that the other person is typing. But the message doesn't appear. I wait for it a long time. But it isn't until the taxi turns onto our street that he answers me.

Let's talk about this tomorrow, he says. *I don't want to put you in a rough position. But I can do better. I can make this not a problem.*

I close my eyes and picture his body stretched out on the ice, his chin lolling to the side like a dead man.

And then I picture the way he mostly ignores me when we're both at the practice facility together. The heavy secret of his attraction. The dark secret of my conflict of interest.

It's too much tonight. Too complicated. More pain than gain. More hurt than love.

So I don't answer his text. I pay the driver and I go inside my apartment, where everyone is quiet. I go into Jordyn's room and pull the covers up on her sleeping body. I kiss her forehead.

She rolls over. Her eyes flicker. "*Daddy*," she whispers. Then she goes to sleep again.

My heart is full, and a little bit broken.

That's my baseline.

All systems normal.

TWENTY-NINE

Hudson

GAVIN IS AVOIDING ME.

The only communication I've gotten out of him was when I told him the results of my doctor's final concussion screening. *Guess what? No concussion diagnosis.*

Very happy to hear that, he'd replied right away. *Great news. So lucky.*

Totally. They said I have a hard head, I'd replied.

No response.

I spent the day hoping he'd reach out again. Now it's ten p.m. and my phone is silent.

You home? I tap out, like the desperate guy I am. Then I send it.

He makes me twist for ten minutes. And then: *I'm home, but pretty tired.*

Well, ouch.

I pace my apartment for a few minutes, trying to decide what to do. I've got sad Maroon 5 songs playing in stereo, like an emo loser.

I've never been this guy before—hung up and hurting. It's not a good look on me. Or on anyone, I guess. But I'd honestly thought I was above this—that my heart wasn't breakable. I'd thought heartbreak was one more thing that discipline could overrule.

Seems pretty stupid now.

I grab my phone off the coffee table and text him again. I don't hold back, either. I just let it fly. *I miss you. I know you're pissed at me, or pissed at the world. Or something. But you haven't let me get close enough to you to apologize. And it's not like you to be cold.*

After I send it I have immediate regrets. Maybe that was too much truth.

The truth is so messy.

I'm staring at my phone, willing him to respond, when a finger taps quietly on my door.

Thank fuck. I trot to the door and whip it open, revealing Gavin in the hallway. "Hi," he says quietly.

I open the door wider and step aside, closing it again after he walks in.

He doesn't sit down, though. He stands in my living room, hands jammed into his pockets. "You're right. I don't do cold very well. It's not my style. But you have me all twisted up. I don't know what to do about it."

"I'm sorry," I say immediately. "I know I was a dick...No—not a dick. Dicks are good. I was a jerk, and I made your job harder by questioning your authority."

He looks down at the wood floor. "Athletes lash out at the trainer. It happens. That's not really the problem."

"Then what is?" I demand. The sad look on his face is twisting my insides.

"We need to take a step back," he says quietly. "The other night just proved it, okay? Neither one of us could function in that scenario. You were potentially injured, and not expected to be rational. And I couldn't function in my job because of our relationship."

"But you *did* function," I point out. "You did everything right. It's only me who was an ass."

Slowly, he shakes his head. "It's cute that you think that."

"What are you talking about? I was *there*."

His chin snaps up and those gray eyes are full of fury. "You weren't *there*, Hudson, when you were unconscious. That's the whole damn problem. For a few minutes, I was in charge of making sure you were going to be okay. And I couldn't even finish a thought because I'd just watched your skull *bounce off the ice*. Apparently this is going to come as a surprise to you, but it kind of fucked me up to watch that."

"Oh," I say stupidly.

Oh.

"It was, like, the perfect storm," he says, hugging himself tightly and beginning to pace in essentially the same spot I'd done the same thing a few minutes ago. "You, flat out on your back. You looked *dead*, Hudson." He gives me a furious glance, and my heart slides a little further into my guts.

I wasn't anywhere near dead. But Gavin has way too much experience with men dying on him. And maybe it took me way too long to clue in, but I finally understand that I shouldn't argue the point.

"...And then you did the whole macho athlete thing and fought off the care protocol." He raises his eyes toward heaven. "Which is honestly no big deal. Henry probably gets a lot of attitude on the bench. It's not personal. Except when it is, baby." He turns to me again, looking devastated this time. "It's great that you didn't get seriously hurt. I believe that you're fine. But I can't be there next time. Your job is to think about winning games. Not to think about danger. But my job is to expect the worst and then make it all better."

"But you're really good at your job," I point out. "And you only work a game, like, three nights this year, right?"

"There will be more," he says softly. "He told me that his wife is hospitalized with preterm labor. They're trying to keep her from having her twins too early."

"Oh, shit. That sounds bad."

"It's touch and go." He makes a face. "But he asked me if I would mind taking a couple of home games as the season finishes up. He also asked me if I wanted to take the LGBTQ night. So there'd be one guy representing pride on the Brooklyn bench."

My stomach does a sideways slide. "One guy," I repeat stupidly.

Gavin shrugs. "Just telling you what he said. I turned him down, though. Told him I'd promised to take Jordyn to that game."

Hell. "But you're mad at me for not coming out."

"No." He shakes his head vigorously. "I care about you, and I realize you're in a bind. And everybody does it in their own time. But you have to understand that I'm in a bind, too. We can't do this anymore, Hudson."

I feel it like a blow.

"...Because I don't want to be the guy who decides whether you come out of a game with an injury. And there's no way I can be honest with my boss about the problem. I can't tell Henry why it's inappropriate for me to work at games."

I sit heavily on the sofa and tip my head into my hands.

"The better things go for me at work, the more often this is going to come up."

"...And I'm the reason you felt like you had to turn down a game."

"You probably think I'm making too big a deal over it," he says quietly. "I can see your side of it, too. But the job is new, and my reputation is all I've got. Besides..." He swallows hard and then stops.

I look up. "Besides what?"

"It sucked, okay? You didn't see what I saw—a guy I have feelings for, laid out on the ice, not moving. And suddenly I'm the guy who's in charge of making medical decisions for you, while you fight me over it?" He spreads his arms wide. "I just don't want to be in that situation again."

"God, I'm sorry. I don't want you to be, either."

"So we need to stop seeing each other."

"...At least until the season ends," I add, grasping for a loophole.

He nods, but it's not a promise. I'll still have to convince him.

"All I have to do is play my ass off, get an early contract renegotiation—with a no-trade clause—and make myself indispensable to Brooklyn."

He gives me a tired smile. "That's all, huh?"

"I like a challenge. And you're already indispensable. So when I come out to management, they'll help us find a path forward."

Gavin looks at his shoes. "I like the sound of that, but there are no guarantees."

He's right. There's no easy solution. But it gives me something to shoot for. "I'm sorry this is so hard."

"Don't be sorry. I'm not trying to blame you. But shit got complicated real fast. And I just don't have room in my life for complications. I wish I did. Because Hudson?" He looks up and gives me a sad smile. "You're my favorite complication."

I'm still processing that when he turns toward the door. And I rise like a puppet on a string, because the sight of him walking out cuts me deep.

"Gavin, wait." The words are out of my mouth before I can help myself. It's not like I can change his mind. That would just be selfish.

He stops, though, right beside the door. And now he's waiting for me to say something.

"Take care of yourself." My voice is gravel. I step a little closer. The urge to kiss him is so strong. But that's not what *taking a pause* means. So I hug him instead.

And, whoops, it's actually worse. As his arms close around me, he sighs, and rests his chin on my shoulder. I feel his strong heartbeat against mine. "Thank you for listening," he whispers.

"Always," I whisper back.

All I want is to listen to him. I want him in my life, and in my bed.

But my whole life is set up to want hockey more.

So a moment later he leaves my arms. And then he leaves my apartment.

And I'm all alone again.

THIRTY

Gavin

I KNOW I did the right thing. I removed Hudson from my private life. No more flirty texts and no more late night meet-ups in his bed, burning up the sheets.

The problem is that he's still lodged in my heart. No matter where I am, at home or at work, my subconscious is still tuned into the Hudson Newgate channel. Whenever I hear the rattle of his keys in the hallway, he's all I can think about. While I'm treating another player, I'm still listening to his laugh from the other room.

Jordyn keeps asking about him, too. "Can Hudson come over for dinner again?" she asks the next time I serve ramen. "He liked it."

"He's probably too busy," I argue.

"Nope," she argues. "He came home when Reggie and me did! Let's call him."

I make another excuse, feeling like a heel. And she drops it. But when I'm ladling up bowls of steaming soup, I almost break down and make him one. What would be the harm, right? It's just soup.

But with Hudson, it was never just soup. Or just sex. My interest in him was deeper than I'd let myself believe.

We can't be a couple, though. He's not ready. I've always known that.

Doesn't make it easy, though. The playoffs start after just two more regular season games, and tensions are high. Morning skate is packed. The gym is crowded. And the training staff is as busy as ever.

Henry is working with Hudson today, though, so at least I don't have to touch him. But he's right there, a few feet away, and it's a struggle to keep my focus where it belongs.

"How's the childcare crisis?" Castro asks me as I work out a charley horse in his calf. "Did you find your little girl a day camp?"

"No," I say with a sigh. "There's one at the Brooklyn Academy of Arts that would be perfect, but they'll fill up before I can register. Plus it's two thousand dollars. I put us on the waiting list, but…"

"Ouch," he says. "Kids are expensive."

"Sometimes," I agree. "And then other times they'd rather have mac and cheese from a blue box than daddy's homemade three cheese extravaganza."

Castro shakes his head. "Bad call, kid. But I'm available to eat your homemade leftovers. Anytime."

"Good to know." I glance up and find Hudson watching me. He looks away quickly, like he didn't mean to be caught.

Henry is on the phone, though, leaving Hudson to his own devices. And the whole room hears him say, "Okay, I can be there in twenty minutes! On my way."

Then he pockets his phone, and I realize that bigger things are afoot than my stupid broken heart. "Is everything all right?"

"Oh yeah." He gives a nervous smile. "But my twins are coming. Gavin, I need you tonight…"

"No problem," I say quickly. Reggie has already been warned. "You go have some babies."

This is the first time I've ever seen Henry look nervous. "She made it to thirty-four weeks, so it's going to be okay."

"It totally is," Castro chimes in as he swings his legs off my table. "You're gonna be on the hook for a lot of Cuban cigars though, man. Don't forget about us."

"Like you'd let me," Henry says with a nervous smile. He grabs his bag and checks his pockets.

Castro starts clapping as he turns for the door. "Good luck, dad! We need updates!"

The rest of us clap, too, and everyone in the vicinity cheers. He pumps a fist in the air and strides out.

Suddenly my day is twice as busy. "Okay, fellas. Who's next? I've got one hour left here and then I have to set up the stadium."

From the moment of Henry's departure, the entire day is like a long skid into chaos.

I've never worked a home game before, and the setup is unfamiliar to me. It takes me two hours to do what Henry probably accomplishes in thirty minutes.

At five o'clock, when the players are trickling in, my sister calls. "There's no need to panic, but where do you keep the Children's Tylenol?"

My heart drops. "Why? Is Jordyn sick?"

"She's cranky and a little warm. At pickup, her teacher passed out a note that said the flu is going around. There were eight kids absent from her class today, including Lila."

Lila is her new best friend.

Hell.

"The Tylenol is in a shoebox at the top of my closet." I don't keep any drugs in the bathroom where Jordyn might find them. "There's one of those forehead thermometers in the medicine cabinet. Keep me posted, okay?"

"She's going to be fine, little brother. I'm going to order soup for dinner."

"Good call," I say uselessly. "Thank you for handling this."

"It's fine," she repeats. "We're fine. Go beat Boston. Jordyn wants to see you on TV."

"Okay. Bye." But when we hang up, I feel dread in the pit of my stomach.

The team captain is waiting on my table, though, so it's time to get to work.

"It's great that you're doing this," O'Doul says as I work on his shoulder. "Before you came along, Henry never took a game night off."

"He has a lot on his plate right now," I say as I work my thumbs into his left trapezius muscle.

"Yeah, but he trusts you," O'Doul says. "So now he gets to stand by his wife and not think about us for once."

"Thanks, man."

"No problem," he says as he vacates the table just in time for Hudson to sit down on it.

"How's the hip?" I ask.

"It's doing well," he says. Then he clears his throat. "O'Doul is right. The team needs you tonight. We're, uh, lucky to have you."

"Thanks," I say quietly.

He drops his voice. "Kind of wondering who you're rooting for tonight, though. Boston's playing."

I let out a bark of laughter as I rotate his hip. "Look, we had a deal. No mention of that."

"Aw, fine. Steal my fun." He gives me a rugged smile, and my heart does a stupid little backflip.

It might have been my call to end things with him, but I miss him so much.

Hudson leaves, and my night becomes a blur of other faces and other body parts. I tape and stretch and manipulate amidst the pregame chaos.

Game time comes before I'm ready. I hustle out to the bench with my kit and watch the players skate their warm-ups. And when the puck drops, I'm full of tension. *Please no Brooklyn injuries tonight*, I beg the universe.

The universe listens—sort of. Crikey gets into a fight with a Boston player. I watch the way some people watch horror movies—through squinted eyes. I still don't really understand why fighting has to be part of this game, and Crikey still has a bandage over his stitches.

Seriously, I don't get it.

But the fight ends quickly when Crikey lands a punch to the Boston player's torso, and his opponent goes down hard with a blood-chilling scream.

Whenever a fighter goes down, the officials swarm the fight, ending things immediately. This fight is no different, except the official whose job it is to restrain Crikey doesn't even have to touch him. Our player is just standing there, his fist still curled, staring down at the guy like he can't understand what just happened.

Meanwhile, the poor guy from Boston is curled up on his side in obvious pain, and Boston's trainer is trotting across the ice with a look of dismay on his face.

The game stops for a few minutes, and the player is carted off. Crikey skates to the boards, and the whole bench leans in to listen as he tries to explain. "My punch was, like, right to his chest pad but something *snapped*, man." He makes a horrified face. "I've never seen anything like it."

He serves a five minute penalty, and the injured player doesn't return to the game.

Afterward, I'm standing here feeling like I dodged a bullet. Does it make me a bad person to feel super lucky that it's not me assessing that injury?

I'm not the only one, though, who's a little startled, apparently. The game gets a little chippy after that, and both teams look put out.

"I've seen better play in the junior leagues!" Coach reprimands them during the intermission. "Get it together. Especially you, Drake. You look asleep out there."

"Yeah, got it," the forward says. But he's visibly pale, and his game doesn't improve much during the second period. We're down 1-2 already, to a team we should be beating.

"I got déjà vu," Hudson grumbles to me before he vaults over the wall for another shift.

During the second intermission I sneak a look at my phone. Reggie informs me, via an emoji, that Jordyn has vomited. "Only once, though," she says cheerfully.

But she follows that up with a photo of Jordyn watching the Brooklyn game and smiling.

People love to say kids are resilient. And yet half the people I know are in therapy for things that happened in their childhoods.

I can't believe I'm here instead of at home with my sick baby girl.

"Gavin!"

My chin snaps up, and O'Doul is waving me across the room. "Help! Drake is acting weird."

"I'm not acting weird," the forward grumbles, rubbing his forehead. "I just have a headache."

"You just fell *asleep*," O'Doul snaps. "In the middle of a fucking game."

"I was resting my eyes."

Even as they play out this ridiculous argument, I'm grabbing for my phone again and opening up the app that tracks Drake's blood sugar. I didn't get any notifications, though.

And the app likes Drake's numbers a lot right now. *Great job, keep up the good work!* it gushes.

"Your numbers are normal," I say, squinting at him.

"I know," he says, looking up at me with a bleary gaze. "That's not my problem. I just feel icky."

"Icky like how?" I demand. "Give me more to go on."

"Like my body is made of concrete. And I have a headache."

"Huh. Like flu symptoms?"

"Yeah, like that." He shrugs. And now that I look closer, his skin is a pale gray color that I don't really like.

"But you're good to play?" Coach asks from right behind me.

"Of course," Drake says.

Uh-oh.

Shit.

It's not really my call whether Drake plays the third period with

203

a fever. But is this a good idea? I'm going to have to watch his blood sugar like a hawk. I have no idea what a fever does to the metabolism. Or whether hockey players ever call in sick.

I'm really out of my depth right now. All I can do is lean forward and plant my palm on Drake's sweaty forehead.

He's burning up.

"Um..." I start to say.

But then Drake flicks my hand off his face and stands abruptly. His color is suddenly more green than gray.

Players and support staff part like the sea as Drake makes a dash toward the toilets.

"Well, fuck," Coach says. "Everybody! Sanitize your hands. That's an order. This team will not be taken out of the playoffs by a fucking virus."

I start handing out alcohol wipes, while Jimbo frantically sanitizes all the equipment and the water bottles.

"Huh. I feel kinda funky, too," another player says. "Thought it was something I ate."

"You can feel funky after the third period," Coach barks. "Let's win this thing."

The boys try. They really do. But the scoreboard is stuck at 1-2 when the final buzzer rings. And we all clomp back to the dressing room, defeated.

But none of my guys are bleeding, so I guess tonight is a win for me personally.

Meanwhile, the team doctor has been paged from his box seats. Doctor Herberts makes the rounds, giving Drake and a couple others a rapid test for flu, and three players come back positive.

"It's going around," he says. "Rest and fluids. No need to panic."

Coach is pacing the rug, looking stressed, though. "New rule!" he bellows. "No morning skate tomorrow. Everybody stay home and rest. I need you all healthy before the playoffs start."

The mood in the locker room is grim. I pack up my kit in silence, eager to head home and take care of my sick kid.

But when I check my phone for messages, I see one from Henry.

And when I open it up, there's a photo of him in a hospital mask, holding two tiny, swaddled babies—one in each arm.

It's a boy and a girl! boasts the message. *She's four and a half pounds, and he's five.*

I can't see his smile behind that mask. But his eyes are smiling. And suddenly my throat is thick.

It must show on my face, because Hudson is standing in front of me now. "What is it? Everything okay?"

Wordlessly, I turn the phone around for him to see.

His expression softens. "Look at that. Something good happened tonight after all."

I clear my throat. "It sure did." I wonder if Henry is as nervous right now as I usually am. This daddy stuff is not for wimps.

THIRTY-ONE

Hudson

IN THE MORNING, I wake up at ten o'clock, feeling bleary. I haven't slept that late since the ninth grade. My father never allowed it.

I stare at the ceiling for a while, wondering what to do with myself. Some guys crave a day off. But I'm not that guy. Being alone at home just makes me twitchy.

It doesn't help knowing that Gavin is right next door. It's tempting to call him. I just want to hear his voice.

But I stay strong. I decide to do some laundry instead.

By two p.m., I've folded my T-shirts, paid all my bills, and ordered birthday flowers for my mother. I've watched a movie and eaten a healthy brunch.

I do some push-ups. Then some sit-ups. Then some yoga stretches. Another hour passes, but I'm still at loose ends.

There's nothing like a day alone to remind me that I don't have much of a personal life.

Okay, any personal life.

It gets so bad that I open my email inbox and respond to everything I've let slide during the run-up to the playoffs. There's a message in there from the PR department.

Hi Bruisers,

I'm still two players short for the photo session happening before our game tomorrow night. Three local LGBTQ organizations are bringing teenage hockey fans to the game, and I'd like to offer the full hour-long session with players. If you can spare ten minutes from your pregame routine, our new fans would treasure it.

—Georgia

I'm not proud of this, but my first reaction is irritation. How dare she make me overthink this again?

Yeah, that's obnoxious. I should be grateful that my team supports these organizations. Just like I should be grateful that my team embraces Gavin. They love him. Full stop.

But every time I think about it, I feel shame. And it starts me on another loop around the *what-if* ferris wheel.

What if I told the world my truth? What if people look at me differently?

Some of the dumber fans would yell ugly things at me. Some of my ex-teammates would wonder if I used to check them out in the showers.

Spoiler alert: I did not. But they'll still wonder.

But what if I could handle all that? What if dreading it is worse than the reality?

I've had this conversation with myself so many times. There comes a point in almost every day when I'm ready to just toss a lit match on my bonfire of fears, and let it happen.

But then doubt creeps in. What will happen to my career?

It's enough of a burden that the league sees me as Derek Newgate's disappointing son. I hate that narrative. Would I then become Derek Newgate's son who never seems to land on a team... because he's queer?

This is why I shouldn't ever have a morning off. I can't stand to be alone with my thoughts.

The email is still sitting there on my screen, though. Before I can overthink it again, I hit the reply button. *Sure, Georgia, I'm in. Just tell me where and when.*

Then I hit send before I can second-guess myself. Or million-guess myself.

It's just some photos. No big deal, right?

I turn off my computer and find some running shoes. Sitting still isn't working for me. I need to sweat some of the stupid out of me.

The next morning I get up at eight, like always. My apartment feels like a prison cell, and I'm eager to get out of here.

But as soon as I sit up, I know something's wrong. My head aches, and it hurts when I move my eyes. And when I get a drink of water, my throat feels scratchy and odd. Lifting a hand to probe my neck, I discover that my lymph nodes are swollen.

Well, fuck. This is bad. But pro hockey players don't call in sick unless they're half dead.

On the other hand, if I'm the guy who spreads illness around before the playoffs, the coach will *not* be happy.

Reluctantly, I find the number for the team doctor and leave him a message, asking for guidance. Then I climb back in bed and wait for his phone call.

But that's not what happens. An hour later, there's a knock on my door. And it's Gavin standing there with a bowl in one hand and his trainer's kit in the other.

He pushes forward like a bulldozer the moment I open the door. "Get back in bed! Why didn't you tell me you had the flu? Where should I put the ramen?"

In spite of feeling like shit, my tummy rumbles when he mentions those noodles. "Whoa, is this your homemade stuff?" I take the bowl out of his hands. It's piping hot.

Then I lower myself to the sofa and take a sip of the broth, right from the lip of the bowl.

Gavin drops his kit and hustles to my kitchen to find me some silverware and a napkin. He pulls a bottle of fresh squeezed orange juice out of his bag, too.

And for a split second I feel like getting the flu on game day is maybe not the worst thing that could happen to a guy.

But then Gavin sits down next to me and unpacks a rapid test. "We've got to swab your nose."

"Hold on," I argue. "Why are you even here? I don't want to get you or Jordyn sick."

"Too late!" he says. "Jordyn is already down for the count. Actually, she's already improving. And I never get sick."

"Me neither, until now."

"Hold still," Gavin says. And when I put down my spoon, he assaults my nose with a swab.

"Argh," I complain as the swab goes too deep for comfort. "Never thought I'd see the day when I didn't want your paws all over me. But here we are."

"Hold *still*," he snorts, going for the other side.

I put my hands on his rib cage and sigh. He feels so good. But I'm not supposed to touch him.

"There," he says, getting up and heading for the kitchen counter, where he does something complicated with the test, and then washes his hands.

I try to console myself with soup, but five minutes later he's showing me a positive test for influenza A.

"Do not leave this apartment," he instructs me. "Coach is calling up some players from Hartford for tonight's game. He wants his A-team rested and healthy."

"That sucks," I complain. "What about the photo op? I signed up."

Gavin's perfect gray eyes blink slowly. "You did?"

"Yeah." I turn my eyes back to the soup. "Took me long enough. And now I can't even go?"

"Not unless you want to give the flu to a bunch of homeless queer kids."

"When you put it like that."

Gavin puts a hand on my messy head and sighs. "I'm sorry."

"I know. But I'll get over it."

"No," he says quietly. "I'm sorry this is so hard. I spent yesterday watching bad TV with Jordyn and wishing I could see you."

"Oh. That sounds awfully familiar."

He chuckles, and then his hand checks my forehead for fever. "Did you take any Advil?"

"Not yet." I wasn't going to bother. But when he fishes some out of his bag and puts them in my hand, I swallow the pills, because I like him fussing over me. "Nobody's ever brought me soup when I was sick. Not since grade school, anyway."

"What? Why?" he asks, handing me the juice.

"My dad doesn't believe in babying anyone." I shrug. "And my mom goes along with it."

He narrows his eyes. "It's not *babying* you to feed you soup, or look after you when you're sick. And you never mention your mom."

I shrug again. "We're not close. Not since I was little. And then the minute my dad retired, he turned all his focus onto me. Like I was supposed to carry the flag for the family."

"Yikes," Gavin says, pulling a forehead thermometer out of his bag and pressing it against my head. "That sounds healthy."

"I liked it," I admit. "He knew a lot about hockey, and I liked the attention."

"But you never had a choice," he points out.

I guess that's true. But it's also a problem for another day. "How many guys are out?"

"Seven," he says. "Nobody is super sick, though. Coach is just trying to keep it that way."

"Fair enough."

"Yeah," he agrees. "Your temperature is a hundred and one. How do you feel?"

"Achy and tired. My throat is rough, and my head hurts. But I've had worse days."

Gavin stands up. He puts a hand on my jaw and meets my gaze. His look is assessing—as if he's trying to decide if I'm underplaying my symptoms.

Then he leans over and gives me a kiss on the jaw. Just one. "Take care of yourself. Text me if you need anything. I'm supposed to call Dr. Herberts with updates. We're both making house calls."

He's holding the place together. Just like always. "Aren't you supposed to take Jordyn to the game tonight?"

He winces. "I was. But now she's sick, and apparently I'm a big meanie for keeping her at home."

"Oh hell."

"Yeah." He shakes his head. "Text me if you need anything."

"I will," I say, and it's so damn tempting. Because I can think of a million things I need from Gavin.

Many of them are sexual, however. Sue me.

He leaves, which makes me sad. I wash the bowl and set it in my drying rack. At least I'll have a reason to stop over there sometime and return it.

In bed, I watch two movies back to back. I take a nap.

Two whole days at home. I don't even know myself right now.

Just when I start to despair that I will never leave home again, my phone rings. And it's Gavin.

"Hi," I say. "I'm fine. My worst symptom is boredom."

"I'm very happy to hear that," he says, and his voice is tired. "Because I have a favor to ask. It's a biggie."

"Anything," I say without hesitation.

"Henry got a positive flu test a few hours ago. He got sent home from the arena."

I look at the time—five o'clock. "Holy shit. So you're working the game?"

"Yeah. And Reggie has to go...somewhere. Her band is counting on her. I thought I had found another babysitter, but she just bailed."

Oh shit. "You want *me* to do it?"

"I wouldn't ask..."

"It's fine," I say quickly. "I'll be there in five."

"Bless you. Because I'm already late."

THIRTY-TWO

Hudson

I TAKE the world's fastest shower, put on clean clothes, and head over to Gavin's apartment, wondering how I'm going to entertain a sick seven-year-old. But when I get there, it's quiet, and there's no sign of Jordyn.

"She's sleeping," Gavin explains as he throws on his jacket.

"Oh." Suddenly this job got easier.

"Make yourself comfortable," he says as he grabs his gear. "The couch is not great, so you can spread out in my bed. She'll find you when she wakes up. Hell—she'll be ecstatic. There's a pot of ramen in the fridge, but if you're sick of it, order whatever sounds good to you guys. I've got to run..."

"Go." I shoo him toward the door. "Don't worry about us."

From the taxi he sends me a string of texts. *She should drink more fluids. If she gets hot or cranky, give her children's Tylenol, but only after 6 p.m.*

After reading them, I promptly fall asleep on his couch, waking up in the pitch dark a little later. The clock on the cable box says it's 7:30. So I stumble around to turn on some lights, and I pour myself a glass of water.

And I must be loud, because Jordyn comes shuffling out of her bedroom in a set of purple flannel pajamas. She squints up at me.

"You're not Daddy."

"See, I knew you were a smart one."

She laughs suddenly. "Did Daddy go to work? Why aren't you at the game? Omigod, do you have the flu, too?"

"True story. Want some water? Daddy said you needed fluids."

"Okay. Can we eat dinner?"

I'm not very hungry, so I'd forgotten about dinner. "Sure, kid. Any suggestions? There's ramen, or takeout."

Her eyes brighten. "Could we order Italian? Reggie lets me get the stuffed shells."

"Do you know the name of the restaurant?"

"I can find it!" she chirps. "Give me your phone?"

Once again the key to babysitting Jordyn appears to be handing over my phone. She finds the restaurant and reads me the menu. I make my choices, and she handles the whole thing. I don't have to do anything, except pay. Which seems fair.

Then I put on the hockey game, and when our dinner arrives, we eat it in front of the TV. Jordyn applauds whenever the camera shows the bench—and the spot behind it where Gavin is standing.

I'm winning this babysitting thing.

Brooklyn is struggling, though, which makes me blue. And the stands are full of rainbow pennants for the LGBTQ event.

"I should have been there," I mumble as the other team strips a rookie of the puck.

A very small hand pats my back. "Everybody gets sick sometimes. You just have to roll with it."

I give her the side eye. "Is that something your daddy said?"

"Yep. Can we have ice cream? There's some in the freezer. And I promise to brush my teeth after."

Huh. Gavin didn't say anything about dessert. "I think anything goes when you have the flu."

She bounces off the sofa, and I help her put a scoop of chocolate chip into a teacup, and I get her a spoon.

Afterward, I tidy up Gavin's kitchen a little bit as Brooklyn scores a goal to pull into the lead. But when I look over at Jordyn, she's asleep again, her head at an awkward angle on the sofa's arm.

Hmm.

I wait a few minutes to see if she's going to wake up. But my neck is sore just looking at her. So I tiptoe over there and contemplate moving her. Is that a thing Gavin would do?

Yes. I think it is. He'd want her to be comfortable.

Okay. Fine. I squat five hundred pounds, right? This will be a piece of cake.

Gingerly, I lean down and spatula her small body off the sofa. She smells like toothpaste and fruity shampoo. I pick her up as carefully as I can.

But sleeping little girls are floppy. It's like carrying an octopus, and I'm afraid I'm going to bonk one of her limbs into a doorframe.

We make it, though. I carry her into a messy room with fish on the bedsheets, and lay her head on the pillow. She rolls over and grumbles as I pull the covers up to her elbows.

Feeling pleased with myself, I text Gavin to let him know she's in bed. The game is over now—and we won. I shut off the TV and contemplate my next move. I'm exhausted, so I walk into Gavin's tidy room and stretch out on his bed.

When I wake up an hour later, though, Jordyn is standing over me, whimpering that she doesn't feel good.

I put a hand on her forehead, and it's hot. "Does your tummy hurt? Do you, uh, think you'll be sick?"

She shakes her head.

"Tylenol it is, then." I check Gavin's texts for the dosage, and I give her the medicine.

But she doesn't go back to bed. Instead, she climbs onto one side of Gavin's queen-sized bed. "Why isn't Daddy here?"

"He will be," I promise. "It takes a while to pack up after the game. People need his help."

"But *we* need Daddy more," she whines.

Girl, I hear you. I stretch out awkwardly beside her, and then take her smaller hand in mine. "Listen, pumpkin. He's not far away.

Your daddy is really good at taking care of people. He wouldn't let you go too long without him. And we're not doing *so* bad, am I right?"

"I guess." She rolls closer to me and snuggles up, her head on my shoulder. "You could tell me a story while we wait for him."

Oh boy. That sounds like it's beyond my pay grade. "What, uh, kind of story?"

"Tell me about when you were little. My papa had good stories about that. He was a little boy in Boston. That's by New Hampshire. Where were you?"

"I was born here in New York, but I was too little to remember living here. Then we lived in Toronto. That's in Canada. And then Denver, which is in Colorado. My papa was a hockey player, so he traveled a whole lot. My mom and I used to go on some of his trips. One time he took me skating on the river in Ottawa. You could skate for miles."

She lifts her head and looks at me in the dark. "Really?"

"Really. It was cool." Honestly, this babysitting gig isn't so hard. I smooth the hair away from her forehead and let myself think about a winter day from over twenty years ago. "I'd never skated on a river before. There were lots of people out there. Like a party. Some men sold hot chocolate and waffles from carts at the edge."

"Did you get to have both?"

"Yup. It was really cold out, and I was hungry. But you could skate right under the bridge, with cars going by right over your head."

"Cool."

I keep talking, telling her more about the sled dogs I saw on that same trip. And eventually she falls asleep again. Her small face looks peaceful, her dark lashes touching her cheeks.

When I glance at her sleeping face, I feel an unfamiliar sense of pride. Like I've done something important. Objectively, I know it wasn't much—all I provided was some TV and takeout food. But comforting her is strangely satisfying.

Hockey is great, but I rarely end the day feeling like I made a difference for anyone other than me.

I close my eyes and listen to her soft breathing. The pillow smells like Gavin. And his words come back to me. *There's no other place you need to be right now.*

Truly there's not.

THIRTY-THREE

Gavin

IT TAKES me a long time to get out of the rink tonight. We gave rapid flu tests to the whole team after the game, and luckily none of them came back positive.

But it's after eleven when I climb out of a taxi and drag my tired ass up the stairs. When I let myself into the apartment, it's dark and quiet. Reggie isn't home yet. Hudson is not on the sofa, which means he must be asleep in my bed.

I don't trust myself to go in there, though. He needs his rest. And if he looks at me a certain way, I might accidentally give him a get-well-soon blowjob.

But then I tiptoe into Jordyn's room to give her a goodnight kiss...and find her bed empty. So I go looking for her in my room.

And the sight I find there makes my heart swell. Hudson is asleep on his back, on top of the covers. Jordyn has snuggled herself against his side, her skinny bottom tucked up against his hip, her feet pushed against his calf, her head pillowed on his biceps.

It's so cute that I stop breathing. There's a greedy place in my heart that craves having a family again. A man to come home to—someone my daughter trusts.

I push that thought away, and I carefully lift my sleeping daughter off the bed.

"Daddy," she murmurs while I carry her into her own room.

"It's late," I whisper. "You feel okay?"

"Mm-hmm," she says, and wraps her arms around me.

I tuck her in and kiss her on the forehead. She doesn't feel feverish.

Then I brush my teeth and change into sleep shorts before returning to my bedroom. I sit down on the side of the bed and palm Hudson's forehead. It's also cool to the touch. So that's progress.

His eyes flutter open. "Hi," he says thickly.

"Thank you," I whisper. "You have no idea how much I appreciate this."

He takes my hand and holds it. "S'no trouble. We had Italian food and watched the game. She made me tell her a story."

My heart doubles in size. I lie down beside him and put a hand on his strong chest. "What's your genre? Sports? Ghosts?"

"Childhood memories. Her pick."

"Ah. I'm not good with those, so I have to make stuff up."

"I shouldn't have slept here," he says, glancing around. "With my flu germs."

"Doesn't matter," I point out. "If I didn't get it from Jordyn, I'm not getting it. My test was negative again tonight."

"In that case..." He rolls onto his side and pulls me to his chest. "I miss you like crazy."

"I know."

He chuckles.

"I meant that I know because I miss you, too."

"You have principles," he whispers. "And reasons. I'm trying hard to respect your boundaries. It's just that you look so fuckable all the time."

"I don't want to violate my own rules," I mumble against his T-shirt. "But I still want you to violate me. It's a problem."

His chest shakes with laughter. "You know that's not all I want, right? It's not just sex. It's never just been the sex. I'm falling for you."

Those are heady words, and my needy heart dances the tango inside my chest. But I know it's not that simple. "It's way too easy to fall for you, too. But hockey is your first love, and hockey is a jealous bitch. You're basically cheating on hockey to be with me."

"That is frighteningly accurate." He sighs. "I know you think it can't work out. But I'm going to prove you wrong. I'm going to get my early contract renegotiation, and then I'm going to find a way to live my life. It will all come together."

"Uh-huh," I say, rubbing a soothing hand on his chest.

"I know you don't believe me, but I'm going to convince you."

"Okay." I smile in the dark. "Now we need to sleep, though. You can convince me tomorrow."

His arms tighten around me. "You're not kicking me out, right? I think I deserve to sleep here. That's my payment for babysitting."

"Fine. But you have to be a good boy." I'm reminding myself as much as him, though.

"Will do."

I disentangle myself from him and lock my bedroom door, so Jordyn won't see us in bed together. Then I get under the covers. "Good night."

With a snicker, he slides into bed next to me. Then he curls up beside me and puts an arm around my waist. "Good night, hottie."

"Thanks for taking care of my little girl."

He kisses the back of my neck. "It's easy. I just say yes to whatever she asks for."

I groan, but it's half-hearted. His embrace feels like the best thing that ever happened to me.

And I fall asleep not five minutes later.

When I stumble out of bed at eight the next morning, Hudson is gone, and Reggie is smirking at me from over the rim of her coffee cup on the sofa. "Fun night?"

I shake my head. "Not in the way that you mean. Where's Jordyn?"

"Playing with my iPad in her bedroom."

"Did she see...?"

Reggie shakes her head.

I don't want to confuse her, so that's a relief.

Or so I'd thought. But that night, as I'm combing out her wet hair, she suddenly asks me a question. "Is Hudson your boyfriend?"

Gulp. "No, honey. Why do you ask?"

"He went to sleep on your bed. Like Papa always did."

Oh. "I told him to make himself comfortable, because he's getting over the same flu that you had."

"But he *could* be your boyfriend," she presses. "If he wanted to."

It's a good thing she can't see my face right now, because I am truly at a loss for words. I won't lie to her. Or discuss Hudson's private business, either. But where does that leave me? "Hudson is very special to me. But I don't think he's looking for a boyfriend."

"He should be," she says, as if it were up to her. "He's nice, and he likes you."

"I'll keep that in mind," I say lightly. "In case it comes up."

Hudson is a busy man, though.

Here's another thing I didn't know about the NHL schedule—there are only four days between the last regular season game and the first playoffs game. And the playoffs encompass four rounds of up to seven games each—a month and a half of additional play. The two teams who make it to the final round will have their time off shortened to six weeks before training camp starts up again.

Hockey is bonkers. The human body isn't built to work that hard for so long. When I think about it too hard, my muscles ache in sympathy.

Luckily, our little flu epidemic fades away. But that still means long hours at the practice rink. I stretch and evaluate and tape and massage people from dawn until the moment I run out of the building to pick up Jordyn from school.

By the evening of game one, I've done my part for the team. I'm unloading groceries in my kitchen in preparation for making Jordyn a game night dinner of chili and corn bread.

She's pumped up about watching, and riveted by the concept of a playoffs bracket. She picks Brooklyn to win everything, and then chooses her other picks based on their jersey colors and logos. But everyone needs a system, right?

"They'd better win," she says, dancing in front of the TV. "I'm counting on it."

"Baby, there's still two hours until the puck drops," I point out. "Better find something else to do for a little while."

"Two *hours*?" She slumps onto the sofa, like a deflating balloon. "I hate my life."

"Jordyn!" She sounds seventeen, not seven. And I'm not used to it.

"I don't hate all my life," she says, rolling over to smile at me. "Just a little part."

"Okay, good. Want to help me make corn bread?"

"Sure!" She pops off the couch like there are springs inside her body. "Can I measure the flour?"

Before I can answer, the apartment's door buzzer rings.

"Ooh! I'll answer." She's already dashing for the door. "Hello? Okay." As I watch, she presses the button that unlocks the door.

"Who is it?" Nobody ever rings our doorbell.

"A carrier delivery," she says.

"A what? Do you mean a *courier*?"

She shrugs.

"Let me deal with it," I insist, and when I open the apartment door, a young man wearing a delivery company's vest is just jogging up the stairs, an envelope in his hand. "Gavin Gillis?" he asks.

"That's me."

"Sign here."

I do, and a few seconds later I'm holding a nondescript envelope with no return address. And I'm filled with dread.

It must be a summons. Eustace has really done it—she's sued me for custody of Jordyn.

I set the unopened envelope down on the counter and go back into the kitchen. But I can't even remember what I was supposed to be doing. My mind is overloaded with panic.

"Daddy?" Jordyn asks softly. "Aren't we making corn bread?"

Right. Corn bread. "Yeah, baby. Can you find the measuring cups?"

"What did the man bring?" she asks, yanking open a kitchen drawer.

"I don't know," I say heavily. "I'll open it later." My hands are actually shaking as I pull the bag of flour out of the cupboard. I can't open that thing in front of Jordyn. I'll probably cry. "Did you wash your hands?"

"Oh, whoops." She darts out of the kitchen for the bathroom, probably because the stepstool in there makes it easier for her to reach the faucet.

So I grab the envelope and tear it open briskly. Like tearing off a Band-Aid. Then I hold my breath and pull out...

Two tickets. To Game One of the playoffs, starting in two hours. There's also a gift card for the concession restaurants, and a hastily scrawled note, too.

G—sorry for the awfully short notice. I had to scrounge for these. But Jordyn was so sad to miss that other game, so please enjoy this one. —H

"Holy shit." I whisper.

"Daddy! You sweared."

"Jordyn, *look!*" I have so much emotional whiplash right now. "Forget the corn bread, we have seats in row E for the game."

"Holy shit!" she chirps.

"Hey!"

She cracks up laughing and starts jumping up and down. "Can we go right now? Wait—we have to wear purple!" She does a dizzyingly fast one-eighty and streaks toward her bedroom.

My grin is so wide it hurts my face.

THIRTY-FOUR

Hudson

YOGI BERRA ONCE SAID: "Ninety percent of baseball is mental and the other half is physical."

But I consider it the perfect hockey quote, too, and the fucked-up math is the whole point. Some nights you know you're capable of giving a hundred and forty percent, and those nights are magic.

That's the kind of confidence I'm bringing with me tonight, and we haven't even left the dressing room yet. But this is my year, as my father is so fond of saying. I'm healthy, my team is mostly healthy, and we are here to make some noise.

I'm so fired up tonight that even my father's pregame sermonizing didn't annoy me much. The fact that he's watching tonight doesn't bother me, either.

Because Gavin is watching too. By the time I shut my phone down, I'd already received an ecstatic text of thanks, and a photo of Jordyn in purple face paint.

"Let's roll, boys!" O'Doul hollers, and we all hoot wildly in response.

Tonight is a gift. And maybe I'm a little sensitive about the number of times I've been traded, but I can honestly say that the trade to Brooklyn was also a gift. I want this team, and this game, and this chance. I belong here.

"Step lively, New Guy!" Castro says, poking me in the ass with his stick. "Let's bring some doom down upon these goons from Philly."

"Bring the doom!" someone else brays as we move in a heavily padded column toward the tunnel.

The crowd sounds grow wild as we clomp across the rubber floor pads and into the brightly lit arena. I step out onto the ice at a sprint, my skates biting the slick surface as I pump forward. Twenty thousand fans scream for Brooklyn. I'm going to give them something to scream about, too.

We skate our warm-ups, and then a gospel choir sings the national anthem. With my hand on my heart, I center myself. And I visualize the game ahead of me. Philly gets a lot of mileage out of their quick center, so tonight I'm going to become his worst nightmare. That's my job. I'm good at my job.

And after the playoffs, Brooklyn's GM will be clamoring to offer me a new contract with all the fixings.

When it's time for the face-off, my focus narrows to the men in front of me, and the puck the ref suddenly drops. Trevi wins it, firing it back to me.

And I'm off, skating like a demon, finding an opportunity to advance it to our winger. And then I get in the center's face. His name is Cuzkic. Nickname Cujo, of course, because hockey players are easily amused.

But Cujo is going to be whimpering like a week-old puppy when I'm through with him.

For the first period, I'm merely frustrating. Doggedly, obsessively frustrating, though, as I stick to him like bubblegum on the sidewalk.

I make it nearly impossible for him to pass the puck in a productive way. And when the buzzer rings at the end of the period, it's a zero-zero game.

"Good work," Coach says to me in the dressing room. "Brilliant. Keep it up, and when he finally cracks, be ruthless."

"Yessir."

"Fluids, boys," Henry prods us, walking around the room with a tray of paper cups. "Water, energy drinks, juice. Something for everyone."

I gulp down some water, but I'm already feeling great. I go back out for the second period ready for more.

Cujo puts up a good fight. He's wily. He varies his routine, trying to shake me.

But I am nothing if not patient. I've been waiting years to make my mark on this game, and I could keep this up all night long.

Late in the second period, it finally happens. Cujo gets tired—mentally as well as physically. When I block yet another pass, he lets his anger overrule his patience. So I double down and crowd his personal space.

Instead of backing off for another try, he yanks me out of the way, his hand gripping my jersey.

I fall, but knock the puck out of his reach on my way down.

Castro swoops in, grabs it and skates hard toward the goal. I don't breathe as Philly's D-man closes in on him. But Castro fires toward the net.

The whole stadium gasps as it streaks right past the post and goes in.

Twenty thousand people scream as the lamp lights, and the ref blows the whistle.

Delayed penalty on Philly.

I hop to my feet. Then I tilt my face toward the rafters and cheer. "Thanks for that laugh, Cujo."

"Cocksucker," he jeers.

Only when I'm lucky, dude.

Then I hear the announcer call the first goal of these playoffs.

And the assist goes to me.

There are no easy games, though, and the third period is tense. Philly ties it up, and then we answer back with another goal. When the final buzzer rings, it's 2-1 in our favor.

On my sweaty trip back down the tunnel, a journalist sticks a microphone in my face. "Can we expect more of this from Hudson Newgate in the postseason?"

It's a dumb question, but I smile anyway. "Sure thing!"

"Your father must be so proud of tonight's effort."

"One in a row!" I say cheerfully.

But the journalist wasn't wrong. My dad is elated with my performance tonight. After the game—and my shower, and the press conference—he can't stop gushing about my speed and focus. "More of that the day after tomorrow," he says, even as my mother rolls her eyes and leans heavily against the wall in the corridor outside the dressing room.

"Right on," I say, finally tired. "I'd better head home and get some z's. You guys, too, right? Mom looks like she's asleep on her feet."

My father glances toward her, like maybe he's forgotten she's there. "Yeah, good plan. We need you rested." His eyes narrow, though. "You're heading straight home?"

"Sure." Then I narrow my eyes. "Emphasis on *straight*, right?"

"*Hudson*." He actually looks over both shoulders, making sure nobody is within earshot. "Don't be careless. Not now."

"I'm never careless," I hiss. "But one day soon I'm going to live my truth out loud. And I'm going to do that with all the care in the world. So brace yourself."

I go home alone, of course. But in the taxi, I check my texts. There's a selfie of Gavin and Jordyn at the game, smiling happily. And another selfie of Gavin drinking a beer, and giving me silly eyes over the rim of the cup. And a picture of Jordyn jumping up and down with her Bombshells pom-poms in her hands.

That last one is from your assist! We screamed. Amazing game! Thanks again for this gift. So awesome.

I tuck my phone into my jacket pocket and watch the lit-up store fronts glide by. Making Gavin happy is almost as satisfying as playing well tonight.

He has no idea how motivated I am to prove myself to him. We can have a real life together.

I just have to make it happen.

THIRTY-FIVE

Gavin

MAY

THE PLAYOFFS ARE A THRILLING, grueling experience for everyone who works for the Bruisers. That's because everything that happens during those tacked-on weeks is handled a little differently than during the regular season. Ticket sales, travel, transportation—it's all done on the fly.

There are new faces in the locker room, too, as extra players are called up from the minors to practice with the Brooklyn coaches, just in case our top team suffers injuries during the race for the cup.

I love my job, but the pace is overwhelming.

Management knows that, though, which is why they treat the whole staff to a catered lunch the day after that first victory.

I'm eating a world class fish taco and chatting with Henry when the team's General Manager walks up to greet us. "Hey, Henry. Any new issues I should know about after last night's game?" Hugh Major is an imposing man in his mid-fifties, with a shaved head and broad shoulders. His voice is deep and commanding, with a steely edge that probably makes the rookies quake.

"My report will be on your desk this afternoon," he says. "I'm waiting on MRI results for a sore knee, but I don't anticipate any nasty surprises."

"Excellent!" the GM crows. "Gavin, we haven't properly met," he booms, offering a hand to me. "Have you settled in? I know we're a lot to take on. But it's great that you've been able to give Henry some crucial backup."

"I'm doing my best," I say, setting my plate down so I can shake his hand. "The learning curve is steep, but you have a great group of people here."

"Gavin is being modest," Henry says. "The guys love him. The women's team would like to steal him. I interview guys all the time, but when I interviewed Gavin, I knew he was special. It's rare to find someone who has a deep understanding of anatomy as well as impressive communication skills. We're so lucky he said yes to joining us."

"That is a really nice thing to say." My face is on fire now. "If you could give that same speech to my mother-in-law, that would be helpful."

The GM laughs. "I know *that* feeling. We're never quite good enough for their precious daughters, right?"

"Her son in this case," I say quickly. "But yeah."

His eyes widen only slightly. "Oh, sorry. Stupid assumption on my part." He claps me on the arm. "Thanks for joining the organization, Gavin. The manager's office is always open. Is there anything we can help you with during the postseason?"

Yeah. Please don't trade Hudson Newgate. "No, sir. Things are going well in the training room."

"Wonderful," the big man booms. "You've met my assistant, Heidi Jo?"

"He sure has!" Heidi Jo pops around his square body to join our group. "Boss, you should know that Gavin has a wicked backhand at the ping-pong table. Be careful how you place your wagers. Now Hugh—you have a call in fifteen minutes. Henry—here's the receipt for the supplies you ordered." She passes a sheet of paper to my boss. "And Gavin, this arrived for you this morning, by courier."

She hands me another sealed envelope, just like the one my tickets arrived in last night. This time I'll withhold my panic. But two couriered envelopes in one week is a lot of high-level mail. So I make my excuses, grab a can of seltzer water for the road, and retreat downstairs to Henry's office, where I tear it open.

The letter inside is from the Brooklyn Academy of Arts. And it's very confusing.

Dear Mr. Gillis,

We are pleased to recognize your Gold Circle Membership to the Brooklyn Academy of Arts. Enclosed, please find our program of events for the current year. Your Gold Circle Membership entitles you to fifty percent off and priority registration for either one adult class or a children's summer day camp.

Your assistant mentioned that the day camp was in your plans, so please let us know before May 30th which program that is, and your camper's name and age. Priority registration ends on June 1st, and we wouldn't want your family to miss out.

Warmly,

Judith McPhee, Director of Membership

Wait, what? My assistant?

I pull out my phone and dash off a text to Reggie. *Did you do this?*

My sister feels guilty about abandoning us this summer to go on tour. And she knows I'm worried about my summer plans.

Do what? she asks, and I send a scan of the letter. *No way,* is her quick response. *I'm broker than you. Didn't you tell me the membership costs more than two thousand dollars?*

That's all true.

Looks like Hudson's work, she writes. *That man is trying to make a statement.*

Hudson? I try to remember if I ever mentioned this particular organization to him, and I realize I must have babbled about my summer childcare options at some point.

What the hell did he do?

I leave Henry's office and head straight for the weight room, where some of the team is putting in an off-day workout. Hudson isn't there. But then I spot him on the mats in the stretching alcove —just like on my first day at work.

"Newgate," I snap. "Can I have a word?"

I don't even give him a chance to argue, I just reverse my tracks back toward Henry's office. But I hear his footsteps following me before I duck into the small space and fold my arms defiantly.

"Problem?" he asks as he steps inside. A smile is playing at the corners of his mouth.

"What is this?" I hiss, waving the paper in front of him.

He takes it. "Looks like you got Jordyn into that summer program after all. She'll enjoy it."

"Hudson! You can't do this. It was, like, thousands of dollars to join the Gold Circle."

He shrugs. "It's a charity, Gavin. I get a tax deduction, yeah? And what's done is done—I can't call up the charity and ask for my money back. That wouldn't be nice."

"But..." I let out a hot sigh. "I would have figured something out. I could have handled it."

He puts both hands on my shoulders and looks me in the eyes with that wide brown gaze. "Of course you would have. That was never the issue. But Jordyn's fancy friends like *this* camp, yeah? Now she can go be with her friends. It wasn't easy for her to make them."

Maybe it's the feeling of his warm grip on my lonely body, or the fact that he's right. But all the fight seeps out of me. "Hell. She'll love it. Thank you."

Still, his face falls. "I didn't do it to make you feel bad, Gav. I just wanted to ease your mind about August. I wanted you to be able to tell your monster-in-law that Jordyn was going to the best summer program in Brooklyn."

"Oh, I will definitely be mentioning that." Just the idea cheers me up a little bit. "I hate that you had to bail me out, though. I moved Jordyn here without a plan."

"I didn't bail you out." He releases my shoulders and slaps me on the back. Then he pushes the door to Henry's office all the way closed, and wraps me into a hug. "Look, I've never been a parent," he says as I take a deep, comforting breath against his shoulder. "But isn't parenting just, like, constructing a parachute on the way down? If it were easy, there wouldn't be so many experts."

That sounds eerily close to something Eddie might say. But I don't tell him that, I just tighten my arms around him instead. "Thank you. It's still a lot of money."

"I have a lot of money," he points out. "And a lack of ways to show you that I'm serious about us. So just let me have this one."

"Okay, but rein it in from here on out," I mumble, trying to convince myself to let go of him.

"Does that mean I can't send you tickets to game five?"

I think about it for a half second as I finally step back. "No way. I want to watch you win."

He smiles, and starts to say something else, but the doorknob turns suddenly.

I guess it's true what they say about professional hockey players —they have excellent reflexes. In that split second, Hudson leaps back from me like I'm on fire. By the time Henry's face clears the doorway, Hudson is a healthy distance away.

"Hey, gents," Henry says with a frown. "Is everything okay?"

"Fine," Hudson says tightly. He looks rattled. "Just having a chat. Later, guys." Then he leaves so fast there's practically a vapor trail behind him.

"Anything up with him?" Henry asks, hooking a thumb in the direction of Hudson's departure.

"No," I say, even as my heart quakes.

Even though I understand why Hudson's been hiding for years, it still sucks to see him go cold like that.

And now I have to think fast. "His, uh, dad is pushing him to pick a nutritionist to work with this summer, and so I googled a few of them for him."

"Oh, interesting," Henry says, putting his coffee cup down on his desk. "I've heard that his dad is pushy as fuck. Some players like that style of high-energy hustle. But I'm not sure Hudson ever had a choice. What does your afternoon look like?"

"Um..." I've got whiplash again, which happens so often when

I'm dealing with Hudson. "Working with rookies in the weight room. Taking inventory of our supplies."

"Sounds good," Henry says, shaking the mouse of his computer. "If we're short of anything, rush the order to Heidi Jo."

"Will do."

That night I'm just getting into bed when my phone rings. And it's Hudson calling.

"Hey," I answer, glancing instinctively to my right. "Are you just on the other side of this wall?" My room is so small that I can put one foot on the floor and knock my knuckles three times against the plaster.

A moment passes with nothing but a creak of floorboards. And then I hear the same tap tap tap against the bedroom wall. "So close, and yet so far." He sighs. "My fault, of course."

"Oh come on. The universe deserves some blame for this one. Not your fault that we stumbled into each other in a bar four months ago."

"Still." He clears his throat. "I called because I'm not happy with the way I reacted today. When Henry came in."

"Oh." I try to think of what else to add, but I can't. It hurt me to see him leap away from me like that. But I'm not going to say so, because he already knows.

"I told you that I wasn't conflicted about my sexuality," he says quietly. "That I'm not ashamed. But I've been trying to hide myself for so long. I don't know how to stop."

"Yeah," I say softly. "I'm sure."

"But I'm going to learn," he says. "I have to get through the play-offs. And then I have to go to L.A. for a few weeks to work with some fitness guru my father loves."

"Okay," I say patiently. He'd mentioned that before.

"July, though." His voice perks up. "The team will do a bunch of contract renewals over the summer, and I'm hoping to get one of them. And when the ink is dry, that's when I sit down with the team and say—guys, there's something you should know about me. That's my plan—go straight in. No warning management, no PR huddle. I'm going to shoot first and ask questions later."

"Wow," I whisper. Because I can picture it. The guys sitting around in the dressing room, and Hudson standing there with a serious expression in his brown eyes. The team will listen. They'll give him what he needs—their attention and support. I know they will. "That could be life-changing for you."

"I know!" He actually laughs. "And then we can navigate the problem of your conflict of interest at work. You and I can sit down with Henry, if that's okay with you."

I swallow the lump in my throat. "Yeah, I could do that. He might help us find a work-around. I actually, uh...I looked into switching to the women's team."

"Really? That never occurred to me."

"Well, don't get too excited. Their season is so much shorter than the men's that the job wouldn't pay me a living wage. I'd have to get a second job..."

Hudson lets out an unhappy grunt. "No way. Okay, so that's not the answer. But we'll think of something."

The fact that he wants to fills me with hope. "Be well, okay? You should sleep now."

"You could come over and kiss me good night," he says in a flirty voice.

"Hudson..."

"Kidding!" I can feel his gravelly chuckle in my belly. "Good night, hottie. I'll go to sleep now, so I can score some more goals for you tomorrow night."

"I'll be watching," I promise.

We hang up, and I lie down in bed and think of him lying in the bigger bedroom on the other side of the wall.

Some day maybe we'll take a sledgehammer to it and break that wall down.

I register Jordyn for the camp, and then show her the welcome letter.

"Oh Daddy, *really?*" she squeaks happily. "I get to go? To Bella and Lila's camp?"

"That's right. But now it's your camp, too." *This year, anyway.* I don't tell her that Hudson helped us. On the one hand, I feel like a jerk for taking all the credit. But I don't know how I'd even explain it.

He's busy, anyway. Brooklyn wins game two and then loses game three, in Philly. They stay down there, too, gearing up together for game four.

Hudson has shone in every game, though. It's not overkill to say that he's dominating. One sports writer even put it like this: *Hudson Newgate has been a shining star of Brooklyn's deep defensive bench.*

I'm thrilled for him. He's finally getting the attention he's worked so hard for.

On the evening of game four, another courier arrives at my door. This time there's a box with a cheesecake from a nearby Italian restaurant. Plus three tickets to game five—even Reggie gets a seat.

Dreaming of you, says the ticket envelope. I hide it in my sock drawer, like a teenager with a crush.

Then I text him my thanks for the cheesecake and the tickets.

That restaurant is my favorite, he replies. *Have you been there?*

Nope.

How about I make a reservation for two, for the week before preseason games start? By then I will have made my big announcement, and we'll have had a chance to talk to Henry.

My heart bounces around inside my chest. *Sounds like a fun date.*

That will be my happy thought, he says. *That and everything that happens AFTER dinner...*

And now it's my happy thought, too.

THIRTY-SIX

Hudson

WE CLINCH the first round with game five. I haven't scored in the playoffs yet, but I've got three assists.

Plus I have the satisfaction of knowing that Gavin and his family are jumping up and down for me when the buzzer sounds.

Not that I've seen much of him. But it's fine. I'm a patient man. And it's time to turn our attention to defeating Carolina.

Our first two games are at home again, which helps. I'm just heading into headquarters when my phone plays "Under My Thumb."

My father has been thrilled with my performance, so it's more fun than usual to answer his calls. "Hey, Dad."

"Hudson!" My father's voice is as enthusiastic as I've ever heard it. "How's *the man*?"

Huh. I guess I'm *the man* now. "I'm good. Feeling rested. Morale around here is pretty high."

"Good, good!"

It's weird, but I've been waiting my whole life for my father to sound as fired up talking to me as he sounds when he's on the phone with his biggest clients. And it suddenly doesn't matter so much anymore. "Is this a social call, or business? I'm on my way to a video meeting."

"Ah. Well. I just needed to run something by you. I got a funny call about you this morning."

"Uh, *funny?* What does that mean? Who called you?"

My father seems to choose his words carefully. "The GM from Colorado called, and he asked me how you're liking Brooklyn."

"God, why? As if they care."

"That's the thing," my father says slowly. "It sounded like they do. Maybe they regret letting you go."

I snort. "Sure they do, now that I'm killing it in the playoffs. They might have a short memory, but I don't. That team wanted nothing to do with me."

"There's a new sheriff in town, you realize."

He's referring to Powers, the newly promoted coach. "Like that makes any difference."

"Doesn't it? Apparently he's been watching you all season. They said that if you weren't sure about Brooklyn, that you shouldn't be hasty to sign anything with them. Sounds like Colorado assumes we'll push for an early renewal. And he's trying to tell us he's interested."

"Not happening."

"But hear me out a second," he says. "There's no rule that says we need to bring Brooklyn to the bargaining table early. Now that there's two teams who want you, it pays to wait out the last year of your contract. Your value could double if there's more demand."

"Dad, no," I say emphatically. "You're assuming that money matters to me. It doesn't. I want security."

He's quiet for a moment. "The thing is? Brooklyn has a bunch of guys up for renewal this year—guys who've been around longer than you. Right now you're in line behind them. Next summer you'll be the main course. I think we should wait."

Everything inside me deflates. "That isn't the tune you were singing before."

"I've been doing some more research."

"Since when?" I demand. "I thought the plan was a new contract this summer."

"Plans change."

"Mine won't," I say in a stony voice. "Your job is to get me what I want, right? And what I want is a Brooklyn contract before next season. With a no-trade clause. I want to stay here. I don't care what the money is."

"You say that *now*," my father huffs. "But if we push Brooklyn for a contract, and they have a year to go, they're smart enough to lowball you. Why are you so hot to stay in Brooklyn all of a sudden?"

"I like it here. That's all you need to know."

He sighs theatrically. "Hudson…"

"Dad—do you give your other players a hard time when they tell you what they want?"

"No, and I'm not giving you a hard time, either. I'm just making sure you've thought this through."

"I think of nothing else. Tell the nice man in Colorado thanks, but no thanks."

"Yeah, I did that already," my father says. "—Because the less interested we sound, the better his offer will get."

"Not that I'll care," I remind him.

"You might," he insists. "That team owes this family something. I'd still like to take a pound of their flesh."

I stop myself from making a very dirty, very queer joke. "Take it for one of your other players. I'm heading to a video meeting."

"All right," he says magnanimously. "Don't let me keep you."

I hang up and roll my eyes.

Colorado? They had their chance. Even if the homophobic head coach is gone, I still don't want to give them the satisfaction.

Round two, against Carolina, is a roller coaster. We win the first game, but drop two in a row. Then I get a goal in the second period of game four, and we win that one.

But I wake up the next day with muscle soreness pretty much

everywhere. And a tightness in my hip that's reminiscent of my troubles earlier in the season.

I head to the rink pretty early and walk into the athletic trainers' room.

Gavin blinks at me in surprise. "Hi, stranger. Rough morning?"

"Hi." I give him a secretive smile. "Do I look *that* bad?"

"You look tired," he whispers. "And don't think I can't tell you're favoring your hip."

I climb onto the table, and Gavin wastes no time manipulating my hip. "This hurt?"

"It's tight, that's for sure."

"Is the pain sharp?" he clarifies.

I shake my head. "Just normal tightness."

"All right. That might not be a big deal. Were you worried about bursitis?"

"Yup."

He pats my hip. "Let me work on this for a few minutes. Then you'll take an anti-inflammatory, and keep Henry in the loop."

"Yessir."

"That's what I like to hear." He drops his voice. "But moan it."

"*Stop*," I say under my breath. "Do you know how hard up I am these days?"

Our gazes collide, and his is as heated as mine. But he looks away first. "Sorry. Forgot myself there for a second."

"Same," I whisper. "Last night I thought about taking a giant drill and blasting through the bedroom wall."

He snorts. "God, get out of my brain."

We both laugh. And that's when Henry walks in. "Hey, guys. How's the hip?"

"Stiff," I grumble. "But Gavin doesn't think it's fatal."

Henry hangs his jacket on a peg. "I can see why you'd worry, though. We need to get you through the playoffs without a flare-up. Any new drama so far this morning?" he asks Gavin.

He shakes his head.

"That's what we like to hear. Another three weeks of good luck. That's what we need."

Plus a new contract, I silently add as Gavin's skilled hands dig into my muscles. I want to haul him onto my body and kiss him like the world is ending. What's the point of winning hockey games if you don't have anyone to celebrate with?

I'm twenty-five years old, and I never wondered that before this year.

But I think I'm finally onto something.

We dispense with Carolina in six games. Then, in a blink, we're mired in round three. Tampa this time.

I'm exhausted. My teammates are exhausted. The staff is punch-drunk. My dad is ecstatic. He won't stop calling me.

I don't have to answer him, though, when I'm on the team bus, shuttling to Tampa's stadium for game four. I text: *Sorry, on the bus! Can't talk*. And then I silence my phone.

There's a message from Gavin, though, so I turn my phone toward the window and read it.

Hope you're sleeping okay on the road. Jordyn wants to know if the hotel is on the beach.

Nope, but there's a nice pool, and I'll get to take a run by the water if it's not ninety degrees. What are you guys up to?

Going to see some mimes in Prospect Park. Then we'll watch the game.

If we make the playoffs next year, I hope there's a game somewhere fun, on the weekend. So I can fly you and Jordyn out to watch the game.

That sounds like fun.

We'll need adjoining rooms. So you can sneak into mine for postgame adult activities.

This trip just keeps getting better.

"All right. Who's got you smiling like that? Didn't even know your face could do that."

I look up quickly and find Castro, my seatmate, watching me. "Oh. Just a friend." And, yup, I feel an instant slap of guilt, because Gavin is so much more to me than that. "A friend for now, anyway." Even if Gavin can't hear me, the correction feels important.

"Ahhh," Castro gives me a knowing smile. "That kind of friend. Who is she? How'd you meet her?"

That's the problem with lying. You have to keep doing it. I don't correct his pronouns, of course. "In a bar, actually."

"You sly dog," he says. "You don't even spend much time at the bar. You're, like, one drink and then *I need my beauty sleep*. Unless you're cheating on your teammates."

"Nah," I say quickly. "Not much of a drinker. Alcohol makes me groggy. But also..." I hesitate.

"Also what?" he presses.

Sharing is so foreign to me that I am suddenly self-conscious. "Well, It's exhausting to always be the new guy. I probably stopped trying to make friends like two teams ago. I figure as long as I shoot the puck straight, that's all you guys really want from me."

"Huh." Castro scratches at his playoff beard. "Not criticizing, here, but that sounds like a hard way to live. We spend so much time together at the rink, on this damn bus. Hockey is the best, but it's a grind. So I figure I gotta make all the minutes count."

"I'm not so good at that," I admit. "Something to aim for, right?"

He shrugs. "I've got it easy, I guess. My wife works for the team. Hope your girl is a hockey fan at least."

I picture Gavin's face and smile. "Yeah, no problem there."

Except it's a lie. Gavin and I still have plenty of hurdles. When it's my turn to explain to the team who I'm dating, that conversation is going to hit different.

Still gives me the cold sweats just thinking about that conversation, and the whispers and sideways glances that will happen afterward.

But I'm going to do it anyway. I promised.

"Who do you think is going to win the Western Conference?" Castro asks, changing the subject.

"Colorado," I say without hesitation. "I need it to be them."

"Your dad got a ring there. And then they drafted you, yeah?" Castro asks. "You want to play them in the finals?"

"I want to *bury* them in the finals. First team to trade me."

He barks out a laugh. "Still bitter? Just against them, or all the teams who traded you?"

"Just them." I clear my throat. "My first bad breakup, so to speak. You wouldn't understand."

"I guess I wouldn't," he says easily. "Hope I never do."

"Amen. Let's grow old together."

He hoots, and smacks my thigh. "Yo! New Guy just made a joke! Someone call ESPN."

"Yeah, yeah."

The bus pulls up in front of the stadium, and I prepare to do battle.

Before we get off, I sneak one more look at my phone.

Play hard! We'll be watching.

I intend to.

THIRTY-SEVEN

Gavin

I LOVE SPORTS–THAT'S why I became an athletic trainer instead of an accountant.

Okay—maybe accounting was never in the cards. But I digress.

Sports is agony and ecstasy. It's hope and disappointment, often during the same game. The highs are really high, but the lows are really low.

So I'm basically losing my mind in front of game seven against Tampa. It's the third period. Brooklyn is down by one goal.

It's way past Jordyn's bedtime, but I can't send her to bed before the final result. I'm not an ogre. We're both strung out, bouncing off the couch every time someone makes a great play.

"I wish we could be there," she keeps saying.

Maybe next year. I can't voice that, of course. But if Hudson and I are somehow a couple, things will be different. Jordyn and I would be able to sit in his comp seats, and nobody would blink.

His arrogant dad can buy his own tickets. I hear they're four grand a pop on StubHub. He can afford it.

My phone rings. I glance at the screen.

"It's Grandma," Jordyn says.

"We'll talk to her tomorrow." After a beat of indecision, I decline the call. "She probably doesn't know our game is on."

Unfortunately, the phone rings a couple more times.

"What if it's important?" Jordyn asks. "What if something is wrong?"

Lord. This is one of those *what-now* moments in parenting. Twenty years from now, I don't want Jordyn declining *my* calls. So what kind of example am I setting?

Although my nerves can't really take a call from Eustace right now. We haven't spoken since her threats to me.

"*Daddy,*" she says, her eyes pleading.

I answer the damn call. "Hello, Eustace. Jordyn and I are a little tied up in the hockey playoffs."

"It's nine forty-five!" she gasps. "Jordyn should be asleep."

Eddie would be glued to this game, too, if he were here. But I don't mention that. I get up off the couch and walk into the bathroom, closing the door behind me. "Did you have something important to say? Or did you just call to question my parenting?"

"Why do you push my buttons?" she asks. "I only called to check in about the summer."

I close my eyes and inhale slowly. "Eustace, the last time we spoke, you threatened to take custody of my child. If that's not pushing buttons, I don't know what is."

She's silent for a moment. "I thought you should know that Chad and I speak of it often. We want to raise Jordyn as our own."

"Yeah? Well I want a winning lottery ticket. But the only way to get it would be to *steal it from its rightful holder*. Which, unlike you, I'm not willing to do."

"There's no need to be dramatic! We wouldn't *steal* her, Gavin—"

"STOP," I insist. "Just stop saying awful things, and trying to pass them off as normal or helpful. Eddie would hate what you're doing to us."

"Not true," she snaps. "He'd want us to care for his daughter. He'd hate that you moved her away from us! To some crappy little apartment in a violent city!"

That's it. I won't take this anymore. "Eddie had a *ten-page* will!" I snap. "If he wanted you to have custody, then you'd have it. But he didn't. And I'm sorry you lost him, and I'm sorry you're upset. But here's a tip—if you want access to Jordyn at all, you'll stop acting like a shrew, and you'll apologize for lawyering up."

"You are so *disrespectful!*" she screeches.

"That's what a good father sounds like!" I yell back. "When someone tries to *take his child.*"

"Listen—"

"No, *you* listen. Eddie would be *furious* with you over this. I'm doing everything I can for Jordyn, and he'd be so ashamed of you right now. Is this how you honor the memory of your only son? By trying to intimidate his husband and invalidate his wishes?"

She sniffles.

"I wanted Jordyn to have her grandparents in her life. She loves you. But if you can't stay in your lane, we're done here. I will *never* back down."

She sobs.

"You're not going to break me with your insults. There is nothing wrong with the choices I've made. I'm doing the best I can. If you can't be gracious, then you can't be in our lives. That's it. The end. Please think about it."

Then I hang up the phone, and take a deep, gasping breath. I'm shaking. Anger isn't my go-to emotion, and I barely know how to handle the rage in my heart. So I lean against the tiled wall and try to slow my breathing.

Until Jordyn suddenly pounds on the door. "Daddy! Hudson scored! He got a goal!"

A goal? Holy shit.

On pure adrenaline, I fling open the bathroom door and gallop back to the TV, just in time for the replay. And there he is—evading a Tampa skater, then deking the goalie. He shoots with the barest flick of his wrist, and then everyone in the crowd jumps to their feet.

"YES BABY!" I shriek.

He's tied up the game. There's only two minutes left on the clock, and they're probably headed into overtime.

There goes Jordyn's bedtime. Again.

I push Eustace's criticism out of my mind. "Sweetie, how about you put on your pajamas and brush your teeth? So you'll be ready for bed when the game finally ends."

She looks down at her purple clothing. "I can't change *now*, Daddy! This is what I wear when Brooklyn wins!"

My heart stops. And for the first time in months, I hear Eddie's laughter in my head again. His beautiful laugh.

Tears spring to my eyes, and I sit down on the couch.

"Daddy?" she asks, wide-eyed. "What happened?"

I swipe my eyes with the back of my hand. "Nothing, Ducky. I was just remembering how your Papa liked to wear his Boston jersey when the game was on."

She comes over and sits on my knee. "I'll go to bed right after somebody wins."

"All right," I say, pulling her into my lap. Then I explain how sudden death overtime works. Although I don't call it that.

"So Brooklyn just has to get one more," she says. "And it's over?"

"Yup," I agree. "Just one more."

They resurface the ice, and then we watch, tense, as Brooklyn goes on the attack one more time. Our guys must be exhausted. But Hudson is skating as hard as ever.

He comes off the ice after a shift, though, and Coach sends Ian Crikey out in his place. Another talented young defenseman. He wants it bad, too.

But sometimes you can want something so badly that you strangle it. And that's what happens to Crikey. In his zeal to get the puck, he hauls a Tampa player off his feet by grabbing his jersey.

The ref calls the foul.

"Oh no," Jordyn breathes.

Oh yes. Coach sends out the PK team, but the disruption gives Tampa a second wind.

They score twenty-two seconds into the penalty. The red light goes off behind Beacon, and all our guys deflate. Just like that. The season is over.

"Oh NO!" Jordyn's lip is quivering. "This is terrible."

I feel heavy inside. I thought Hudson would get to play for the cup. He must be devastated.

But I turn off the TV, and scoop my daughter off the couch. "I'm sorry, Ducky. But they made it almost to the tippy top. They're one of the best four teams in the world. But sometimes that's as far as you can go."

She wraps her arms around me, exhausted. "Is it really over? I wanted Hudson to win."

"He wins a lot," I remind her. "And tomorrow is another day. Another chance to get it right."

I'm not sure she's buying what I'm selling. But that's okay. I ask her to brush her teeth and change her clothes. Then I put her to bed. "Don't think sad thoughts," I whisper as I turn out the light. "Now Hudson gets to take a summer vacation."

"Oh," she says sleepily. "That's nice."

"Yeah." I kiss her on the forehead. Then I leave Jordyn in her room, only to pace around my apartment. I'm still processing the end of the season. Hudson's done. But so am I. If they'd won, I'd be back at work tomorrow taping ankles and palpating sore muscles.

But now I'm done, too, for eight whole weeks.

Just like Hudson. I wonder if he's shell-shocked like I am.

I grab a sticky note and scribble a message on it. Then I step into the hallway and stick it onto his door.

Proud of you. Amazing goal!

Brutal ending, tho. :(

Call me if you want to talk. No matter what time.

THIRTY-EIGHT

Hudson

LOSING ALWAYS BLOWS. But this time it blows a little less, because I'm surrounded by a team that finally feels like mine.

We're all at the tavern. The GM is buying drinks, and the coach is shaking hands. There's lots of back-slapping and tired smiles.

"Everyone, gather 'round!" Coach Worthington says. He picks up a butter knife off the bar and bangs on his pint glass.

Everybody shuts up pretty fast, too.

"I just want to say that you should be proud of your season. We accomplished a lot together. I feel great about our chances next year, too. Train hard before I see you again in August. But first, I want you to be well-rested."

That gets a round of applause. We're tired.

"Before we part for the season, I want to give out one more game puck. Jimbo?"

The equipment guy pulls a puck out of his pocket and passes it to the coach.

"Folks, this one's for Hudson Newgate. Not only did he have a great season with us these past five months, but his goal tonight was flawless. We're going to have to find you a new nickname next year, though. Nobody can be the New Guy forever, yeah? Here you go, son."

My teammates shift out of the way so I can come forward and take the puck from him. "Thank you, sir."

"Terrific season," he says to me, with a bracing clap on my shoulder.

"It's been my pleasure to play for you this season."

Everyone claps, and I can feel my face redden. It's weird to suddenly be the center of attention. I shove the puck in my pocket and try to look humble.

But there's no denying this is a big moment for me. I finally did what I came here to do. I played my heart out, and I gave it my all, and I made a difference to this team.

And for once, everybody knows it.

Coach ends his speech by thanking a few people, and then everybody goes back to drinking and carousing.

I finish my beer and look around. Castro and Heidi Jo are trying to get a game of darts going. Trevi is nose to nose with his pretty wife, deep in conversation. Those guys know who they're going home with tonight, and they don't have to hide it.

As I set my bottle down on a table, something crystalizes inside me. I can have what they have. Even if Brooklyn doesn't offer me an early contract renegotiation, that shouldn't stand in my way.

I want a real relationship with Gavin. And I'm willing to take some risks to have it. Next season is going to be different for me. No matter what.

It's already past one a.m., so I shake a few more hands and then head for the door.

The walk home is short. I take the same path as with Gavin the first night we met, when I did everything wrong. I made so many mistakes with him, but by some miracle he likes me anyway.

As I mount the stairs, I picture him asleep in his bed, on the other side of the wall from mine. And I know I'm ready to knock that wall down. I have big things to say to him. Big, scary things.

So when I find his note on my door, I don't even unlock my apartment. I stand in the hallway and phone him, even though it's really late.

He declines the call, but I hear shuffling feet a moment later, and a bleary Gavin—clad only in boxers—unlocks the door.

"Hey," I whisper.

He beckons me inside, so I quietly close the door behind myself and follow him into his bedroom. I close the door there, too, and kick off my shoes. Then I remove my tie and suit coat and drape them over his doorknob.

Gavin flops back into the bed. I remove my trousers and my dress shirt and drape them over his heater before climbing in there without an invitation.

I belong here with him. I know that now. I don't remember the moment he went from being my obsession to becoming my dream. But here I am, wrapping my arms around his sleepy body, and resting my heart against his.

Gavin's arms close around me. "I'm sorry about the loss. Jordyn cried. But you were awesome. I hope you're proud."

"I'm feeling a lot of gratitude," I say, tugging him closer to me. He's sleep-warmed and heavy. "And I came here to tell you that I made a decision."

"You did?" His arm snakes sleepily around my waist.

"Yeah. When training camp starts again, I'm going to come out. No matter where I am with my contract."

His head pops off my shoulder. "Really?"

"Really. I can't put my life on hold forever. If Brooklyn doesn't want me now, there's nothing I can do to make them change their minds."

"Whoa." He's awake now. "So how would that work?"

"I still have to go to L.A. for a month. But I'll miss you like crazy. What would you say if I rented a nice beach house? You and Jordyn could come out to California for a week-long vacation."

"Sounds fun," he says. "If I can swing it."

"It's my idea. I'd be the one buying your tickets."

"But..."

"No buts. I'm the guy who has to train across the country, right? That's my problem to solve. And I want to solve it by bringing you guys out to see me. We can take Jordyn to Disneyland. I guess you could pay for that, if you're so inclined."

He thinks about it for a moment. "Wow. All right. But I don't know if I'm giving in because you're right, or because I want to stay in a California beach house with you."

"Look," I rub his back. "I have more money than time. If you don't let me spend it on you sometimes, I'll see less of you. And that will make me sad. It's selfish, but I think I'm onto something here."

"Okay," he says wearily. "But then what?"

"I'll be back to Brooklyn in late July. I'll get myself into the right headspace to come out to my team. And then—with your permission—we'll tell Henry about us, and you can discuss your job protocols with him. If you still think I'm worth complicating your life for."

"Baby, I won't be able to help myself." He plants a kiss on my bare chest. "I want to be part of it. I want to watch what you can do next season. I want to watch you put down roots with that team, even if it means I can't work there, too."

"That would be unacceptable," I say immediately. "There *has* to be a way for the team to get their heads around the idea of us."

"Guess we'll find out," he says quietly. "We won't know unless we try."

"Think about it," I beg. "I don't want to bring this to Henry unless you're really okay with it. If you want to take the chance."

He kisses my chest slowly. Twice. "Fortune favors the bold. I don't want to walk away from you. Not if you're willing to take a big risk for me."

"*All* the risks. I'm ready." I slide a hand right onto his ass. "And guess what? As of tonight, we don't have any more gametime conflicts for a while. So now we can do whatever we want, yeah?" I give his ass a slow, dirty squeeze.

"You make a few good points." He moves his mouth to my neck, sucking gently on my skin.

That's all it takes for my dick to harden inside my briefs. "Fuck, baby. Give me that mouth. It's been too long."

He obviously agrees, because we come together in a heated kiss. When our tongues meet, I feel a rush of gratitude. It's been weeks since I've tasted him, and I can't get enough.

"Mmm," he says between kisses. "I know our dry spell was my idea. But I don't think I can hold out any longer." His hands are already shoving my briefs down my hips.

My body is totally down with this. My cock springs free, and I scramble out of my underwear, and then get to work on his.

Mere seconds later, we're buck naked and making out like champs on his sheets. Our cocks knock together as he ruts slowly against me. I feel like a wildfire that's about to get out of control.

"I've got...to slow down," he says between kisses.

"Uh-huh," I agree, panting against his mouth. "Don't come yet."

"You could fuck me," he whispers against my lips. "I want it."

I groan. And then I grasp his hips in firm hands and hold him still. "Okay, time out. Actually, there's one more thing I forgot."

"Condoms?" he rasps. "I've got some."

"Awesome. But that's not what I meant. Would you believe I didn't come here for sex? And then you answered the door in your underwear, and I kind of lost my mind."

He tucks his face into the hollow of my throat and laughs.

I run my fingers through his hair and smile. "Here's the thing. I want very badly to put you on your hands and knees and fuck you."

He lets out a muffled, horny groan.

"But you should know that I'm also falling for you. You're the only guy who's ever made me feel this way—like I want everything with you. And I'm probably gonna make a lot of mistakes, okay? I'm not good at this stuff, but I care about you. A lot. Maybe you aren't on the same page yet. Maybe you'll never get there. But I'm not just here for a quick fuck."

He sits up suddenly, blinking at me in surprise.

"You don't have to say anything," I whisper into the silence. "But I wanted you to know I care about you."

When he finally speaks, his whisper is hoarse. "Swear to God I don't know what I ever did to deserve you."

I snort. "Let's not pretend you couldn't do better than me."

"*No*," he insists, covering my mouth with one hand. "Don't do that. You don't get to make that speech—which is just about the most romantic thing anyone has ever said to me—and then walk it back. There's nothing harder than putting your heart on the line."

"Nah." Sitting up, I brush his hand away so that I can respectfully disagree. "Falling for you is the easiest thing I've ever done. You smiled at me that first night, and it was game over. It's just taken me a few months to admit how much I'd risk to wake up next to you every day."

He straddles my lap, and takes my face in two hands. "You deserve everything. But I've been pretty dead-set on never loving anyone again."

"Getting widowed will do that to a guy," I whisper. "And you have a child to think of. My eyes are wide open, okay? I just want you to know that I'm here for you. I'll take whatever you can give me."

He blinks back at me, like maybe I've stunned him into silence. Too much talking, I guess. So I kiss him.

THIRTY-NINE

Gavin

HUDSON'S KISSES are slow and deep. As if his tongue is on an exploratory mission, and my whole soul is uncharted territory. I've never been kissed more thoroughly in my life.

And I realize I'm terrified.

It isn't that I don't think I can fall in love with Hudson. The problem is that I already am.

He breaks our kiss and whispers to me. "Baby? Are you okay?"

"Yup. Never better."

His hands go still on my skin. "Then why did you get so tense? I didn't mean to scare you with my big speech."

"I know." And I can't really explain myself without sounding like an ass. But wanting Hudson was easier when I thought I couldn't have him. It felt safe to have feelings for a guy who wasn't ready to take any risks for me.

But here he is, proving himself to be the big-hearted man that I already knew him to be. Boldly asking for the things I'm too afraid to hope for again.

You must think I'm such a coward. He said that to me once when he was explaining why he was still in the closet.

Tonight, the coward in this bed is me.

"I want this. It's just that…" I swallow roughly.

"…Moving on is hard?" he guesses. "You still love Eddie."

"I'll always love him. But I never want to go through that again. You are every bit as amazing, though, and I don't want to die alone. So, yeah, I'm the picture of mental health right here."

He chuckles warmly. "You want to continue this some other time? We can see each other tomorrow."

"No," I insist. Then I wrap my arms tightly around him, just to make the point clear. "Sending you away isn't going to help. I need you right here, and it scares me."

"I'd only be on the other side of the wall." He kisses my jaw, and runs a hand down my flank. "You were patient with me, Gavin. I can be patient with you."

"Don't go. I want you here. I want to visit you in California, but only if I tell Jordyn that you and I are dating."

His eyes brighten, and he smiles at me. "Really?"

"Really. But only if you want that, too. We're a team, though. If you don't consider yourself the kind of guy who wants a child in his life, that's kind of a deal breaker."

He kisses the corner of my mouth. "Baby, I know you guys are a two-for-one special. And even if I never saw myself as the kind of guy who wanted to make babies, that doesn't mean I can't love your kid. She's pretty great, too. If you tell her we're dating, I will be just as careful with her feelings as I plan to be with yours."

My heart practically bursts. "She'll be thrilled if I tell her we're dating. I'm honestly a little afraid for you. You have to practice saying no before we go to Disneyland."

"What? Why?"

"Because I know you. And I don't want to bring home three suitcases full of souvenirs."

He snickers. "Fine. Let's practice."

I press myself a little closer to him. It's hard to be this happy and also think at the same time. "Okay. Saying no to a little girl is hard. It's advanced work. You should practice saying no to me first."

"Sure," he says. "Hit me with anything."

I lick his neck. "Okay, hot stuff, how about we eat seven cookies, each, and some cotton candy?"

"No way, you naughty boy." Hudson runs his finger down my abs, and I get goose bumps. "Sugar is poison."

"Good work." I whisper into his ear. "That one was a softball, though. What if I suggested that we play ping-pong all night, and stay up past our bedtime?"

"Well..." He considers. "That doesn't sound so bad, because ping-pong is life. But let's not, okay? There are other things I'd like to do with you instead." He kisses my shoulder. And then my nipple.

"Mmm." I flop back onto the mattress to make more of my skin available to him. "Do you want to fuck me?"

He raises his head. "Are we still role-playing? I could try to say no. But it might come out as a yes. A guy only has so much willpower."

I laugh, and then run a hand down his abs, stopping just short of his cock. "Fine. If I'm going to do this big, scary thing—if I'm going to get involved for real—I deserve a good banging. Don't you agree?"

When I curve my hand around his length, he tips his head back and groans. "You deserve something all right."

Bracing my hands on the mattress, I dip my head and take him onto my tongue. I've missed this so much—the salty heat of him. His gasp of pleasure, and the way his thick fingers tangle in my hair.

"Fuck," he curses as I take him all the way into my mouth. "Yeah. Just like that."

I pop off him. "Lie down."

He immediately complies. But then he rolls onto his side, stretches out diagonally, and beckons to me. "Flip around. I've got work to do, too."

When I realize what he's suggesting, my shiver is pure anticipation. I stretch out, sixty-nine style, taking him into my mouth again.

He doesn't make me wait. A roughened palm takes me in hand. It's glorious.

I prop myself up on one elbow, so I can glance over my shoulder at his handsome face. The sight of my cock in his hand is wildly stimulating. I clench my thighs together and remember to breathe as he lowers his mouth to my tip.

Wet heat envelops me, and Hudson lets out a moan of pleasure. Not to be outdone, I turn back to the matter at hand. His taste and his scent are making me crazy. And that's not even counting the hot heaven of his mouth on my cock.

Every last doubt leaves my mind as we lick and nibble and stroke each other. After a time, Hudson releases me. I gasp for air and try to slow my heart rate as he opens my bedside table and pulls out the lube. "Can I?" he asks.

"Yeah," I croak. Then I shiver, just anticipating what's to come.

"On your stomach," he demands.

Another shiver. And the sound of the lube bottle as he coats his fingers. I grab a pillow and hug it under my chest as his naughty hand begins to massage into my crease.

"Christ," I mumble. My body relaxes against the bed, as if commanded by a higher power.

I haven't done this in years. But I want it so bad. Hudson is shameless, teasing me open, penetrating me with a thick finger. My legs splay open and my brain goes fuzzy with static. I sigh into the pillow as he finds my spot with his fingertip.

"Good boy," he whispers. "So hungry for this, yeah?"

My response is a sexed-up moan.

"You ready for two?"

"Anything," I slur, thrusting my hips against the bed.

Hudson chuckles. I hear the sound of a condom wrapper opening, and then he goes back to playing with me. Stretching me with his fingers. Scissoring them while I try not to make too much noise.

He's doing all the work, and calling all the shots. It's exactly what I needed—someone else to hold the reins for a minute. Someone to make all the decisions.

Like magic, I'm so turned on that I'm humping the bed. I'm human Jell-O. He could mold me into any shape, and I'd go willingly.

"You want my cock? Lift up, honey."

Even my liquid brain can follow that instruction. I cock my hips toward him a few degrees, and he slowly enters me, letting out a deep sound from his chest. "You're killing me," he whispers. "Sexiest man alive. Taking me like a champ."

I close my eyes and thrust back against him, and hear his breath catch.

Rising up onto all fours, I rock back again. "Give me more. I need it."

"You're going to get it," he says, rubbing my back with one strong hand. "For once in my life, I'm not in a rush."

"But what about my needs?" I look over my shoulder and see him smiling down at me. Then he takes my hips in two hands and gives me the thrust I'm looking for. "Thank fuck."

He starts to move, and I drop my head, letting even more tension drain out of me. There's a reason I didn't look at another man for two years until I met Hudson. I was waiting for the right guy. And it's not just chemistry, either. It takes a lot of trust for me to get this naked with anyone. I'd forgotten how magical it feels to let go so completely.

We find a rhythm. The only sounds are the gentle squeak of the bed, and his low-voiced praise of my blissed out self. At some point he pulls out and urges me onto my back.

I go where I'm told, lifting my knees. His hands land on my shoulders, his hooded gaze on my face. We are made of heat and friction.

"Good boy," he whispers, taking my cock in one hand and stroking me firmly. "You're perfect. I need you to come now."

"Okay," I slur, and suddenly that seems like a super good idea. I gaze up into his dark eyes and reach for it as his strong body works above me, his arms flexing. It's the most erotic thing I've ever seen.

But I don't climax until he closes his eyes and gasps. "Fuck, I need you."

The room blurs and I paint my abs with my release, gasping that I need him, too.

It's not poetry. But it's still true.

FORTY

Hudson

JULY - SIX WEEKS LATER

"HEY, sleeping beauty. I brought you some coffee."

My eyes slit open to find Gavin standing over me. He's wearing shorts and a Brooklyn Hockey Training Staff T-shirt that hugs his chest, and he's holding a steaming mug in one hand.

"What time is it?" I croak over the whir of Gavin's air conditioning.

"Almost nine. The kid and I are heading out soon for her checkup."

I sit up quickly. "God, nine? I never sleep late." At least I never used to. "You wore me out," I whisper, reaching for the coffee.

He plants a kiss on my messy hair. "It might have been me. Or it might have been the hundred weighted sit-ups you did during our movie."

The season starts in mere days, so I've been working out like a beast. "Thanks for the coffee. I'll get out of your way."

"You're not in our way. I knew you had a call this morning, though. I think you said nine-thirty."

"Oh, yeah." I rub the sleep out of my eyes. "That damn nutritionist. Waste of time, but it makes my father happy." I swing my feet over the edge of the bed and stand up. I'm wearing a new pair of sleep shorts and a T-shirt. Had to start sleeping in clothes, just in case Jordyn walks into the bedroom.

"Hi, Hudson!" she says as I emerge like a zombie. "I have to go to the doctor. And Daddy won't tell me if there's going to be any shots."

"Because Daddy doesn't know," Gavin says as he sits on the sofa. "Now come and sit down for me, or the doctor will think we don't know how hairbrushes work."

"What if I don't like this doctor?" Jordyn asks, popping to the rug between his knees. "She won't be like our doctors at home. In New Hampshire," she adds quickly, but not before Gavin winces.

"If the doctor isn't nice, we'd find another one for next time." He begins to gently brush out sections of her hair with a practiced stroke. "But this is your friend Bella's doctor, and she's known her forever. Bella wouldn't steer us wrong."

"Okay," Jordyn says warily.

"Nobody likes getting weighed and measured by the doctor," he says lightly. "But her job is to make sure you're healthy. It doesn't take long, and there's probably a sticker in it for you at the end. Or something like that. And don't forget—you're going to Bella's house afterwards."

"Right," she says. "I need to bring my bathing suit for the playground."

"I already put it in your backpack," he assures her. "Braids?"

"Yes. *Please.*"

I take a sip of my coffee, and admire the blond hairs on Gavin's muscular forearms as he fixes his daughter's hair.

Now that we're officially a couple, I don't feel guilty for staring at him anymore. And he's totally on the same page, because I've caught him giving me hot glances many times during the past few weeks.

It's been a great summer. The best one of my adult life. Our California vacation was the highlight—I'd rented a house with a pool, and walking distance from the beach. We did a barbecue on the sand, and went to Disneyland. Twice.

My phone currently holds about seven million photos that Jordyn took. And I can't bring myself to delete a single one.

Telling her that Gavin and I are dating had turned out to be easier than I'd thought. Her eyes had widened comically. And then she'd asked: "Does this mean I can go to *all* the hockey games now?"

"No," Gavin had said at the exact same time I'd said "yes." So then I had to backtrack, because hockey games on school nights are apparently a bad idea.

But she's taken our relationship in stride. It's blown my mind a little, if I'm honest. Now if only my upcoming conversation with the team would go that well, too.

If it doesn't, there's always whiskey.

"All set, Ducky. Now we'd better head out," Gavin says to his daughter. Then he turns to me. "What should we do this afternoon?" he asks. "I had an idea."

"Did you now?" I ask in an innocent tone. Although my implication is anything but innocent. Tomorrow, Gavin and Jordyn are leaving for a two-week stay in New Hampshire. After several difficult conversations with his monster-in-law, he got her to apologize. She even admitted that she has no shot at custody.

Gavin—proving himself the bigger man once again—has agreed to a lengthy visit before Jordyn's fancy summer program begins. I'm going to miss them.

But with Jordyn at a friend's house, we'd have the afternoon to ourselves.

"Here's my idea," he says with a smirk. "Any chance you'll be hitting the gym this afternoon? I'd like to lift, too. And the place will probably be empty."

"Hell yes." I carry my empty coffee mug to the sink for a wash. "We can do that."

"Cool. See you there?" He crosses to me, and I turn my head for a kiss.

"Eww!" Jordyn complains. The first time she said that, I was worried. But then I realized she's against *all* kissing. Any time a TV character kisses, she makes gagging noises.

Gavin ignores her and plants a second one on me. "I'll text you when I'm on my way."

"Can't wait," I say a little dreamily.

Once they're gone, I rinse my mug and leave it in the dish rack. After scanning Gavin's apartment for any of my stuff I might have left lying around, I go back to my apartment on the other side of the wall.

Still hate that wall. I've actually browsed the rental listings for a big apartment in a nicer building. Just to see what's out there.

It's too soon, though. When I brought it up with Gavin, he wasn't ready for that. "We need to take things slow," he'd said. "For Jordyn's sake. Besides—our current setup is pretty convenient, right? We have a lot of privacy here."

He isn't wrong. But I still fantasize about a day when he's only an arm's reach away.

While I'm setting up my laptop for my Zoom call with the nutritionist, my father calls. I let it go to voicemail, because he's not my favorite person right now.

Last week I'd finally broken the news to him that I'm planning to come out to my team. He'd immediately tried to talk me out of it. "Wait until we've got a contract," he'd argued. "Brooklyn isn't ready to negotiate with you yet. But any day now! Just cool your jets. What's a few more months?"

But I've been listening to this argument for years. "I'm done waiting. And I can't do that to Gavin," I'd insisted. "I'm not the only person in this relationship."

He hadn't liked that argument one bit. "You're smarter than this. You shouldn't do anything to make yourself less valuable."

That's when I'd snapped. "God, do you hear yourself? You just said out loud that I'm less valuable to you than a straight guy."

"To *them*," he'd roared. "Jesus. Don't put words in my mouth. Any player who draws media attention around his personal life is a liability. I don't make the rules."

The shitty thing is that he's probably right. It's just that I can't live on those terms anymore. My life is worth more than my contract value. Even if it took me way too long to realize it.

Since that call, I've been avoiding my father. Coming out is scary enough without his opinions echoing around in my head. But he texts a moment later. *Pick up. I need to speak to you. It's important.*

For a long minute I just stare at the phone, wondering what he wants to talk about. He's being vague—possibly intentionally. I'm tired of his games.

On the other hand, I want a new contract so badly I can taste it. And so curiosity wins out. I pick up the phone and dial him.

"Hudson, glad I caught you," he says.

I roll my eyes.

"Now, don't panic."

"Great opener, Dad. Why am I panicking?"

"A buddy of mine heard your name mentioned. There's some big three-way trade in the works."

My blood goes cold. Literally cold. My hands feel suddenly clammy. "That doesn't make any sense. Brooklyn won't trade me. Not after that season I just had."

"That's what I think, too. But this is a good thing—we want the sharks circling. The more interest there is in your name, the better."

"Makes sense," I say mildly. But my heart is thumping madly.

"You need to delay, though," he says.

"Delay what?" I demand, even if I have an idea.

"Your big, uh, announcement. You know what happened last time."

He can't even say it. "Until when? I was thinking August fifteenth, Dad. The team goes to the Hamptons for a golf thing and some scrimmages."

He sucks on his teeth. "That might be a little fast. We want that roster solid. How about October?"

My heart slumps. My literal nightmare is getting traded right after I come out. *Again.*

And my dad has a point about the timing—lots of trades go through during training camp, as the rosters are gelling.

"I'll think about it," I say grudgingly.

"Good man. Hey—aren't you late for your call with the nutritionist?"

I want to scream.

Two hours later I'm lying on a mat in the stretching room at the gym, trying to sort out my hip flexors, and also my life.

Only one of those things is working.

"Hey!" Gavin says, dropping his gym bag on the mat when he finds me there. "Let's do this. Is it legs day?"

"Yeah," I say roughly. "How was the doctor's?"

"Piece of cake. Nice office. No shots."

"Sweet."

Then, stretching his quads, he launches into a story about the first time he had to take Jordyn in for shots.

But I'm only half listening. All I can hear is my father telling me not to do anything that would *lower my value.*

"...And she screamed right up until the moment the lollipop went into her mouth!"

It takes me a second to realize that Gavin has fallen silent. I turn to him regretfully. "Sorry."

His brow furrows. "Something the matter?"

"No," I say immediately. "Just spaced out for a minute."

"How'd your call go?"

"With my dad?"

He tilts his head, a quizzical expression on his face. "You spoke to your dad? Is that why you're in a mood?"

"I'm not in a *mood*," I grumble.

Oops. That's what it sounds like when a guy is truly in a mood.

His eyes narrow. "What did that asshole say now?"

"He, uh, asked me to announce in October. After the flurry of preseason trades."

"What?" His jaw drops. "You said August fifteenth."

"I know I did. But..." I clear my throat, trying to choose my words carefully.

But he doesn't wait for me to finish. "You chose August fifteenth. That date gave me plenty of time to work out the thorny job questions with Henry, before the season officially starts."

"Gavin, I'm going to do it. I *swear*. I just need to think a little harder about the date."

His hurt look says that he doesn't believe me. "What if October comes, and your father says—*It's not a great time. How about January?* What then?"

The question lands like a punch to the chest. Because that is absolutely something my father might do. "I'm going to do it," I whisper, climbing to my feet. God, I need some air. "Just—I need to think about what he said. Maybe I'll go for a run."

"You do that," he says sharply.

Then I hear footsteps out in the hallway, and I practically dislocate my shoulder turning to see if anyone is out there listening.

Gavin watches this reaction with a cold look in his eye. Like he can see right through my cheap, twisted words.

Like I've just proven once again that I am a goddamn coward.

My teammate—Crikey—sticks his head into the room. "Hey guys. Just wondered who was around on a hot July day."

"Hey," I say stiffly. Then I walk right past him and leave the gym, barely stopping in the dressing room to grab my phone and keys.

FORTY-ONE

Hudson

TEN PACES outside the practice facility, I already feel like an asshole. But I don't turn around. Instead, I start running. It's hot as blazes, and I don't have any kind of plan. I just take off down the street.

Five minutes later I'm in an unfamiliar neighborhood. The big buildings give way to smaller houses. They're old in an interesting way. If I were in a better mood, I'd look closer.

But I keep running, baking in the sunshine, until someone gives a loud catcall. And then I hear my name.

I stop suddenly, turning to look around. And I spot our team captain—O'Doul—sitting on the stoop of one of the houses. "Yo! Crazy man! You lost?"

Yes, I am. "Just, uh, running," I say brilliantly.

"I can see that." He gets up off the porch. "Want to have a burger with me?"

"Well..." I don't, really. But my brain is static and I can't think of a reasonable excuse on the fly.

"You do, trust me," He says. "Come on." He leads me literally across the street, and into a sleepy little French bistro. Most of the other customers are elderly women sipping coffee and eating pastries.

"This doesn't look like a burger joint," I point out.

"They know me here."

Sure enough, a smiling waiter with a thick accent seats us at the nicest table in front of the window.

"Two of my usual, Pierre," O'Doul says.

"Oui monsieur." Then he pours sparkling water into two fancy glasses and retreats.

I glance around the restaurant, which is quirky and cool. And I wish I could have brought Gavin here already. God, if I get traded, I might never see him again.

"All right," O'Doul says, smoothing the napkin onto his knee. "Why do you look so bummed out?"

"You're a regular here," I say insensibly.

He just nods.

"I've never been a regular *anywhere*."

He lifts a curious eyebrow, but waits for me to continue.

"There's a rumor. I might..." A wave of nausea nearly overcomes me. "I might get traded again."

He blinks, surprised. "Any reason to think it's true? Players don't usually hear that shit."

"My father," I mutter. "He hears a lot of shit."

"Ah." O'Doul picks up his glass and takes a drink. I never really pictured him as a fancy restaurant guy. Then again, I don't spend a lot of time with my teammates. Figures I wouldn't know them very well.

Suddenly, this feels like a huge loss.

"Your dad is an interesting guy," he says carefully. "What's the point of telling you there's a trade rumor if it might not come true?"

"To warn me, I guess?" *Or to control me.*

Shit. That's probably the real reason.

O'Doul looks out the window, like he's thinking. "I know your trade history is a burden. You feel like you can never relax."

"Because I can't. I'm always remaking my game to suit the new team."

His gaze returns to mine. "I came to hockey a much different way than you. I didn't have a family. No real mentors. Twenty bucks in my wallet to feed me for a week. But it was easier that way. Nobody telling me how to be. I had no choice but to be a hundred percent me, all the time. Didn't know any better."

I'd heard snippets of his story in the locker room. O'Doul was an orphan who grew up on the streets. "Yeah, it was different for me. There's pictures of me skating in diapers on an NHL practice rink."

He snorts. "Excellent blackmail material. But I don't envy you that family dynasty thing. Or the feeling that getting traded again would be a failure."

"It would be," I point out.

"Would it, though?" he shrugs. "Getting traded right now would suck, but it would also mean that somebody wants you."

"Yeah, but I have no *life*."

He nods slowly, my anguish ringing between us. "I hear that. Except for one thing—did anyone at this table get traded today?"

"Not yet. Day ain't over, though."

He taps the table with two thick fingers. "You're here right now. And you can't live your life looking over your shoulder. Maybe it's easy for me to say, because I've never been traded. But you have to make every day count. Otherwise what's the point?"

I shrug.

"Sure hope you don't look at your career as a series of *almosts*," he says. "How many NHL games have you played? Two hundred?"

"Almost three hundred."

He smiles suddenly. "Dude, that's a *real* career. There's guys out there living off the memory of a single season. Or a single game. You are already living the dream. Don't be so het up about trades that you can't enjoy it. That'd be a crime."

I take a sip of my water to cover my reaction, because those truths land hard on me.

Then a waiter appears, setting two loaded plates down in front of us. There's a burger—with avocado and bacon on it—inside a glossy homemade bun. And a stack of deeply golden hand-cut fries. "Wow. Looks amazing. But I shouldn't have the bread."

"Oh, it is." He picks up his burger immediately. "It'd be a crime not to eat that bun, dude," he says, reading my mind. "But you do you."

"Fuck it," I grumble, picking up the burger and taking a very satisfying bite. Then I shove a fry in my mouth and groan. "*God.* What makes that taste so good?" It's more than just a fried potato. It's heaven.

"Truffle oil," he says. "I don't even know what a truffle is. All I know is that I eat these fries a couple times a week."

"You're a smart man, O'Doul."

He laughs. "Hardly. Not even a little. What I am is *old*, and with age comes wisdom. It's not the same as intelligence. Wisdom is shit you learn by being around long enough to make a lot of mistakes."

"Old at thirty-six, huh?"

He points a fry at me. "Trust me. Hockey years are like dog years. That makes me—what's 36 times 7?"

"Old," I grunt. "Too hungry for math."

"It goes by fast, though. Blink, and you'll be at the final days of your career. That's why you need to make 'em all count."

"Yeah, I'm eating fried potatoes. For me, that counts as living."

He grins. "Good work, kid. I knew you could do it."

O'Doul treats me to lunch, and I leave the restaurant feeling shored up and grateful.

The first thing I do as I walk toward home is call Gavin. It goes to voicemail, and my heart plunges.

Shit. I've really fucked up now. He's not even taking my call.

But then my phone rings thirty seconds later. It's Gavin.

"Hey," he says as soon as I answer. "I was on a chair at the top of Jordyn's closet, looking for her extra bathing suits."

"Oh. Sorry." I clear my throat. "Let me start over. I want to apologize for running out on you today. That was stupid. I was in a panic over something my dad told me. Trade rumors about me. That's why Dad wanted me to wait."

He sucks in his breath. "Why didn't you just *tell* me that?"

"Because I let him get into my head. O'Doul just asked me why my father would even tell me something like that. He has to know it would make me crazy, yeah?"

"He *should* know," Gavin agrees. "And if he doesn't, then he hasn't really been listening to you, has he?"

Stopping on the sidewalk, I consider the question. "He's always trying to keep me in line. There's a reason his ringtone is Under My Thumb."

"I did notice that," Gavin says quietly. "You already know his flaws, but you fell for it anyway. He's got you all twisted up on a rumor."

This is true. But my father knows a lot, and the crappy things he says are based in reality, even if they're hard to hear.

"Serious question—does he have to be your agent?" Gavin asks. "What if there were someone else you could talk to about this? Someone with a clear head."

"You have a clear head." I start walking again.

"Not so much," he says with a sigh. "I have big feelings about you coming out. I'm definitely in the pro column, here. Your dad is against it. Maybe you need more guidance than the people who care about you can give."

Now I'm smiling, right here on Gold Street. Gavin always has my back. "I appreciate the concern. I really do. You're trying not to be pushy, while my father doesn't bother restraining himself. But I can't switch agents. He'd never speak to me again."

Half a second later, I realize what I've just said to a man whose parents literally don't speak to him. "Wait. I'm sorry. I don't mean that literally. But it would be very awkward, and embarrassing to him if his own son fired him."

Gavin sighs. "Okay. I guess I'll shut up about this."

"Don't ever shut up," I insist. "I value your opinion more than you could know. But I called to tell you that it doesn't matter what he thinks. I'm going to come out on the fifteenth just like I said. He won't like it, but I don't really care."

"Wow," Gavin whispers. "Okay."

"O'Doul hit me with some hard truths today. I'm watching my life go by, and all I've got to show for it are a few million dollars and a lot of sore muscles."

"To be fair, they are very attractive muscles," Gavin says.

"You sweet-talker. But I'm not joking. And, yeah, kinda scared to rip the Band-Aid off, but I'm going to do it anyway. I swear."

"All right. You're coming over tonight?"

"Of course I am. Wish you didn't have to go away tomorrow."

"Me too. But once the season starts up again, I'll see you every day at work."

"Yes, you will." What was I even thinking, listening to my dad? I need to come out so we can get right with the organization. "Dinner tonight is on me. Let's order something glorious, and split a bottle of wine."

"Can't wait," he says.

And that's exactly how I feel.

FORTY-TWO

Gavin

TWO WEEKS in New Hampshire with Eddie's parents is a long time.

If he were still here, even Eddie would agree.

Don't get me wrong—their new mansion makes for a great vacation. The pool is glorious, and Jordyn and I swim every day. She and I take several hikes in the White Mountains, and Jordyn goes horseback riding with her grandmother. Twice.

In the evenings, we sit on the grandiose patio of their McMansion and dine on lobster rolls and grilled corn and ice cream. Or steak and Caesar salad.

I don't even have to do dishes, because they have staff for that.

Still, I can't wait to get back to New York. My inbox is full of training camp schedules and new player files. I can feel the preseason excitement from two hundred miles away.

And I miss Hudson like crazy.

When the sun goes down, I get lonely. I've already read four thrillers and a memoir, and listened to hours of podcasts in my room alone.

I've even googled job openings. While I believe that the team might accommodate my relationship with Hudson, I need a backup plan. He doesn't want me to leave my job, and it would be hard work finding a new one.

I will if I have to, though. I'm employable, and a job is a job. But there's only one Hudson. I honestly never expected to risk my heart again. It's terrifying. But it's worth it.

On the last night in New Hampshire, I close all my job-hunting tabs and open up our secret messaging app. That app probably has a big boner just from all the horny texts we've sent each other late at night.

Sex, and hockey gossip. Those are our only two topics. One of his teammates—another defenseman—got traded a few days ago. That's a bummer, of course. But it seemed to relax Hudson. As if he'd dodged a bullet.

I'm lying in bed, the windows open to admit the fresh breeze, as I tap out another message to him.

Is it still hot in New York?

Yes it is. Or maybe I'm just hot for you, baby.

Fair enough. How was your workout?

Lonely.

And how's the hip?

Which one? Never mind—I'll update you on both. Hold, please.

For a moment I worry that his bursitis is back. But then he sends me a closeup photo of his six-pack and hips, clad only in boxer briefs. His hand is placed casually at the waistband, his thumb hooked into the elastic, like he might peel them off at any moment.

And there's a prominent bulge on display, too.

Okay, that's mean. Still have to survive another night without you.

Nah. THIS is mean.

He sends me two more photos—one from either side. This time the underwear is gone, and his cock juts haughtily upward in front of those lickable abs.

Holy heck. Hudson Newgate sent me two dick pics.

My mouth actually waters, and I spend about sixty seconds

pondering the ethics of sending my new boyfriend a dick pic from the guest room of a mansion owned by my dead husband's parents.

But then I realize that Eddie would totally approve. He'd been a big fan of inappropriate texts.

You realize this is war, right?

Kinda counting on it.

I kick off the covers and lock the bedroom door. Then I get naked, and get hard. Not like it's difficult. All I have to do is look at my boyfriend's cock and picture myself licking it.

I tap the camera icon, pose my shot, and send back an equally horny photo of me stroking myself.

It's not that surprising that my phone rings a moment later with a video call. I carefully shut down the private app and answer the call.

The screen is black. "Hey, baby. You're alone?"

"You bet I am."

The screen resolves to a closeup shot of Hudson drizzling a little lube onto his cock. And then his broad hand begins to stroke.

Whew. It's very hot in here all of a sudden.

"Wish this was your mouth," he growls.

"Give me twenty-four hours, and it can be." My hand closes around my dick and begins an erotic massage. But then I realize I haven't bothered to show him the goods. So I turn the phone to show him what he does to me.

Hudson groans. "If I were there, I'd ride you. I'm in the mood to get fucked."

"Are you, now?" My balls tighten just thinking about it. I'm often the bottom, but once in a while Hudson switches things up. "And people say you don't know how to have fun."

He snickers. "They probably do say that."

"Dead wrong," I pant. My videography leaves plenty to be desired. The picture is bobbing all over the place. But so is my dick. I'm on some kind of mission to have the world's fastest orgasm. "This isn't gonna take long."

"No kidding." He swirls his hand over that glorious cock head and grunts with pleasure. "You know what would get me there?"

"What?" I gasp.

"Let me see your face. I love your dick, but I really miss your sexy eyes."

My heart flutters dangerously. I've always understood that it's a privilege to fall in love, and to be loved by someone who appreciates you.

How extraordinary that I'm offered that chance twice in one lifetime.

I move the phone, resting it on my book. I capture my bare chest and my flushed face. Self-conscious now, I look away from the camera and stroke myself to Hudson's feverish dirty talk.

"That's it, baby. Can't wait to get you home and take care of you myself. Love it when you're desperate. Love to make you shoot."

I glance at the screen and see him jerking his thick cock between muscular thighs. It's my little secret how much I like the press of his strong legs around my body when he holds me in bed. The security of it.

"You crave this, don't you?"

"Yes," I admit, throwing my head back. "Can't wait to have you in my bed again."

"Show me how much," he pants. "Love it when you come for me."

So I do.

The next morning, I am the picture of cheer. I don't even try to hide my enthusiasm for going home. I speed-eat my breakfast and then hurry to pack up all our belongings.

Eustace fusses over Jordyn, and gets a little teary when I begin to pack up the rental car.

Outside, Jordyn hugs her grandparents tightly. After making

sure that Jordyn is seat-belted in the back, Eustace walks around the car to bid me goodbye.

"Thank you for bringing her," she whispers to me.

"It was my pleasure," I say as genuinely as I can manage. To her credit, Eustace didn't say any of the manipulative things that I imagined her saying on this trip. She didn't even bring up the idea of Jordyn moving here for good.

I'm a good father, whether she likes to admit it or not. And she's not a stupid woman. So maybe this truce will hold.

"I hope you'll call me if you need anything," she whispers. "I know childcare is expensive."

"Appreciate that," I say with genuine gratitude. "But I've got it covered for now." Jordyn's summer program starts on Monday. She's excited to go.

Thanks to Hudson, of course. But I don't mention that.

"Take care," she says, placing a hand on my arm. "I can't wait to see you both again soon."

"You too," I manage. "Be well."

She gives me a shaky smile, and I climb behind the wheel. *Here's to you, Eddie. Hope you're smiling down at us right now.*

He doesn't weigh in, of course. But I'm not as anxious about it anymore. I feel like I've found my feet. Sure, it took a while.

Just like this drive is going to take a while. Four hours to be exact. Eustace had offered to fly us from New York to Boston, but I'd stubbornly rented a car instead, because I didn't want more of her charity.

Seems foolish in retrospect.

Jordyn must agree with me. She's fidgety the whole way back. "Are we there yet?" she keeps asking from the back seat.

"Nope. Soon," I say at the three hour mark. "We're still in Connecticut."

"Ugh. Connecticut is *huge*."

I guess geography isn't taught in the second grade. But maybe they'll get around to it in third.

"Can we stop for a soda and chips?" she whines.

"Seltzer water," I bargain. "And pretzels."

"Okay," she mumbles. "Fine."

I let the lack of gratitude go, and point the rental toward a roadside rest stop. There are lots of families gassing up and ferrying children to the bathroom.

Jordyn is too old to go into the men's room with me, so I stand right outside the ladies' room and wait for her. My phone rings, and it's Hudson, probably wondering when I'm going to get home.

"Hi!" I say, answering the call. "We're somewhere in Connecticut. Want to have dinner later?" There's only silence on the phone, though. "Hudson? Did I lose you?"

He answers me in a broken voice. "Yeah. You did."

"What?" Icy chills roll down my back. "What are you saying?"

"I'm headed to the airport in an hour."

"Why? To go where?"

"Back to Colorado. I got traded."

Wait, what? "That's not possible. Tell me this is a joke."

In the ensuing silence, my heart slides down my throat. "It's real," he finally says.

"But..." My head spins. "Now what?"

More silence. And then, "Now nothing. It's over, Gavin. I get on another plane and I leave everything behind. The end. I'm sorry."

Then he hangs up.

FORTY-THREE

Hudson

I'M numb as I pack my suitcase.

Really numb. Dead inside.

I pack on autopilot. Workout gear. Shoes. Suits. Toiletries. IDs and financial documents. That's all a guy needs to start his life over again.

I should know. I've done this before. I could go pro.

My phone is buried deep inside my carry-on. My father's calls unanswered. I can't talk to him right now. That ass was right about the trade rumors, and I didn't believe him.

Now a car is coming for me in the next ten minutes.

Someone is suddenly banging on my door. "Hudson? You in there?" And my heart bottoms out.

Gavin.

Swear to Christ, I almost don't answer it. Saying goodbye to him might kill me. I was *this* close to having the life I wanted.

Or maybe I was just fooling myself the whole time.

But I open that door, and he's standing there, his luggage at his feet, a wild look in his eye. "What *happened*? Why didn't you stay on the phone?"

"You said you were on the road, and I didn't want Jordyn to over-hear. Where is she?"

He points at his apartment door, and then pushes past me into mine. "Hudson, I'm dying here. Talk to me."

"I did. There is nothing left to say. That's how my life works. I tried to tell you that. You should have listened."

"Stop it." His face reddens with anger. "I know you're hurting, but I drove home as fast as I could to ask you—what do we do now?"

Does he really not get it? "There's not one thing we can do now. I'm going to Colorado. You're going to training camp, with the team I thought wanted me. Unless the universe hates both of us the same amount, you'll meet another great guy and get on with your life."

He blinks. "That's it, huh? All the things we said to each other. All the plans we made. You'd just throw that away? What about coming out?"

"Are you *joking?* I have to start over now. Again. With a coach who helped them FedEx my ass across the country the first time I came out."

He rubs his face with two hands. "None of this makes sense. I don't know what just happened."

"I don't either," I clip. "I never do. I was in the weight room with Silas and I got a message on my phone. *If you're in the building, please come to Hugh's office.*" The memory burns already. "Swear to God, I thought it would be good news. Maybe a contract, or a PR thing, you know? Then I walked into that office and saw their faces."

"Oh honey," Gavin whispers. His eyes get red. He takes a step toward me.

My heart lurches. I want to touch him so badly. But I can't do it.

If he hugs me, I won't be able to stay angry. I won't be able to walk out of here.

So I step away, toward my luggage, and watch the hurt slice through his eyes. "For what it's worth, they said they hadn't planned on trading me at all. But Colorado kept sweetening the deal. And sweetening the deal. So they decided to send me to the team who was panting for me." I roll my eyes, but it's a half-hearted gesture. "But if I was so damn valuable, they would have just said no."

"You *are* though," Gavin insists, his eyes wet. "To me. Maybe we can make this work."

A bitter laugh stings my throat. "Long distance? I travel seventy nights a year, minimum. That's not even a little bit fair to you— trying to date an unavailable guy who's going to be in the closet until he dies."

"Don't say that." He swipes at his eyes. "You don't *know* that."

"Don't I?" Anger surges through my veins again. It feels powerful. It's what sees me through. "I'm going now. My car is going to pull up any minute." I pick up my luggage.

"Call me later," he says.

"Why?" I demand. "So we can be sad together?"

"*Hudson.* Don't leave it like this! You're not this guy."

"Yeah, I am," I insist. "I tried not to be, and look how that turned out?" My voice cracks on the last word, betraying how hard it is to hold myself together. "Tell Jordyn I'm sorry. I'll send her a new jersey to add to her collection."

He makes an anguished sound. But he doesn't stop me as I walk toward the door.

Maybe he finally understands there's no point.

FORTY-FOUR

Hudson

THE COLORADO COUGARS play their games in Denver, but they're headquartered twenty-five miles away, in Boulder.

It's a beautiful little city in the mountains. A hub for hipsters, hikers and foodies. I watch dispassionately as the streets slide by, until the young woman who picked me up from the airport pulls into a tidy development of sleek stone and wood townhomes.

She navigates to a space in front of one of them and parks. "Here we are, Mr. Newgate." She kills the engine. "The GM didn't want you to have to look for housing right away. This townhouse is available to you on a week to week basis for as long as you need. Or, if you decide to stay here, say the word and you can sign a longer term lease."

As if I were dumb enough to sign a longer term lease.

"Let's get you settled," she says, exiting the car. "You have a meeting with Coach Powers at seven p.m., sharp. He's staying late for you, so there's no time to waste."

I climb robotically out of the car and then extract my luggage from the back.

The woman is already unlocking the front door with a code with precise taps of her index finger. She's in shiny heels and a skirt with those pleats that look like an accordion fold.

I search my memory for her name, and come up blank. Leila? Lilah? It's something with an L. I've barely said four words to her for the past hour. Numb guys aren't great with conversation.

Nonetheless, I troop up the stairs and follow her into the house. It's surprisingly nice, with high ceilings, a stone fireplace, a tastefully casual L-shaped sofa, and a thick rug on the floor of the living area.

Her heels click on the wood floors as she heads for the granite and steel kitchen. "I'm writing down the front door code here. But it's not hard to remember—1979, the year the team joined the NHL."

"1979," I repeat dutifully. "Thank you..." I clear my throat, and it's suddenly obvious that I've forgotten her name. "...For all your help."

She turns to me with a stern expression. "It's *Liana*. I know trades are disorienting, Mr. Newgate. But you do have a meeting in..." She checks her smart watch. "One hour and fifty minutes. It's a ten minute drive to the facility. Do you know where to find it?"

"Yes. But I don't have a car."

She marches to the front window and points outside. "That blue Toyota SUV is also rented to you on a week by week basis. You will need to sign the short term lease agreement immediately, so we don't run afoul of the salary cap."

"Right, Liana. Thank you."

"Let me show you the kitchen," she says, beckoning me toward the back, as if I couldn't find it myself.

She's a little terrifying. But at least she's snapped me out of my stupor. I follow her through an arched doorway into a kitchen done up in wood and granite. "Look," she commands. Then she opens a cabinet that turns out to be a fully stocked refrigerator. "I wasn't informed of any dietary restrictions, so I went with your basic Whole Foods assortment. This should get you through for a few days until you get your feet on the ground."

I blink at a banquet of high protein and high fiber choices. Salads and meats and an entire roasted chicken. Fruits and vegetables. Eggs. Bottled seltzer. "Thank you," I say again, as heat creeps up my neck.

This is not how trades usually work. I'm always stumbling around a hotel room, clutching the business card of a real estate broker and wondering what just hit me.

"Breathe, Mr. Newgate. Then put your stuff upstairs and get to the coach's office."

"Yes ma'am."

"Here's the car key. Your new address is on this keychain." She hands me the fob. "What's the door code?"

"1979," I answer dutifully.

"Good work. See you at seven." Her heels click across the floor again as she lets herself out.

When the door closes, I go back into the living room, grab my bags and carry them upstairs.

One room holds a king-sized bed made up in white linens. I drop my bags on the floor and contemplate a face-plant onto the bed. Fuck the meeting. Fuck everything.

But I don't do it. If I lie down on that bed, all I'll do is brood. I'll picture Gavin following me out the front of our building. I didn't kiss him goodbye. I didn't even shake his hand.

Always the braver man, he'd followed me outside anyway. He'd watched as I'd tossed my luggage into the taxi's trunk, and then climbed into the back seat.

I'd raised a hand in a wave, which must have seemed cruel to him. But it was all I was capable of at the time.

My last view of Brooklyn was the devastation he wasn't afraid to wear on his face.

At one minute before seven, I approach the players' entrance with a kind of sick déjà vu.

Once upon a time I felt so proud to walk through these fucking doors. I thought I had the world hanging off the end of my dick.

Now I just feel tired. I'm too old to start over. And yet I don't have a choice.

There's a security desk just inside, and I don't recognize the older man behind it.

But he recognizes me. "Mr. Newgate? Welcome back to Colorado!" He smiles, which makes his handlebar mustache twitch.

"Thank you, sir," I say with about as much enthusiasm as a dead man.

"Coach Powers is waiting for you in his office. Do you know where that is?" He points toward the elevator.

Sadly, I do. So I give him a nod and a wave, and ring for the elevator, which takes me all too quickly to the third floor.

Before I'm ready, the elevator burps me out into an attractive room carpeted in Colorado Cougar blue. Liana rises from her chair to greet me. "Welcome to headquarters," she says with the same serious frown she wore before. "Thank you for being on time."

"Kind of scared not to be. You know where I live."

I was hoping for a laugh, but I don't even get a lip twitch. "He's waiting for you. Can I bring you anything to drink?"

"No, thank you." I don't plan on staying long enough to chug a beverage. "I'll just go on through, if that's okay."

She nods, and I head for the walnut door of the head coach's office. My body feels like lead.

This malaise won't last, I remind myself. As soon as I hit the rink with the other players, the old instincts will kick in. The feeling of steel against ice will work its old magic.

It won't hurt this much tomorrow.

It couldn't possibly.

Coach Powers looks up from his laptop when I walk in. I'd expected to be greeted by the GM, too. But the coach is alone in his office.

I brace myself for a jocular greeting that I'll be expected to return. But he regards me thoughtfully instead. "Come on in, Hudson. Close the door if you wouldn't mind."

I do it. Then he rises from his desk and stretches out a hand to shake, his icy blue eyes holding mine. "It's really good to see you here."

Swear to God, I almost can't respond. But that's no way to start off with a new team. And I'm kind of an expert on that. So I force myself to extend my hand and shake.

His grip is strong, but not obnoxiously so. And he takes his seat again gravely, like he understands my hesitation. "I'm sure getting traded was a shock. Your father tells me you would have preferred to remain in Brooklyn."

"Nobody asks to get traded," I point out, my voice scratchy from disuse. "Not often, anyway."

If he disagrees, he doesn't say so. And his smile is fleeting. "I've been watching you, Newgate. And when they gave me the top job last year, I decided that Colorado needed you back. So I sincerely hope that bargaining hard for you is not deeply disruptive to your life."

There is nothing positive I can say about that. And I don't have the energy to tell a white lie. The tank is empty. So I end up just staring at him. It's awkward, but I don't care that much.

He sighs. "Getting traded is hard. I get it. But I need you. I need your experience, and your tenacity. I need your leadership. And we both need a championship ring. You want that, right?"

"Of course," I say quickly. "You know I do."

It's just that I want a lot of things now, and they aren't all compatible. It's so confusing. Life was easier when I only let myself care about hockey.

He nods thoughtfully. Like he knows there's more I'm not saying. "First things first—this is your early renewal contract." He opens a folder on his desk and passes a stapled sheaf of papers across the shiny wooden surface. "I haven't even sent it to your father yet. I'll do that tomorrow. But I didn't trade for you just to get a cheap test drive. I'm already sold. Have a look at the terms."

Numbly, I take the contract and glance at the cover sheet. The terms are bulleted neatly onto the first page. Four years at three million dollars per year.

And a no-trade clause that kicks in on my twenty-seventh birthday.

If I were one-percent less stoic, I might actually break down crying. This is exactly the contract I've always wanted.

From exactly the wrong team.

"You can take your time with it," he says. "The offer doesn't expire until the start of regular season play, in October. It's the best terms we can provide. And if you choose to sign, it will give you a lot of insurance against any injury you might suffer. But I realize that Colorado wasn't in your travel plans. So if you decide to wait until your contract expires next summer, I won't take it personally."

I grip the contract in my hand, and I'm literally speechless. I can't believe I've finally gotten exactly what I've always wanted.

And I still want to howl.

He's watching me, too. I think he can read the struggle right off my face. He turns away for a second, swiveling his leather chair to open a mini fridge that's built into the shelving on the wall. He pulls out two cans of flavored seltzer water, and passes me one without comment.

I sort of snap out of my trance when he passes me the cold drink. I pop the top and take a deep gulp. "Thank you," I say stupidly. It's not clear whether I'm thanking him for the soda, or for the twelve million dollars.

He decides it's the latter, I guess. "You think on that. Meanwhile, we need to go back to the last time you sat in this office. There are some things that need clearing up."

I actually chuckle, although it hurts my throat. "No need to discuss *that*, right? Some things are meant to be brushed under the rug."

He doesn't even crack a smile. "I disagree. You are under no obligation to discuss your private life with me. But I'm going to tell you what I think, and you can do whatever you want with that information. Okay?"

I only nod.

He takes a sip of his soda and then sets the can on the desk.

"Five and a half years ago, you sat here in this office and did something incredibly courageous. I've never seen anything like it."

Startled, I swallow hard.

"I admired the hell out of you, Hudson. Still do. But timing is everything, and I can only assume that you felt burned by that experience. That must be why I never heard another word about it."

People say that time heals, but right this second I know they're wrong. Even after all these years, I just don't want to talk about this. At all.

"Like I said, it's none of my business. But I need you to know you could still do that. If the timing was right again for you to—"

"*Timing?*" It comes out angry. "It wasn't *timing* that fucked me over, sir."

He blinks. "Why do you think that?"

"I *know* that." Rage boils inside me. "It wasn't a coincidence that I got traded right after my big, *courageous* revelation. This team did not want to deal with me, and they wouldn't even say it to my face."

He's already shaking his head. "That's not true. Although the thought crossed my mind when I heard about your trade. I went right into the GM's office, demanding to know what happened."

"And?" I spit.

"And," he says quietly. "The manager showed me that the trade predated your announcement by about two hours."

"What?" I snap. "That can't be true."

"Sure it can. The terms were finalized, but they were waiting on the call with the league. It was rescheduled after the league's attorney got into a fender bender. Took 'em another day and a half to finalize."

"But my father said…" I brace my hands on my knees and try to think.

"He said what?" Powers presses. "Hudson, breathe."

I gulp air. "He and I need to have a chat. Like immediately."

"Okay." He looks concerned. "Let's take a walk first."

"Why?"

"Because you look like you're going to pass out. Come on." He rises from his desk. "Bring your drink. Let's go outside. It's a beautiful night, and you can see the new track we put in. Besides, it's hard to feel stress when you can see the sky."

Whatever, dude. Still, I follow him out of the office and down another corridor, because it's easier than talking. We pass a glass wall with views down onto an expansive weight room. There are a couple of players down there right now. I recognize my old roommate, Davey Stoneman seated on the bench. He's talking to a younger guy I've never met.

They don't look up. But I can picture how the next week will go —with me trying to learn everybody's names. Trying to figure out their style of play, and the vibe in the dressing room.

In exchange, I'll get to skate hard and fast and win games.

That's how I've survived the past few years. Hockey is always there for me. It doesn't care if I'm queer, or grumpy or worried about the next game or the next contract. When muscle and steel meet the ice, you glide forward. Every time.

We pass through to a set of stairs, descending to a back exit I'd forgotten about. Powers pushes open the doors, and then we're approaching a state of the art running track I've never seen before. "Nice," I say listlessly.

"It is. And there's a view of the mountains on the opposite side. Come on." He crosses the track and cuts through the oval of green grass in its center. I follow him, the slanting evening sunshine warming my face. When we reach the other side, there's a broad dirt path through a stand of trees. And beyond that, a stone wall that's guarding a rocky cliff of sorts. And a big view of the Rockies.

"This is where I go when I need to sort things out," he says, his hip parked against the wall.

"Does it work?" I hear myself ask.

His lips quirk. "Sometimes. Depends on how fucked up the situation is. Try me."

"Huh." I lean heavily on the wall. "Five years ago, my father told me I got traded because I came out to management."

He lets out a low whistle.

"You're really telling me that didn't happen?"

"I *know* it didn't happen like that. But I can see why the timing would make your father suspect it. He obviously made an assumption."

Except that's not what he said. *I have it from the inside. They didn't want to deal with that from a rookie.*

"He lied," I say flatly. Honestly, it's the only explanation that makes sense. If I'd been traded for being queer, my father would be the *last* person an insider would tell. Why incriminate the organization like that? We could sue them.

Fuck. My father *lied* just to shut me up. He's the one who didn't want to deal with my sexuality. Not the team.

"That's a hard thing to carry around for five years," Coach Powers says carefully. "No wonder you look so pissed off to come back here."

I turn my face away, feeling stupid. "I did wonder."

Coach gives me a minute before he speaks again. "After I pushed the GM on it, he and Coach Reynolds had a post-mortem meeting. Reynolds thought he was right to ask you to hold back your statement to the team, until you had all the information about your trade. But I've always wondered if there wasn't a better way we could have handled it."

It's so hard to rearrange my thinking. I've been carrying around a lie for so long. "That whole meeting looks completely different to me now," I say slowly. "Everybody was so quiet. The silence was, like, deafening."

"Because they weren't sure what to do," he says. "And you know they couldn't just tell you about the trade before the league's approval. It would have been a rule violation."

"Yeah," I say lamely.

"The silence bothered me, too, though. It still bothers me. Even in their confusion, words of support aren't so hard to pronounce, right?"

"For some people they are," I mumble.

"Not for me," he says firmly. "Not anymore. I was the junior flunkie in the room back then, but if I could turn back time, I would have offered you those words of support. I'm sorry that I didn't, Hudson. I hope you can forgive me."

"You're forgiven," I say immediately. I stare at the red rocks in the distance, and try to regulate my breathing. My father betrayed me all those years ago. I wonder how he feels about it now—whether he has any idea how deeply it screwed up my life.

I pull my phone out of my pocket and send him a two word text. *You're fired.*

Then I pound the rest of my soda. "Do me a favor?" I say to Coach Powers. "Don't send that new contract to my dad. I need a change of representation."

"All right," he says. "You let me know where you land on that. I can probably get the GM to extend the deadline if you need to get the new guy up to speed. I assume you have friends you can ask for recommendations?"

"Yeah," I grunt. Although it's barely true. I have more acquaintances than friends. "Thanks."

He claps me on the shoulder. "No rash decisions, okay? Sit with it. Meet the team. Get acclimated to the altitude. Drink a lot of water tomorrow, and take a break if you get winded or headachy."

"Will do," I mumble.

"And Hudson? There's a long list of reasons I wanted you here. Last season's success is only one of them."

"Thanks," I say. But my mind is starting to shut down. I woke up in Brooklyn, having a normal day. And now my head is exploding.

"You may find that there are others in the organization who share some of your recent challenges."

"What?" I force myself to focus on what he's saying. "What kind of challenges?"

He fingers his soda can. "I have a feeling that one or two of your new teammates might struggle with their sexuality."

"Why do you think that?" I demand.

He shrugs cryptically. "It's a hunch. It's my hope that someday soon nobody will have to struggle. That any person—hockey player or not—will feel free to express themselves. If somehow you help the Cougars move toward that future, I'd be grateful. But if you just want to skate fast and make goals, I'll take that as a consolation prize."

I stare at him.

"Get some rest. See you tomorrow," he says.

Then he walks away.

FORTY-FIVE

Gavin

"WHAT ARE WE WATCHING, DUCKY?" I ask Jordyn. "Anything but Frozen."

Now that Reggie is living here again, she and Jordyn have resumed singing all those songs. A guy can only take so much.

"Isn't there a hockey game on?" Jordyn asks me. "The season started, right, Daddy?" She grabs the remote control and points it at the TV.

"Yeah," I say begrudgingly. But the game holds no appeal. "The game isn't as interesting to me without Hudson on the team, though."

Jordyn clearly hasn't lost interest. Not in hockey and not in Hudson. She constantly asks me how he's doing, and whether he likes Colorado, and if he misses us.

What I believe: *I don't know. I doubt it.* And *probably, but it's really fucking hard to tell.*

What I've said: "Great! Sure!" And "He told you he does."

A week after he left, I received a FedEx package from the Colorado Cougars' main office. Inside I found a youth-sized jersey and a program with all the players' signatures on it. And a postcard of Boulder, Colorado.

Dear Jordyn, I'm so sorry I had to leave without saying goodbye. It was a real shock. I sure hope you had a great summer. Here's a new jersey for your collection. —Love, Hudson

Love? My ass.

I'm still bitter. Part of me thinks that Hudson really did love me.

The other part is just plain upset at the way he acted. I've been abandoned before, and the cold way he left was triggering for me.

Since then, I've had dreams about him leaving. Either I'm chasing the car, or I'm yelling and he can't hear me. I've had some lonely late night hours, lying awake and staring at the ceiling. Sometimes I walk into the weight room at work, and instinctively look for him before I catch myself.

It's brutal. Not quite as brutal as losing a husband in a car crash. But still bad.

"Daddy, is it?"

My attention snaps back to Jordyn. "What, sweetie?"

"Is Hudson's game on TV, too?"

"Sure, somewhere," I tell her. "But we probably don't have that channel."

I happen to know that Colorado is hosting Chicago tonight. I may have checked Colorado's game schedule. For science.

Which means I also learned that Colorado will be visiting Brooklyn next month for a game.

If Reggie is still in town, maybe I'll ask her to babysit that night. I'll go out to a bar nowhere near the stadium and get good and drunk.

My child disappears into her room, emerging a minute later with her iPad. She's googled: *How to watch Hudson play hockey.*

And Google, being shrewd to the point of being creepy, has promptly responded with a link to the Cougars' schedule, followed by a link to the ESPN+ subscription page.

"That will cost money," I tell her as she's clicking the link.

"Daddy, it says *free two-week trial.*"

"But that's how they hook you," I grumble. "They want you to forget about the end of the two weeks, so they can charge your credit card."

She looks thoughtful. "We could do that thing with your phone that reminds us about doctor's appointments? And then they won't charge you the money, right?"

Kids are way too smart these days.

You have to learn to say no, I'd told Hudson. And yet here I am typing my Amex number into the subscription site.

Why? Self-torture, apparently. That's the only explanation that makes sense. Jordyn finds the game in the hockey directory, and when the camera sweeps Colorado's bench, I lean forward, looking for his rugged face.

Jordyn squeals, and there he is, right in front of us in HD, wearing an unfamiliar blue helmet and a serious game-day expression.

My heart contracts with longing. Then an unfamiliar coach taps him on the shoulder, and he vaults over the wall for a shift.

"Whoa," Jordan says, because Hudson skates like he's on fire. He's fast and aggressive as he halts the progress of a Chicago forward and strips him of the puck. "Hudson is angry tonight. Can I make popcorn?"

"Sure, baby."

She heads for the kitchen, finds a bag of microwave popcorn, rips off the plastic and puts it into the microwave.

When it's done, I shove some into my mouth when she offers it. But I don't leave the couch until intermission.

He's magic. I'd forgotten. Or maybe I'd wanted to forget. But that guy on the screen is at the top of his game.

After grabbing a beer, I find my phone and google his stats. In just four games, he's got two assists and a goal.

I smile in spite of myself. I'm still angry, damn it. But also joyous. Because I know how badly Hudson wants to prove himself. Look at him go.

As the second period starts, I keep googling. I look up his teammates. A couple of them were there for at least five years. So Hudson probably knows them. Maybe they're friends.

I hope he has friends.

"The coach looks nicer than our coach," Jordyn decides, her eyes glued to the TV. She has popcorn in her hair. "What's his name?"

So I google Colorado's coach. "It's Clay Powers. He's only thirty-eight years old—the youngest head coach in the league."

"He's cute," she says. "I like his face."

It is a nice face, I guess. And he wears the heck out of a suit. Just for kicks, I google *hottest NHL coach* and his photo comes up immediately.

Figures.

The whistle blows, and the camera pans the bench again. I scrutinize Hudson's teammates, looking for any clues of what it's like there, and whether he's happy. There's a young equipment manager behind the bench. And a trainer in a blue quarter-zip jacket.

Of course there's a trainer. But Hudson used to *date* a trainer in Colorado, didn't he? Maybe *that* trainer.

I pop up off the sofa and pace my way to the fridge, where I grab a second beer. I'm usually a one beer kind of guy, but now my head is full of awful thoughts. Hudson and the trainer rediscovering one another. Having sex on a giant bed in a mountain chalet, while snow falls gently past the window outside.

Wait. Is it snowing in Colorado yet? Should my unhappy subconscious be picturing autumn leaves instead?

I take a gulp of my second beer and pace behind the sofa. On our screen, Hudson skates like a Tasmanian devil. He trips a Chicago player and doesn't get called for it, and his teammates high-five him when he returns to the bench. I squint at the screen, trying to see if the trainer says anything to him, or smiles.

Jesus Christ. It's going to be a long season. I'm definitely canceling this channel when the trial is over.

I take out my phone and open up our secret app, tapping in my pass code. There's our old thread, from the morning he got traded, frozen in time. Eggplant emojis and smiley faces and hearts. *Can't wait to see you*, he'd written.

If only.

Later I'll blame it on one and a half light beers, which is bull-shit, but there isn't a better reason for me to tap out a message.

Jordyn made me get ESPN+ tonight so we could watch your game. You look great.

On the ice I mean.

Whatever. You probably look great in general, you dick.

I'm still so mad at you. But I honestly hope you're doing okay. I hope someone in Colorado makes you play ping-pong and eat carbs once in a while.

I hit send, but then I read it back and realize how stupid it all sounds. So of course I double down.

Really, she made me subscribe. She held me down with her short little arms and threatened to sing Frozen from start to finish unless I said yes to the free two-week trial.

Which I'll cancel. It's probably expensive so at least I only have fourteen days for self torture.

Please score another goal in the next two weeks. Kthx.

PS: Your coach is hot. I can't see the trainer well enough to know if he is also hot, but if that's your ex please never tell me. I really don't want to know.

I read it back, and groan.

"Whatsa matter, Daddy?" Jordyn asks from the sofa.

"Nothing. Just, uh, need to see if this app lets you delete stuff you sent."

It doesn't.

Fuck my life.

Colorado scores, and Jordyn applauds, and I power my phone all the way off so I'm not tempted to embarrass myself any further.

FORTY-SIX

Hudson

WE BEAT CHICAGO.

That game felt good. Really good. I've been skating like a super-hero at practice. I work out like a beast, eat a great diet, and watch game tape like there will be a quiz later. From the moment I wake up in the morning, I'm all about hockey.

Brooklyn is going to be sorry. Those are the only two things keeping me going—revenge, and hockey. Plus, wearing myself out at the gym and on the ice is the only way I can get any sleep.

I drive the blue SUV home from Denver to my townhouse, and park in my designated spot. Four other players on my team live in this development, in a highly desirable neighborhood. It's a sweet setup, and I have no complaints with management.

Except for the only one that matters—I'd rather not be here at all.

After tapping in the code for the front door, I step into the quiet space. I bought the furniture from the rental company, and haven't added anything much to the house except for my favorite rug, which Heidi Jo shipped to me a week after I left Brooklyn.

She arranged for a moving company to ship me the rest of my belongings. She arranged for a charity to pick up my Brooklyn furniture, and mailed me a donation form for tax purposes. Erasing my life in New York was surprisingly easy for her. A few phone calls, and it's like I was never there.

Gavin probably has a new neighbor already.

I climb the carpeted stairs and drop my gym bag inside the bedroom. I hang up my suit jacket and tie in the closet, and change into shorts and a T-shirt. When I put my phone on the charger, it lights up with a notification. And I freeze. It's the encrypted app that I used to chat with Gavin.

And there's a new message.

Even though I've made it a point not to reach out to him, I'm not a strong enough man to resist this. I grab the phone and log in so fast that I'm in danger of breaking the thing.

I miss him so much. It takes all my focus not to think about him when I'm alone.

The first message makes me smile. The second one causes a burning sensation behind my eyes. It kills me to think that I hurt him. He has every right to be mad.

But somehow he's still buoyant, too. Still Gavin. I can hear his voice when he tells me the coach is hot.

Which he would be, I guess? If he wasn't my coach, and a dozen years older than me.

The last message, though, requires a reply.

Hey. If you were watching, I'm glad I didn't stink it up tonight.

Is it horrible that I've wondered if you watched? Not that I deserve it.

I'm really sorry for the way I left. I didn't know how to handle it. I still don't. The truth is that I was afraid of what would happen if I let you touch me. Like I might have broken in half.

I was just trying to hold myself together so I could get into that car.

And I had to get into the car.

I bet you wish you never went into the tavern that fateful night last winter.

I'm sorry.

PS: The team trainer here is a stranger. And he couldn't hold a candle to you.

PPS: Dicks are nice. That's not an insult. We've been over this.

After I hit send, I put the phone down. I'm still so confused. I wish I had behaved differently. And yet the outcome would be the same.

Our story got cut short. That's not my fault. My biggest sin was believing it could have ended differently.

I can't believe I have to play Brooklyn next month. Just thinking about it makes me want to hurl. I'll spend the whole trip wondering where Gavin is, and whether he's thinking about me, too.

This anxiety spiral is cut short only when the doorbell rings downstairs. Which is just weird. Nobody even knows my address. Must be a food delivery gone wrong.

I walk downstairs and open the front door, and find a woman standing there under my porch light. A redhead in business casual with a blazer and a pin on the lapel that reads *Either You Like Hockey or You Are Wrong*.

It's Bess Beringer, my new agent. "Hi," I say stupidly. "I didn't know you were in town."

"That's because you boogied out of the stadium so fast that I missed you. Can I come in?"

"Of course." I open the door a little wider. "Sorry. I would have stayed if I'd known."

"It's okay," she says. "I don't travel that much these days, but I had to go to Vegas for a negotiation, so I thought I'd pop by and see you play. What a game! You must be thrilled. Thought you might be out celebrating with the guys."

"Not much of a drinker," I say by way of explanation. "Can I get you a soda?"

"Sure," she says. "That would be great."

I head to the kitchen and rustle up a couple of seltzers with lime. When I return, Bess is admiring my fireplace. "Nice house they set you up with here."

"Isn't it? Happy to avoid the nightmare of finding something of my own. I'll just stay on the month to month lease until they get sick of me."

She takes the soda from my hand. "Keep playing like that, and they'll never get sick of you."

"Here's hoping." We raise our glasses in a mock toast, and Bess smiles.

I'm phoning it in pretty well right now, I guess. Even though my phone is burning a hole in my pocket. I wonder if Gavin read what I wrote.

I wonder if he'll ever forgive me.

"Can we talk?" She sits on an armchair, so I take the sofa.

"Sure."

"I don't know you very well. I only met you that one night at the bar in Brooklyn."

"Yeah, in March, I think?" It was one of the rare nights that I'd gone out with my teammates, and Bess had been there with her husband, Mark Tankiewicz, who's still happily employed as a defenseman in Brooklyn. It's hard not to be jealous.

A lot of the Brooklyn players work with Bess, and when I'd called to ask Castro for a recommendation, he'd sung her praises to the sky. "She's super smart and a straight shooter. A little scary when she's angry, but that's probably a good thing."

Now she's fixed me with a penetrating gaze, and I think I understand what he meant. "Can I ask you a question?"

"Sure. You probably want to know why I haven't signed my contract yet, right?" The contract in question is sitting, unsigned, in a bathroom drawer upstairs. Bess already got me an extension on the decision. I have until Christmas to decide whether to sign.

Whenever I think about it, I feel a strange detachment. Like it's someone else's decision.

"I would never rush you," she says. "But like I said before—I don't know you very well. My job is to get you whatever you want. That's hard to do when I can't figure out what that is. In the first place, you haven't told me why you fired your dad. If it's personal, maybe you don't need to share. But if you two had a difference of opinion about how business gets done, it might help me to know what happened."

I take a deep drink of soda and try to figure out how to respond. "He lied to me," is what I decide to go with. "It happened years ago, but I just found out, and it was a pretty big betrayal. We're not, uh, speaking at the moment." The one time I answered his call, and tried to explain why I was so mad, he started yelling at me.

So now I've blocked him.

"Hell, I'm sorry." Her gaze turns sympathetic. "That's a big rupture in your life."

"I guess." The more I think about our relationship, the less healthy it seems. "To be honest, I'm enjoying the silence. He was really, um, hands-on."

She nods thoughtfully. "I can only imagine how complicated it would be to have a parent as an agent. You and I don't have that kind of messy history, but I hope you know you can always tell me if you need more or less support. I have a different relationship with each of my clients. But it takes a while to get that right."

"I'm sure," I agree. "But I'm not worried. You're nothing like him, anyway. I don't need you to follow me around and question my nutritional choices."

She cringes. "Yeah, you don't need to comment on mine either, okay? Pact?"

"Pact," I agree, and she smiles.

"Now can we talk about your contract extension? You still have a couple months to make up your mind. But I want you to know that I think it's a good deal. And signing now would protect your finances in the event—"

"—Of an injury," I finish. "Yeah, I know. It's a factor."

"But more to the point—if there's something else you want from your next contract, you'd have to actually tell me what that is, or I can't find it for you. And if it's more money, I'll need you to be specific," she says carefully. "If you have a number in your head, let's talk about that. But you might have to settle for two years instead of three if you want a higher salary."

"It's not the money," I say gruffly. "That's not the issue."

She regards me with a tilted head, like she can't quite do the math. "All right. Then what is it? You're not sure you like Colorado?"

"Yeah, but it's not, uh, Colorado's fault." I set my glass on the coffee table and stare at it. "I left someone behind in Brooklyn. I didn't want to leave, and I hesitate to lock myself in here for four seasons."

"I see," she says gently. "So you might want to be a free agent next summer? That's a little risky."

"I know," I say quickly. "Brooklyn let me go. I'm sure they had their reasons."

She sets her drink down and folds her arms, to make it easier to stare at me, I guess. "And there's no chance that your special someone would move here to Colorado?"

"Uh, probably not." I swallow. "It was kind of new, and awfully complicated. I fucked it up pretty good anyway."

"Oh honey," she says.

I attempt a casual shrug, but I feel like I'm sitting here bleeding.

The doorbell rings again, and Bess raises her eyebrows. "Are you expecting company?"

"Nope." I get up. "This is already more visitors than I've ever had in this house."

This time when I open the door, I see my teammate, Davey Stoneman, standing there. He's lost his jacket and tie, but he's still wearing his suit pants and button down shirt. His hair is flopped too close to his eyes, and he's wearing a big grin. "Hey! You ran out before I could invite you out for beers."

"Oh, uh...Sorry. I'm not much of a partier these days. Not like before." Five years ago he and I were rookies together for Colorado, and briefly roommates. Now he's an alternate captain for the team, but still the least serious person I have ever met.

My quick disappearance tonight was intentional, of course. I wasn't in the mood for Stoney's antics.

I don't know if I'll ever be in the mood.

"That's cool," he says with a shrug. "I just brought the beers over here. You still drink beer?" He holds up an Igloo cooler in his hand.

"Sometimes?"

"Awesome." He gives me a grin and pushes past me into the house. "Hey! It's Bess Beringer, agent to the stars!" Stoneman—or Stoney, as the guys call him—is one of those people who knows everybody's name.

"Nice to meet you," Bess says, rising to shake his hand.

"You want a beer? I also brought chips and dip." He puts the cooler on the table and starts removing things from it.

"I'm always good for chips," Bess says.

"Awesome. Newgate—get us a bowl and some napkins?"

"Sure. Make yourself at home," I grumble, heading for the kitchen. I grab a few things and head back to the living room.

"Aww, Newgate is grumpy," Stoney says with a grin. "That's why I came over here. To see why you're such a shut-in. The guys think you hate 'em. And I'm like—*no, Newgate is cool. Give him a chance.*"

"Uh-oh." Bess raises her gaze to mine and grins. "Got a rep already?"

I groan and throw myself onto the sofa. "Is it illegal to be grumpy?"

"Not if you got a good reason," Stoney says. "So let's hear it."

Bess crosses her arms and waits, probably wondering what I'll say.

"Getting traded is rough," I complain. "I had a life in Brooklyn. For six whole months, I had a life."

Stoneman fishes an opener out of his pocket and uncaps several beers, one of which he pushes toward me. "See, I knew there was something wrong. Five years ago you were kind of a gregarious guy, you know? Chatting us up in the dressing room. Good for a party as long as your dad wasn't breathing down your neck. So this is all about a bad breakup?"

"Basically," I mutter. I grab the beer and take a gulp.

"Want me to set you up?" he flips his hair off his face. "Maybe you just need a little fun in your life to forget about your broken heart."

My neck heats. "I don't think I'm ready for that."

"Oh, man." He manages to guzzle his beer and shake his head at the same time. "This is bad. Amazing that it hasn't wrecked your game, right?"

"I guess? The game is the only thing I got right now. For years I've been *all* about hockey. And I thought it was working for me. But this is the first time ever that I'm just not really sure what I'm doing, you know? If I have to choose between hockey and my life..."

Fuck. Is that even a choice I could *make*? I fight off a shiver.

"Why is this breakup so complicated?" Bess asks.

"Yeah—who is this girl?" Stoney demands.

I flop back on the couch and stare up at the ceiling. It's a really nice ceiling, with dark wooden beams making a pattern across the space. And I know without a doubt that I'd rather be back in my crappy little Brooklyn apartment. No question.

It hurts so much that I take a deep breath, and then jump off a cliff. "What if it's not a girl?"

Immediately, I want to suck it back in. It's been years—literally years—since I dared to talk about my sexuality with anyone in hockey.

And I'm afraid to even look at Bess or Stoney. So I stare up at the ceiling instead.

"Okay, not a girl, a *woman*," Stoney says. "Sorry. My bad."

Bess snorts. "Pretty sure that's not what he meant, buddy."

The ensuing silence almost kills me, and I give in and look at Stoney. He's taking a sip of beer. And I see the moment he figures it out. His eyes widen. "Oh, fuck! Goddamn, man. My bad again!" He snaps his fingers. "You used to date a dude from some gym, right? Just before you got traded?"

My jaw unhinges. "You knew about that?"

"Roommates." He shrugs. "Forgot my phone one day the boys and I were goin' biking. Heard you guys in the bedroom. Kinda loud." He shrugs again.

Bess laughs so hard that she chokes on her beer, while I roll face first into the sofa, wishing the room would swallow me whole.

"This new guy did a number on ya, eh?" Stoney muses. "Want me to key his car when we play Brooklyn?"

"No," I say into the leather upholstery. "He didn't do anything wrong. That was all me."

"Oh, buddy." Stoney sighs. "So what's your plan to get 'im back?"

I lift my head. "I can't get him back. He can't move here. He has a job and a kid and family on the East Coast."

"Oooh." Stoney winces. "That's rough. We might have to just drown our sorrows on this one, eh?"

"Yeah," I grunt, because I don't want to talk anymore. I'm all talked out.

Two beers later, Stoney gets up to leave. ("Gotta hit the hay and do it all over again tomorrow, eh!")

"This is all in the vault, okay?" I say, following him to the door.

"Sure, sure! Don't keep it all bottled up there, though. We can't have you hiding out in this house all season. Nice place and all, but it makes you seem aloof."

"Noted. Thanks for stopping by."

"Oh, I'll do it again. You got a great pad, Newgate. Can't wait."

I finally close the door on him.

Bess is cleaning up beer bottles and carrying the dip bowl to the kitchen.

"You don't have to do that," I insist. "I got it."

"I'm sure you do," she says. "I can already tell you're one of my more high-functioning clients. Some of these boys can't tie their own shoes. But do me a favor?"

"What?"

"Take your time signing that contract. I don't want you to have regrets."

"I might as well sign it right now and give it back to you. Otherwise, I'm just waiting around for a miracle that won't come."

She raises both hands. "I'm not taking it tonight. You have too much up in the air. Sleep on it, okay?"

"Fine," I grunt. Like that will change anything.

Back in the living room, she heads for the door, her hand on the knob. "Listen, thank you for sharing your truth with me. I'm sure that was hard, but it helps understand your needs."

It was hard. "Thanks for listening."

"It doesn't have to be a secret, you know." She shrugs. "Just a thought."

I smile for the first time tonight. "Hey, thanks. My dad disagreed. I knew I liked you."

She smiles, too. "Good night, Hudson. Take care of yourself. Call me anytime."

"I'll do that."

It isn't until I go upstairs again that I remember to check the app. Just in case Gavin left me another message.

He did. But it's a voicemail. My heart kicks into a higher gear as I tap the play button and brace myself to hear his voice.

"Look," he says, as I close my eyes so I can imagine he's in front of me. "I might have done some more drinking after the kid went to bed. Because I don't think you get it at all. I'm *not* sorry I went into that bar, okay? I'm not sorry we met. I'm *very* hurt right now, but that doesn't mean I wish it never happened."

He blows a wheezy breath past the microphone before continuing. "I mean—who thinks that way? Would you really wish away the time we had together? Is heartbreak so terrifying to you that you'd go back in time and erase us? Because I would never do that. Even if I can't sleep at night for missing you. Even if the guys in the gym keep asking me if I'm okay, because I look so tired. Not that I can tell them. It would be nice if I could express that I'm sad and frustrated. But I respect your privacy, so there's nobody to listen to me but Reggie.

"That's what you've done to me—blown through my life like a hurricane. But hey, don't kiss me goodbye because you might shed a tear in the limo afterwards. And then the world would end, huh? Who taught you that? *Someone* must have convinced you that feelings are the worst thing that can happen to a guy. Was it your father? I'd like to kick his ass.

"I mean—how can you listen to a man who thinks that the true measure of success is avoiding *noodles*, for fuck's sake.

"You left. And you decided that it's over between us. Didn't even ask me what I think. Couldn't wait to shut down that discussion. Guess what? The biggest distance between us isn't the miles between Colorado and Brooklyn. It's that I am willing to lay it all on the line, even when it hurts. But your way is pretending it never happened. So you can keep playing hockey, and going home alone afterwards.

"I hope that's what you really want. I hope this was all just a blip for you." He takes a deep, shuddery inhale. "...And I guess I'll just keep being the only one who still cares."

The recording ends. And I realize that I've forgotten to breathe. I take a deep gasping breath, but it gets stuck somehow, and comes out sounding like a sob.

I roll onto the bed, clutch the phone to my chest, and squeeze my eyes shut.

But my despair doesn't ebb. Because every damn word was true.

Somehow I'd come to believe that big emotions are a luxury only for other people. Along with pizza, and cake.

I've been starving myself for years, and I can't even remember why.

FORTY-SEVEN

Hudson

NOVEMBER

OVER THE NEXT FOUR WEEKS, Stoneman drags me out for drinks a half dozen times. Since my nice house is as silent as a tomb, and echoing with my own incriminating thoughts, I let him.

I discover that my new teammates are an army of decent guys. Stoney is the clown, of course. Kapski—the star forward—is the sharp-tongued ladies' man. Those two are the social butterflies of the group.

I'd wondered if Kapski would be slow to warm up to me since he's the one I humiliated in last winter's Brooklyn game. But he likes me fine now that we're playing for the same side.

Their favorite hangout is a popular Boulder brew pub with too many carbs on the menu. But otherwise I like the place. It's famous for its artisan beers on tap, but they stock a light beer in bottles. Every time I order one, my team makes fun of me. They bang an actual gong that's hanging on the wall of the bar.

I am not deterred. "If you want my ugly face at your party, I can drink what I want," I tell Stoney.

The clock is ticking down on the Brooklyn trip. I'm trying not to think about it, which is how I end up holding a low carb beer on a Tuesday night while the sound of a gong reverberates in my ears.

"How come you guys give me grief for drinking this, but you don't give Cockrell grief for being a vegetarian?"

Ivan Cockrell, one of our goalies, looks up from his plate of buffalo-style cauliflower and frowns at me. He's a stoic guy with a carefully trimmed beard and serious brown eyes. "Nothing wrong with being a vegetarian."

"No kidding," I agree. "Just trying to understand the team psychosis."

He gives me a fleeting grin. "Hey, I got a question for you. How do you like Red Rock Circle? There's a house for sale on your street."

"I like it. Great street. Quiet, but not dead, you know? Lots of young professionals. Some families. But you should ask someone who knows more than I do. I've only been there a couple months, and real estate isn't really my thing."

He carefully wipes buffalo sauce off his fingers. "I think I'll make an appointment to see it."

"Wow, home ownership," Stoney says. "That's scary stuff. My biggest commitment is a one-year lease, and three fish in a tank. Used to be five, but one of them is a cannibal." He shrugs.

Someone puts a hand on my shoulder, and it's DiCosta, another blueliner like me. He's a big, bearded guy who doesn't say a whole lot. But tonight he says, "Talk to me about your boys in Brooklyn."

Oof. My heart drops into my shoes. "What do you want to know?"

"Can we take 'em?"

"It'll be a fair fight. You got two snipers to watch, though. Drake and Castro are dangerous. Tankiewicz is sneaky. But so am I."

"Should be a blast!" Kapski says. "Let's make 'em cry."

I take a sip of my beer and wish for a moment that I was more of a whiskey drinker.

The night before we're set to leave, I can't sleep.

Gavin had said that he wasn't sleeping well either. I wonder if that's still true.

I used to hate that wall dividing us. Now it's 1800 miles.

Sitting up in bed, I pick up my phone and check the time. 4:14 a.m. Hell. Almost time to get up and head to the airport, anyway.

There's a text from Bess.

How are you holding up? I'll be thinking about you tomorrow, and I'll see you at the stadium. Okay if I show up before the game?

I'm not used to getting supportive messages like that. Warmth wasn't my dad's style.

Would love to see you. Kind of a mess here.

It's not like me to admit it. But hell, it's true.

Even though it's the middle of the night, my phone rings a minute later. *Bess calling.* "Hello? I hope my text didn't wake you up."

"Nope. My teething toddler did," she says. "But what are you doing up at...whatever hour it is in Colorado?"

"Just getting a little extra anxiety in before the road trip," I joke.

"Are you worried about the game?"

"Nah. That part's easy."

"Coming back to Brooklyn is hard," she says.

"Right," I admit.

"Are you going to see him?"

I hesitate. "Not sure it's up to me. Not sure what it would accomplish, except misery."

"Is there something you could do—a gesture you could make—that would show him you still care?" she asks.

"Like...flowers or something?" I wouldn't even know where to start. "That's not us."

"What *is*, though?" she presses. "Favorite food? Favorite beer? Favorite activity?"

"Italian takeout. Amber ales. Uh. I can't send him a gift. Too superficial. What he really wanted was for me to come out of the closet."

"So do that."

I open my mouth to argue, and then close it again.

"If that's what's holding you back...It's your life, Hudson. You've got a contract locked up if you decide to sign it. You've got a great team and every other worldly comfort. If the thing you want most is this guy, then show him."

No way! says a decade of fear.

"How would I, uh, go about doing that?" says my mouth.

FORTY-EIGHT

Hudson

IT TAKES ABOUT seventy-five years to get to Brooklyn. But when the plane lands in New York, Bess has already texted me.

All set! We can bring both teams together on the loading dock, where they usually play elimination soccer before games.

My stomach rolls. The idea of standing in front of fifty guys to announce my attraction to men makes me want to yack on my shoes.

On the other hand, I know I need to do this. I've known it for a long time. Even if it's too late for me and Gavin, I'm so tired of holding everything in.

I'm so tired, period. I look like the Bugs Bunny cartoon where he props his eyelids up with toothpicks.

We check in at the big hotel across the street from the stadium. For once in my life I skip the morning skate and take a nap. When my alarm goes off at four, it feels like waking from the dead.

I eat a protein bar and put on a suit. I check my messages. Bess writes:

All systems go for 5:30! You are an inspiration.

I'm an inspiration whose hands are shaking. Even so, I open up my thread with Gavin and send him a short message.

I know this is out of the blue and you probably don't want to hear

313

from me. But I'm making a big announcement to both teams on the loading dock at 5:30. If there's any way you could be there, it would mean the world to me.

Then I shut down my phone and go.

"You sure you want to do this?" my agent asks me.

"Of course," I snarl. "Why would you second-guess me *now*?"

Bess holds up her hands in submission. "Only because you've turned a peculiar shade of green, and I'm a little afraid of the consequences."

I take a calming breath through my nose.

It's not very calming. The loading dock is filling with guys dressed in athletic wear. No, it's *full*. And they're all staring at me.

My pulse is racing, and I might pass out.

Coach Worthington claps his hands. "Okay, boys. Newgate wants to talk to all of you for a minute. Please give him your full attention. Afterward, it's back to your respective dressing rooms, and the usual protocol." He turns to me. "Okay, Newgate. Your meeting."

The subtext is: *get on with it, dumbass.*

But I'm panicking inside. I take a step forward, and even though I rehearsed this in my head for two thousand miles, I'm not sure how to begin. "Uh, thank you for gathering around for a minute. There's some things I need to say, and I won't take up much of your time."

They stare back at me.

"Usually, on the team, I keep to myself..."

"You?" Castro hoots. "Nah."

That gets a chuckle, and I'm grateful to him for breaking the tension.

"Yeah, I know. Here we've got two of the best groups of guys in the league, right? And I've done a shitty job of getting to know most of you. I used to blame that on being the new guy. Honestly, it was just my favorite excuse. There's another reason I don't engage much. For years I've convinced myself that I wouldn't be accepted by the team, or by management, if you all knew me better. If you knew I'm..." *Breathe.* "The only bisexual man I know of in professional hockey."

After I choke the words out, I pause to take a look around the circle. I've built this moment up in my mind for years. It was this Rubicon I couldn't ever cross.

Strangely enough, the world hasn't ended yet. There's no bolt of lightning. Nobody throws tomatoes, or vomits.

I don't know what I was expecting. The players are just watching and waiting for me to continue. Their expressions are curious, but not even shocked, really.

"So..." I clear my throat. "Maybe you think that's dumb. Maybe you're right. But if I've been distant, I'm sorry. I honestly didn't know how to talk about it. I didn't try very hard, though. I convinced myself that what a team wanted most from me were game points, and to shut up about my personal life..."

Movement near the corridor catches my eye, and I glance over there. And my knees almost buckle.

It's Gavin, leaning against the doorframe, hands jammed into his pockets, a grumpy expression on his perfect face.

I take another deep breath and force myself to continue. "But I've realized a few things. There's a *reason* you guys are two of the best teams in the league. It's because you trust each other. Team play means more to you than connecting passes and accurate shots. It's about loyalty and having each other's backs. Maybe if I'd figured that out sooner, I wouldn't have been traded so many times. I guess we'll never know." I chuckle awkwardly. "I'm bi, and I always have been. I'd like to be a better teammate, and for whatever reason, I needed to be open about that so I could stop worrying what you all might think."

There is a brief, deep silence. I stand utterly still, and nearly stroke out.

But my new coach starts clapping. Hard. And a few others join in.

Half a second later it's the whole room. I risk a glance at Castro, who's standing more or less right in front of me. When we make eye contact, he gives me a manly chin lift. And then a grin.

Okay. Well. I hold up a hand to indicate that I'm not quite done, and they quiet down. "Thanks for that. Some of you might think I'm an idiot for worrying so much about this. But who knows? Maybe there's something holding you back, too. Maybe you're dyslexic, or depressed, or carrying around some burden I can't see. Let me just tip you off that holding it in doesn't make it go away. Please learn from my mistakes. The time and energy I've spent on my fear could have been put to better use..."

I risk another quick glance at Gavin. He's red-faced and scowling.

"...Finding someone who will listen," I add. "Last season I found that person. I met the greatest guy in the world. And for a little while, I was living my best life. But fear is a shitty teacher, so I messed that up pretty badly, too. I would like that guy to know that I am so sorry." My voice cracks. "Maybe one day he'll forgive me. Thank you."

The minute I'm done speaking, Stoney applauds loudly, and the rest of my teammates—and my former teammates—do the same thing.

My face heats with embarrassment, but also relief.

After all that time, I did it. I told the truth, and it didn't kill me.

Not yet, anyway. I'm swarmed with the sort of back pats and well-wishes that you'd crave if you were me. And I appreciate it. I really do. This moment was a long time coming. Even if it's come too late.

When I glance at the doorway, Gavin has disappeared. I search the room for his clear gray eyes.

But he's nowhere to be found.

FORTY-NINE

Gavin

I SHOULD HAVE GOTTEN a babysitter and gone out to get drunk.

Instead, I sit numbly on the sofa and watch the game with Jordyn.

The poor kid is deeply confused. "Daddy! I don't know who to root for! I want Hudson to win. But I want Brooklyn to win. They can't both win!"

"Tell me about it," I grumble, rubbing my forehead.

I still can't believe he came out to everyone he knows tonight. It was incredibly brave. Twenty thousand spectators have no idea, of course. The game is hard fought and well-matched.

Every time the camera zooms in on the players' faces, I'm scrutinizing their interactions with Hudson. What I see is the same game-night concentration as always. The same chirpy conversations. The same shoulder bumps and butt pats and sweaty brows.

The first period is scoreless, which doesn't help my mood. Because I don't know who I'm rooting for, either. It's a battle of wills on the screen. A sweaty battle, and Hudson is right in the mix, skating hard to stop his former teammates from scoring.

Nothing has changed for him, and yet everything has changed for him. I can't look away. I want to know why he did it. But I also don't want to ask.

Maybe he met somebody new.

Brooklyn scores early in the second period, but then Colorado answers with another goal.

Jordyn shrieks and buries her face in my shoulder. "Daddy, I can't watch. This is torture."

"It's only a game, baby."

She looks up at me like I've lost my mind.

Then the door buzzer rings. I almost don't bother answering. It's kind of late for deliveries, even if Reggie is expecting some more moving boxes.

My sister is moving out. Her band got signed by a label. They're headed to L.A. to try to make it big.

The buzzer rings again. I answer it this time.

"Delivery!" the guy calls out.

But when I open the door, a dozen roses are thrust into my face. And a six-pack of my favorite beer. "Sign here, sir."

"Whoa, Daddy!" Jordyn says when I close the door. "Did Hudson send you *flowers?*"

"Maybe," I mumble. Then I open the card.

G—I want to see you. I'm at the Hilton. Or I could come to you, but I won't show up uninvited. I miss you like crazy. And I couldn't come all this way and not tell you. —H.

Well shit. Me and him at a hotel? What good could come from that?

I stare at the flowers.

But how can I stay defensibly angry in the face of a dozen roses and some very expensive craft beer?

The truth is that I want to see him. So bad. But I don't want the ugly emotional hangover that will surely follow.

"Is it from him?" Jordyn demands.

"Yup." I shove the card in my pocket and stomp over to the table with the roses. I don't even have to put them in water, because Hudson sprang for an expensive arrangement in a vase.

"He still loves us," Jordyn announces with a shrug. "He wishes he didn't move away."

I have no response. If only it were so simple.

The door opens again ten minutes later. It's Reggie. "Ooh, flowers! Are you going to see him?" She practically has hearts in her eyes.

"That would be a terrible idea," I whisper.

"Overtime!" yells Jordyn.

We line up on the sofa to watch. "This is so exciting," Reggie says. "Who are we rooting for?"

"Brooklyn," I grumble at the same time that Jordyn says "Colorado."

I don't know why Hudson thinks he can sweep into town and make me watch his big announcement. It's too late for me to be won over.

That's how it should be.

Right? My heart is very confused.

It was hard watching him come out, because it made me realize something unflattering about myself: I doubted him. All last summer, when he was planning to come out, part of me doubted that he'd ever do it.

Which is why I lie awake sometimes now and console myself thinking that Hudson would have chickened out, and we would have broken up anyway.

But now he's free to be himself, and I still miss him. There's a Hudson-sized hole in my chest.

"Oh my GOD!" Jordyn shrieks, and my eyes fly to the screen, where Hudson has stripped Crikey of the puck. "SHOOT!" my daughter yells.

Hudson doesn't have a shot, though. He makes a lightning fast pass to Kapski instead.

Who scores.

The lamp lights. The buzzer sounds. And twenty thousand fans howl their frustration.

The Colorado team is ecstatic, though. They crowd Hudson and Kapski for helmet thumps and butt pats and a hundred other little masculine warrior rituals.

Then it's time for the handshake line. Hudson is grinning from ear to ear as he tries to skate by his former teammates for a quick handshake or fist bump. But it takes forever, because they all want to hug him instead.

I slump down on the sofa, wondering what's wrong with me. I should be happy for him. I gave him a big, angry speech about how much I still care.

"Bedtime," Reggie says, clicking off the TV. "Brush those teeth, kid. I'll tuck you in."

"What about Daddy?" Jordyn asks.

"Daddy is going out for a beer with the team." She winks at me.

"No, I'm not," I mumble.

"Maybe we have time for a Frozen sing-along?" My sister giggles.

"Awesome!" my daughter yells.

"Cheap trick," I mutter.

But then I get up to find my jacket.

FIFTY

Hudson

I'M at the hotel bar with my new teammates.

It wasn't really a choice. They're so busy buying me drinks and snacks that I can't sneak away to decompress.

I'm grateful, though, and a little drunk. So I've kept my smile intact. Bess is standing at my side, too, quietly shoring me up with glasses of seltzer water and her calm demeanor.

"We needed that overtime win, amirite?" Stoney asks before downing another shot of tequila. "Good pass, New Guy," he says.

"Hey," I sputter. "Knock it off with that nickname. I've known you for *years*."

He shrugs. "It's kinda the obvious choice. Although maybe I could do better." He puts a hand to his chin, and adopts a thoughtful pose. Then his eyes light up. "I got it! You should be Noogie!"

"Wait, what?"

But it's too late. Stoney steps in and grinds his knuckles into my scalp, for a classic noogie.

"That is not a nickname," I growl.

"Be careful what you wish for," Bess snickers.

"Hey, Noogie?" Kapski says. "Want one of these potato skins?"

It takes great self-control to ignore the nickname. That won't stick, right? I glance at the platter. Fried carbs with cheese. But it smells so good. And I've already broken so many traditions today, what's one more? I pick up a crispy, oozing potato skin and eat it in two bites.

Bess passes me a napkin. "Hey, don't look now. But a certain hunky Brooklyn athletic trainer just came in the front door. Could that be your guy?"

My gaze leaps to the lobby area where I see Gavin standing there looking devastating in tight jeans and a leather jacket. "How'd you know that's my guy?"

"Prolly from the pissed-off look on his face," Stoney snickers. "How badly did you fuck up this relationship?"

"He's here though, right?" Cockrell points out.

"Cute, too," grunts DiCosta. At least I *think* that's what he said, but I can barely believe that big, burly DiCosta would call another man cute. Then he gives me a shove. "Don't just stand here, dumbass."

Right. I take a step forward.

"Good luck," Bess says. "I'm rooting for you."

I hurry toward Gavin, about twenty long paces away. For a second he doesn't spot me. But then those gray eyes lift to mine. His face is a stone, though.

Mine isn't. Everything inside me relaxes, because Gavin is right here in front of me. I just want to drink him in.

Instead, I lean in and kiss him on the cheekbone. Then I start to say hi, but the bar behind me erupts in cheers.

Fuck.

He takes a step back and folds his arms across his chest. "Can we go somewhere and talk?"

"Yeah, of course. But curfew is in twenty minutes, so do you mind going upstairs with me?"

He lifts an eyebrow, as if considering. But then he crosses to the elevators and presses the button.

The bar erupts in hoots and catcalls.

Without even turning to look at my teammates, I lift my middle finger and flip them all off.

"Ignore them," I beg.

They're still laughing as the doors open and we step in.

He looks down at the floor and sighs as the elevator begins its quick ascent to the sixth floor. "I greatly admire what you did today. I want you to know that."

"But you're still mad at me." The elevator doors part again, and I lead him to my room, opening the door with a flourish. He steps inside and crosses to a chair and the other window, sitting down unhappily on it.

"I'm confused," he says quietly. "It took a lot for me to get to a place where I was ready to take all the risks for you. I was even looking at jobs outside the organization, in case I needed one..."

"Whoa." I sit down on the bed. "I never wanted you to leave your job."

"Yeah, I know. But it might have come to that." He leans back in the chair, catches the back of his head in two hands, and looks up at the ceiling. "I wanted to believe in us. And then you ran out of here like you were on fire, and I had no say in what happened. I couldn't believe you did that to me. Just left me behind."

I feel sick, knowing that I hurt him so badly. "It was selfish of me. I knew it the whole time. But deep down I thought maybe you were too good for me anyway. That maybe I wasn't brave enough to give you what you deserve."

He brings his gaze back to mine. "All you had to do was *love* me. I didn't need you to be a big shot, or a genius, or a romantic."

"What *did* you need?" I ask, because I'm sensitive about this. "I'm no good at relationships. It's like everyone got the manual but me."

"You say that, but every time you let yourself relax, you're a great partner. You consider my feelings, you're kind to my kid. It's not that tricky." He rubs his temples. "It was good, up until you panicked. I know the trade wasn't your fault. I just wish you'd handled it like a grown-up, so I didn't spend the last three months in so much agony."

My heart breaks right in half. "If it helps, I learned a lot. And I'm hoping you'll still talk to me, because I have so much to tell you."

"Like what?" he cocks his head.

"Fired my dad."

"Whoa. Really?"

"Yeah." I clear my throat. "You were trying to tell me how toxic that relationship was, and I finally listened."

He whistles.

"Came out to my team." I grin at him. "You saw that part. And, uh, I'm trying to figure out if there's any way we can be closer again. On the planet, I mean."

He blinks. "How would you do that?"

"If I go free agent, I could beg one of the New York teams for a spot. Or maybe New Jersey. If I don't get injured this season, they could get me for real cheap."

"That sounds risky. What's your other option?"

"Well..." I rub my chin. "Colorado offered me a three year extension for twelve million."

He sits forward in his chair. "Twelve million...*dollars?*"

"Yeah." I shrug. "Contract is sitting in a drawer at home. I have until Christmas to decide. But money isn't everything. You are, though. I'm looking for ways to prove it to you. So I'm thinking of turning the contract down and trying to get back to the East Coast."

He shoots out of his chair and starts pacing the room. "Hudson, I say this with love—you cannot turn down a twelve million dollar contract for me."

"Why?" My stomach drops. "I want another chance with you."

He stops pacing and throws his arms out to the sides. "And I want it too, you dickhead!"

"I like dickheads," I remind him. "That's not an insult."

He stomps over to the minibar, grabs a glass and fills it with water. Then he guzzles it down. "Twelve *million* dollars."

"It's just money."

"God." He blows out a breath. "There's something you should know."

"What?" If he says he's dating someone else, I'm probably going to lose my mind.

"I love my job. But the hours are weird. And now my sister is leaving New York, so I'm going to have childcare problems again. Plus, you're not there. So..."

I stop breathing.

"...I've started looking for a new job. New York City isn't a hotbed of athletic opportunity, so I've been looking at university jobs. All over the place. I don't know where I'll land."

"Oh..." I'm trying not to get excited. "I hear Colorado has some good schools."

He rubs the back of his neck. "How well do you like Denver?"

"It's actually Boulder. Which is one of the most livable, beautiful towns in the world. Red rocks, hiking. Craft beer. Biking. I bet there's even a horseback riding camp around there somewhere."

He snorts.

"...I have a three bedroom house with a fireplace that would be fun to make out in front of. That's not verified yet, for obvious reasons. The furnished bedroom has a king-sized bed. There's another room at the front of the house with a window seat, at a good distance from the, uh, grown-ups room. And even a guest room which might accommodate a sister from time to time. Or even a set of ridiculous grandparents."

He sits down on the edge of the bed, a few feet away from me, and puts his head in his hands.

"Gavin," I say quietly. "If you would ever consider putting Boulder into your travel plans, now would be a good time to say so. I would have asked you this question already. But when I brought up living together before, you definitely weren't interested."

"That's when we were sharing a wall." He flops backward suddenly onto the bed. "I spent all of August waiting for you to come to your senses and invite me out for a visit."

My heart skips a beat. "Too bad I'm such a dumbass. If I thought you would have gotten on that plane, I would have flooded your mailbox with invitations."

He rolls to the side to look up at me. "See, I would have swallowed the last bit of my pride if you told me you couldn't live without me. Maybe that sounds reckless. But I needed a sign, Hudson."

Ohhhhh shit. He needs a sign. *I'm so bad at this.* "I…"

He waits.

"I *LOVE* you," I wheeze.

Gavin's eyes go wide. "Are you okay?"

"Yes! I'm fucking fine. But I love you. I want you. I need you. Please come to Colorado. Come for Christmas," I beg. "Please. No—that's too far away. Come for Thanksgiving."

His expression softens. "I want to. Tell me this is a rational thing to do."

"I can't, because I don't know how to be rational with you. Since the day we met, I've wanted you all to myself. And that's never going to stop."

He reaches out a hand and finally, *finally* touches me. He plants his palm at my cheek and strokes his thumb through the stubble over my lip. And it feels so good that my skin heats in appreciation. "I love you, too. You matter to me," he whispers. "So much. I tried to get over you, but it didn't work out."

I reach for him, placing my hands tentatively on the T-shirt inside his jacket. And apparently I have a lot more to say. I'm like a broken dam. "I can't close my eyes without seeing your face. I can't climb into bed without wishing you were there. I was never really living until I had you. And I've never said that to anyone. Ever. Any of it."

"Jesus, Hudson." He pulls away, only to shake off his jacket, kick off his shoes, and then belly flop onto the bed. "That was so hard for you, wasn't it?"

"You have *no idea.*"

His clear gray eyes blink back at me. "Don't be afraid to feel things. That's what we're here for."

"I'll try, baby. Because you're my number one. I've got no pride left. I'll give it all to you."

He reaches over to play with my hair. "I want to kiss you now. But I don't want to stop you from talking. We've been needing to talk for so damn long."

"Yeah, that's true. But may I also point out that I'm leaving town tomorrow at nine? We can talk on the phone, baby. The kissing, though..."

He gives me a secretive smile. "Pretty smart for a dumb jock." Then he rises up on his elbows. Locking eyes with me, he slowly closes the distance.

I need it too badly to wait. I haul him onto my body, and he sinks down with a moan. His kiss is generous, and I wrap my arms around him, at long last.

I *am* pretty smart for a dumb jock. Finally smart enough to never let him go. "Will you come for Thanksgiving?"

"Yes," he whispers against my lips.

"Will you consider jobs in Colorado?"

"Yes."

He kisses my neck, and I shiver. "Gavin?"

"Hmm?" He tongues my earlobe.

"I'm really happy I walked into the tavern that night. I'm sorry I ever said I wasn't. Will you forgive me?"

He kisses me. "I already have."

Epilogue: One Year Later

DECEMBER

JORDYN SETS down her pencil with a thwack on the kitchen counter. "I thought you said five o'clock. It's almost *six*."

I glance at the clock on the microwave. The townhouse kitchen is the nicest one I've ever had, and we often spend time here together, even when we're not waiting for Hudson to walk through the door. "Ducky, he told me he wouldn't come home until after you finish those math problems."

"*Daddy*." She rolls her eyes at my ridiculous gambit. "*Please*."

I bite back my smile. "The plane landed at five, but he has to get out of the Denver airport and drive home in the snow. Plus, it's rush hour."

She picks up her pencil with an aggravated sigh.

Hudson has been on a weeklong road trip, and we're both eager to see him. Jordyn's eagerness is probably compounded by her boredom with long division and her empty belly. I've outdone myself with a welcome home dinner. There's a chili-rubbed brisket braising in the slow cooker, and we've been smelling it all afternoon.

I'm impatient, too, although food has little to do with it. A seven-day road trip is just mean, and I'd have a word with the GM if he'd listen.

I miss Hudson like crazy when he's gone. He got a goal against New Jersey, though, in the last away game before the Christmas holiday, so at least my suffering has a higher purpose.

"What's twenty-seven divided by...?" Jordyn stops mid-sentence and tosses down her pencil. "*He's here!*"

My daughter must have supersonic hearing, because it's another couple of seconds before the back door swings open. "Hey!" he cries, dropping his suitcase on the mat. "It's almost like you're waiting for me or something."

Jordyn flings herself at him, and he catches her in a hug.

But I just stand there smiling at him for a moment admiring him in his suit and overcoat. The man really rocks a suit. I hope they never nix that NHL rule and let the boys dress down, because I'm really going to enjoy unbuttoning that finely woven shirt later.

"Now can we eat?" Jordyn asks, releasing him.

"Just a minute," Hudson says. "There's something I gotta do." He rounds the kitchen island and steps closer, drawing me into his arms. "Happy to be home, baby."

Then he smiles before his lips touch mine. He smells like a crisp snowy evening and feels like magic, so I kiss him hard.

"Ew," Jordyn complains. "Can't you do that later?"

Hudson draws back just far enough that I can see the smile in his brown eyes. "If you insist." He winks, and it's a wink that comes with a promise.

We sit down for dinner together, and Hudson and I play footsie under the table while Jordyn gives him a lengthy play-by-play of last night's school's holiday concert.

After we moved here last spring, I had *so* much guilt about sending her to a new school for the second time in two years.

It's really hard to be the new kid, after all.

But after I landed a good job at U.C. Boulder, everything seemed to fall into place. It's not pro hockey, but my hours are great, and the athletes I work with are young and full of enthusiasm.

And the move wasn't as hard on Jordyn as I'd feared. She's learned a few things about how to be the new kid. Over the summer, she talked Hudson and two of his teammates into throwing her a skating party at the practice rink for her birthday.

Hudson has gotten a little better at saying no to her. But he said yes to this, on one condition—"You have to invite every kid in your whole grade, okay? It's a big rink. And nobody should feel left out."

He must have been right, because the party was *very* well attended.

I'm not sure whether it's good parenting, or not, to let your kid increase her social status by leveraging the team's popularity to the unsuspecting fourth grade residents of Boulder. But here we are.

"Wish I could have seen your concert," Hudson says, setting down his wineglass. "You know I would have come if I was in town."

She shrugs. "Daddy made a video. You can watch it with me after dinner. Then we have to watch the next episode of Hawkeye."

He picks up his fork and smiles at her. "Sure, but only if we can do both of those things before bedtime. It's a school night."

She squints at him. "But I'm on Christmas break."

"Oh. My bad."

"The episodes aren't that long. Maybe we could watch two of them."

"One is plenty," I say, just in case Hudson forgot how to say no on his road trip.

He gives me a knowing smile, because he can see right through me. Jordyn should go to sleep at a reasonable hour tonight, because it's good for her health.

And because I want some time alone with him.

He winks at me.

After dinner, he instructs her to put on her PJs and brush her teeth. Then they settle onto the sofa in the living room.

While I make a fire in our fireplace, they watch the concert video on his phone. And then we all watch an episode of Hawkeye. They squabble over the plot, but I haven't been watching the show with them, so it goes over my head. I'm just here for cozy family time in front of the Christmas tree and the fireplace. Fine. And for Jeremy Renner in a form-fitting costume.

"Bedtime!" Hudson announces when the credits roll.

"Piggyback ride up to bed?" she wheedles.

"Absolutely."

She climbs onto his back, and I watch them disappear up the stairs from my perch on the sofa.

With the TV off, the crackle of the fire is the only sound except for the low murmur of Hudson's voice from Jordyn's room.

I'm still "Daddy" while he's "Hudson." And he is careful to defer to me on parenting decisions. But it's nice to have some support. Like I told Hudson recently—"I still feel like a clueless dad sometimes, but I no longer feel like a clueless *single* dad."

"So we're both clueless? Sounds accurate," he'd replied. "But I think we're pretty great, and Jordyn is a lovely kid. We must be doing a few things right."

I recline on the sofa, the wineglass on my belly, and I listen to their voices. Once again, I'm living the dream. A healthy family, a home, a good job. I'm grateful every day, because I know how perilous it all is.

And how wonderful. The fire warms me, and I know in my bones that there's nowhere else I need to be right now.

It's almost Christmas. And just afterwards, Jordyn's grandparents will fly out to whisk her away to an Aspen ski vacation for a few days. They bought an overpriced condo, which they have visited four times so far.

Eustace loves Colorado, apparently. We visited them in New Hampshire again over the summer, too. The monster-in-law is as pleased with me as she'll ever be, I guess.

My thoughts are interrupted by the doorbell, which is not entirely unexpected. Several players live in this development. And now that Hudson has become more social with his teammates, they pop by from time to time.

I get up to open the door and find Davey Stoneman on the front porch wearing his trademark lopsided grin. "Yo, Gavin! How's it hangin'?"

"Uh, doing well, Stoney. What's up?"

He holds up a bottle of red wine. "Thought you and Noogie might want a glass."

Yeah, that nickname stuck. And Stoney's timing isn't the best tonight. But Stoney has great taste in wine. I enjoy big, plummy cabernets almost as much as I enjoy this man's sense of humor, and the way he's embraced me as his teammate's family without a moment's hesitation.

On the other hand, I haven't seen Hudson in a week.

"Come right in," I say, opening the door a little wider. "And if you were hoping for some leftovers, I can help you out."

He brightens even further. "How did you guess?"

"Perpetually single guy who's been out of town for a week...It wasn't that big of a leap. Sit down, I'll fix you a plate, and fetch you a wineglass."

"You're the best, Gavin."

I head to the kitchen, and when I come back, he and Hudson are standing by the front window, peering out into the darkness. "Whatcha looking at?" I ask.

"DiCosta," Hudson says.

"What's he doing outside?" I ask. "Shouldn't you let him in?"

"It's not like that," Stoney says gleefully. "He's moving in to the place across the street."

"Really?" I set down Stoney's plate on the coffee table. "Does he need any help?"

"Nope!" Hudson laughs. "I'm not touching that. Look." I move to the window and stand beside my boyfriend, who wraps an arm around me. "See? He's got help."

As I watch, DiCosta and another man stand arguing on either side of a giant fir tree that's stuck halfway into the front door of the townhouse across the street. "They should have taken that in the other direction," I point out.

Hudson gives me a squeeze. "Pretty sure they realize that, baby."

"Who's that guy?" I ask.

"The decorator," Stoney says. "DiCosta is goin' upscale."

"*That* is hard to picture," Hudson scoffs.

Outside, the two men are arguing. I'm just about to suggest that we offer to help, when DiCosta waves the other guy off the stoop. He warily backs up onto the snow-covered yard.

With a shout so loud I can hear it through our double-glazed windows, DiCosta gives the tree a mighty shove, and it pops out of the doorway like a champagne cork from a bottle and lands in the snow.

The three of us crack up.

"Daddy? Hudson?" Jordyn's voice comes from the top of the stairs. "What's so funny? Is Stoney here to eat leftovers again?"

"Oops, busted." Stoney clamps his hand over his mouth. "Sorry for being loud, sweetie!" he calls up to her.

"He's not staying very long!" Hudson adds, giving Stoney a nudge toward the couch. "Eat your dinner, you freeloader."

"I'll go tuck her in," I say, heading for the stairs. "You two behave. And pour me some wine."

Hudson

Ninety minutes later I'm toweling off from the thirty-second shower I needed after saying a very thorough hello to my boyfriend.

I hang up my towel and pad back into the bedroom from the en suite bath, naked, and carrying only a warm washcloth.

"Thanks," Gavin murmurs, taking it from me and wiping off his stomach. "Don't let me fall asleep. I don't want to miss out on round two."

I laugh. "Is that because round one lasted about seventeen

seconds? When I told you I missed you, I wasn't joking." I take the cloth from him and toss it into the empty wire hamper. And when I climb onto the bed, he pulls me close.

"It was mutual, though." He kisses my neck, because he knows it drives me crazy. "Phone sex just isn't the same."

"No kidding." I lean in and kiss him properly, and we make out like teenagers who just discovered kissing. It sucks to leave him so often.

On the other hand, coming home again is always pretty great.

"Hey," he says, running a hand down my happy trail. "I have a tricky question for you."

"Tricky?"

"Well, it's a question about Christmas." He frowns. "I got you a present. But now I'm, uh, a little worried that we got each other the same thing. And it's, uh, hard to return."

I let out a bark of surprised laughter, because that would be pretty funny. And touching, honestly. But if he's right, it *would* be tricky. "Well how do you want to sort this out? Maybe you should give me one clue. Like, how much space does this gift occupy? And if that's not conclusive, we'll move on to another clue."

He chews on his lip. "I kinda don't want to disclose the size if I don't have to. It's too telling."

Uh-oh. Maybe we *did* get each other the same thing. This is probably about to get awkward. But also sweet.

"How about the color?" he suggests. "Is your gift green?"

"Nope," I say with immense relief. "Definitely not."

"Awesome." He falls back against the pillow with a smile. "Okay, this is great. I can stop worrying."

"Yeah, you totally can."

We lie there in the dark for a second. And I try to think of something green that Gavin might have gotten me. A green sweater? A green tie?

Nah. If it were something simple like that, he wouldn't have been stressed about it. I close my eyes and think of green stuff.

Trees. Grass. The green felt on a billiard table. Which makes me think of...

My eyes fly open. "Baby. Did you buy me a ping-pong table?" I sit up fast, because the idea is so exciting to me.

Gavin plops a hand over his eyes and sighs. "Fuck. I spilled my secret for nothing."

I laugh. "Did you really? What a great fucking idea. Almost as great as mine."

He sits up too. "Wait, really? Is your gift going to take up the whole basement? Do we have a problem here?"

"No way." I shake my head. "It's all good. How were you going to hide that, anyway? You think I wouldn't have gone down into the basement before Christmas?"

"Pfft." He makes a face. "When's the last time you did your own laundry?"

"Fair. Sorry."

He smiles. "Nah, it's fine. Just don't go down there. Jordyn wants to surprise you before I whip your ass at the table."

"Please, bitch."

We both crack up. And then we lie back down, his head on my shoulder. I run my fingers through his hair. And I think about the gift that's been burning a hole in my consciousness all week long. It's either the best idea I've ever had, or the worst. Could go either way.

"You okay?" he asks after a time. "I can practically hear your gears grinding over there."

"Just hoping you like my gift half as much as a ping-pong table." If he doesn't, I've got bigger problems.

"I'm sure I will. But if you want, you could just tell me now." His smile is teasing.

"Uh, I think I want to," I say. "I wasn't saving it for Christmas morning anyway. Is that okay?"

He rubs my chest. "Whatever you want, babe. I don't really care about presents, though. Being here with you is all I need."

That bodes well for me. So I prop myself up on an elbow and fish a small wooden box out of my bedside table.

Here goes nothing.

My heart starts to pound.

"Baby, look. This has been the best year of my life. And I don't know if you're ready to marry again. But if you are, I hope the lucky guy is me."

I open the box and show him two rings inside.

"Holy...!" Gavin stares. "Do you mean...?"

"Yes," I whisper hoarsely. "Yes. I want to marry you, but I understand if that idea is difficult for you. So I got these with no expectation that it would be a quick decision. Look—see how they're not the same?"

"Oh." He fingers the box, where one ring is a single platinum band, and the other is two bands fused together.

"The double one would be for you," I say, my voice rough with emotion. "I know how it's always upset you that you lost Eddie's ring." He'd told me that story about a year ago, when we went skiing. "We could both be there on your finger, when the time was right. Think about it."

Gavin suddenly lifts a hand to his face and flicks a tear away. "That is...wow. That's the most thoughtful..." He takes a sharp breath. "Wow."

"Aw, honey. Didn't mean to wreck you." I grab him into a hug. "I'm sorry."

"No, it's good. It's...I *want* to. I want to get married. To you. It would be an honor. I love you so much."

My heart swells. I can't even speak. All I can do is hold him tightly. "I love you so much, too," I manage to grind out.

There is more kissing after that. And then Gavin takes the ring out of the box and slips it on his finger. "It fits."

"I measured your finger while you were sleeping."

"Really?" He laughs. "And here I thought my gift was romantic."

My eyes blaze with emotion, because my ring looks so good on his finger. "It is, baby. Totally. So romantic."

He kisses me to shut me up. And I know without a doubt—no matter what the future holds—I'm finally home.

THE
END

Also by Sarina Bowen

Hello Forever

And co-written books
HIM by Sarina Bowen & Elle Kennedy
US by Sarina Bowen & Elle Kennedy
EPIC by Sarina Bowen & Elle Kennedy
Top Secret by Sarina Bowen & Elle Kennedy
The Best Men by Sarina Bowen & Lauren Blakely